THE FOLKLORE OF WALES:
GHOSTS

THE FOLKLORE OF WALES: GHOSTS

Delyth Badder and Mark Norman

2023

www.uwp.co.uk

British Library Cataloguing-in-Publication Data
A catalogue record for this book is available from the British Library.

ISBN: 978-1-915279-50-7

Illustrations by Katie Marland
Cover artwork by Andy Ward
Typeset by Agnes Graves
Printed and bound by CPI (UK) Ltd, Croydon CR0 4YY

The publisher acknowledges the financial support of
the Books Council of Wales.

I Wil,
y gorau oll am ddeud stori fwgan
a gyda'r gobaith nad yw ei ysbryd byth ymhell
Delyth Badder

To the people of Wales,
who have so much lore to enjoy and celebrate
Mark Norman

Contents

Preface

*

There are already many very fine books examining the folklore of Wales, and within those, a subset of books which examine the theme of Welsh ghosts. Why should there be a need for another at this time? And, more importantly, what makes it different from all the rest?

For many years, there has been a market for 'visitor guides' or 'coffee table' books which discuss the strange histories, spooky goings-on and possible paranormal events of any given geographical area. New books come and old books go. Often the same stories, or at least different versions of the same underlying stories, appear in successive titles. However well presented or entertainingly written these books are, there can be an inherent problem associated with them for people who want to know more about the subjects under discussion. This problem stems, in a large part, from the nineteenth century.

The Victorian and Edwardian periods saw a marked acceleration in people's interest in customs, traditions, folklore and social history. This was fuelled by the work of many antiquarian scholars and financially well-positioned 'collectors'. They had the resources to create museums, to finance books and to devote much time to gathering stories from the classes which, often, they considered to be beneath them – the superstitious 'common folk' or the 'uneducated' rural communities.

Thankfully, times have changed since then. Today, the legacy of these collectors lives on in our museums, our libraries and, indeed, our beliefs. This legacy is not, by definition, bad; much of it is excellent, but it does also carry problems. Not all of our stone circles and rows, ancient forests or other sacred sites are Druidic, for example. But due to eighteenth-century concepts, which were supported initially by the antiquarian William Stukeley (1687–1765) and followed by many others, this idea took hold and now can be very difficult to shake off. It is especially true in Wales given the continuing relevance of poet, scholar and master forger, Edward Williams, more commonly known by his bardic name, Iolo Morganwg (1747–1826), who fabricated many of the country's 'ancient' traditions and lore. This is an example of where we still find issues today.

With the rise of the rail network during the nineteenth century, and the ability to ferry tourists into remote areas which consequently became 'honey-pots' for a holiday economy, a lucrative market for guidebooks was identified. With the public interest in folklore, it felt only natural to put plenty of local colour into these titles and we find ourselves left today with the remains of this 'guidebook folklore'. Misrepresented and embellished stories have been told and retold so many times that we find them quoted on websites and within other information sources for buildings, locations and events to this day. Recycling does not always come with fact-checking.

In this book, we aim to dispel some of the myths surrounding ghosts in Wales but, more importantly, to highlight large swathes of the country's overlooked history. We go back to sources that have remained un-accessed for many years and, crucially, many of these sources have been translated and published in English for the first time. Our aim is to preserve and make more accessible many of these pockets of Welsh folklore that have traditionally been neglected outside Wales.

Dr Delyth Badder has channelled a lifetime's interest in Welsh folklore into academic study, and an extensive library of some of Wales's rarest antiquarian folkloric texts. She has an academic interest in Welsh death omens and apparitions, in particular the appearance of spirits within the Welsh tradition, as well as the nineteenth-century neo-Druidic movement in Pontypridd, and the life and work of archdruid and surgeon, Dr William Price. She is a regular contributor in the media to discussions on Welsh folklore. As a fluent Welsh speaker, Delyth has been able to access material previously overlooked in texts which have been solely dependent on more common English-language sources.

Delyth otherwise works as an NHS consultant paediatric and perinatal pathologist and a medical examiner for the Welsh Medical Examiner's Service.

Folklorist Mark Norman is working alongside Delyth to examine and contextualise this information against a broader folkloric landscape. Mark is the Founding Curator of the Folklore Library and Archive, an organisation dedicated to the collection and preservation of folklore materials for the future. Many people know him as the creator and host of The Folklore Podcast. Ranked in the top half per cent of shows globally and approaching two million downloads behind it, it has for many years been making folklore accessible to a wide audience.

Mark also acts as a council member for the Folklore Society and is the Recorder of Folklore for the Devonshire Association.

Joining Delyth and Mark to provide visual reference for some of these tales is fine art illustrator Katie Marland. Katie recently completed her master's degree at the Royal Drawing School, where she discovered a penchant for drawing from grimoires, folklore and esoteric texts. Her practice is research-led, typically taking inspiration from books, medical history and museum collections, where she can most often be found haunting the halls with a sketchbook. Her most recent exhibition, 'Folklore', is an ongoing body of work dedicated to the chronicling of British folklore, myth and legends.

Together, we are delighted to be able to shine a light on these uncanny stories and explore how they sit within the wider Welsh folkloric culture.

Bwgan bo lol a thwll yn ei fol,
Digon o le i geffyl a throl.

Bo lol bogey with a hole in its belly,
Plenty of room for a horse and trolley.

CHAPTER ONE

Introduction

*

Cofio wna hoglanc iefanc,
Yn llwyd hyn a glybu'n llanc;
Gelwais i'm cof, adgof oedd,
Hanesion o hên oesoedd;
Ganfod o rai hergod hyll,
Du annillyn dân ellyll;
Drychiolaeth ddugaeth, ddigorph,
Yng ngwyll yn dwyn canwyll corph;
Amdo am ben hurgen hyll,
Gorchudd hên benglog erchyll;
Tylwyth têg ar lawr cegin,
Yn llewa aml westfa win;
Cael eu rhent ar y pentan,
A llwyr glod o b'ai llawr glân;
Canfod braisg widdan baisgoch,
A chopa cawr a chap coch;
Bwbach llwyd a marwydos,
Wrth fêdd yn niwedd y nôs.
Goronwy Owen, 'Cywydd y Cynghorfynt'
('The *Cywydd* of Jealousy')

A young lad, when he has gone grey, will remember what he heard
as a boy; I called to mind, it was a memory, tales of long ago;
that some had seen an ugly hulk, a dark unsightly will-o'-the-
wisp; an apparition black, bound, bodyless in the gloom, bearing
a corpse-candle; a shroud over a horrid wraith, covering a frightful
old skull; fairies on the kitchen floor, guzzling many a wine-feast;
their payment found on the hob, full marks if the floor were clean;
seeing a lusty witch in her red petticoat, a giant's head with a red
cap; a pale bogey with embers, beside a grave at the end of night.

A cursory glance along the shelves of any self-respecting bookshop or museum gift shop in Wales will uncover innumerable books on ghost lore, aimed predominantly at tourists and those who crave an overview of some of our most well-known and beloved stories and legends.

These texts provide an invaluable service, introducing many of the fundamental aspects of Wales's unique culture and heritage to a greater number of readers. The retelling, reimagining and recontextualisation of such stories is of course a key component of folklore. However, reading one book after the other, cover-to-cover, reveals that many of the same stories within them have been re-hashed repeatedly; there are only so many times one can read about the singing ghost of Adelina Patti at Craig-y-Nos Castle or the vengeful criminals and callous judges of the Skirrid Inn.

Yet most of these texts barely scratch the surface of what Wales has to offer.

This is not the first volume of Welsh ghost-lore in recent years which concentrates on accounts which, for one reason or another, have not been so widely reproduced. However, most popular collections of this type tend to concentrate on English-language material. A survey of the ghost stories which have been retold in these texts over the years would reveal a disproportionate number located in the industrial south-east and north-eastern Clwyd – all areas in which the Welsh language has historically struggled to hold its ground in the face of continued societal pressure and cultural influence from over the border.

The earliest written accounts of Welsh hauntings were predominantly collected by the English gentry – people such as John Aubrey (1626–97), Joseph Glanvill (1636–80) and Thomas Pennant (1726–98) – wealthy, educated, upper class men. While their accounts are invaluable to our understanding of Welsh folklore during this time, these men had little experience of the Welsh lower classes and their customs, and had a tendency to present their own societal or religious biases in their work.

The gentry would not typically have been privy to the age-old custom of gathering at the hearth after dark, or congregating at a *Noson Lawen* (Merry Evening), to swap tales and scare the audience with stories of local *bwganod* (bogeys), as described below by Erfyl Fychan (Robert William Jones) in *Bywyd Cymdeithasol Cymru yn y Ddeunawfed Ganrif* (The Social Life of Wales in the Eighteenth Century) (1931):

Yr oedd y gred mewn ysbrydion yn gryf, ac yr oedd i aml i lidiart ei geffyl gwyn neu hwch a pherchyll. Trosglwyddid yr hanesion hyn o genhedlaeth i genhedlaeth. Adroddid y straeon wrth y tân fin nos, a chan y tystiai'r tadau a'r mamau fod y straeon yn wir, nid rhyfedd i'r plant eu derbyn.

The belief in spirits was strong, and many a gate had its white horse or sow and piglets. These stories were passed down from generation to generation. The stories were told by the fire in the evening, and since the fathers and mothers testified that the stories were true, it is not surprising that the children accepted them.

It is likely that the first folkloric study of a region by a born-and-bred Welshman wasn't conducted until 1802 by William Williams of Llandygái in *Observations on the Snowdon Mountains; With Some Account of the Customs and Manners of the Inhabitants*, intended, as he wrote, 'for the private use of the Right Hon. Lord Penrhyn', who employed him in 1782 as the supervisor of the Penrhyn estate. The book was written as a guide for Richard Pennant, the first Lord Penrhyn, providing a description of the landscape, community and lore of Eryri, and was written from a purely Welsh perspective rather than that of the English gentry; for this reason alone, its contribution to Welsh folklore study and understanding is immeasurable.

Williams pulls no punches when discussing the collections of his antiquarian predecessors:

It would be endless to point out the absurd conjecture and misrepresentations of those, who have of late years undertaken to describe this country. Some give manifestly wrong interpretations of the names of places, and others, either ignorantly or maliciously, have, as it were caricatured its inhabitants. Travellers from England, often from want of candour, and always from defect of necessary knowledge, impose upon the world unfavourable, as well as false accounts of their fellow-subjects in Wales: yet the candour of the Welsh is such, that they readily ascribe such misrepresentations to an ignorance of their language, and a misconception of the honest, though perhaps warm temper of those that speak it. And it may be, travellers are too apt to abuse the Welsh, because they cannot, or will not, speak English. Their ignorance ought not to incur disgust: their reluctance proceeds not from stubbornness, but from diffidence, and the fear of ridicule.

The one exception to this rule, and unique to Wales, is the work of the Reverend Edmund Jones, 'Yr Hen Broffwyd' ('The Old Prophet') of Transh in Pont-y-pŵl (Pontypool), Monmouthshire. An eighteenth-century Independent minister, Jones spent a remarkable and gruelling seventy years travelling the length and breadth of Wales on horseback, not only preaching the gospel to the sinners of the country, but also collecting stories of ghostly sightings (as well as encounters with witches, devils and fairies) as proof of God's message on Earth.

What makes Jones's work so valuable is his propensity for collecting first-hand accounts from all social classes without discrimination, from servants to the gentry; his only criterion for inclusion was that he considered the source a God-fearing Christian. While his methods are far from unbiased, his writing paints a broad and relatively unfiltered picture of Wales's supernatural belief system during the eighteenth century. Despite many subsequent antiquarians, folklorists and authors making heavy use of his accounts in the centuries since, his 1780 book, *A Relation of Apparitions of Spirits, in the Principality of Wales*, is an exceptional, and in many ways unrivalled, chronicle of the country's ghost-lore. As such, it may come as no surprise that we have also drawn on the knowledge of 'Yr Hen Broffwyd' throughout this book.

Later collections from the nineteenth to the early twentieth centuries, with the emergence of folklore study as a worthy recognised discipline within antiquarianism, show a shift in the importance of obtaining accounts from the lower classes, while still placing much reliance on the content of earlier works. In Wales in particular, many of these collections come from the life's work of various clergymen scholars, often with a vested interest in preserving and amplifying Welsh culture, and more often than not local to the area they were writing about.

Their clerical background often imparted a degree of bias within their collections, as too did the social standing of the previous century's antiquarian gentry. Whereas Edmund Jones had argued for the existence of ghosts as proof of the divine, later clergy were very quick to dismiss superstitious tendencies within their flock. Even by the end of the nineteenth century, Welsh antiquarians were writing cynically of superstitions within their communities, as exemplified by Trebor Môn (Robert Thomas Williams) in *Derwyddiaeth* (Druidism) (1890):

Ni welir ofn 'Hwch ddu gwta', 'Aderyn y corph', 'Canwyllau cyrph', a 'Thylwythion Teg', na thyaid o bobl ddiniwed yn eistedd yn haner-cylch o flaen tanllwyth o dân mawn i sôn am ysbrydion, drychiolaethau, cŵn annwn, a gwiber Penhescyn.

There is no fear of 'Tailless black sow', 'Corpse bird', 'Corpse candles', and 'Fairies', nor a houseful of innocent people sitting in a semi-circle in front of a blazing peat fire to discuss ghosts, apparitions, hounds of annwn, and Penhescyn's viper.

These clergymen were often the very same folk who were responsible for collecting parish histories in Wales, which also offer an invaluable and often overlooked source of local ghost-lore. With their shared interests in spirits of both holy and supernatural origin, many a local ghoul has also found its way into the pages of Welsh theological texts. This combination meant that these authors were able to provide more accurate and reflective accounts of the folklore of a particular region.

While reference to these records is not uncommon in contemporary Welsh-language books pertaining to folklore, the use of parish history accounts and more purely religious texts are notably absent from English-language works on the supernatural in Wales. We hope that including these less-reported Welsh-language sources will help increase the collective understanding of ghost-lore in Wales, both inside and outside the country.

Whereas nineteenth- and twentieth-century antiquarians were focused on recording local historical traditions, in contemporary contexts there has been a growing tendency to erase all regional variation within Welsh folklore, and to portray any and all such customs as having taken place in a nebulous 'Wales'. This modern trend may be due to the character limits placed on social media posts. Simply put, claiming that a certain tradition was commonplace in Wales gives you a lot more room for manoeuvre than stating that it was confined to Rhosllannerchrugog or Llanrhaeadr-ym-Mochnant.

Another somewhat prosaic explanation for this phenomenon is that some broadcasters or presenters, when discussing Welsh folklore, are unwilling to attempt some of the pronunciations which seem difficult to those unfamiliar with the language – and so, certain spirits or entities become 'common in Wales' rather than being confined to a specific area.

Throughout this book, we will endeavour to give regional variations in ghost stories their due, and hopefully draw the reader's attention to the fact that Welsh ghost-lore is enormously diverse across county lines, and even between neighbouring villages.

Similarly, Welsh ghost-lore – and its folklore as a whole – is often presented as over-romanticised and overembellished. While it would be easy to blame this on the need for likes, clicks, views and subscriptions, this is not a new phenomenon. We will see later in this chapter how many of the ghosts in Wales are presented as simplistic, often abstract forms; however, late nineteenth- and early twentieth-century folklorists were also rather fond of 'enhancing' their tales – the works of Wirt Sikes and Marie Trevelyan being two prime examples of this.

This is not altogether surprising, given these folklorists were writing during the tail end of the Industrial Revolution, when Wales as a whole, but especially the south, had been transformed beyond recognition. This occurred with such rapidity – overwhelming the landscape, language and culture – that many of its inhabitants, including some of these authors, and in particular their readers and their contributors, were desperately yearning for some semblance of their traditional heritage. While these folklore collections remain invaluable today, a degree of caution is required when interpreting their content, as with any source.

But the ghost-lore of Wales need not be confined to dry, musty books on the regional history of Methodism. The *hwiangerdd* (nursery rhyme) printed at the very beginning of this book serves as a perfect example:

> *Bwgan bo lol a thwll yn ei fol,*
> *Digon o le i geffyl a throl.*

Bo lol bogey with a hole in its belly, plenty of room for a horse and trolley.

Bwgan can be translated as ghost, hobgoblin or bugbear according to *Geiriadur Prifysgol Cymru* (The University of Wales Dictionary). It also means 'bogey', and is translated as such throughout this book. The term *bolól*, however, can also mean bogey, hobgoblin or even the Devil himself; it is also sometimes used idiomatically to describe pitch darkness. (For further reference, we have provided a glossary of terms at the end of this book.)

The use of this particular word is found in the north-west of the country, predominantly areas in and around the old county of Meirionnydd; the term *bolól* is included in *The Welsh Vocabulary of the Bangor District* (1913). *Llygad y bolól* (eye of the bolól) is a colloquial name for the field poppy in Gwynedd owing to the black spots at the base of its petal, and *Sioni bolól* is north Ceredigion's answer to the bogeyman.

Reference to the *bolól*, therefore, indicates that this nursery rhyme originated in north-west Wales. Certainly, Delyth, who hails from this area, distinctly remembers being terrified of *bwgan bolól* as a child, believing it to be a devil that hid in the boughs and hollows of trees in the dark, probably more so as a result of the wonderfully sinister illustrations of Jenny Williams that accompanied the poem within *Llyfr Hwiangerddi y Dref Wen* (Y Dref Wen Book of Nursery Rhymes) (1981)!

The purpose of this nonsense rhyme mirrors a theme we will see several times during the course of this book. It serves as a warning of danger on the roads, for truanting children as well as those travelling home at night from work or the market. This theme is discussed in more detail in Chapter Three: 'Ghosts in the Landscape'.

At a passing glance, this traditional rhyme is an amusing, simplistic couplet concerning an ambiguous phantom, yet it tells us so much more about the richness and complexity of Welsh folklore than first meets the eye. Most importantly, perhaps, it presents the perfect example of traditional ghost-lore that is still active and used to scare children within Welsh communities today.

This brings us to one of the most important points in relation to the accounts presented in this book. While these tales may not be well-represented or widely available in print, we should avoid describing them as being somehow 'lost' or 'forgotten'.

Dafydd Iwan's 1983 folk anthem 'Yma o Hyd', given a new lease of life in recent years due to its association with the Welsh national football team, begins with the lines:

Dwyt ti'm yn cofio Macsen?
Does neb yn ei nabod o
Mae mil a chwe chant o flynyddoedd
Yn amser rhy hir i'r co'.

Don't you remember Macsen? No one recognises him. A
thousand and six hundred years is too long a time to remember.

Here is Dafydd Iwan berating the good people of Wales for having 'forgotten' Macsen (Magnus Maximus), the reimagined Roman emperor who
married a maiden from Caernarfon called Elen in the legend of *Breuddwyd
Macsen Wledig* (The Dream of Macsen Wledig). While Dafydd Iwan is
clearly making an exaggerated political point, figures like Macsen Wledig,
or similarly venerable characters – many of whom are alluded to within
the pages of this book – are indeed remembered throughout Welsh society,
from primary school to universities and beyond. Wales has an extremely
long memory, and this is rarely more apparent than with regard to the
survival and re-invention of the country's folklore over the centuries.

Generally, words like 'lost' or 'forgotten' are too readily applied to even
the most famous Welsh legends, simply because audiences outside Wales
have traditionally struggled with their contextualisation or translation,
and those of us who are aware of them have not always succeeded in our
attempts to transmit them to a wider audience. At best, these accounts
are overlooked; at worse, ignored. Despite the lack of representation from
both antiquarian and contemporary Welsh-language accounts within
today's popular collections of ghost-lore, the vast majority of these stories
are actively shared in various forms today within the communities of
Wales – they are certainly not 'hidden' or 'obscure'.

There is a wider point to be made about the misrepresentation of Welsh
folklore on a British or even international stage. This is often more relevant to discussions relating to Welsh mythology and legend – examples
include the straightforward pairing of the Welsh otherworld Annwfn (or
Annwn) from the *Mabinogi* with the Christian concept of Hell, and the
pervasive personification of any and all figures from Welsh mythology as
deities; however, it is also relevant to the country's ghost-lore.

Despite the close proximity, there is evidence that the folklore of Welsh
ghosts has developed and survived separately from English ghost-lore.

For example, the presence of the 'ghost in a white sheet' motif is notable in its absence from Welsh accounts until the case of the 'Fighting Ghost of Tondu'. This was a cadaverous figure which appeared around the disused Ynysawdre colliery in Pen-y-bont ar Ogwr (Bridgend) in 1904 – described as being 'shrouded in white' in only one newspaper report from the time, and most certainly representing a rather violent hoax. We are unaware of any earlier cases that neatly conform to this stereotype.

By way of explanation, it is worth exploring whether there were any significant differences in the beliefs surrounding ghost-lore in England at the time. We see that texts such as *Dæmonologie* (1597) by King James I of England quite literally describes the Devil as carrying bodies 'out of the Grave to serve his turne for a space'. Conversely, the notion of the ghost 'rising from the grave' is exceedingly uncommon in Welsh folklore; more often than not, a spirit materialises from the ether or is sent down from the heavens. Why would folk therefore envisage them in their burial shrouds?

In fact, ghosts wearing white clothing in general are not a significant feature in the supernatural landscape of Wales, and are often associated with the *Ladi Wen* (White Lady) (discussed in Chapter Seven: 'Ladi Wen'), the *Tylwyth Teg* (fairies), or angelic, and even demonic, visitation instead. It is only in late twentieth-century accounts that ghosts in white robes begin to appear, undoubtedly due to the pervading influence of popular culture.

It is probably no coincidence that the Fighting Ghost of Tondu appeared, as it did, in 1904. This was the year of the religious revival in Wales, the largest of its kind within the twentieth century, which brought with it a whole new slew of ghostly visions sent as a sign from the heavens. Nineteenth-century revivals, such as that of 1859, had been associated with phenomena such as *canu yn yr awyr* ('singing in the sky') which is discussed in Chapter Five: 'Holy Ghosts'. These revivals were responsible for converting thousands of households across the country, as described by Myra Evans in her autobiography, *Atgofion Ceinewydd* (Memories of New Quay) (1961):

Fel y gŵyr y rhan fwyaf ohonoch, effeithiodd diwygiad mawr 1859 ar bob ardal ymron yng Nghymru, a daeth llawer o hoelion wyth y cyfnod i bregethu yng nghapel bach Ffos-y-ffin. Synnent at anwy-

*bodaeth y plant yn yr ysgrythur, ond ar ryw olwg nid oedd hynny'n
rhyfeddod, waith 'r oedd bryd yr oes ar straeon ysbryd, y toili, y Tylwyth Teg, gwrach-y-rhibyn, a phethau o'r fath. 'R oedd angen llawer
o dân y diwygiad i ddifetha'r holl syniadau hyn ym meddyliau'r bobl.*

As most of you know, the great revival of 1859 affected almost
every area in Wales, and many stalwarts of the time came to
preach in the small chapel of Ffos-y-ffin. They were surprised at
the children's ignorance of the scriptures, but in a way that wasn't
surprising, as people of that age preferred ghost stories, the *toili*,
the fairies, *gwrach-y-rhibyn*, and such things. Much revivalist fire
was needed to destroy all these ideas in the minds of the people.

In 1904, visions were commonplace, predominantly comprising of
religious imagery. Interestingly, some of these accounts are readily comparable with those more abstract apparitions recorded in sixteenth- to
eighteenth-century Wales, such as wheels or balls of fire (discussed below).

An understanding of the Welsh cultural and religious landscape is
therefore necessary to fully appreciate the nature and evolution of its
ghost-lore. While the stories presented in this book serve as interesting standalone accounts, they have much wider implications for our
collective understanding of Welsh social history and identity when
considered within a cultural context.

In this vein, the use of the Welsh language features heavily within
the pages of this book. When providing locations, the Welsh place-
name is always used where one is available, with translation provided
where necessary.

Our approach reflects the need to safeguard place-names in Wales –
with recent examples being the official use of 'Yr Wyddfa' and 'Eryri'
rather than 'Snowdon' and 'Snowdonia', 'Bannau Brycheiniog' rather
than the later 'Brecon Beacons', and the ongoing campaign to prevent
the names of houses and historic buildings from being changed into
English, erasing much of their inherent meaning in the process.

Where the account is derived from a Welsh-language primary source,
this text has been included verbatim along with an English-language
translation. Whereas we have endeavoured to capture the context of each
account accurately in our translations, invariably some of the character

and depth of the original source material has been lost – whether this is through the loss of a particular phonetically written dialect in the text, or simply the inability to translate a given word neatly and succinctly without losing some of its nuance. This unavoidable limitation should not be to the detriment of Welsh-speaking readers.

We hope it goes without saying that Welsh words cannot be simply mapped onto their English equivalents on a one-to-one basis. The language hides a myriad of secondary meanings which are not always apparent from a cursory glance, and the misunderstandings which were already all too common in pre-twentieth-century accounts have become all the more prevalent in the age of Google Translate, when mistranslated inaccuracies can be uploaded or streamed within seconds to an eager global audience.

In adopting this approach, not only are we inviting Welsh speakers to provide their own interpretations of the source material, but we also hope it will encourage non-Welsh speakers to expand their knowledge and understanding of the language.

A primary example of the loss of nuance through the erasure of the Welsh language can be seen in the tale of the Leckwith Ghost. It was first recorded by Thomas Henry Thomas, or 'Arlunydd Penygarn' ('The Artist of Penygarn'), in his lecture, 'Old Folks' Tales', presented to the Cardiff Naturalists' Society in 1902, of which he was a prominent member. It was also later printed in their 1903 *Transactions* under the title 'Some Folk-Lore of South Wales'. Thomas was a nineteenth-century artist, and while his illustrations in Wirt Sikes's *British Goblins* (1880) will probably be most recognisable to many of our readers, in Wales, his illustrations of Welsh people, the architecture and landscape of the time, and his heavy involvement in the Eisteddfod (a competition-based festival celebrating the culture and language of Wales) and the Royal Cambrian Academy, as well as his interest in geology (which resulted in a fossil being named in his honour) are among his many varied accolades still remembered to this day. The tale is written as follows:

the participator, who was walking from Canton to Leckwith at night … was joined by a silent man who dogged his footsteps and gazed upon him imploringly. He would not be shaken off.

'I called him names and threatened him. He only kept looking, looking at me, but said nothing, I got into a rage and said, "'N'en o Duw, what do you want?" Tears ran down his face and he said, "I couldn't speak till you asked me in the name of God. I am dead but I cannot rest till my head is buried" (the bone he meant, what you call skull). "I was boatman," he said "down the Ely river, and my head is on the bank and devils do play football with it. If you will come and bury it I shall rest." So I agreed to go in search of the skull and he took me down the river to a bend, just above the Taff Railway Bridge as is now, and there by a bluish light was a lot of people kicking football like hurrah with the poor man's skull. I thought I would go to them praying, and as I came to them they all flew away. So I took the poor man's head and buried it in a soft place, digging a hole with my knife, and the ghost he stood and looked at me, till he went out like smoke.'

This fantastical tale is shortly picked up by Cadrawd (Thomas Christopher Evans), a prominent Glamorganshire antiquarian and folklorist, for an article that appeared in *The Cardiff Times* in 1903. While Thomas's version strongly suggests the spirit and protagonist conversed in Welsh – '*N'en o Duw*' being recognised by the ghost as meaning 'in the name of God' – in this instance, Cadrawd places even more emphasis on the ghost's understanding of Welsh:

At last I says, 'Yn neno Duw,' or, more correctly, 'Yn enw Duw, beth wyt ti'n fofyn?' (in the name of God what do you want?) At that the tears ran down his face, and he said, very slowly, 'I couldn't speak until you asked me in the name of God! I am dead, but I cannot rest till my head is buried.'

Six years later, Marie Trevelyan provides her version of the same account in *Folk-Lore and Folk-Stories of Wales* (1909). Another prolific Glamorganshire writer, Trevelyan is well known for having a penchant for tweaking and embellishing her vast (and usually unreferenced) collection of Welsh folklore, being heavily influenced by writers of the south Wales neo-Druidic movement such as Iolo Morganwg and Morien (Owen Morgan), who were arguably even more prone to fabrication.

This tendency to romanticise Welsh folk tales and custom has undoubtedly contributed to the enduring popularity of her work within the general population. Her account runs as follows:

> The old man saw imploring glances in the sunken eyes, but not a word was uttered. 'At last,' said the old man, 'I called nine names, but it did no good. He only kept looking at me, and then I got into a rage, and cursed him, but he didn't say nothing. At last I says, "In the name of God, what do you want?" Then tears ran down his face, and he said very slowly: "I couldn't speak until you asked me in the name of God. I am dead, but I cannot rest till my head is buried."'

Any reference to the Welsh language has, by this point, disappeared, taking with it one of the most interesting elements of the story – not the more fantastical detail of the ghoul's skull being used as a football, nor the common motif in Wales of the spirit with unfinished business, but rather the fact that this restless ghost could not find peace until it found another soul to converse with in its mother tongue.

It is safe to say the Welsh are yet to solve the age-old riddle of what a ghost actually is, as evidenced by the lecture delivered to Cymdeithas Cymreigyddol Bangor (The Bangor Society for the Promotion of Welsh Culture) on 1 March 1844 by Thomas Lewis:

> *Nis gallodd un Athronydd erioed, trwy ei fawr wybodaeth, nac un Pheryllydd erioed, trwy ei fanwl ymchwiliad, ddywedyd pa beth ydyw Yspryd. Cymmaint ag a all y dysgedigion penaf ei ddywedyd am Yspryd, sydd mewn ffordd nacäol, dywedyd y peth nad yw – nid yw y peth yma – nid yw y peth arall.*

> No Philosopher has ever, through their great knowledge, nor ever any Apothecary, through detailed researches, said what a Ghost is. All that our most learned can say about a Ghost, is in the negative, saying what it is not – it is not this thing – it is not the other.

However there are various characteristics that appear common to the Welsh ghoul within our folkloric texts and parish accounts. Daniel

Silvan Evans and Ivon (John Jones), writing in the folklore text, *Ysten Sioned: Neu Y Gronfa Gymmysg* (Sioned's Pitcher: Or The Mixed Collection), first published in 1882, describe three such features:

> *Y mae tri pheth neillduol yn nodweddu pob bwgan, os bydd o'r iawn ryw, ac yn uniawn ei gred; sef nas gall, neu nas myn, siarad ond â rhyw un pennodol o holl ddynion y byd; nas gall, neu nas myn, siarad â'r un hwnw, ond pan fyddo ar ei ben ei hun; ac nas gall, neu nas myn, ddechreu yr ymddiddan. O fewn holl gylch llenoriaeth bwcïod nid oes hanes fod neb o honynt erioed wedi agoryd ei ben wrth neb, os byddai rhywun arall yn wyddfodol. Nid gwaeth i chwi geisio cael bwch i'r odyn na cheisio gan fwgan ddechreu siarad cyn y siaredir ag ef; rhaid i'r dyn y byddo ef wedi penderfynu siarad ag ef, neu wedi cael ei orfodi i wneuthur hyny, ei gyfarch ef yn gyntaf; os amgen, ni fynega yr ellyll mo'i neges; a hyd oni chaffo arllwys ei gwd a thraethu y chwedl sy ganddo i'w hadrodd, ni chaiff y dyn hwnw byth lonydd ganddo.*

There are three particular things that characterise every ghost, if it is of the right kind, and orthodox; which are that it cannot, or does not want to, talk to any but one specific person in all the world; that it cannot and will not speak to that person unless they are alone; and that it cannot, or does not want to, start the conversation. Within the whole literature of ghosts, there is no mention that any of them have ever opened their mouths to anyone, if someone else was there to hear them. You might as well try to get a goat to a furnace as to persuade a ghost to start talking before it is spoken to; the person with whom it has decided to speak, or has been forced to do so, must greet it first; otherwise, the demon will not say what its message is; and until it can reveal its secrets and tell the tale it has to tell, that person will never be at peace from it.

This is a universally held belief in Welsh folklore writing – that a ghoul will only appear to one person, who must then begin the conversation when both souls are alone. The ghost should most commonly be commanded to relay its message in the name of the Trinity. Once that message was forthcoming – avoiding any unnecessary chatter, remembering that 'questions about its condition were a very embarrassing business, and they were rarely answered' (*'odd rhoddi cwestiynau yn nghylch ei gyflwr yn beth tra thranglwyddus, ac anfynych yr atebid hwynt'*) – one would be bound to complete the task set or else prepare for the worst:

> *Os wedi yr ymrithiad cyntaf yr esgeulusai y personau hyny eu dyledswydd, ymrithiai yr yspryd i'w golwg yn barhaus; yn gyntaf, yn anfoddlon; yn ail, yn ddigllon; ac yn drydydd, mewn gwedd gynddeiriog, gan fygwth rhwygo cyrph y pleidiau yn ddarnau oni chwblheid y mater dan sylw yn fuan.*

If after the first apparition those persons neglected their duty, the spirit would manifest itself to them continuously; first, discontented; secondly, displeased; and thirdly, in a furious manner, threatening to tear the bodies of the parties to pieces if the matter in question was not completed promptly.

The above sage advice comes from Tudur Clwyd (the Reverend Thomas Frimston), writing at the beginning of the twentieth century, in *Ofergoelion yr Hen Gymry: Mewn Pymtheg Dosparth* (The Superstitions of the Old Welsh: In Fifteen Categories).

Many of the themes surrounding ghosts with messages of unfinished business relate to hidden items of treasure or such like – this is one of the most common motifs in Welsh ghost-lore and is discussed in depth in Chapter Two: 'Unfinished Business'.

The manner in which these ghosts sometimes appear is also noteworthy within Welsh lore, tying in with both the religious and the cultural landscape of the country at any particular time. We have already looked at some of the elements that are not prevalent in Wales, such as the motif of ghosts in white sheets; however, there are reports of commonly experienced ghostly forms from across the country which warrant closer inspection.

It is evident in the earliest recorded hauntings made by clergymen such as the Reverend Edmund Jones that, rather than spectral shrouded figures, folk were more prone to reporting distorted or abstract forms and shapes. Within Jones's body of work, we see accounts of 'the likeness of a man, but could not see his arms, and he was without a hat' in

Pembrokeshire, 'a white thing in the form of a pyramid' in Monmouthshire, and 'a strange fire which kindled in the night about Harlech-Town' in Gwynedd – that is, familiar forms presented in a supernatural light.

When considering the history of religion in Wales, this is not an altogether surprising finding. Much of the medieval religious iconography that existed within places of worship was destroyed during the suppression of the monasteries, and later under increasing puritanical influence during the sixteenth century. By doing so, the largely illiterate lower classes could no longer depend on this imagery for their ghost-lore, and instead had to rely on their own limited imagination. It is therefore little wonder that the phantoms of the seventeenth and eighteenth centuries resemble perversions of the mundane, or distortions of universal fears, such as wild animals, weather phenomena, or fire. We will see many tales of shapeshifting ghosts, or spirits appearing as 'wheels' or 'balls' of fire throughout this book – an example of their endurance in Wales.

Great balls of fire aside, another common trope which may be found within the general ghost-lore of the country is that of the 'living ghost'. There are many reports throughout the world, and throughout the centuries, of eyewitnesses seeing the apparitions of living people. Modern pseudoscientific theories have attributed the phenomenon to astral projection, while traditional folkloric accounts have associated bad luck with seeing one's own counterpart. 'Spirit doubles' are especially prominent within Irish folklore, most commonly known as the *fetch* – the counterpart to the Welsh *lledrith*.

Spirits of the living feature at least as often within the ghost-lore of Wales. So common are these apparitions, that they are treated as pure 'matter of fact' within both folkloric and parish history accounts. In the small village of Llanegryn in Gwynedd, William Davies provides the following example in *Hanes Plwyf Llanegryn* (The History of Llanegryn Parish), first published in 1948:

Ffynnai dau neu dri o draddodiadau am ysbrydion ym mhlwyf Llanegryn. Un traddodiad oedd mai ysbryd y byw a gymdeithasai gyda dynion; tystiai amryw y byddent hwy beunydd yn cymdeithasu â'r byw ar wahan i'r corff a phellter lle. Credai'r lleill mai ysbrydion y meirw a ddychwelai o'r byd anweledig i gyfeillachu â dynion ar y ddaear.

Two or three traditions about ghosts flourished in the parish. One was that the spirit of the living had contact with others; several people attested that they were in daily contact with the living, despite the fact that they were removed in the flesh and a long way off. Others believe that the spirits of the dead came back from the invisible world to communicate with people in the land of the living.

He continues with an exceptionally delightful account of such an apparition in the form of a local elderly woman:

> *Adroddai eraill yn ddifloesgni iddynt weled ysbryd dyn a dynes fyw. Adroddid am hen wraig a drigiannai yng Nghefn-coch-bach a fyddai yn rhodianna oddi amgylch ar lasiad y dydd ar hyd y meysydd yn y gwanwyn a dechrau'r haf. Gwelai morynion Waun-fach hi beunydd yn rhodio ymhlith y meillion yng nghae Llety Dyfrgi pan fyddent hwy yn mynd yn gynnar yn y bore i odro. Ond cysgai hi ei hunan yn dawel yn ei bwthyn bach gerllaw.*

Others told unequivocally how they had seen the ghosts of a man and woman who were still alive. The story was related of an old woman who lived at Cefn-coch-bach who, in the early hours, would roam the fields in spring and early summer. The maids at Waun-fach had seen her daily among the clover in the Llety Dyfrgi field when they were on their way to milking early in the morning. But in fact she was sleeping quietly in her small cottage nearby.

Similarly, the Reverend William Hobley in *Hanes Methodistiaeth Arfon* (The History of Methodism in Arfon) (1910), provides a slightly bleaker outlook on sighting the wraith:

> *Gwelodd un ffarmwr wr ar ochr y mynydd pan y gwyddid fod y gwr hwnnw yn ei wely adref. Y goel ydoedd na byddai'r gwr a welwyd yn y dull hwnnw ddim byw yn hir; ac fel y coelid am dano, felly y digwyddodd iddo.*

One farmer saw a man on the side of the mountain when it was known that this man was in his bed at home. It was believed that the man seen in that manner would not live long; and as it was believed, so it happened to him.

These forms of premonitory apparitions are introduced in Chapter Ten: 'Death Omens', which by no means covers the breadth of this particularly prominent phenomenon in Wales, but hopefully provides a starting point.

While there are entire libraries of accounts that we could not fit within the pages of this book, in the following chapters, you will meet a trove of treasure-guarding, shapeshifting, fantastical spirits, along with ghostly priests, princes and donkeys, and a *Ladi Wen* or two for good measure. We hope you will be sufficiently inspired to delve into the vast array of Welsh texts on ghost-lore that we have not yet referenced, and the many hundreds of stories within them – not lost or forgotten, just waiting to be found.

CHAPTER TWO

Unfinished Business

*

Hir yw'r dydd, a hir yw'r nos,
A hir yw aros Arawn.
Trad.

Long the day, and long the night, and long the wait for Arawn.

One of the earliest accounts of a haunting comes from the writings of Pliny the Younger in the first century CE. In a letter, Pliny discusses the frequent manifestation of an emaciated, bearded man in chains in a house in Athens. The ghost eventually drives away the owners of the property, and the house is subsequently purchased by the philosopher Athenodorus, who does not believe in the story of the spirit … until it appears to him one night. Being a rational person, Athenodorus follows the apparition, which leads him into the courtyard of the house, where it points at the ground before disappearing. Athenodorus places a marker on the spot to which the ghost gestured, before returning to bed.

The next morning, Athenodorus has the ground under the marker dug up and a skeleton is discovered. The body has been secured with iron chains. The philosopher has the bones removed and interred in a proper burial, and the ghost of the bearded man in chains never appears again.

There are many stories where apparitions are described as 'restless spirits', unable to find peace until they have obtained justice for a wrong done to them in life, or unless they are able to deliver a message which they were not able to convey themselves before their death. In many cases, this relates to pointing out the location of a lost item or treasure. As we learned in the introductory chapter, bringing a conclusion to some unfinished business is one of the main reasons for ghosts appearing in Welsh folklore, and the earliest recorded Welsh ghost tales from the seventeenth and eighteenth centuries have many such examples.

Tudur Clwyd, in *Ofergoelion yr Hen Gymry: Mewn Pymtheg Dosparth* (The Superstitions of the Old Welsh: In Fifteen Categories), written sometime at the turn of the twentieth century, summarises succinctly the purposes of the ghost returning on 'unfinished business':

> *Rhith* (ghost) *yw yr hyn a dybir ei fod yn yspryd person ymad-*
> *awedig, yr hwn a anfonir i'r byd yn ei ol ar neges neillduol, megys*
> *i ddynoethi llofruddiaeth, i hawlio ad-daliad arian neu dir, a*
> *gamattaliwyd oddiwrth weddwon neu amddifaid, neu a gyflawn-*
> *odd rhyw annghyfiawnder yn ystod ei oes, ac nas gall gael llonydd*
> *hyd oni iawn drefnir pethau. Brydiau ereill, amcan yr ysprydion yn*
> *ymweled â'r byd ydyw cynnysgaethu etifedd â hysbysrwydd yn mha le*
> *cyfrin, neu ym mha gell mewn hen gist y mae gweithredoedd hawl yr*
> *ystad yn guddiedig; neu mewn adeg o gythrwfl, yn mha le cuddiodd*
> *arian neu lestri.*

An apparition (*ghost*) is what is thought to be the spirit of a deceased person, who is sent back to the world on a special errand, such as to expose a murder, to claim the repayment of money or land, which was confiscated from widows or orphans, or who committed some injustice during his life, and cannot rest until things are properly arranged. At other times, the purpose of the spirits visiting the world is to endow an heir with information as to which secret place, or in which compartment in an old chest, the deeds of the estate are hidden; or in times of trouble, where they hid money or dishes.

It is worth mentioning that, while Tudur Clwyd's chapter on the various types of spirits is of interest, he neglects to provide a single Welsh account!

A few such examples are included in the Reverend D. G. Williams's 1895 prize-winning essay at the National Eisteddfod in Llanelli, 'Casgliad o Lên-Gwerin Sir Gaerfyrddin' ('A Collection of Carmarthenshire Folklore'). It was well known by the townsfolk of Llandeilo that a strange gentleman appeared one night to Evan y Gwëydd (Evan the Weaver) outside his home to ask for a single favour which Evan, in politeness, granted without hesitation.

*'Purion,' meddai'r boneddwr, 'dyna addewid sydd raid ei chadw,
oni ddwr ni fydd i ti lonyddwch, ac ond ei gwneyd, ti gai lonydd byth
gennyf i; enwa di yr amser, ond goreu pa gyntaf.'*

'Very well,' said the gentleman, 'that is a promise that must be
kept, or else you shall have no peace, and until it is done, you
shall never have peace from me; name your time, but the sooner
the better.'

Now realising his error, Evan fearfully suggested they should meet to
conclude the matter – whatever that may be – in three weeks' time.

When the agreed time was upon him, overcome with regret, Evan hid
in his bedchamber with the door bolted. Despite his efforts, he found
himself thrown to the floor and unceremoniously pushed outside by
unseen forces, where the gentleman stood waiting, ordering Evan to
follow him to a large rock that sat atop Glan Ty'nybedw. Under this
rock, Evan found an old iron vessel with something rattling inside,
which he was commanded to throw into the depths of Llyn y Fan lake
in order to be released from his promise. The spectre then carried him
through the air to the sound of tumultuous thunder, and poor Evan
awoke half-frozen and alone near the banks of the river Tywi.

While this tale was often repeated and much feared by the inhabitants
of Llandeilo, several similar examples of tales relating to a ghostly request
to dispose of hidden or buried iron items can be found throughout
Wales – a motif which is discussed later in this chapter.

Once business had been concluded satisfactorily, the ghost would
usually be able to rest and would not trouble anyone further. Williams
further suggests that should the hidden item be tampered with without
the ghost's express permission, such an act of discourtesy would cause
a terrible storm, as exemplified in a tale from the Carmarthenshire
border. Local tradition states that a crock of gold lies hidden beneath
Carreg y Bwci (Bogey's Rock), found on top of Craig Twrch mountain,
and will remain hidden owing to the disastrous storm that would strike
should it ever dare be unearthed. A similar legend is also associated
with the Frenni Fawr summit in Pembrokeshire, and in Dyffryn-bern,
Ceredigion – a tale which is recorded in the manuscripts held at the
Nantgarw archives, Amgueddfa Cymru (Museum Wales) (1925/2).

Writing in his 1885 prize-winning essay at the National Eisteddfod in Aberdâr, 'The Folklore of Glamorgan', Cadrawd suggests that the only alternative way of removing these spirits was through the agency of a cunning man or religious person with a knowledge of laying ghosts:

> It was a general belief that the ghosts of those persons, who, whilst here upon earth, had hidden coins, or even pieces of brass, copper, or iron, would re-appear, and that they could not be prevailed upon to return until the hidden treasures were discovered, unless someone who was conversant in the Black Art were near, for it was supposed they had power over such disturbers of the peace; and that by the said Art all kin of spirits were invariably transported to the Red Sea to ride in Pharaoh's chariots.

A spirit described as being particularly angry used to be resident at the Maltsters Arms on Bridge Street in Pontypridd. The haunting went back many years, pre-dating the current name of the property to a time when it was known as the White Horse Inn. The story can be found in a number of coffee-table and tourist books relating to hauntings in Wales, but these lack the detail found in the older Welsh-language sources, such as an example recorded by Glanffrwd (the Reverend William Thomas), in *Plwyf Llanwyno: Yr Hen Amser, Yr Hen Bobl, Yr Hen Droion* (Llanwynno Parish: Its History, People and Customs) (1913).

Although there are no details as to the identity of this particular ghost, Glanffrwd goes to great lengths to point out that the manifestations took place in the cellar of the building. It had, according to Glanffrwd, his tongue firmly in his cheek, demanded permission to be there.

One night, a young maid working in the property went to the cellar in order to fill a quart jug with beer and saw the spirit standing soberly between the barrels. She chose not to mention this to anybody else, but the next time she needed to venture into the cellar she was naturally scared. This time, the ghost was sitting on top of one of the barrels. It clearly looked annoyed with the girl; Glanffrwd suggests that this was because she had not wished the spirit a good night during their first encounter!

After a time, the maid became too frightened to visit the cellar on her own and so relayed the story to her mistress who accompanied her when the next quart jug needed to be filled. The landlady, however, did not see the apparition even though the maid insisted that it was standing next to her and 'gnashing its teeth terribly' (*'yn ysgyrnygu ei ddanedd yn ddychrynllyd'*).

Having failed to convince her employers, the maid took to using a candle to light her way when braving the cellar, but the ghost promptly extinguished the flame, causing the maid to cry out:

> *'O'r anwyl, beth sydd yma?'*
> *'Ie,' ebe'r ysbryd, 'Da genyf i ti ofyn y cwestiwn, ac mae arnaf eisieu cael dy gwmni i fyned oddiyma i Gwmpistyll Goleu, o dan Eglwys Wyno. Nos yfory am ddeg o'r gloch ni a gychwynwn ein dau.'*

'O dear, what is here?'
'Yes,' said the spirit, 'I'm glad you asked the question, and I want your company to go from here to Cwmpistyll Goleu, under Wyno Church. Tomorrow night at ten o'clock we will both start.'

The girl agreed. When they met the next night, they went to the spot, where the spirit described to her where to uncover some silver gaffles – steel spurs which, in life, the spirit had attached to fighting cockerels, causing the death of many a poor beast. Prior to his death, 'the old gambler' (*'yr hen gambler'*) had buried the gaffles – an act which now weighed heavily on his conscience. He instructed the maid to remove them and take them to the river Taf, near Pontypridd, where she should throw them into the water. Once she completed this task, the ghost was never seen again.

The tale of a cellar-dwelling ghoul apparently persists in the Maltsters Arms, with sightings reported as recently as 2006, when the ghost of a young woman in a long Victorian dress was seen by a member of the staff. However, these accounts do not make as much sense as they might at first appear. The current Maltsters Arms is a different building, constructed around 1875 to replace the previous property in which the haunting took place. The original building stood on an adjacent site and not in the same footprint as the current pub, proving perhaps that, much like the poltergeist of the Emlyn Arms in Llanarthne (see Chapter Six: 'Poltergeists'), a good ghost story is rarely ever bad for business.

Ghosts often appear to maids and servant-boys in many older stories, most likely owing to the condescending attitude of the middle- and higher-class collectors of folklore in the Victorian and Edwardian eras.

Daniel Silvan Evans and Ivon, writing in *Ysten Sioned* (Sioned's Pitcher), first published in 1882, recount another story of a ghost who troubled a serving maid, this time in a farmhouse in an otherwise unspecified location. Although there were plenty of other people present, the spirit always seemed to target and understandably terrify the same person, and so the other members of the house contrived to ensure that the maid was never left on her own, either during the day or at night when sleeping between two other maids.

One summer morning, after the other two had risen, the maid inadvertently fell asleep again, and as it was bright daylight her companions erroneously thought that it would be safe to leave her. But once they had gone, something 'seven times colder than a lump of ice in January' ('*saith oerach na thalp o ia mis Ionawr*') took her hand, causing her to wake in a fright. She knew that she could not avoid a conversation with the spirit this time.

While we know from the account that the ghost wanted the maid to find an item or items which had previously been hidden, the authors are rather vague on the specifics:

> *Dywedodd wrthi fod hen bedol, neu ryw ddarn o haiarn, neu ryw faint o arian, neu ryw gêr o'r fath, yng nghudd yn rhywle, a'i bod hithau i fyned yno a chyrchu y cyfryw, a gwneuthur y peth a'r peth â hwynt.*

> He told her that an old horseshoe, or some piece of iron, or some amount of money, or some such equipment, was hidden somewhere, and that she was to go there and find it, and do such and such with them.

Once the girl had completed the task the spirit had requested of her, she was left in peace.

The description of the ghost's icy touch is far from unprecedented across the British Isles, with several accounts of cold corporeal spirits being recorded as early as the seventeenth century. Professor Owen

Davies has previously suggested that this unpleasant sensation likely reflected the coolness of corpses, with further inference that the Devil himself is said to possess an icy touch. This notion certainly appears to be supported in earlier Welsh accounts, as we find in *A Relation of Apparitions of Spirits, in the Principality of Wales* (1780), where the Reverend Edmund Jones proclaims:

> They are in a cold place indeed, who after death are sunk below the mercies of God, and the comfort of his mercies, where the warmth of his mercies never reaches ... There is the eternal cold of discomfort, and the tormenting fire of God's wrath.

Silvan Evans and Ivon appear less certain than the reverend in their speculations when concluding their tale of the ghost's icy hand:

> *Pa ham y mae dwylaw bwganod mor ddychrynllyd o oer? Ai rhy wylaidd ydynt i nesu at dân ac ymdwymo? Ond bid yr achos y peth y byddo, dwylaw oerion ofnadwy sy ganddynt; ac os ydynt felly yn yr haf, fel y tro hwn, rhaid bod yr ewinrew wyllt ar bob cymmal iddynt yn y gauaf; gan fod eu hoerni ar bob amgylchiad y cafwyd prawf arno, yn ddigon i dreiddio trwy fêr esgyrn y neb y gorfydd arno eu teimlo.*

> Why are ghosts' hands so terrifyingly cold? Are they too shy to approach a fire and warm themselves? Whatever the cause, they have terribly cold hands; and if they are like that in the summer, as on this occasion, there must be severe frostbite on their every limb in the winter; as their coldness in every circumstance that has been tested, is enough to penetrate the marrow of the bones of anyone who has to feel their presence.

Edmund Jones provides a further example of a frosty spirit, this time appearing in Llanfigan, Breconshire. In this account, a young woman, called Ursula Powel, saw the ghost of her recently drowned fiancé materialise at her bedside, whereupon she felt his face, which 'she thought as cold as stone'. This spirit's message was one of comfort, requesting she cease her mourning for him, as 'he was where it was the will of God he should be'.

Not all messages are those of reassurance, and it is not uncommon for spirits of the dead to return to terrorise those perceived to have wronged them in life. The Reverend Evan Isaac records such a case from the Tŷ Cerrig area in Montgomeryshire in *Coelion Cymru* (Welsh Beliefs) (1938), as told to him by Wmffre Cyfeiliog (the Reverend John Humphreys). He describes how a gentleman widower, who was responsible for the poor within the parish, burnt his recently deceased wife's will and forged one that stood him in better favour. It was said that he dragged the paper between her lips so that he could state under oath that the words had indeed come through his wife's mouth, and used her hand to hold the pen before signing her name to it. An uncle of Wmffre Cyfeiliog from Comins Coch, Ceredigion, had once worked for this gentleman, and recounted how one evening, while he sat basket-making by the fire:

agorodd drws y gegin megis ar ddamwain. Gan ei bod yn oer caeodd fy ewythr ef, ond nid cynt yr eisteddodd nag yr agorodd y drws eilwaith. Caeodd ef drachefn. Daeth y forwyn i'r gegin, ac agorodd y drws y drydedd waith. 'Yn enw'r annwyl,' meddai f'ewythr, 'meddyliais i mi gau'r hen ddrws yna'n ddigon ffast.' 'O,' meddai hithau, 'waeth i chi heb boeni, y mae o'n agos, mi wn.' 'Y fo,' meddai ynau, 'Pwy fo?' 'O, meistr. Fel hyn y mae pan fydd o'n dod tuag adre', y mae'r drysau yn agor a chau a chlecian, ac yn aml daw yntau i mewn wedi ei orchuddio â llaid, ac yn gwaedu weithiau. A dyma i chi beth rhyfedd. Yr oedd ganddo gwmni yma i de un diwrnod, a pharodd i mi roddi llestri te gore meistres ar y bwrdd, ond pan euthum i'r cwpwrdd a cheisio tynnu'r llestri allan, yr oedd dwy law yn cydio ynddynt ac ni allwn eu symud o'u lle.' Yn fuan wedyn wele'r gŵr yn cyrraedd, ac yn ymddangos fel pe bai wedi ei dynnu trwy'r drain.

the door opened as if by accident. As it was cold my uncle closed it, but no sooner had he sat down than the door opened a second time. He closed it again. The maid entered the kitchen, and the door opened a third time. 'In God's name,' said my uncle, 'I thought I'd closed that old door tightly enough.' 'Oh,' she said, 'there's no use worrying, he's close now, I know.' 'He,' my uncle inquired, 'Who is he?' 'Oh, master. It's always like this when he's on his way home, the doors open and close and rattle, and he'll often come in covered in mud, and bleeding sometimes. And this is the funny thing. He had company for tea one day, and bade me put the mistress's best tea-set on the table, but when I went to the cupboard to try and take the crockery out, there were two hands grasping them and I couldn't move them an inch.' Soon enough the husband arrived, and looked as if he'd been pulled through a hedge.

In 1973, the Trawsfynydd branch of Merched y Wawr (Daughters of the Dawn), a Welsh organisation not unlike the Women's Institute, published a book on the history of the area called *Hanes Bro Trawsfynydd* (The History of the Trawsfynydd District). Within its pages is a local ghost tale – the account of 'Annie Holborn', found to be Anne Hugh of Holborn cottage by a researcher from nearby Blaenau Ffestiniog, Moi Plas (Morris Davies). The church registers showed Annie as having been interred on 4 April 1753.

The cottage had apparently been named 'Holborn' in memory of a visit which Hugh, Annie's father, had made to London while driving cattle to Kent. Nearby, on the road between Trawsfynydd and Hugh's birthplace of Moelfryn Uchaf farm was another farmhouse called Brynhir. A strange and particularly reclusive family had recently occupied the property, consisting of a husband and wife, and their son and daughter. The local drovers believed that the husband was a highwayman because of his scarred face and rough appearance.

When she was eighteen, Annie and the son of Brynhir fell in love. The family at the farm did everything they could to try and dissuade their son from entering into a relationship with the girl, considering her to be beneath him:

> *Ond er yr holl helynt, ni fynnai'r llanc roi'r gorau i'w gariad, a dywedodd, 'Nid oes ond llaw angau fedr ein gwahanu.' 'Llaw angau' meddai'r tad, 'llaw angau gaiff eich gwahanu,' a chydsyniodd y fam â'r awgrym.*

But despite all the trouble, the youth did not want to give up his love, and said, 'Only the hand of death can separate us.' 'Hand of death' said the father, 'then by the hand of death you shall be separated,' and the mother consented to the suggestion.

In nearby Dolgellau lived Jac Pegi, who was known as a notoriously unscrupulous villain. An arrangement was made that Pegi would murder Annie for money, and so 'Jac Pegi murdered the most beautiful girl in Trawsfynydd and there was great sadness in the parish' ('*[l]lofruddiodd Jac Pegi yr eneth brydferthaf yn Nhrawsfynydd a mawr oedd tristwch y plwyf*').

The funeral was the largest that had ever been seen in the village. After the burial, a wake was held at the nearby pub, which had a door that conveniently opened out on the cemetery. Talk naturally turned to the murder and many people believed that the owner of Brynhir had been responsible for arranging it. It was decided by a group of them that they would go to the farm, find the man, and flay him alive for the crime, but they were talked down by the local rector who told them that they should leave it to God to avenge any wrongdoing.

After the funeral, the son of Brynhir left Trawsfynydd, and nothing more was heard of him. His sister also left home and never returned. From this point on, things continued to deteriorate for the remaining inhabitants of Brynhir:

> *Ni ddeuai gwas na morwyn yn agos i'r lle, ac ni chawsai'r gŵr na'r wraig ddim cwsg oherwydd bod twrw fel tarannau yn y tŷ drwy'r nos. Dro arall clywid llais merch yn canu ac yn griddfan bob yn ail. Yr oedd y defaid, y gwartheg a'r ceffylau yn marw o un i un. Bu farw'r wraig, a chododd yr ardal fel un i wrthod iddi gael ei chladdu ym mynwent y plwyf.*

Neither servant nor maid came near the place, and neither the husband nor the wife had any sleep because there was a noise like thunder in the house all night. Another time a girl's voice was heard singing and moaning alternately. The sheep, cattle and horses died one by one. The wife died, and the area rose as one to refuse her burial in the parish cemetery.

Alone, the husband invited Jac Pegi to live at the farm, but Jac's body was found in the river Prysor the following day. For years afterwards, the lake near Brynhir (which eventually went on to submerge most of its farmland) became known as Llyn Jac Pegi (Jac Pegi Lake). Unsurprisingly, the husband also soon left, and local tradition claimed that for the next twenty years, Annie's ghost was seen riding her horse through the area. Such was the gentle nature of Annie in life, that nobody was afraid of her spirit in death.

We will see several examples within this book of ghost stories which appear to emerge as a result of a community's distrust of outsiders; a theme which also seems relevant to this unpleasant tale.

While accounts of the spirits of victims pursuing their oppressors are easily found within Welsh folklore, it has been suggested that the ghosts of people who were wicked in life far outnumber the good. This should come as no great surprise when we think about the reasons why such stories might arise. The violent, cruel and unjust members of a community were often those who held power over others. Disliked, and even despised for their deeds in life, it follows that when these characters died, narratives would naturally form around them. With their death, the rest of the community could find some closure through the stories that they told, further tarnishing the reputation of the deceased. Unlike the living, the ghosts of the dead could be laid, trapped or banished, the power of the community ultimately proving greater than that of their tormentors.

Not only did these stories target the 'unreachable' higher classes, hauntings also often served as cautionary tales within communities, reflecting the current values and moral ideals of the parishioners – an approach which is often still appreciable in more contemporary sightings. Underpinning these accounts, themes such as infanticide, thievery and suicide are commonly found, as seen in the nineteenth-century haunting of Corlan yr Ŵyn, a sheep's fold on top of Bwlch-y-Rhiwgyr cairn in Eryri, where the spirit of a mother who murdered her baby was said to appear, along with the sounds of the crying infant.

In a similar vein, in 1912, a pupil of Ysgol Lewis (Lewis School) recorded a story in *Llen Gwerin Blaenau Rhymni: O Gasgliad Bechgyn Ysgol Lewis, Pengam* (The Folklore of Blaenau Rhymni: Collected by the Boys of Ysgol Lewis, Pengam), detailing an apparition that appeared to Rhys Dafis when he was staying the night at Penllwyn – 'a very large old house' ('*hen dy mawr iawn*') dating from the sixteenth century, which shares its name with the community in Pontllanfraith, Caerffili.

Despite being given an excellent room at the house, Rhys struggled to sleep. In the middle of the night, he suddenly felt a great pressure on his chest, pinning him to the bed with sufficient force that he was unable to move. Even in the bright moonlight streaming through his window, he could see nothing on the bed, but was trapped nonetheless. After what felt like an age, Rhys saw the apparition of a woman appear in the room and cross to the wash-basin where there stood a jug of water.

Arllwysodd y dwr i'r ffiol, ac yno bu yn golchi, ac yn golchi, ac yn golchi ei dwylaw am amser maith. Wedi hynny cododd ei llaw i gyfeiriad ei llygaid, ac megis wedi ei thrywanu gan fraw, syrthiodd yn wisg ei chefn; mewn moment yr oedd wedi diflanu o'i olwg yn llwyr. Yna daeth yn ol iddo'i hun, fel tae, a chysgodd. Wedi codi, a myned i lawr y bore canlynol, dywedodd ei helynt y noson cynt, a dywedodd ei gyfaill wrtho, – 'Flynyddoedd yn ol, bu gwraig ieuainc brydferth fyw yn y plâs. Lladdodd hon ei gwr yn yr ystafell yr oedd efe yn cysgu ynddi. Ar noson oleu leuad byddai ei lledrith yn dod yn ol i'r ystafell, lle gwnaeth ei chamwri, ac yno ceisiai olchi y gwaed ffwrdd oddiar ei dwylaw – yn union fel y gwelodd efe hi.'

She poured the water into the vase, and there she washed, and washed, and washed her hands for a long time. After that she raised her hand in the direction of her eyes, and as if she had been stabbed by fear, she fell backwards; in a moment she had completely disappeared from his sight. Then he came to, as it were, and slept. After getting up, and going down the following morning, he told of his trouble the night before, and his friend told him, – 'Years ago, a beautiful young woman lived in the mansion. She killed her husband in the room you were sleeping in. On a moonlit night her apparition would come back to the room, where she committed her crime, and there she would try to wash the blood off her hands – just as you saw her.'

The most obvious rational explanation for this story is suggested by Rhys's temporary immobility. Believed in more superstitious times to be a night-time visit from a demon or hag, the inability to move is one of the main symptoms reported in episodes of sleep paralysis – a condition that is yet to be fully medically characterised, but is thought to result from dysfunctional sleep cycles. A hallucinatory component is also very common and will often draw on local superstitious imagery, sometimes taking the form of an unwelcome intruder. The Welsh writer and antiquarian Myrddin Fardd (John Jones) notes an interesting cure for *Yr Hunllef* (The Nightmare) – the colloquial term for sleep paralysis in the Caernarfonshire area – in *Llên Gwerin Sir Gaernarfon* (The Folklore of Caernarfonshire) (1908). The afflicted are advised to 'draw the fingers of both hands through the toes and then to place them under the nose and inhale strongly for around two minutes' ('*tynu bysedd y dwylaw drwy fysedd y traed, ac yna eu gosod hwy wrth y trwyn, a thynu arogl i fewn yn gryf am oddeutu dau funyd*'); the treatment was considered infallible!

A more recent haunting recorded in 1976 in Llanbedr Pont Steffan, and held at the Amgueddfa Cymru (Museum Wales) archives in Nantgarw, deals with the unfortunate taboo surrounding suicide within the community, and the impact of such a haunting on surviving relatives. The author of the manuscript, J. Ann Thomas, describes inheriting an oak chest from her recently deceased great aunt, which then found a new home when she sold it to her brother-in-law. From the moment of its arrival in his house:

> *roeddynt oll fel teulu (3 plentyn) yn clywed sŵn cerdded ac roedd estyll y llawr yn sgrechian. Digwyddai'r sŵn yn ystod y nos, wedi iddynt oll fynd i'r gwely; deuai'r sŵn nôl a 'mlaen trwy bob nos tra bu yno – rhyw 2/3 wythnos i gyd.*

> the entire family (3 children) could hear footsteps and the floorboards would scream. The noise was heard during the night, after they'd all gone to bed; the footsteps would go back and forth throughout the night while it was there – around 2/3 weeks in total.

An attached letter, dated 27 September 1976, from John Owen, the curator of Ceredigion Museum, provides further information regarding the haunting, describing how the noise in the first instance was akin to someone climbing out of the chest.

Mrs Thomas further states that her great aunt's brother died by suicide in 1946 while living at the address from which the chest had come; conclusions may be drawn as to whether this was considered the underlying cause of the haunting. In any case, following weeks of disturbed sleep, the chest was unsurprisingly re-homed in her parents' cellar and the ghostly footsteps were heard no more, the Reverend W. John Gruffydd of Ffair Rhos having suggested at the time that the chest be returned to the family to finally lay the ghost.

A similar familial haunting was once said to be associated with the author and clergyman, Ellis Wynne, whose early eighteenth-century volume, *Gweledigaethau Y Bardd Cwsg* (The Visions of the Sleeping Bard), is considered among the most important Welsh prose ever written in terms of Wynne's rich grasp and idiomatic use of the language.

Wynne was born at Y Lasynys farm, near Harlech, Gwynedd, in 1670/1, where he lived for the vast majority of his life. It was in 1703 that he wrote the darkly humorous literary masterpiece for which he is best remembered. The year after its publication, Wynne, a graduate of Jesus College, Oxford, was ordained as a priest and deacon at Bangor Cathedral, and served in Arfon as a rector at Llanbedr and Llandanwg, and as the incumbent at Llanfair, Harlech, and Llandanwg. He would go on after ordination to publish his own translation of *Llyfr Gweddi Gyffredin* (The Book of Common Prayer) in 1710.

A story exists not about Wynne, but about the ghost of his first wife, Lowri Moel-y-glo, whom he married in 1698. The following year, she sadly died giving birth to their son, Edward. The tale of her return to Y Lasynys first appeared in an article penned for the quarterly Welsh periodical, *Taliesin*, edited by the antiquarian and cleric Ab Ithel (John Williams) – the author of this particular article. The story was published in February 1861, and was subsequently quoted by William Davies in his 1898 prize-winning essay at the National Eisteddfod in Blaenau Ffestiniog, 'Casgliad o Lên-Gwerin Meirion' ('A Collection of Meirion Folklore'):

Dywedir y byddai Lowri Wynn ar ol ei chladdu, neu yn hytrach ei hysbryd, yn d'od ar brydiau i'r Lasynys, ac mai oddeutu cafnau'r moch y byddai yn gwneud cryn dwrf. Un noson aeth Elis Wynn allan ati, a bu'n ymddyddan am yn hir hefo'r ddrychiolaeth. Y canlyniad fu, na chaed byth wedi hyny ddim anesmwythder na thrallod oherwydd ymweliadau nosol Lowri Wynn.

It was said that after being buried, Lowri Wynn, or rather her spirit, would visit Y Lasynys occasionally, and would make a considerable noise around the pig troughs. One evening, Elis Wynn went out to her, and was in conversation with the apparition for a long time. The result was, that he never after experienced any difficulty nor adversity because of Lowri Wynn's nightly visitations.

Ellis Wynne, having by all accounts alleviated Lowri's restlessness, later took a second wife, also conveniently called Lowri – Lowri Lloyd from Hafod Lwyfog, Beddgelert. The couple would have a further nine children together. Ellis Wynne died in 1734 and lies peacefully under the altar at Eglwys Santes Fair (St Mary's Church) in Llanfair.

In *Hanes Plwyf Llanegryn* (The History of Llanegryn Parish), first published in 1948, William Davies describes another similarly poignant account. The son of one Nansi William had died when he was still quite young, and people had begun to report that they had seen his spirit wandering the parish. His grieving mother would spend every night pacing the road between the village and the churchyard in the hope that he would appear to her, allowing him the chance to relay whatever message troubled him, and to find peace.

Davies records another story where the spirit of a deceased husband would appear to his widow on days when she was particularly anxious:

> *Yr oedd siopwr yn ei herlyn am arian, a chredai hi'n sicr fod ei gŵr wedi eu talu cyn ei farwolaeth, ond methai yn lan â chael hyd i'r llyfr cyfrifon a ddangosai hynny. Un noson yn nistawrwydd ei bwthyn unig, ymddangosodd ei phriod iddi yn y man lle'r oedd yr hen lyfr cyfrifon wedi ei roddi i'w gadw.*

A shopkeeper was suing her for money and she was certain that her husband had paid it while he was alive, though she was unable to find the accounts book which would verify that the payment had been made. One night in the quiet of her lonely cottage, her husband appeared to her in the very place where the old accounts book had been put for safekeeping.

Such was the strength of belief in Wales that many restless spirits were returning to Earth because they had unfinished business.

It was also believed that certain people could be brought in purely to pass on messages. In *Hanes Rhosllannerchrugog* (The History of Rhosllannerchrugog) (1945), clergyman and author John Rhosydd Williams recorded an example of this from a letter submitted by one of his parishioners, W. O. Hughes (1848–1938) of Johnson Street. The letter described how it was usually the case that people would 'invite a pious old man from the area to stay in the room with his Bible open and his candle lit, until he saw the spirit and received its message' (*'cael hen ŵr duwiol o'r ardal i aros yn yr ystafell a'i Feibl yn agored a'i gannwyll yn olau, hyd nes y gwelai yr ysbryd a derbyn ei genadwri'*). Hughes noted that his own grandfather had apparently done this for people on many occasions.

While there could be a variety of reasons for a spirit wanting to return and pass on a message, many of them involve money or hidden treasure. Such was the case in the story of 'Crochon Our Penpistyll' ('The Golden Cauldron of Penpistyll') which was recorded by Daniel E. Jones in his book *Hanes Plwyfi Llangeler a Phenboyr* (The History of Llangeler and Penboyr Parishes) (1899), a text which had previously been submitted as a prize-winning local Eisteddfod essay in 1897.

William was a servant working at Penpistyll. One night, the apparition of a woman appeared before him when he was in the hayloft above the cattle. After lingering in front of him for a short time, but doing nothing remarkable, she disappeared again. The same thing happened again the following evening.

As we have already discussed in the introductory chapter, in Welsh folklore a ghost cannot speak unless the witness speaks first, and so on the third night when the woman appeared again, William plucked up the courage to ask what her message was. The spirit requested William follow it, and led the boy to the middle of a field, indicating a boulder which she told him to lift. Underneath lay a pot of gold coins: '"Take those," she said, "and take care of them."' ('"*Cymer di rheina,*" mynte hi, "*a gofala am danyn nw.*"').

William had nowhere safe to keep the pot and so, the following morning, he dug a hole in Allt Penpistyll (Penpistyll Hill) and sunk the pot there. The story tells that William's work did not go unobserved. He was seen by people from across the valley who went to the site under the cover of darkness and stole the treasure. They used the gold to buy a large farm and cattle, which they would then drive over the border to England. The place was subsequently called Pantyporthman, which translates as 'Drovers' Dell'.

While this story may have arisen in order to explain a particular place-name, Daniel Jones notes that a descendant of William recalled how, when he was a child, the family involved had quite firmly believed in the tale.

Jones provides a further example from the same area:

> *Yr oedd Mr. Bowen, Llangeler, yn gweld bwci un noswaith ar ol y llall yn Mhenlon Bwci, ar bwys Coedstre, ac wedi gofyn beth oedd ei neges, fe aeth ag ef dan ffenestr Coedstre a dangosodd swm o arian iddo yno. Ni chafodd neb wybod erioed faint o swm ydoedd.*

> Mr. Bowen, of Llangeler, after seeing a bogey over several nights on Penlon Bwci, near Coedstre, and having asked what his message was, was taken to the window of Coedstre and was shown a sum of money there. No one ever found out how much of a sum it was.

Whether the name 'Penlon Bwci' existed prior to the origin of this tale, or arose as a direct result of this particular ghost, or simply that this story was concocted as a retrospective explanation, this common feature is seen throughout Wales, and is discussed further in Chapter Three: 'Ghosts in the Landscape'.

While the tale of apparitions leading people to hidden treasure is popular in Wales, the more common conclusion is for the ghost to demand that the items are destroyed, often by throwing them into running water, as already exemplified in the case of the Maltsters Arms' cellar-dwelling ghost. This motif can be seen as early as the accounts collected by the Reverend Edmund Jones – an example of which is recorded in Ystradgynlais, Powys, where the spirit of a woman who hanged herself in 1769 bade a man cast into the river a 'great sum of money' which she had hidden in the wall of her home; and in Breconshire, where a ghost called 'Howel' appeared to his cousin, requesting that a hidden hatchet be thrown into the nearby lake 'with all the strength of thine arm'.

A similar story, recorded by Cadrawd, tells of the discovery of gold, although the finder manages to hold onto it in this case. It is noteworthy, however, because it introduces an unusual piece of lore that does not seem to be mentioned beyond Wales.

The events in this tale occur at a property called Havod in the old county of Glamorgan, where a spirit was said to torment a servant. Finally, the servant spoke with it, after which he was conducted to a spot outside Neath. Here, the ghost revealed a buried crock of gold. The servant dug up the crock and was made a gift of the gold by the ghost, who was then able to rest. In evidence for the veracity of this story, the teller described how the servant used the gold to leave Havod and pay for the construction of a row of houses which secured his financial independence. The interesting postscript to this story is in the final sentence, which describes how it 'was also said of this man, and of every one had had the misfortune or the opportunity of speaking to a ghost, that he could never look a man in the face!' This is not a belief generally reported outside Wales, where there are several recorded examples.

Undoubtedly, one of the most extraordinary (and inconvenient) ghostly requests was recorded by Edmund Jones, who described how the son of an innkeeper, again in Ystradgynlais, was asked by the spirit of 'a well-dressed woman' upon their third encounter, and after he had finally plucked up the courage to address her, to travel to Philadelphia in Pennsylvania to retrieve her property! From here, he was to obtain a box containing '200 pounds in half-crowns', and was charged to meet her the following Friday night.

In some state of confusion, the man agreed to attend a prayer meeting that was being held until midnight on the Friday evening by the parish curate, presumably hoping he could avoid the fateful rendezvous. But as he was leaving to fetch his horse, the apparition was said to have lifted him up in the air and carried him 'without seeing sun and moon' to a strange house where he found the box of money under a board in a fine room. The spirit then carried him three miles to 'the black sea', which he perceived to be a lake of clear water, where he was asked to cast the box.

He eventually returned home on the Monday night, three days after his disappearance, looking 'rather sickly' and unable to look into another man's face, much as in Cadrawd's preceding account. It was later remembered that a woman called Elizabeth Gething travelled from her hometown to Pennsylvania some eighty years earlier, and this was most likely the true identity of the roving spirit. While the Reverend Jones was convinced this encounter provided unquestionable proof of ghosts, which he believed were one of God's creations, whether or not the disappearance of an innkeeper's son for three days only to reappear looking 'rather sickly' is of convincing supernatural origin is up to the reader to decide!

A historically significant figure with a ghostly message is recorded in the village of Aberllefenni, Gwynedd. The spirit in question is that of Owain Lawgoch (Owain of the Red Hand), or Owain ap Thomas ap Rhodri. As the great nephew of Llywelyn ap Gruffydd, better known as Llywelyn ein Llyw Olaf (Llywelyn the Last), Owain was the last claimant to the title of prince of Wales (that is, before the uprising of Owain Glyndŵr, discussed in a later chapter). With his grandfather, Rhodri, having renounced his claim to the throne to lead a life of relative obscurity in England, Owain instead travelled to France as a young man to fight the English in the Hundred Years' War as 'Yven de Galles' ('Owain of Wales').

In 1372, while still in France, the house of Gwynedd's successor announced his intention to claim back the Welsh throne, with the support of Charles V of France, and attempted to raise a fleet to invade. In 1378, he was eventually assassinated by a spy for the English, John Lamb. While the real threat he posed to English rule in Wales is doubtful, it is unsurprising that many legends have arisen in association with this flamboyant character, who offered hope to the people of Wales during their brutalisation by the English invaders. Two such stories are discussed below.

In *Cantref Meirionydd: Ei Chwedlau, ei Hynafiaethau, a'i Hanes* (Cantref Meirionnydd: Its Legends, its Antiquities, and its History) (1890), author Robert Prys Morris notes:

> *y byddai ysbryd un o'r enw Ywain Lawgoch, yn ol ei gelwid gan rai, ond gan eraill, Ywain Goch, yn ymweld âg Aberllwyfeni gynt. Dywedir y byddai yr ysbryd hwn yn arfer dangos ei law, a dywedyd, 'Fy llaw goch i.' Ond dywedir hefyd y galwai ei hun yn Ywain Goch o Dan y Castell. Cyfeirir ato yn Nghywydd Canmoliaeth Tal y Llyn, gan Fychan y Gwyndyll, fel Owain Goch, ond ar ymyl y ddalen dodir Owain law goch; a gelwir y llyn y dywedir ei hoffrymwyd iddo yn Llyn Ywain Lawgoch, ac hefyd yn Llyn Ywain Goch.*

the ghost of one called Ywain Lawgoch [Ywain of the Red Hand], as he was called by some, but by others, Ywain Goch [Red Ywain], used to visit Aberllefenni of old. It is said that this spirit used to show his hand and say, 'My red hand.' But it is also said that he called himself Ywain Goch from Dan y Castell [Red Ywain from Under the Castle]. He is referred to in the Tal y Llyn Cywydd [poetry measure] of Praise, by Bychan y Gwyndyll, as Owain Goch, but on the edge of the page is written Owain red hand; and the lake that is said to have been offered to him is called Llyn Ywain Lawgoch, and also Llyn Ywain Goch.

One reason given for the appearance of Owain's ghost is that he had buried a pickaxe and trowel under the foundations of Plas Aberllefenni (Aberllefenni Hall), a property which he is traditionally said to own (despite there being no historical evidence to support this claim). While the loss of two such prosaic tools seems at first glance an unusual excuse for the persistent haunting by such a significant figure within Welsh history, this is in fact not the case at all when considering the location of this particular account.

Aberllefenni is a small village, and was until recently almost exclusively the home of the slate quarry workers of Chwarel Aberllefenni (Aberllefenni Quarry), one of the oldest quarries in Wales, comprising Foel Grochan, Hen Chwarel and Ceunant Ddu quarries. It is said to have been operational from as early as the sixteenth century (Plas Aberllefenni was reported to have been roofed with local slate in 1500) up until its closure in 2003. For local folk, the pickaxe and trowel would have been vital, everyday tools of the trade. With this in mind, it is therefore not surprising to find their significance also being mirrored by the local restless ghoul.

It was also believed that iron could attract spirits, which may account for Owain's return to retrieve his pickaxe and trowel. This belief is recorded by Myrddin Fardd in *Llên Gwerin Sir Gaernarfon*:

Byddai ysbryd yn fynych yn cael ei anfon i gadw meddiant o dŷ dros lawer o flynyddoedd, oherwydd i hen wreigan cyn marw guddio ychydig sylltau ynddo; neu bod yn werth ceiniog neu ddwy o hen haiarn, oblegyd yr oedd fod mewn lle felly ddarn o haiarn cuddiedig mor sicr o dynu ysbryd i'r fan ag yw tynfaen ... o dynu nodwydd cwmpawd y morwr ato ei hun.

A spirit would often be sent to keep possession of a house for many years, because an old woman before dying hid a few shillings in it; or being worth a penny or two of old iron, because having a hidden piece of iron in such a place was as sure to draw a spirit to the spot as a lodestone is to attract the sailor's compass needle.

Perhaps the Reverend Edmund Jones demonstrated the most sensible approach when questioning why so many of our Welsh spirits return to Earth to request the recovery, and often subsequent destruction, of their past property:

My answer is: that we know little of the manner of the world of spirits, and there are many instances in the apparitions of spirits of eternity that they were very short in giving account of the other world. And why? Because the strong human corruption, which corrupts everything, would be sure to make some ill use of a larger and more particular knowledge of the things of the other world, as it doth of his.

Another story suggests that on returning home from an extended trip away, Owain Lawgoch was murdered by a man who had usurped his inheritance. An old milkmaid, Elin ach Ifan (Elin daughter of Ifan), who worked at the hall, claimed:

yr aflonyddai yr ysbryd hwn arnynt wrth odro, pan ydoedd hi yno yn gwasanaethu; ac yr ydoedd yn aros yno o flwyddyn y rhew mawr, pryd, yn ol a ddywedai, y rhewid y llaeth o'r picyn at deth y fuwch wrth odro.

this spirit disturbed them while milking, when she was serving there; and it stayed there from the year of the big frost, when, according to what was said, the milk froze from the pail to the cow's teat during milking.

The lake mentioned in the previous quotation – Llyn Owain Lawgoch, now known as Llyn Cob (not to be confused with Llyn Llech Owain in Carmarthenshire, which also boasts a legend associated with Owain) – lies across the road from Plas Aberllefenni.

Another tale relating to Owain stated that his spirit was eventually trapped in a bottle by a local conjurer and thrown into the river at Llyn Du, described as being 'an old deep basin in the river Dulas' ('*hen grochlyn dwfn yn afon Ddulas*'). What happened next is retold in *Llen Gwerin Blaenau Rhymni: O Gasgliad Bechgyn Ysgol Lewis, Pengam*:

Elai pawb i fynny i Lyn Du i edrych a welsent y botel. Yno yr oedd ar waelod y llyn, yn amlwg i bob un a llygad craffus ganddo. Oedd yn amlycach ar rai adegau na'i gilydd. Rhai blynyddoedd yn ol, aeth Dic y Dychymyg, fel y gelwid ef, i fynny un diwrnod, wrth ei hun. Daeth ar garlam gwyllt yn ei ol, a thystiai iddo weld y botel, ac i'w ddychryn, yr oedd bys coch yn gwthio ei hun allan o'i gwddf. Credodd fod ysbryd Owain Lawgoch bron dod allan o'i garchar – a mawr oedd dychryn plant y gymdogaeth, o ganlyniad. Cadwai pob un ym mhell o'r Llyn Du am fisoedd, o ganlyniad i eiriau Dic.

Everyone went up to Llyn Du to see whether they could spot the bottle. There it was at the bottom of the lake, clear to everyone with a keen eye. It was clearer at some times than others. Some years ago, Dic y Dychymyg [Dick of the Imagination], as he was called, went up one day, by himself. He came back at a wild gallop, and professed that he saw the bottle, and to his horror, a red finger was pushing itself out of its neck. He believed that the ghost of Owain Lawgoch was about to come out of its prison – and the children of the neighbourhood were greatly frightened, as a result. All kept away from Llyn Du for months, as a result of Dic's words.

This paragraph reads, of course, like a story concocted as a warning to keep children away from a dangerous location – in this case a deep water course. Many stories that we find in folklore today share this origin, as seen elsewhere in this book. In this case, however, we may need to consider the postscript of the emerging finger from the bottle with an especially large pinch of salt.

The book in which it is found was compiled from an exercise set for the students at Ysgol Lewis in Pengam, Cwm Rhymni. The boys were tasked with writing an original piece of work based solely on otherwise unpublished stories, the purpose being that they would not be able to translate any existing texts; this meant that each tale was transcribed from verbal accounts. The resulting work has added greatly to the collected folklore of the Rhymni area, and as every story is printed exactly as presented by each young author, they often read more like fairy tales than folk narratives. A degree of artistic licence in accounts such as this one is only to be expected.

We often find similar stories occurring in folklore from different geographical areas. These themed groupings of stories are sometimes referred to as tropes, although this term is falling out of favour in folklore study. One such trope revolves around a recurring sentiment howled by all manner of Welsh ghouls with unfinished business.

The first example, to the best of our knowledge, can be found in *Cambrian Superstitions* (1831) by William Howells. The author claims to have acquired the tale from 'one of those receptacles of stories *yclept* [called] an old woman', who related an account from Pembrokeshire, where a traveller called Noe (an archaic Welsh spelling of Noah) arrives at an unspecified inn one night. After he is refreshed, he makes as if to continue his journey, at which point the landlord intervenes with the warning: 'you will not travel to night, for it is said that a ghost haunts that road, crying out "The days are long and the nights cold to wait for Noe."'

The traveller answers mysteriously, 'O, I am the man sought for', before departing. After this night, neither he nor the ghost are ever seen again, with some speculation that the spirit was that of a jilted lover, or that Noe was a murderer; in either case, folk were quite certain that he was destined 'to no good place'.

This version was later recounted verbatim by Wirt Sikes in his 1880 publication, *British Goblins*, and a similar ghoul awaits the elusive 'Noah' in Glanffrwd's *Plwyf Llanwyno*. This story revolves around a spirit that was said to haunt Twyn y Cefn Bychan and which could be heard periodically 'wailing during the night in a ghastly voice, cold and melancholy' ('*i ruddfan yn ystod y nos mewn llais erchyll, oer a phruddglwyfys*'):

> *Hir yw'r dydd, a hir yw'r nos,*
> *A hir yw aros Noah.*

Long the day, and long the night, and long the wait for Noah.

According to this story, the spirit had been trapped for many ages, and was neither able to move on nor relay its message until it had spoken to Noah. Eventually, this same Noah passed by one night to hear the spirit's message and settle the matter once and for all. The message itself remains a mystery, as does Noah's identity, and his reason for passing by in the first instance.

A variation of this tale was recorded by Daniel Silvan Evans and Ivon in *Ysten Sioned*. In this story, which takes place in a farmhouse in an unspecified location around the south-west of Wales, the family keep a room out of use because of the many frightful noises that emanate from it, violent enough that a witness would believe furniture was being smashed. Of interest, however, was a voice that could be heard bawling angrily from the room late each night: 'Long the day, and long the night, and long the wait for Arawn.' (*'Hir yw'r dydd, a hir yw'r nos, a hir yw aros Arawn.'*).

The occupants of the farmhouse were gathered around the fire one winter night before supper, when there was a knock at the door. The unexpected stranger was duly invited in to enjoy the warmth of the house, and after the pleasantries of introduction had been made, he asked whether he would be able to partake of some food and lodgings. The family offered him food and drink, but told him they could not provide a bed because of the nightly disturbances in the only spare room. They described the nature of the problem, but the visitor was undeterred: "'I would not be the worse for that," said the weary traveller; "there is nothing that will harm me; I will take it gratefully, and do not be uneasy because of me.'" (*"'Nid gwaeth am hyny," ebai'r teithiwr blin; "nid oes yno ddim a wna niwed i mi; mi a'i cymmeraf yn ddiolchgar, ac na fyddwch anesmwyth o'm plegid.'"*).

The family were uncertain, but they could see how tired the traveller looked, so they conceded and allowed him use of the room, feeling rather guilty that he would probably be no better rested by the morning. They asked the man his name, and whether he had travelled very far: "'My name," he said, "is Arawn; I have come a long way, and have walked hard.'" (*"'Fy enw," ebai yntau, "yw Arawn; yr wyf wedi dyfod o bell ffordd, ac wedi cerdded yn galed.'"*).

The man's name naturally unsettled the family but they showed him to the room nonetheless, doubting he would spend a restful night. Their concerns, it would turn out, were unfounded as there was no disturbance heard from the room at all. In the morning, as in the previous accounts, the visitor was nowhere to be found and the room was silent from that day on.

While this adaptation of the tale provides us with no further clues as to the origin or purpose of the ghostly cry, the protagonist's name here is of particular interest, as it denotes a reference to Arawn, who is first presented in the First Branch of the *Mabinogi* as king of the Welsh otherworld, Annwfn (also known as Annwn). Whereas preceding versions could generally be considered a metaphor for the need for patience, the use of such a prominent figure from Welsh mythology somewhat muddies this interpretation. It may represent a commentary on the inevitability of death – Arawn, when looked at through a later Christian lens, was sometimes referred to as the king of the underworld or even Hell.

In order to fully appreciate any nuance, it is worth considering the political and cultural landscape in Wales at the time Silvan Evans recorded this account. Over the course of the eighteenth and nineteenth centuries, the scale and rapidity of the changes brought on predominantly by the Industrial Revolution saw Welsh identity and culture being increasingly oppressed. In a mere century, Welsh had gone from being a universally used language to being spoken by barely half the population. The secondary effects of mainly English and Irish immigration in previously rural and close-knit communities, especially within the mining communities of the south Wales valleys, and the introduction of the despotic 'Welsh Not' in schools across the country, saw the attempted eradication of an entire culture by the British state. Professor Jane Aaron has theorised that Arawn in this context may therefore 'be taken here to represent the full plentitude of Celtic culture', with a call for his return representing the 'instinctual repressed yearning for his presence' – bringing peace not only to this household, but to the wider country. A Welsh scholar and pioneer of Welsh lexicography, it can come as no great surprise that Silvan Evans might seek to invoke a strong and enigmatic character such as Arawn to return to Wales in its time of need.

Further examples of this trope have been noted by Daniel E. Jones in *Hanes Plwyfi Llangeler a Phenboyr*, and by the Reverend William Jenkin

Davies, the vicar of Ystalyfera, in *Hanes Plwyf Llandyssul* (The History of Llandysul Parish) (1896), where an elderly parishioner called William recalls how the 'Bwci Pen-mol-ym-or' ('Pen-mol-ym-or Bogey') would shout: 'Long day of summer, long night of winter; A very long time to wait for Owen' (*'Hir ddydd ha, hir nos eia; Hir iawn i aros Ŵan'*).

A similar adaptation is also recorded by Dewi Cynon (David Davies) in *Hanes Plwyf Penderyn* (The History of Penderyn Parish) (1924), this time involving the cry of an apparent 'wood nymph' that was said to manifest on a stone known locally as Stôl yr Wyddones, translated by Dewi Cynon as 'Wood Nymph's Throne'. Here she would cry at night for her presumed lost partner: 'Long the night, and cold the weather to wait for Aron' (*'Hir yw'r nos, ac oer yw'r hin i aros Aron'*).

The word *gwyddones* (a variant of *gwiddon*) more commonly alludes to a giantess, witch or sorceress rather than the image of a wood nymph.

Similar themes of howling ghosts may be seen elsewhere within the country's rich lore (see Chapter Nine: 'Fantastical Ghouls'), and there are doubtless more hidden examples of this particularly intriguing motif waiting to be discovered.

Our final closing account of unfinished business has something of a touch of black comedy to it, as do many of Glanffrwd's other tales.

The haunting centres on a couple, Dafydd and Rachel, and a spirit with a message to impart. The ghost tried very hard to disturb Dafydd in order to gain his attention, but it proved to be a difficult task because, unbeknown to the spook, Dafydd was incredibly hard of hearing and was known locally as Dafydd Fyddar, or Deaf Dafydd.

The ghost appears to have been relentless in its attempts to engage with him, but could only be understood when Dafydd was able to see it. Despite this, the couple seem to have been quite troubled by its antics, and ended up moving to different houses and parishes to evade it.

After some years, Dafydd and Rachel finally settled at Craig-yr-Hesg and for a time it appeared that the spirit had not followed them there. But then, one night, Dafydd saw the ghost in the form of a foal walking along the top of the house. He pointed this out to Rachel and together they finally decided to relent and ask the spirit what it wanted and why it had followed them for so long – a decision which one might ask wasn't reached earlier in the proceedings.

They approached the ghost to receive its message, and the spirit led them to a location described simply as a place near Cendl (Beaufort, Gwent). Here, they were shown a hearth stone in a house, under which was buried a knife in a box which Dafydd was tasked to throw in the river. While doing so brought an end to the disturbances, the memory of the events were said to have haunted Dafydd Fyddar to his grave.

CHAPTER THREE

Ghosts in the Landscape

*

*Ac yspryd Dai Brondinî
Yn gwneyd i'r wlad ddychrynu,
Ni theithia neb heb gwrdd ag ef
O farchnad tref Llanelli.*

Deio Bach, 'Can yr Ysbrydion' ('Song of the Ghosts')

And the ghost of Dai Brondinî, bringing terror to the country, no one could travel without meeting him, from the market in Llanelli.

Llawer gŵr syber a moesol, uniawn ei ymddygiad, a chredadwy ei air, a glywodd ac a welodd bethau rhyfedd o bob lliw a llun yn y nos ar hyd 'Lon-ceryg-bychain' a 'Lôn-nant-Iago,' yn mhlwyf Llanbedrog. Meddiannid yr holl ardal ar fachludiad haul y gauaf gan breswylwyr byd yr ysbrydoedd, fel nad gwiw oedd i neb o breswylwyr cyfreithlon yr ardal fyned allan ar ol iddi nosi heb gael ei aflonyddu gan fodau o'r byd anweledig, naill ai preswylwyr hudoliaethus byd tanddaearol y Tylwyth Teg, ai cenadau oddiwrth ei fawrhydi brwmstanaidd, neu o'r ardal dawel lonydd lle y peidia y trigolion a'u cyffro. Yr oedd bwgan yn llechu yn sawdl pob clawdd, canwyll gorff yn goleuo pob Eglwys, ladi wen yn gwylio pob croesffordd, a drychiolaethau mor aml a llwyni eithin.

Many a sober and moral man, upright in his conduct, and trustworthy in his word, has heard and seen strange things of all shapes and sizes at night along 'Lon-ceryg-bychain' and 'Lôn-nant-Iago,' in the parish of Llanbedrog. The whole area was occupied at sunset by the inhabitants of the spirit world, so that

it was not possible for any of the legitimate inhabitants of the area to go out after nightfall without being disturbed by someone from the invisible world, either the beguiling dwellers of the underground world of the Tylwyth Teg, and their messages from his sulphuric majesty, or from the quiet and peaceful area where the inhabitants cease their excitement. There was a ghost lurking at the foot of every hedge, a corpse candle lighting every Church, a white lady watching every crossroad, and apparitions to be seen as frequently as gorse bushes.

This passage from Myrddin Fardd in *Llên Gwerin Sir Gaernarfon* (The Folklore of Caernarfonshire) (1908) suggests that anyone venturing out of their house at night to walk the roads of Llanbedrog, or by extension any similar Welsh parish, would be likely to stumble upon a phantom around every corner. While we are not supposed to take this literally, but rather as a commentary on the high number of superstitious beliefs and stories of ghosts and fairies at the time, haunted highways and byways in Wales often feature at the forefront of Welsh ghost-lore.

At the opposite end of the country in Carmarthenshire, the Reverend Tom Beynon compiled another list of roads one might seek to avoid after dark in *Cwmsêl a Chefn Sidan* (Cwmsêl and Cefn Sidan) (1946), a collection of letters and columns which first appeared in various Welsh newspapers and periodicals:

> *Yr oedd gan yr ysbrydion heolydd arbennig i ymddangos ynddynt –*
> *Heol Rogerly, Heol Cefn y Maes, Heol Gellidêg, Heol Cwm Cadwgan,*
> *Heol Capel Teilo, Heol Ferem, a Heol Pont Spwdwr.*

> The ghosts had specific roads they would appear on – Rogerly Road, Cefn y Maes Road, Gellidêg Road, Cwm Cadwgan Road, Capel Teilo Road, Berem Road, and Pont Spwdwr Road.

Similar warnings of haunted paths, fields and landmarks are commonplace in Welsh parish histories and folklore accounts. Within the later chapters of this book we will learn more about animal ghosts, white ladies, phantom funeral processions and corpse candles, all of which were frequently seen traversing the Welsh landscape. However, there are many more roaming spectres that cannot be so easily categorised, as described in some of the older Welsh-language sources.

An example of such a haunting can once more be found in the pages of *Llên Gwerin Sir Gaernarfon*, where Myrddin Fardd records a well-known ghost at a *camfa* (stile) in Abererch called Camfa Angharad:

> *Pawb yn gwybod am 'Gamfa Angharad,' a'r arswyd i fyned trosti bron cyn i'r nos ymddangos, yn dod i lawr genedlaeth i genedlaeth ar blant a phobl weiniaid.*

> Everyone knows about 'Camfa Angharad,' and the horror of going over it at twilight, passed down from generation to generation between children and servants.

The haunting at Camfa Angharad took on a shapeshifting element, a motif to which we will return. In this case, the ghost (or possibly ghosts) appeared in different forms, including a group of men in bright white clothing who seemed to move through each other and then change into greyhounds, jumping over the wall and into an adjacent field.

The appearance of a group of men in uniform clothing might also lead us to suspect this account has as much to do with the *Tylwyth Teg* (fairies) as it does with ghosts. Groups of supernatural beings are often seen as fairies; an early example recorded by the Reverend Edmund Jones describes a company of spirits 'with speckled clothes of white and red colour' who appeared to an innkeeper in his bedchamber in Llangynwyd Fawr in 1767. Jones speculates that 'by their appearing with speckled clothes ... I'm inclined to think they were the fairy sort'. The transition into greyhounds at Camfa Angharad might also put us in mind of the dogs of the *Tylwyth Teg*, sometimes known as *Cŵn Bendith y Mamau* (see Chapter Ten: 'Death Omens'), although as we will see in the next chapter, ghostly greyhounds are not without precedent in Wales.

A tangential story from Camfa Angharad describes how a rock exhumed from underneath this same stile was said to bear an inscription that was legible only to Dic Aberdaron. Born Richard Robert Jones in 1780, Dic was a wanderer from Pen Llŷn (Llŷn Peninsula) – a shabby and eccentric character. He had received little in the way of education but proved to have a love of languages and was said to have taught himself a dozen or more, including Latin, while still a child. The actual number reported varies, with one of the obituaries written on his death in 1843 putting the total as high as 35! Unfortunately, we do not know if the inscription on this stone had any relevance to the haunting because, if Dic was able to read it, he seems not to have had the inclination to record its meaning anywhere.

In folklore, boundaries are usually significant. These boundaries may be represented by physical barriers, such as stiles, but less tangible boundaries, such as time, can also serve the same purpose; the transition from one day to another is an important boundary, as is the transition from day to night. We might note that in his account, Myrddin Fardd refers to the 'horror' of Camfa Angharad at twilight.

Alwyn and Brinley Rees note in *Celtic Heritage: Ancient Tradition in Ireland and Wales* (1961) that:

> boundaries between territories, like boundaries between seasons, are lines along which the supernatural intrudes through the surface of existence … the fact that unbaptised children used to be buried at boundary fences suggests that these lines, like the unbaptised child, did not really belong to this world. Stiles were favourite perches for ghosts.

The motif of ghosts on stiles is especially common in Wales on 31 October, known as *Nos Galan Gaeaf* (Winter's Eve, or Hallowe'en). Regarded as a seasonal boundary, it was once celebrated nation-wide, most commonly through various divination practices and the lighting of bonfires. *Nos Galan Gaeaf* was also considered the most ominous of *Y Tair Ysbrydnos* (The Three Spirit Nights), the other two falling on *Nos Galan Mai* (Mayday Eve) and *Noswyl Ifan* (St John's Eve), when ghosts were believed to be particularly active. As Glanffrwd recalls from his youth in Llanwynno:

> *Credid yn gryf ys llawer dydd fod Satan i'w weled yn marchogaeth pob camfa ar nos Galan Gauaf! Ac yr wyf yn cofio i mi basio llawer camfa ar nos Galan Gauaf a'm llygad yn nghau, fel os oedd yr 'hen fachgen' yn cael ride arnynt, yr oeddwn yn penderfynu peidio edrych arno, na rhoddi cyfle iddo i ddangos ei hun i mi, oddieithr iddo ddyfod oddiar y Gamed.*

It was strongly believed in days gone by that Satan could be seen riding every stile on Hallowe'en! And I remember passing many a stile on Hallowe'en with my eyes closed, so that if the 'old boy' was having a ride on them, I elected not to look at him, nor give him a chance to show himself to me, unless he came off the Gamed [stile].

It is little wonder that Glanffrwd was scared witless by this imagery, as physical boundaries such as stiles also feature prominently in well-known *hwiangerddi* (children's nursery rhymes) associated with *Nos Galan Gaeaf*:

Mae heno'n nos Glangaea',
A bwci ar bob camfa

Tonight is Hallowe'en, with a bogey on every stile

Hwch ddu gwta
Ar bob camfa

The tailless black sow, on every stile

Bwci Bal yn y wal,
Bwci Beto nesa' ato

Bal bogey in the wall, Beto bogey next to him

Historian William Davies refers to the same phenomenon of haunted Hallowe'en stiles in *Hanes Plwyf Llanegryn* (A History of the Parish of Llanegryn), first published in 1948. It was another noteworthy open-air apparition that troubled this particular locality, as it was believed that '[s]ome glades were troubled by the ghost of a child; it cried all night from a holly-tree, year after year' ('*[p]oenid ambell lannerch gan ysbryd plentyn; nadai gydol y nos ar goeden gelyn, a hynny'r naill flwyddyn ar ôl y llall*').

William Hobley, in *Hanes Methodistiaeth Arfon* (The History of Methodism in Arfon) (1910), mentions a similar crying ghost child in Clynnog, Gwynedd. He reports that '[a] child could be heard crying in

Llwyn Maethog, so that nobody was of a mind to travel that way late at night' ('*[y]r oedd plentyn i'w glywed yn crïo yn Llwyn Maethog, fel nad elai neb o'i fodd y ffordd honno yn hwyr o'r nos*').

This seems very sensible. If anything is likely to deter a person from walking a lonely road late at night, it is probably the disembodied voice of a crying child. While the spirits of children were generally considered rare in Wales, a further example of a ghostly crying boy can be found in Chapter Nine: 'Fantastical Ghouls'.

Folklore has a habit of leaving its mark on the landscape by way of the stories that become ascribed to place-names. Whether these stories are an accurate record of the origin of the place-name is often the cause of much debate.

In 1874, the book *Hanes Morganwg* (The History of Morgannwg) by the Welsh poet and historian Dafydd Morganwg (David Watkin Jones) gave the following derivation for the village of Abercwmboi:

> *Llygriad yw'r enw hwn o Abercwmbô, neu yn hytrach Abercwm y Bwci. Cafodd y lle yr enw am fod pobl ofergoelus yr oesoedd gynt yn credu fod bwci neu ddrychiolaeth yn trigianu yn y lle.*

> The name has been corrupted from Abercwmbô, or rather Abercwm y Bwci. The place gained its name because superstitious people from previous times believed that a bogey or a phantom dwelt there.

The generally accepted etymology of Abercwmboi today reflects its association with the nearby Cynfoi water course rather than a long-forgotten bogey. During the nineteenth century, however, the village was in fact known as Cap Coch (Red Cap) – a name which allegedly arose due to the antics of an eccentric publican who was prone to wearing his red cap on cockfighting day.

The supernatural etymology of various points within the landscape is not unusual, and there are numerous historical landmarks which can be found simply by searching the Royal Commission on the Ancient and Historical Monuments of Wales's database of historic place-names. Myrddin Fardd also collected an exhaustive list of place-names derived from local ghost-lore within the boundaries of Llŷn and Eifionydd in 1908:

Cae'r Bwgan (Bogey's Field), Pwlldefaid, Aberdaron; and
Trefgwm, Sarn Meyllteyrn; and Botacho Ddu, Nefyn

Cae Bodwiddan (Sorceress / Giantess / Nymph's Field),
Gyfelan Fawr, Llangwnadl

Nant y Widdan (Sorceress / Giantess / Nymph's Stream),
near Garn Fadryn, Llaniestyn

Perthen Bwbach (Bogey's Orchard), Nyffryn, Llaniestyn

Carreg y Bwgan (Bogey's Rock), Pigstryd, Llanbedrog

Lleiniau'r Bwgan (Bogey's Patch), Hobwrn, Nefyn

Cae Pwll y Widdan (Field of the Witch's Pool), Plas Boduan;
and Hendref, Boduan

Erw'r Bwgan (Bogey's Acre), Mathan Isaf, Boduan

Cae Pwll Bwbach (Field of the Bogey's Pool), Gwynfryn, Llannor

Cae'r Widdan and Cae'r Widdan Uchaf (Sorceress / Giantess /
Nymph's Field and Upper Field), Hendrefeinws, Abererch

Pwll yr Wyll (Goblin / Demon's Pool), Tŷ'n Lôn, Y Ffôr

Pwll yr Ellyll (Demon / Elf's Pool), Murgwt Lloer, Llanarmon

Cae Pant y Bwbach (Field of the Bogey's Hollow), Tyddyn y Berth,
Llanarmon

Camfa'r Bwbach (Bogey's Stile), on the boundary between
Hen Inn and Tŷ'n y Coed Uchaf, Llanystumdwy

Gallt y Widdan (Sorceress / Giantess / Nymph's Hill),
Penstumllyn, Cricieth

Pant y Gwylliaid (Hollow of the Savages), Pant Glas, Cenin,
Llanfihangel-y-Pennant

Ffynnon y Cythraul (Demon's Well), Llanfihangel-y-Pennant

Yr Ellyll (Demon / Elf), Cwmtrwsgwl, Llanfihangel-y-Pennant

Beddau'r Dewiniaid (The Graves of the Sorcerers), near Dinas Emrys,
Beddgelert

Cader / Castell Ellyll (Demon / Elf's Seat / Castle), near Yr Wyddfa

Melville Richards also records several such places from across Wales in his
chapter 'The Supernatural in Welsh Place-names' in *Studies in Folk Life:
Essays in Honour of Iorwerth C. Peate* (1969), writing that the 'recognition

and fear of the supernatural are so ingrained in human nature that one would expect this to be recorded as an onomastic feature'.

A rather fantastical example of a haunting giving rise to a place-name can be found in William Davies's 1898 essay, 'Casgliad o Lên-Gwerin Meirion' ('A Collection of Meirion Folklore'), in an excerpt entitled 'Ysbryd yn dychrynu Ymladdwyr' ('A Ghost scaring Brawlers') from Dyffryn Ardudwy, Gwynedd. The tale recounts how a spot on Tyddyn-y-llidiart farmland, known as Clwt y Chwareufa (The Games Patch), was often used for all manner of sports and contests within the community. It would not always be clear who the winner of a particular feat was:

Os rhoddid her i ymladd, ymneillduai y pleidiau i'r llanerch olaf a nodwyd [Llety'r Cweryl] i benderfynu y ddadl trwy ornest neu ymladdfa. Ond rhyw dro a hi yn nesau at wyll yr hwyr, ymddangosodd ysbryd yn eu plith ar lun eidion enfawr a hir-glustiog, a chanddo wyneb fel gwyneb dyn, ac iddo draed fel traed llew, ac wedi iddo chwalu y pleidiau ymladdgar oddiwrth eu gilydd, rhoddodd un naid anferth i odreu y Moelfre, lle y gwelir hyd dydd hwn nôd gareg a elwir Llun Troed yr Eidion, sef y man y dysgynodd, yn union gerllaw Penrhos Dinas yn Ardudwy.

If a challenge was issued to fight, the groups would retreat to the last mentioned spot [Llety'r Cweryl: The Quarreling Spot] to decide the argument through a competition or fight. One day as it was approaching the darkness of the evening, a ghost appeared among them in the form of a giant, long-eared bullock, with a face like a man, and feet like a lion, and when he had separated the fighting groups from each other, gave one colossal leap towards the base of Moelfre, where to this day can be seen a mark in the rock called Llun Troed yr Eidion [The Form of the Bullock's Hoof], which was the place it landed, very near Penrhos Dinas in Ardudwy.

While this story either represents a retrospective folk tale concocted to explain the pre-existing name of the rocky outcrop, or an opportunistic and somewhat creative naming of the landmark to serve as a deterrent to the quarrelling children of the community, Moelfre hill itself is strongly anchored within the folk tradition of Meirion.

Another north Walian hill sharing the same name features in Wirt Sikes's seminal *British Goblins* (1880):

> There is a curious legend regarding three stones which once stood on the top of Moelfre Hill, in Carnarvonshire, but which were long ago rolled to the bottom of the hill by 'some idle-headed youths' who dug them up. They were each about four feet high, standing as the corners of a triangle; one was red as blood, another white, and the third a pale blue. The tradition says that three women, about the time when Christianity first began to be known in Britain, went up Moelfre Hill on a Sabbath morning to winnow their corn. They had spread their winnowing sheet upon the ground and begun their work, when some of their neighbours came to them and reprehended them for working on the Lord's day. But the women, having a greater eye to their worldly profit than to the observance of the fourth commandment, made light of their neighbours' words, and went on working. Thereupon they were instantly transformed into three pillars of stone, each stone of the same colour as the dress of the woman in whose place it stood, one red, one white, and the third bluish.

Contemporary retellings of the above tale consistently attribute this story to the aforementioned Moelfre hill in Meirionnydd. However, Sikes's account is instead located in the old county of Caernarfonshire. While it is entirely possible that Sikes conflated his counties, other possible topographical candidates exist in the Caernarfonshire area, such as in Llanaelhaearn and Llanfairfechan.

The notion of communities being punished or shamed for the acts of 'Sabbath-breakers' is a universal motif throughout British folklore, and Wales is no exception. While the Devil in Welsh folklore was more often depicted as a dimwitted and farcical figure, the fear of damnation was no laughing matter. Numerous landmarks are therefore found across the country which were used to serve as a stark reminder of the repercussions of committing such a sin as breaking the Sabbath. The Reverend Elias Owen in *Welsh Folk-lore: A Collection of the Folk-Tales and Legends of North Wales* (1896), notes a location of this nature on the slopes of Cader Idris in Gwynedd, known as Carreg-gŵr-drwg (The

Rock of the Evil One), so named from when parishioners congregated on Sunday to play cards. The Devil appeared, as he is wont to do, dancing around the rock and leaving his hoofprints behind.

Leaping monstrosities and devils aside, it is apparent that not every monument with an uncanny name deserves its sinister reputation, as proven by Glanffrwd in *Plwyf Llanwyno* (Llanwynno Parish). Originally published in 1888, the volume was drawn together from a series of articles that had originally appeared in *Tarian y Gweithiwr* (The Worker's Shield), a weekly Welsh-language newspaper published in Aberdâr between 1875 and 1934.

A rocky outcrop once stood next to the main road near the village of Ynysybwl in modern-day Rhondda Cynon Taf, known as Cadair Ysbryd (Spirit's Chair). Its appearance, according to miners from the area, came about when a section of rock fell away at the convergence point of several slips, forming a shape which resembled an armchair. There was a locally held belief, which Glanffrwd places sometime around the 1860s, that this place was haunted by a ghost which sat in the chair. The author, however, thought he knew of a far more rational origin for this tale:

Yr wyf yn cofio i rai o bobl y plwyf er ys mwy nag ugain mlynedd yn ol gael eu dychrynu yn ddirfawr wrth weled ysbryd yn eistedd yn y gadair, a'i wedd mor loew fel y goleuid y ffordd drosti; ond gan fy mod yn gallu cyffesu i mi fy hun, fel hogyn drwg, oleuo canwyll y noson hono a'i rhoddi mewn darn o glai yn y gadair, nid yw yn deg i ni ddyfod i'r penderfyniad fod ysbryd wedi bod cyn ffoled a threulio oriau i eistedd ar galedwch y gadair gareg hon. Onid tebycach mai goleuni fy nghanwyll i a welwyd gan y bobl a ddychrynwyd mor ddirfawr?

I remember that more than twenty years ago some of the people of the parish were terrified when they saw a ghost sitting in the chair, and its appearance so pale that it lit up the road; but as I can confess that myself, as a naughty boy, lit a candle that night and put it in a piece of clay in the chair, it is not fair for us to come to the decision that a ghost was such a fool as to spend hours sitting on the hardness of this stone chair. Is it not more likely that the light of my candle was seen by the people who were frightened so dreadfully?

It seems quite likely that this prank played by the young Glanffrwd was responsible for spawning a ghost story at this spot. The geological feature may remain, but the name, to the best of our knowledge, does not.

Sometimes ghosts in the landscape arise, not because there is any specific associated tradition or historical event, but rather because the nature of the area lends itself to the telling of atmospheric, uncanny stories. Glanffrwd recalls just such a place:

> *Llawer gwaith y cerddais o Gwm Clydach i Ynysybwl yn ofnus a chynhyrfus, trwy dywyllwch y nos, ac yn dysgwyl ar bob cam weled ysbryd, neu ryw fod annaearol arall, yn gwneud ei ymddangosiad ger fy mron. Ac er i ni weled rhai pethau, a chlywed lleisiau hefyd nas gallaf eu hesbonio, ni welais ar fy mhererindodau nosawl yn y plwyf, erioed ddim cyffelyb i ysbryd.*

Many times I walked, scared and agitated, from Cwm Clydach to Ynysybwl, through the darkness of the night, and expecting at every step to see a ghost, or some other unearthly being, making its appearance before me. And although we saw some things, and also heard voices that I cannot explain, I never saw on my nocturnal pilgrimages in the parish, anything similar to a spirit.

Glanffrwd's writings suggest that, although he had a passion for recording local customs and traditions, he thought some of them rather ridiculous. He recalls how, when he was young, one of the first traditional sayings that he heard was 'something dwells under Clwyd Drom' ('*[mae] rhyw-beth yn cadw dan y Glwyd Drom*'); the name literally translates as 'Heavy Gate'. He notes that the saying was in common use among the older generation within the parish, and that children were therefore frightened to walk past the gloomy location, where an old ivy-covered oak tree stood on the bank of the stream. He continues to describe how, later in life, he himself once witnessed a spirit at this very location – it was the spirit of poetry; a tongue-in-cheek reference to how his beloved Llanwynno served as one of the nationally celebrated bard's greatest inspirations.

In *Hanes Rhosllannerchrugog* (The History of Rhosllannerchrugog) (1945), John Rhosydd Williams recorded various accounts of local folk customs and superstitions, some of which, as we have already seen in

Chapter Two: 'Unfinished Business', he gleaned from a letter submitted by parishioner W. O. Hughes of Johnson Street. One such tale is that of the ghost of Allt-y-gwter:

Nid oedd ysbryd Allt-y-gwter bob amser yn gwneud ei hun yn we-
ladwy. Os byddai rhywun yn dod i fyny'r allt rhwng hanner nos ac
un o'r gloch y bore, byddai'r ysbryd wrth giat y Memorial. Gwelid
ef weithiau fel ci mawr du, bryd arall fel ci bychan gwyn (carlwm).
Rai prydiau ni welid dim ond ni chlywais ei fod wedi dilyn neb
erioed ym mhellach na'r Siop Rad, diflannai yno fel olwyn o dân.

The Allt-y-gwter ghost did not always make itself visible. If someone came up the hill between midnight and one o'clock in the morning, the ghost would be at the Memorial gate. It was sometimes seen as a large black dog, other times as a small white dog (or stoat). Sometimes it was not seen but I never heard that it had followed anyone further than the Cheap Shop, it would disappear there as a wheel of fire.

Here we see a return to the shapeshifting motif mentioned briefly earlier. The ghost in this account tends to appear in animal form, and it is to animal apparitions that the idea of shapeshifting is generally applied. The image of a black dog is a prevalent one in folklore from across Britain and the rest of the world, and is one we shall discuss in greater detail in Chapter Four: 'Spectral Beasts'. The motif of a ghost disappearing in a wheel of fire is also common in Wales, as numerous examples in this book attest.

While the ghost of Allt-y-gwter was known only to manifest itself within particular boundaries, in the Amgueddfa Cymru (Museum Wales) archives in Nantgarw, the curious and contemporary tale of a ghostly easy rider can be found in a handwritten manuscript entitled *Ysbrydion, Chwedlau a Dipyn o Hiwmor* (Ghosts, Legends and a Little Humour). The story is told by Robert Henry Edwards of Llwyngwril, Gwynedd, and was collected in 1998 by the author Gwilym Vaughan Jones of Pencoed, Bangor.

This account centres around a caravan park in Brynhyfryd, Arthog, kept by a man called Dei Glyn. One Saturday evening, a visitor arrived

at the park on his motorbike to pitch a tent for the night, before heading out for an evening ride down towards Fairbourne beach:

> *Wrth ddychwelyd ar y beic, teimlodd nad oedd y peiriant yn tynnu*
> *yn dda i fyny'r allt. Trodd i edrych yn ôl, er mawr syndod iddo*
> *gwelodd glamp o ddyn mawr yn eistedd ar y sedd ôl. Pan gyrhaed-*
> *dodd Brynhyfryd 'roedd y dyn o'r sedd ôl y 'moto beic' wedi diflannu.*
> *Yn sydyn sylweddolodd mai ysbryd oedd wedi teithio gydag ef. Yn ei*
> *ddychryn gadawodd y lle y noson honno.*

> When returning on his bike, he felt that the motor wasn't pull-
> ing well up the hill. He turned to look back, and much to his
> surprise saw a very large man sitting on the back seat. When he
> arrived at Brynhyfryd the man on the back seat of the motorbike
> had disappeared. Suddenly, he realised that it was a ghost that
> had travelled with him. In his fright he left the place that night.

Accounts of phantom hitchhikers are certainly not unique to Wales;
neither are they confined to modern-day sightings. An example of a
malevolent horseback-riding ghost from nineteenth-century Dolgellau
is provided for comparison in Chapter Eight: 'Water Spirits'.

The Reverend William Jenkin Davies recorded a story of a field-
dwelling ghost in his book *Hanes Plwyf Llandyssul* (The History of
Llandysul Parish), published in 1896 following his success with the
essay at Llandysul Eisteddfod in 1894. The tale in question was told
by a local elderly man named William to the interviewer, Tomos, and
recorded verbatim by Davies.

This sighting occurs at the village of Faerdrefawr, which lies within the parish. William describes how two local men, Daniel Meical
and Shincin Charls, were returning home on a Saturday night from
Llanbedr Pont Steffan (Lampeter). As dusk fell, they reached Pont Fach
y Ferdre (The Little Bridge of Ferdre), when Shincin suddenly lowered
his head and began mumbling:

> *'Beth yw'r mater,' medde Daniel. Mwmian nath Shincyn am dipyn,*
> *yna gofynnodd, 'Welsoch chi ddim o'r dyn gwyn yn y câ o dan y côd?'*
> *'Naddo,' medde Daniel, 'dos dim yno hefyd os nad ôs cadno, dewch*

nol i weld e.' Ar ol hir gocso, blonodd i fynd, ac i'r câ 'reithon nhw, ond er iddy nhw gynnu gole, ni welo nhw ddim. Fe gychwynon lweth i Landyssul, ond mor gynted ag y cyrddo nhw'r hewl, dyna Shincyn yn mwmian wedyn. Ar hyn trodd Daniel i ben yn ol, a'r tro hwn, gwelodd e yr ysbryd.

'What's the matter,' said Daniel. Shincyn mumbled for a while, then he asked, 'Didn't you see anything of the man in white in the field under the trees?' 'No,' said Daniel, 'there's nothing there either if not a fox, come and see.' After a long time coaxing, he agreed to go, and to the field they went, but although they lit a lamp, they could not see anything. They set off for Llandysul a second time, but as soon as they reached the road, Shincyn began mumbling again. At this Daniel turned back, and this time, he too saw the spirit.

The pair then heard the spirit approaching 'like a trotting horse' (*'fel ceffyl yn trotian'*), and when it came close enough, Daniel tried to grab it but it apparently disappeared in his hands. Needless to say, both men continued home scared witless.

The narrator, William, continues to explain to Tomos that there were more sightings of this particular ghost: 'Ferdre Fowr's ghost plays its tricks still. More recently, Dr Evans saw it, in a white garment and –' (*'Ma ysbryd Ferdre Fowr yn hware'i strancie o hyd. Un nosweth yn ddweddar, fe welodd Dr. Evans e, mywn gwisc wen a –'*).

Unfortunately, at this point in the narrative, Tomos decides that he has had quite enough of the parish ghosts and swiftly changes the subject, so we will never know what happened to Dr Evans!

What is most interesting here is the imagery of the ghost in white. As we discussed in the introductory chapter, this is not a significant motif within Welsh ghost-lore, especially in pre-twentieth-century narratives, and certainly less so than comparable historical sightings from England. This account, along with the white-suited, well-dwelling phantom priest from Llandysul, discussed in Chapter Five: 'Holy Ghosts', are both recorded in the same area, are relayed by the same storyteller (who had not witnessed either of these apparitions firsthand), and have probably circulated within the community for a significant period, possibly generations, with whatever degree of artistic licence each retelling imbues. This makes any analysis of these accounts extremely difficult. We suggest they are enjoyed at face value, as was no doubt intended.

Conversely, a motif that is very much at the forefront of ghost-lore within the landscape is that of guarding hidden treasure. We have already discussed this theme in Chapter Two: 'Unfinished Business' and will see it again later with regards to the *Ladi Wen* (White Lady) in Chapter Seven: 'Ladi Wen'. However, we have included some brief examples that can equally and appropriately find their home in this chapter. As stated by the Reverend D. G. Williams in his 1895 essay, 'Casgliad o Len-Gwerin Sir Gaerfyrddin' ('A Collection of Carmarthenshire Folklore'): 'In many of the places where spirits are said to exist the tradition also thrives among the locals that there will be hidden treasure.' ('*Mewn llawer o'r lleoedd y dywedir fod bwcïod ceir traddodiad hefyd yn ffynnu ymhlith yr ardalwyr fod yno ryw drysorau cuddiedig.*')

He provides a local example from Trelech, called 'Bwci Llwyn Mowr' ('The Bogey of Llwyn Mawr'). It is said that buried treasure attracts the spirit to the large cairn and possible burial chamber, Crug-y-Durn, which lies outside the village – a story that is highly reminiscent of the ones we've already encountered in Chapter Two: 'Unfinished Business', and yet exemplifies how important landmarks within the community are woven into local folklore and acquire new significances.

William Davies notes an interesting and unusual nineteenth-century example of treasure-guarding ghosts that can be found stalking the farmland of Ystum-gwern, again located in Dyffryn Ardudwy. This time, a 'cauldron full of gold' ('*crochan llawn o aur*'), said to be buried under the footprint of where Gwern y Capel monastery once stood, is protected by the odd pairing of a phantom monk and soldier, whose mission in death is to protect the treasure from thieves.

The folklore of roadside ghosts is often intertwined with darker, and often tragic, themes. An account recalling such a spirit that was once seen at Foel Dduallt, a hill near the village of Ynysybwl, where Glanffrwd was born, was recorded by the author in *Plwyf Llanwyno*. People in this area believed that Foel Dduallt was haunted by the ghost of a man who had hanged himself from a tree in the nearby forest; the ghost was known as 'Ysbryd Ysgubor y Clûn' ('The Spirit of Ysgubor y Clûn'), *ysgubor* being the Welsh word for barn.

Glanffrwd notes that the ghost appeared as a blue gaseous light, and 'troubled the old inhabitants for a long time' ('*blino yr hen drigolion yn hir*') – a sight which he admits looked peculiar but would have had a natural explanation. The implication here is that the light was ignis fatuus, the flickering lights of marsh gas emitted from decaying material which then combust, commonly termed 'will-o'-the-wisp' in folklore. The explanation seems plausible at first sight; however, Foel Dduallt was made up of rough pasture at the time, and not of wetland or marshy terrain. It is therefore unlikely that ignis fatuus would form over this sort of land.

In any case, so notorious was this ghost that it was immortalised by a poet of the parish in the following verse:

Mae ysbryd yn trigo ar Gefn-yr-Erw,
Ysbryd rhyw adyn a dorodd ei wddw,
Ac yspryd yn cadw wrth 'Scubor y Clûn,
Ysbryd hen gybydd a laddodd ei hun.

A spirit resides at Cefn-yr-Erw, the spirit of a wretch who broke his neck, and a spirit dwells at 'Scubor y Clûn, the spirit of an old miser who killed himself.

It was said that the local priest had been brought in to banish the spirit. Laying troublesome ghosts, i.e. the act of moving them on or banishing them (either to a remote location, usually cited as the Red Sea because of its religious connotations), or otherwise by trapping them in a vessel such as a bottle or snuff box, was traditionally either the work of magical practitioners such as cunning folk, or clergymen with specialist knowledge in the field. Sometimes, the spirit would instead be given an impossible task to complete, which would effectively trap it for a specific period of time. Common tasks included emptying pools with damaged vessels, clearing areas of grass one blade at a time, or spinning ropes of sand.

The ghost at Foel Dduallt was a curious amalgamation of these things. It was not sent permanently to the Red Sea, but instead, the priest compelled it to:

aros mil o flynyddoedd i gario dwfr o'r Mor Coch mewn gogr, ac ar ol iddo orphen, ei fod i wneyd rhaff o dywod y môr i'w chyflwyno yn rhodd i drigolion y plwyf – y gloch-rhaff Eglwys Gwyno.

wait a thousand years carrying water from the Red Sea in a sieve, and after it finished, it was to make a rope from the sand of the sea to present it as a gift to the residents of the parish – the bell-rope of Gwyno Church.

Eglwys Sant Gwynno (St Gwynno's Church) sits on the edge of Coedwig Sant Gwynno (St Gwynno Forest), a short distance away from Pontypridd. The building is medieval but is built on the site of a much earlier religious establishment. Gwynno was a sixth-century Welsh saint, and a sacred well associated with him, Ffynnon Wynno, arises from under the hillock where the church perches, overlooking the forest. The churchyard serves as Glanffrwd's final resting place following his death in 1890, denoted by a grand monument which was funded by his many friends and admirers. Also among the main attractions in this particular churchyard are the two gravestones dedicated to the legendary Guto Nyth Bran (Gruffydd Morgan), located beside the south porch of the church. Born in 1700, Guto was renowned for being exceptionally quick-footed, and is said to have caught hares and out-run horses. He died after a congratulatory slap on the back, having completed a twelve-mile race in 53 minutes from Newport to Bedwas, Caerffili, in 1737.

While 'Ysbryd Ysgubor y Clûn' still has a long way to go in completing its task, one needn't always go to such elaborate lengths to lay a troublesome ghost. On 28 November 1868, the *Pontypool Free Press and Herald of the Hills* carried a story referring to beliefs in the Snatchwood area that a ghost was appearing as a consequence of a man having died by suicide there. The spirit was said to appear around midnight, near a pear tree beside the road to Abersychan. The newspaper correspondent had no doubts that stories of ghosts were a vestige of less enlightened times, and offered plain advice on how to lay this one:

when one does appear … we recommend all the young fellows in the neighbourhood to provide themselves with stout cudgels, hide themselves in the hedges, and when the ghost makes an appearance (it will be sure to be a 'him,' so that there need be no hesitation on the score of gallantry) to walk up to it and LAY ON HARD! Depend upon it, the ghost will be effectively laid by one dressing!

Murder was also considered an equally tragic excuse for a ghost to haunt a particular location within the landscape. William Davies provides an example from nineteenth-century Meirion, 'Ysbryd Bwlch Oerddrws' ('The Ghost of Bwlch Oerddrws'):

Deuir i'r bwlch hwn trwy esgyn rhiw serth ar y ffordd o ddinas Mawddwy i Ddolgellau. Byddai y lle anhygyrch hwn gynt yn cael ei aflonyddu gan fodau amgen na dynol, 'ar ol i ryw ddyn oedd yn gwerthu nwyddau hyd y wlad gael ei dagu i farwolaeth gan lofrudd er mwyn cael ei eiddo'.

This pass was arrived at by ascending the road from Dinas Mawddwy to Dolgellau. This inaccessible place was once troubled by non-human beings 'after some man who was selling goods across the country was strangled to death by a murderer for his possessions'.

Ghosts aside, Bwlch Oerddrws was a noteworthy location in its own right, being the spot where the most capable men in the area were said to have convened in an attempt to restore the confiscated land and property of those who had sided with Owain Glyndŵr during the Welsh revolt, and create their own rules for local governance. The poet Meurig Ebrill (Morris Davies) (1780–1861) penned a bleak description of the pass, which does nothing to alleviate its ghoulish reputation:

Bwlch Oerddrws serth, gerth o'i go', – lle uchel
  Heb un lloches ynddo;
Ar hin oerllyd, drymlyd dro
Tristwch wrth fyned trosto.

Steep Bwlch Oerddrws, terrible and angry, – a high place, without any shelter; in chilly weather, a sombre journey, sadness while traversing it.

Northwards from Dinas Mawddwy and past the village of Llanfachreth lies Cynefin Bryn Blew — a summit where the site of an equally tragic haunting is reported by William Davies. The ghost was said to be that of Daniel y Milwr (Daniel the Soldier), believed to be a brave horseman, unrivalled in battle and unnaturally strong. One day while fleeing from the enemy, he fell over the side of a cliff in the vicinity of Ystum Gwadnaeth farm and perished. He was buried nearby with a large stone to mark the site, on which the name 'Daniel' was carved. It was said that '[t]here was once terror at passing the place, because huge things were seen there, and worse still, shrill wailing would be heard' ('*[b]yddis gynt yn ofni myned heibio'r fan, oblegyd gwelwyd pethau anferthol yno, a chlywyd dolefiadau gwichlyd erchyllach na hyny*').

It should be emphasised that not all Welsh roadside ghosts are malevolent or doleful characters. Davies also relays an unusual tale from Glyndyfrdwy, Denbighshire, of the charitable 'Ysbryd Hen Ŵr Bryn Goleu' ('The Ghost of the Old Man of Bryn Goleu'):

Gwelwyd ysbryd hen wr Bryn Goleu un tro gan hen wraig o'r gymydogaeth, a phan gyrhaeddodd ei chartref edrychai mor welw a'r wal wen, ei hanadl yn ei dwrn, a methodd am amser yngan gair. Pan ddaeth ychydig ati ei hun dywedodd yn frawychus iddi weled ysbryd hen wr Bryn Goleu wrth lidiard y ffordd oedd yn arwain i fyny at ei thy. Cariai lusern oleuedig yn ei law, agorodd y llidiard iddi, ac arweiniodd hi nes dyfod ar gyfer ei hen breswylfod, pan y diflanodd yn sydyn o'i golwg.

The ghost of the old man of Bryn Goleu was seen once by an old woman in the community, and when she arrived home looked as pale as the white wall, out of breath, and couldn't utter a word for some time. When she had composed herself a little, she said shakily that she had seen the ghost of the old man of Bryn Goleu by the gate of the path that led up to her house. He carried a lit lantern in his hand, opened the gate for her, and led her until they had reached his old dwelling, when he suddenly disappeared from sight.

The motif of the protective ghost is unusual but not unprecedented in Welsh folklore; examples of watchful Black Dog phantoms are discussed in Chapter Four: 'Spectral Beasts'.

Neither were the spirits of the dead the only apparitions that Welsh folk had to contend with along the roads. Later in this book we shall be exploring phantasmal death omens, a motif which is particularly strong in Wales, and as part of this we will look at ghostly funeral processions and corpse candles – portents of impending doom that could also be encountered while traversing the roads. In the same way, apparitions of individuals who are not known to be deceased are also reported to appear. Classically termed 'wraiths', this phenomenon would usually occur at the exact moment of death.

We have already discussed these 'living ghosts' within Welsh folk belief in the introductory chapter, but by way of example we might use a story noted by William Davies in *Hanes Plwyf Llanegryn*:

> *Y traddodiad arall ydoedd y byddai rhai'n gweled eu teulu neu eu cyfeillion yn crwydro ar eu hen lwybrau pan fyddent yn croesi glyn cysgod angau. Clywom am wraig o'r wlad yn mynd adref o'r pentref yn hwyr ar y nos, a'i mab bychan yn ei llaw; a phan oedd ar fan arbennig gwelai ei chymdoges, Beti Llwyd, yn ei phasio ar yr ochr arall i'r ffordd a'i chlog arferol dros ei gwar; a chyn gynted ag y cyrhaeddodd hi garreg ei haelwyd, curai cyfeilles y drws gan ofyn a ddeuai i ddiweddu'r hen chwaer Beti Llwyd, a fu farw ar yr adeg y gwelodd hi yn ei phasio ar y ffordd o'r pentref.*

The other tradition held that some would see their families or friends wandering along their former paths as they were crossing into the valley of the shadow of death. We have heard of a countrywoman going home from the village late one evening and holding her small son by the hand; when she reached a certain place, she saw her neighbour, Beti Llwyd, passing by on the other side of the road, with her usual cloak over her head; on reaching her home the mother heard a friend knocking at her door and asking her to come and lay out old Beti Llwyd, who had expired at the very moment she had seen her go by on the road from the village.

While we have already touched upon the Devil's role in Welsh place-names, the Evil One and his demons are also frequently encountered on the road. Daniel E. Jones in *Hanes Plwyf Llangeler a Phenboyr* (The History of Llangeler and Penboyr Parishes) (1899) provides such an example.

It was once thought that devils haunted the road through the hamlet of Dôl-haidd in Carmarthenshire. Other nearby landmarks associated with local folk tales include Rhiw'r Wrach (Hag's Hill) or Pant y Wrach (Hag's Dell), so named after a type of Welsh portentous hag-like creature – *gwrach-y-rhibyn* – who was said to frequent the area, and about whom we will learn more later in this book. There is also an old trackway, part of which is named Rhiw Cyrff (Corpse's Hill) because it lies on the route of an old corpse road used to carry coffins from Felindre to Penboyr Church. We shall also return to corpse roads briefly in Chapter Ten: 'Death Omens'.

This particular tale recounts how a nobleman of Penllwyncoch farm named Mr Lewes went to visit a lawyer in Castell Newydd Emlyn. The farm was part of the larger Dôl-haidd estate, and the man in this story is possibly John Lewes who lived here between 1740 and 1755, having inherited the property from his father, James. After their business was conducted, the lawyer gave Lewes a sheaf of documents, with strict instructions not to open them until he arrived home. Unfortunately, Lewes was impatient and chose to stop on the way back and look through the papers, at which point:

> *Gydai fod e wedi dachre tro'r dail, dyna haid o wrdrwgied yn dod o byti ddo, ac yn gneyd ryw stumie rhyfedd. Clymodd y papyre nol ar unwaith a threiodd fynd shagadre, ond dodd ddim ffordd cyffro o'r fan, a 'rodd hi'n bacar arno.*

> As he began to turn the pages, a swarm of devils surrounded him, and making some strange expressions. He retied the papers immediately and tried to go towards home, but there was no way of rising from that spot, and he was trapped.

Lewes instructed the devils to go and cut all the gorse in the immediate area and bring it back to him, thinking that he would be able to make his escape while they were gone. The demons did so, but had returned with all the gorse before Lewes had even had time to stand.

The devils then took all of the gorse they had cut and removed it to nearby Bronhyddenfach field where they set it alight, but did so with such speed that they had surrounded Lewes again before he was able to move. He eventually made his escape by sending the demons to fetch water from the river Teifi to put out the fire. Although he managed to get back home, the devils were said to roam the area for years afterwards.

While in this chapter we have outlined all manner of ghosts, bogeys and devils that might be encountered along roads, within fields, and up mountains, we conclude with a protective Carmarthenshire measure which may be employed by the intrepid traveller should they be faced with a supernatural foe, according to the advice of the Reverend D. G. Williams:

> *Ni raid i'r un pererin gymeryd ei orthrechu gan yr ysbryd a arwain y teithiwr nosawl allan o'i lwybr. Yr oll sydd angenrheidiol i'r crwydredig ei wneuthur yw troi rhyw bilyn o'i wisg ar ei wrthwyneb.*

Not one pilgrim should have to be overcome by a spirit that would lead the night-time traveller from his path. The only thing necessary for the wanderer to do is to turn an item of their clothing inside out.

Those familiar with aspects of British folklore may perhaps already be aware that this is a common and universal protective ritual against the mischief and malice of the fairies, and in fact Williams continues to state that in the western areas of this county, it is a tactic used in particular against the goblin, which is a creature all too familiar to the inhabitants there – another example of how the definition of 'spirit' in Wales was generally fluid and encompassed a broad paranormal church.

Williams recounts a tale of an old woman from Brynaman who, try as she might, could not come down the side of a mountain because spirits hindered her journey: 'But she had the idea to turn her petticoat inside out. After that she moved "like a bird" as she put it' ('*Ond meddyliodd am droi ei phais ar ei gwrthwyneb. Daethai wedi hyny "lawr fel aderyn" meddai hi*').

We are of the understanding that adjusting one's undergarments is entirely optional, and that other clothing items will prove just as effective.

CHAPTER FOUR

Spectral Beasts

*

Hwch Ddu Gwta
Nos G'lan Gaea'
Lladron yn dwad
Tan weu sana.
Trad.

The tailless black sow, on Hallowe'en, thieves are coming, knitting socks.

From the mundane to the bizarre, spirits in animal form have been reported in Wales for as long as those resembling humans, and represent a particularly prominent aspect of Welsh ghost-lore when compared to sightings beyond Offa's Dyke. As Professor Owen Davies has noted, phantom animal sightings reported to the Society of Psychical Research across Britain in general only make up a 'very small proportion' of cases, whereas Wales is universally, and often quite literally, crawling with examples.

While we are reluctant to belabour the stereotype, sheep are indeed a common sight in fields across Wales, with sources estimating a total approaching ten million. They outnumber the human population by a ratio of around three to one and account for almost one-third of the total number of sheep farmed across Britain. It should therefore come as no surprise to find that ghost sheep exist within the folklore of Wales. Indeed, in the old county of Meirionnydd, a particular meaning was ascribed to their appearance, as noted by William Davies in *Hanes Plwyf Llanegryn* (History of the Parish of Llanegryn), first published in 1948:

> *Dywedid hefyd os byddai'r ysbryd yn teimlo yn garedig tuag at y neb yr ymddangosai iddo, y cymerai ffurf rhyw greadur caredig ac addfwyn. Ond os teimlai yn gas a chwerw yr ymddangosai ar*

ffurf creadur creulon ac arswydus. Ei ffurfiau cas oedd teirw, cŵn,
hychod, ac adar ysglyfaethus, neu dân. El ffurf garedig fel rheol oedd
dafad. Clywsom hen ferch o'r enw Beti Dafis yn diolch am i ysbryd
arbenning ymddangos iddi hi ar ffurf dafad hynaws.

It was also said that if a ghost felt kindly towards someone to
whom it appeared, it would take the shape of some kind of gentle
creature. But if it felt angry and bitter it would appear as a cruel
and dreadful one. Its vicious shapes were those of bulls, dogs,
swine, and carrion birds, or fire. Its kindly form was usually that
of a sheep. We once heard an old maid by the name of Beti Dafis
give thanks that a certain ghost had appeared before her in the
shape of a gentle sheep.

Conversely, the existence of ghostly sheep was firmly rejected in neighbouring Caernarfonshire according to Myrddin Fardd in *Llên Gwerin
Sir Gaernarfon* (The Folklore of Caernarfonshire) (1908):

*Darlunid [yr ysbryd] bob amser braidd ar ddull rhyw greadur neu
beth sylweddol ag y byddai y sawl a'i gwelai yn gyfarwydd ag ef;
canys gallai ymrithio a chymeryd pob rhyw lun, oddieithr dafad a
cholomen.*

[The ghost] was always depicted somewhat in the manner of
a creature or some sizeable thing which the person who saw it
would be familiar with; for it could assume and take every kind
of form, except a sheep and a dove.

Myrddin Fardd provides no further explanation for this, but the Christian connotations associated with the imagery of a sheep and a dove are
self-evident.

Shapeshifting ghosts often feature in other Welsh animal ghost stories,
as we have already seen in Chapter Three: 'Ghosts in the Landscape'.
One of the most unusual and unique examples is that of a giant ghostly
rabbit recounted in the *Dundee Evening Telegraph* of 22 May 1902. The
story begins:

Llangynwydd [*sic*], which is in the Llynvi Valley, has a ghost scare on just now. Near the village are the ruins of an old British castle, known as Castle Coch. Local tradition has it that in the ruins a chest of gold is buried, and is supernaturally guarded. One evening about a week ago a terrified villager saw the figure of a tall, ethereal-looking nun cross the castle moat, climb to the top of the ruins, and then vanish.

On another occasion, a farmer out with his dogs saw the apparition. The dogs ran at it, but quickly fled when the ghost of the nun suddenly transformed into a giant rabbit, the size of a sheep. It is difficult to say for certain whether the account of the giant shapeshifting rabbit is pure fabrication, as it is notably absent from other sources; what it highlights however are the dangers of working with 'newspaper folklore' reportage.

The ruinous Llangynwyd castle in Bridgend, alternatively referred to as Castell Coch (Red Castle), should not be confused with the famous nineteenth-century Gothic Revival castle of the same name that stands in Tongwynlais, Cardiff. The latter example is also noted for its treasure-guarding phantom, in the form of two enormous eagles, said to guard the iron chest of the twelfth-century lord of Senghenydd, Ifor Bach, in a 'subterraneous passage leading from the Castle to Pontrhydycyff, a distance of about two miles'. According to *Castell Coch: A Gossiping Companion to the Ruin and its Neighbourhood*, written in 1857 by the prominent chemist, antiquarian and naturalist, Robert Drane (who subsequently went on to destroy as many copies of his book as he could find), the giant birds famously saw off a group of men trying to gain access to the legendary chest. The men tried shooting the birds – even casting silver bullets, and bringing with them a minister to read an exorcism, all to no avail.

While the account of the guardian eagles of Castell Coch may be enough to raise a few eyebrows, there are many other examples within folklore of treasure-guarding spectral beasts.

Bwlch Nant Ffrancon runs through the mountains of Eryri. The first road through the glacial valley was constructed in the late eighteenth century by Lord Penrhyn – some may recognise this area from the 1968 film *Carry on up the Khyber* where it doubled as the Khyber Pass. It was locally believed at one time that when the Irish fled from the

Parliamentarian army under Major General Thomas Mytton in 1646 during the English Civil War, they concealed their treasures in caves high up in the mountains until they could return to retrieve them. There are a number of legends that became associated with this belief, some of which were recorded by the poet Hugh Derfel Hughes in *Hynafiaethau Llandegái a Llanllechid* (Antiquities of Llandygái and Llanllechid), first published in 1866, including the following example:

> *Aeth dau frawd o fugeiliaid defaid o Giltwllan, i edrych am eu defaid i'r Benglog, ac yno mewn lle anghysbell, canfu yr ieuengaf dwll yn myned i'r ogof ardderchog, yn yr hon yr oedd bwrdd crwn, ac ar y bwrdd, bentyrau rheolaidd o aur ac arian; ond ni feiddiai fyned i mewn i'r cyrchu, gan fod yn sefyll yn eu hymyl, filgi, a llygaid tanllyd yn tremio arno, ac yn barod i ruthro arno os meiddiai fyned i mewn. Ar hyn aeth y bachgen ar ol ei frawd, ac ar ol ei oddiweddyd, ac adrodd ei weledigaeth, troisant yn ol i chwilio am yr ogof, ond er cymaint eu hawydd a'u hymdrech, methasant ei chael.*

Two shepherd brothers from Giltwllan went to the Benglog to look for their sheep, and there in a remote place, the youngest found a hole leading to the exquisite cave, in which there was a round table, and on the table, orderly piles of gold and silver; but he did not dare to enter, as there was standing near them, a greyhound, with fiery eyes staring at him, and ready to rush at him if he dared to enter. Upon this the boy went after his brother, and after overtaking him, and recounting his vision, they turned back to look for the cave, but despite their desire and effort, they failed to find it.

Another ghostly greyhound sighted in north Wales was reported at the Ty'nyberth crossroads, Clynnog. William Hobley, writing in *Hanes Methodistiaeth Arfon* (The History of Methodism in Arfon) (1910) said that it was:

> *yn ddigon mawr i fyned ar draws y ffordd, gyda'i ben ar un clawdd a'i gynffon ar y llall. Ffarmwr Maesog, yn yr adeg honno, ydoedd un o'r rhai a'i gwelodd ef. Bu'r lledrith hwnnw yno am yn hir o amser.*

big enough to span the road, with its head on one hedge and its tail on the other. The Farmer of Maesog, during that time, was one that saw it. This phantom was there for a long time.

Apparitions of spectral dogs are well established within British folklore, and indeed the world beyond. Many examples of ghostly dogs in Welsh lore may be traced to mythology surrounding the psychopompic *Cŵn Annwn* (Hounds of Annwn), first recorded in the First Branch of the *Mabinogi*. Tales of other spectral dogs, usually termed *Cŵn Du* (Black Dogs) because of their prevalent colouring, are quite distinct stories but are often mistakenly conflated. This is especially prevalent in Wales when the terminology for these spectral hounds is used interchangeably, usually depending on the locality of the sighting, as discussed in Chapter Ten: 'Death Omens'.

While *Cŵn Du* are more generally regarded as malevolent entities, there are many stories in Wales where the ghosts of dogs serve a protective purpose. An example of one such case comes from *Cwmsêl a Chefn Sidan* (Cwmsêl and Cefn Sidan), a collection of letters and columns which first appeared in various Welsh newspapers and periodicals, published in 1946 by the Reverend Tom Beynon.

Born and raised at a farm called Y Cenfu in Mynydd y Garreg, Carmarthenshire, he describes with fondness how his parents would occasionally spend an evening reciting ghost stories and regional superstitions around the hearth. One such story concerned a Black Dog sighting:

> *Y mae gweled ci du yn dwyn ar gof imi bob amser y stori am nhad-cu, Thomas Beynon, yn dychwelyd o Lechdwnni dros y caeau genlli'r nos, pryd y gwelodd anghenfil erch ac y cafodd gwmni gwarcheidiol ci du mawr. Cadwodd y ci at ei ochr gan ymwasgu'n gyfeillgar ato a dal i gydgerdded hyd oni chyrhaeddodd y Gletwyn; yna diflannodd y ci amddiffynnol.*

Seeing a black dog always brings to mind the story of my grandfather, Thomas Beynon, returning from Llechdwnni across the fields in the dead of night, when he saw a frightful monster and had the company of a large black dog. The dog kept by his side and pressing against him in a friendly manner and continued to follow his footsteps until they reached y Gletwyn; then the protective dog vanished.

The tale is also found translated in private correspondence from the archives of the folklorist Theo Brown, who had a particular interest in stories of black dogs, in a letter sent in 1965 by an acquaintance:

> This is the only written proof I can find of this not unusual story. I have heard a variation of it from the lips of a Cardiganshire Baptist Minister, who told it of another Minister in the 18th Century, who was guarded from thieves (? highwaymen) on the lonely roads above Staylittle in Montgomeryshire by a large dog (colour unspecified) who also disappeared when his presence was no longer necessary … The written evidence about a similar belief in South Wales thus suggests it was pretty universal.

Similar accounts of protective hounds can be found spanning the breadth of the country. An example can be heard in the tape recordings held at the archives at St Fagan's National Museum of History, Cardiff, transcribed and published by John Owen Hughes in *Straeon Gwerin Ardal Eryri* (Folk Tales of Eryri) (2008). The storyteller, William Roberts, provides an account from Llanfairfechan, Conwy, which was passed down through the family. His grandfather was returning home one evening from Caernarfon, Gwynedd, where he'd been to sell his horse, when he realised as he was walking through Coed y Glyn – 'an onerous place' ('*lle trwm ofnadwy*') – that he was being accompanied by a giant dog as big as a calf, which would not leave his side. As they reached the gate, he was set upon by thieves on the hunt for his day's profits, but the dog attacked with gusto and the thieves retreated. The dog waited until Roberts's grandfather had made it to the farm gate, before barking once and disappearing.

A similar example from Castell-nedd (Neath), mentioned in the journal *Folklore* in 1945, describes how an old lady who used to cross over the mountains in the dark to sell her wares in the markets of Aberdâr and Merthyr Tudful was protected by a phantom White Dog, which disappeared at dawn. The story was originally relayed to the author's mother by the remarkable Cranogwen (Sarah Jane Rees) – master mariner, teacher, activist, preacher, editor of the women's periodical *Y Frythones*, LGBTQ+ icon, and celebrated poet. In 1865, she also became the first woman to ever be awarded a prize for poetry at the National Eisteddfod.

Another white dog was involved in an incident said to have taken place at Rhosgoch, Ynys Môn. One summer evening after supper, Wil Pritchard, a farm labourer, was returning with two other workmen to the stable loft where he and other servants slept and which was accessed by a flight of stone steps. About halfway along their route, a big white-coloured dog appeared and walked with Wil. He spoke to the animal and it looked up at him in a friendly manner. The other two workmen turned around to see who he was speaking to. They evidently could not see the dog, and accused Wil of talking to himself. Wil was equally surprised when he bent down to pat the dog's head and found that he could not feel the animal when he did so. As Wil continued to talk to the hound, his companions became increasingly annoyed, believing that he was playing a trick on them, and by the time they reached the steps to the loft, both were quite angry. They went up to the loft first, one of them having the key, while Wil looked for the dog, which seemed to have vanished.

Shortly after entering the loft, Wil heard a cry and the two workmen quickly descended the steps, almost knocking him over in their rush to leave the building. Wil asked them what the matter was as he couldn't see anything to cause such a commotion. The older man just muttered, 'What a dog, what a dog!'

The workmen described how they had opened the loft door to see a pale dog as big as a calf, standing to a height of about four feet, blocking their way and snarling at them. As his companions refused to venture back upstairs, Wil went up to the loft instead but found no trace of the beast. The dog never appeared to any of them again, but Wil believed that it had shown itself to the others because they had mocked him when he had been talking to it on the journey home.

While the white spectral hound in the above account had been perceived as gentle and protective by Wil, it is interesting that it appeared as a snarling beast to his companions. In some of these cases, where ghostly dogs appear to be threatening, might it not be possible that they are being protective towards someone, or something, else?

Perhaps this is the case with an incident said to have taken place at the village of Camros (Camrose), Pembrokeshire. The events in the story took place around the year 1830, and were recorded in 1936 for the Lincolnshire folklorist Ethel Rudkin by Mr D. P. Lewis, the grandson of the witness. He had been told the story in the 1880s by his grandfather, who was then eighty years old. Lewis wrote:

> At the time of the described incident, my grandfather was the act-ing steward of the considerable estate of Camrose and his journeys to the neighbouring town of Haverfordwest were fairly frequent and always afoot.
>
> So far as I recollect the story it was on his way home from Haverfordwest in the darkening evening that he became some-what alarmed by a considerable commotion in the wood. In his pastoral mind, this could only be caused by a battle royal between some domestic animals and he wondered whose bull had invaded the territory of his neighbour and what dogs were joining in the melee. However, he was secure enough in the pro-tection of the hedges and it seemed unlikely that the strife would culminate in the vanished being forced through the thick trees to a drop over the crest of the little cliff into the brook beneath.
>
> A few yards walking brought him to the bridge and here he was terrified to see a huge black dog rise over the trees with a frightful roar and swoop downwards within a few feet of him, to the stream beyond the bridge.

A similarly frightening apparition was recorded in the parish of Llan-fachreth, Gwynedd. 'Bwgan y Bont' ('The Bridge Bogey') was said to terrorise the folk of Y Blaenau, a late seventeenth-century farmhouse which is still standing to this day. The ghost was said to appear 'in the form of a dog hanging under the arch of the bridge nearby' ('*ar lun ci yn crogi o dan fwa'r bont sydd gerllaw*').

The account is given in the essay 'Chwedlau a Thraddodiadau Plwyf Llanfachraith' ('The Legends and Traditions of Llanfachraith Parish') by an unknown 'Cofiadur' ('Recorder') in the literary periodical *Taliesin* in 1859. It describes how a local gentleman farmer, 'one who thought of himself as a great icon of courage' ('*un a gyfrifa ei hun yn gawr mewn gwroldeb*'), threw a stone at the spirit with the intention of hitting it, but was instead struck by the 'force of evil' ('*rhyw adwyth*') and spent the rest of his days in ill health. This account also serves as another example of how folk tales often targeted the squirearchy, as we saw in Chapter Two: 'Unfinished Business'.

The journal *Archaeologica Cambrensis* in 1919 gives a curious reference to a church-dwelling *Ci Du* in the town of Llanwrtyd Wells in Powys:

> Within the south wall of the old parish church of Llanwrtyd there is a short flight of rude stone stairs rising from the level of the church floor to the top of the wall, which is not high. This stair passage is quite dark, having no window or opening either inwards into the church or outwards into the open air. It used to be entered from within the church by a small door opening into or out of a large square pew. I believe this entrance is no longer open. It was closed, I think, when the church was last repaired in the early sixties of the last century. The old church is hardly used at all now except for funeral services ... A good many years ago, when the parish school was kept in the old schoolroom attached to the west end of the church, this dark passage was known as Twll y Ci Du (the Hole of the Black Dog), and was a source of considerable dread to the younger children. It does not seem to have been clear who or what this black dog represented, but it appears to have been vaguely supposed to be either the Evil One himself or one of his imps.

As this church passage was connected with the schoolroom, it is quite possible that it was named Twll y Ci Du by some of the older children to frighten the younger pupils. Despite its ominous name, there is no specific record of an appairition having been sighted here.

The same journal contains a reference to Y Rhath (Roath) in Cardiff where, at the beginning of the nineteenth century, stood the old gallows at the end of Heol y Plwca (City Road; originally Plwcca Lane) – a site fondly referred to locally as 'Death Junction' (more so today because of the dangers of that particular stretch of road rather than its gory history of executions). This location was supposedly haunted and guarded at night by a spectral Black Dog.

Accounts in this area are recorded as early as 1578 by the genealogist Rice Merrick in *A Booke of Glamorganshires Antiquities*. This book was the first attempt ever made to record the history of a Welsh county, and makes reference to a place called Beth y ky dy (Bedd y Ci Du, or Black Dog's Grave), supposedly the etymological source for the lordship or manor of Roath Dogfield. However, this suggestion is doubtful; the name 'Dogfield' does not appear until the reign of Henry VIII. Much more likely is its association with William Doggavel (or Docgeuel) who, according to Walter de Gray Birch's *A History of Margam Abbey* (1897), gifted 'all his meadow under Rahat', the earlier form of Y Rhath, to the monks of Margam Abbey in the twelfth century. It is recorded that the monks, in return, forgave William 'a debt of ten silver shillings'.

Glanffrwd in *Plwyf Llanwyno* (Llanwynno Parish) (1913) also records a sighting of a *Ci Du*, heard from his grandmother:

> *Clywais fy mamgu yn adrodd pa fodd yr oedd fy nhadcu o Flaennant un noson yn dychwelyd o'r Dduallt, o garu un o'r merched, a phan oedd yn pasio trwy yr Hen Wern, i Satan fyned heibio iddo fel ci anferthol o fawr, a'i lygaid yn dân gwyllt, ac iddo, wrth gamfa yr Hen Wern, droi yn dân i gyd, a llosgi allan a diflanu, nes y credodd fy nhadcu fod coed y Wern yn myned yn greginion ar unwaith!*

> I heard my grandmother tell how my grandfather from Blaen-nant one night was returning from the Duallt, from courting one of the women, and when he was passing through the Hen Wern, Satan passed him like a huge dog, and his eyes were fireworks, and that he, at the stile of the Hen Wern, turned to flames, and burnt out and disappeared, until my grandfather believed that the trees of y Wern would immediately become burnt shells!

While the particular appearance of this huge dog with its fiery eyes might be attributed to that of the spectral *Gwyllgi* (Wild Dog), Glanffrwd admits that his grandfather possessed a very strong imagination. He suggests that perhaps his grandfather had seen one of the dogs from the nearby farms with its eyes shining in the dark.

The mistaking of real animals for ghostly ones seems to be something of a theme in Llanwynno, or at least as far as Glanffrwd would have us believe. He continues with a similarly sceptical account of a donkey, believed to be the Devil:

Gwelodd Shams Llwynmelyn y gwr drwg wrth y Gelli Isaf wedi cymeryd arno ei hun ffurf asyn, a chafodd Shams gymaint o fraw fel y ffodd nerth ei draed, ond gan fod yr asyn wedi cael ei weled boreu dranoeth yn pori yn mhlith asgell tir Gelli Isaf, yr ydwyf yn credu nad yw y dystiolaeth yn ddigon cryf i brofi fod Satan yn ddigon dwl i ymddangos mewn croen mwlsyn.

Shams Llwynmelyn saw the evil one at Gelli Isaf having taken on the form of a donkey, and Shams was so frightened that he fled as fast as he could, but as the donkey had been seen the next morning grazing among the thistles of Gelli Isaf's land, I do not believe that the evidence is strong enough to prove that Satan is stupid enough to appear in the skin of a mule.

Unusually, this is not the only case of possible mistaken identity with respect to phantom donkeys within this parish. Als, also known as 'Als gwraig Rhys gwr Als' ('Als wife of Rhys husband of Als'), a local shop-keeper in Llanwynno, is described by Glanffrwd as a person who 'knew much of herbs and plants' ('*[g]wyddai lawer am lysiau a phlanhigion*') which, as well as suggesting her role as a folk healer within the community, perhaps also carries a suggestion of her proclivity to attribute supernatural origins to everyday occurrences.

Als apparently had a frightening altercation with a ghost that haunt-ed the gate of Cae'r Defaid (Sheep Field) – a spirit which had been responsible for assuring her of the general existence of ghosts. Als was said to believe that they 'were to be seen on every stile in the country' ('*i'w gweled ar bob camfa yn y wlad*') at Hallowe'en – a concept that we discussed in more detail in Chapter Three: 'Ghosts in the Landscape'.

The ghost of Cae'r Defaid had taken the form of a donkey, braying under the branches of the great oak tree in the field at night. As it trans-pired that a particularly vicious donkey belonged to Mynachdy farm, and had already terrorised some of the parishioners, many believed this was the very same beast. But Als was convinced that when she passed by the site on her return from Gelliwrgan, it was a spirit in the form of a donkey that she had seen, and furthermore, that it still haunted the area.

Like many of the folklore collectors of the time, Glanffrwd, a man of the cloth, regarded the belief systems of the common folk as naive.

A similar view is aired by Gruffydd Prisiart, a Methodist clergyman in Beddgelert, and recorded by William Hobley in the second volume of *Hanes Methodistiaeth Arfon* (1913):

> *Gynt yr oedd y gred mewn ymddanghosiad ysbrydion yn dra chyff-redinol. Nid oedd braidd lwyn o goed na chil adwy na byddai rhyw ysbryd neu gilydd yn y lle. Yr oedd un hen wr yn nodedig am eu canfod. Yr oedd yn yr ardal un bwg a alwai'r ardalwyr yn 'lloicoed.' Dywedai'r hen wr am hwn mai clamp o lo braf ydoedd, a phluen wen ar ei grwper, ac yn brefu yn ddiniwed.*

Previously, the belief in the appearance of ghosts was very common. There wasn't a grove of trees or a gateway that wouldn't have some ghost or other inhabiting it. One old man was noted for finding them. There was one bogey in the area that the locals called 'lloicoed.' The old man said about this one that it was a large fine calf, with a white feather on its rump, which brayed harmlessly.

Another, who had a propensity for seeing ghosts everywhere, according to Hobley, was a man named Morgan Owen Penybont, employed in the workshop of a cobbler named John Hughes. Morgan described the customary way that ghosts would appear to him, 'with the upper part in the form of a man, and the lower part in the form of an animal, horse or goat or the like' (*'gyda'r rhan uchaf ar ddull dyn, a'r rhan isaf ar ddull anifail, ceffyl neu afr neu'r cyffelyb'*).

This is not an uncommon motif in Welsh folklore, and is usually associated with the Devil or his demons appearing in human form but with tell-tale cloven hooves revealing their true infernal nature. The Reverend Edmund Jones in *A Relation of Apparitions of Spirits, in the Principality of Wales* (1780) records an earlier example from Ceredigion of a tailor – 'a profane man and a great drunkard' – who came upon a man on horseback one evening and agreed to make him some clothes. Despite his inebriated state, he couldn't help but notice 'the man's feet who spoke with him were not like a man's, but like a horse's feet'.

In his terror, the tailor sought the advice of Sir David Llwyd, a curate and physician from Ysbyty Ystwyth who was 'known to deal in the magic art' – in short, a cunning man or conjurer. The advice received was 'to delay measuring him as much as possible; not to stand before but behind him; and bid him be sure to be at home the time appointed'.

When the fateful day arrived, the tailor measured the mysterious stranger as instructed. Sir David Llwyd eventually arrived, and simply asked, 'What is your business here? Go away!' Surprisingly, this seemed to have the desired effect.

The Devil and his imps could sometimes appear in unlikely corporeal forms. Glanffrwd provides accounts of both devilish foals and dogs in the Llanwynno area in his usual comical fashion:

> Gwelodd Emwnt o'r Rhiw ef lawer gwaith yn Nghoedcae Shasper, ar lun ebol bach yn wastad; ond yr oedd cynifer o ebolion yn pori yno fel yr oedd yn anhawdd gwybod pa un ai y diafol ar lun ebol neu ebol gwirioneddol a welodd Emwnt fwy nag unwaith. Pe buasai yn marchogaeth un o'r ebolion buasai yn hawddach credu ei Fawrhydi Satanaidd oedd allan am ei evening ride, ond peth lled ddwl a di-dalent i un fel efe oedd ymddangos i neb ar lun ebolyn! Gwelodd Wil Rhyw ef fwy nag unwaith ar lun ci mawr, a'i lygaid yn fflamiau yn ei ben, ond yr oedd William wedi yfed cryn lawer o frandi y noson hono, fel nad ydyw ei dystiolaeth ef yn derfynol ar y pwnc.

Emwnt o'r Rhiw saw him many times in Coedcae Shasper, always in the shape of a small foal; but there were so many foals grazing there that it was difficult to know whether it was the devil in the form of a foal or a real foal that Emwnt saw more than once. If he had been riding one of the colts it would have been easier to believe his Satanic Majesty was out for his *evening ride*, but it was quite stupid and talentless for someone like him to appear to anyone in the form of a colt! Wil Rhyw saw him more than once in the shape of a large dog, with his eyes flaming in his head, but William had been drinking quite a lot of brandy that night, so his testimony is not conclusive on the subject.

Demonic foals aside, one of the most curious animal transfigurations must be the account of a Cardiganshire-born shoemaker called Griffith Edward, also recorded by Edmund Jones. Edward, now living in Tretŵr,

Powys, had recently converted to Methodism, when on coming home one evening from his place of worship, he was followed by the 'enemy':

> in the shape of a turkey cock, piffing after him, and making such a sound with his wings which the turkey cock makes when he makes the piffing noise with his mouth (but something more disagreeable, which everyone that considers it may easily imagine was very terrifying both to see and hear).

The spectral turkey, however, proved no match for Edward, who was 'a man of extraordinary piety' and sent it on its way. Again, we may draw our own conclusions as to the supposed supernatural origins of the aggrieved turkey.

Turkeys play an altogether different role in a tale relayed by Thomas Morgan in *Hanes Tonyrefail: Adgofion Am y Lle a'r Hen Bobl* (The History of Tonyrefail: Memories of the Place and the Old People) (1899). The man at the centre of this story, named Rasmws, worked at Garthgraban Fawr, a farm which was then owned by the Humphreys family. Now known as Garth Grabban Farm, it is situated in the village of Coed Ely, Rhondda Cynon Taf. It is notable for being the birthplace in 1795 of the eminent Welsh Calvinistic Methodist preacher William Evans, a fact celebrated by a blue plaque above the modern garage door at the property. Evans was known as 'Cloch Arian Cymru', or 'The Silver Bell of Wales'. The famous composer, Ivor Novello, was his great grandson.

Thomas Morgan recounts how the farm's servant, Rasmws, frequently returned from his night-time errands reporting that he had seen ghosts while out on the roads. His alleged experiences were quite intense, and included seeing a large dog which would follow him along the path, before turning into a bull: 'in the end the hedges would be aflame on either side of him, and he would come home drenched in sweat and near death' (*'yn y diwedd byddai y perthi ar dan bob ochr iddo, a deuai adref yn chwys mawr ac ar fin marw'*).

So affected was he by his beliefs, that when the farm owner was away on business, Rasmws slept with a gun next to his bed, believing that the spirits went to the nearby Coedmawr woods during the day, returning to the farm after dark.

One night, terrified at hearing a great commotion outside his bed-room window, Rasmws fired his gun through the window until there was 'a great silence' (*'bu yno dawelwch mawr'*). The next morning, he went outside and discovered that six of the farm's turkeys had been shot.

It was said that nobody would pass Garthgraban Fawr, even during the day, because of all the stories told by Rasmws and by those on neighbouring properties. Out of despair, the owners moved to England. The new owners, the Williams family from Gadlys, Aberdâr, were said to have dispelled any phantoms that remained at the property, and no further ghostly hounds or bulls (or burning hedgerows, for that matter) were seen again.

Sometimes, spectral animals would only be heard, and not seen at all. Glanffrwd notes an example of this phenomenon from the Pontypridd area:

> *Er ys amryw flynyddoedd yn ol clywid trwst troed ceffyl yn trotian yn gyflym lawer noswaith ar heol Penwal a Gellilwch. Yr oedd Williams Gellilwch yn adnabod ei swn o bell. Byddai yn trotian wrtho ei hun heibio i wlawty Pwllhowel, i gyfeiriad y Graig Wen, ac yn fynych cyfarfyddai y teithwyr hwyrol a'r swn, ond nid a'r ceffyl; pasiai ar drot heibio iddynt, ond nid oedd un amser yn weledig. Clywais ddynion geirwir yn adrodd hyn droion, dynion na fuont erioed o dan ddylanwad ofn nac ofergoeledd; tystient eu bod wedi clywed y nos-geffyl hwn yn trotian heibio iddynt ar y pryd! Nid wyf fi yn cynyg eglurhad ar hyn, dim ond adrodd y ffaith yn union. Y mae dynion yn byw yn y plwyf a allant dystiolaethu i wirionedd yr hyn yr wyf yn awr yn ei adrodd.*

For several years the clatter of a horse's hooves trotting quickly was heard on many evenings on Penwal and Gellilwch road. Williams Gellilwch recognised its sound from afar. It would trot by itself past the Pwllhowel coalhouse, in the direction of the Graig Wen, and the evening travellers would often encounter the noise, but not the horse; it trotted past them, but was not at any time visible. I have heard truthful men tell this many times, men who have never been under the influence of fear or superstition; they testified that they heard this night-horse trotting past them at the time! I do not offer an explanation on this, but merely state the facts exactly. There are men that live in the parish who can testify to the truth of what I am now relating.

The sound of phantom hooves are a common motif in Welsh ghost-lore, and can be found in some of the earliest eighteenth-century accounts by the Reverend Edmund Jones, right through to this contemporary twentieth-century example relayed by Lonie Williams of a haunting at Bodfan – a Grade II listed farmhouse in Llandwrog, Gwynedd. The interview recording can be listened to at the National Museum of History tape archives in Cardiff, and a transcription may be found in *Straeon Gwerin Ardal Eryri* (Folk Tales of Eryri) (2008) by John Owen Hughes. Williams explains how he was scared of visiting the farm as a child, owing to its reputation for being haunted:

> *o'dda n'w'n d'eud bydda' twrw ceffyla' yn rhedag ar hyd yr ardd, gefn drybeddion nos ynde. A'r ceffyla' yn 'sdabal w'th gwrs. Wel, – a bod ysgolfeistr a'i asusdant o Benffordd Elen wedi mynd yno efo ci – o'dd gin 'rysgolfeistr 'ma hen gi bach go ffyrnig. A bod y nhw ydi mynd yno un noson. Aros ar 'i traed i brofi nad o'dd 'naim ffashiwn beth yn bod. Ond yn y wir, ganol nos, dyma'r ceffyla'n dechra' dŵad, ag yn galpio ar hyd yr ardd. A dyma n'w allan i'r drws. O'dd 'na ddim byd i weld, ond twrw dychrynllyd y ceffyla' 'ma'n rhedag. A'i harnis n'w'n tincian w'th iddy' n'w redag 'yd yr ardd. A mi ddychrynnodd y ddau gymaint mi redon' adra' o'no, efo'r ci. Dyna hanas yr ysbryd 'na, 'te.*

they said there was the noise of horses running along the garden, in the middle of the night, see. And the horses were in the stable, of course. Well, – and the schoolmaster and his assistant from Penffordd Elen had gone there with a dog – the schoolmaster had something of a ferocious old dog. And they'd gone there one night. Stayed up to prove that there was no such thing. But to tell you the truth, in the middle of the night, the horses started coming, galloping along the garden. And they went out of the door. There was nothing to see, but the terrible noise of these horses running. And their harnesses tinkling as they ran through the garden. And it frightened the two of them so much that they ran home, with the dog. That was the story of that ghost, see.

This farmhouse ghoul was also heard in the dead of night, throwing and rolling apples picked from the orchard around one of the upstairs rooms, where they were stored.

It is possible in both the above cases that the landscape in the area formed a natural echo chamber, and the sound of a horse or horses from another road resonated on this one. Folklore, however, does not demand proof of a ghost; its interest lies in the stories and their transmission, not in the explanation.

The sounds of unseen animals are not limited to hooves. An intriguing account of a spectre known as *Yr Hwch a'r Tshaen* (The Chained Sow) exists in Ceredigion, and is recorded by the Reverend Evan Isaac in *Coelion Cymru* (Welsh Beliefs) (1938). This phantom sow is said to frequent the wooded banks of the river Cell, in the mountainous northern part of the county. The author was assured in 1924 by a native of Mynydd Bach, a hamlet near Pontarfynach (Devil's Bridge), that he had heard the ghost often, and even seen it at times. He was furthermore assured by a 'Mr J.B.' in 1925:

ei fod ef un tro pan oedd yn ieuanc yn marchogaeth adref yn lled hwyr ar y nos, a phan ddaeth ar gyfyl afon Cell, i'r ceffyl wylltio drwyddo a rhuthro carlamu fel peth gwallgof onid oedd, pan gyrhaeddodd adref, yn crynu fel dail y coed tan wynt, ac yn foddfa o chwys. Taerai pawb a wybu am yr helynt mai gweled yr Hwch a'r Tshaen a wylltiodd y ceffyl.

that he had at one time in his youth ridden home fairly late at night, and when he came close to the river Cell, that his horse had taken fright and galloped like a mad thing so that, when it arrived home, was shaking like the leaves on the trees in the wind, and was sweating profusely. Everyone who knew of the incident swore that it was seeing the Chained Sow that had frightened the horse.

A local schoolmaster from Pontarfynach, Mr T. Richards, provides us with a slightly more rational explanation for this haunting: that the clanking of the sow's shackles was no more than the noise of the local miners, dragging steel chains late at night to scare their supervisors while they entered the mine shafts to blunt their augers, thereby prolonging their employment. Another of Isaac's acquaintances from Aberystwyth explains that the infrequent sighting of the 'sow' could be explained by the custom of letting pigs loose to graze on acorns that fell from the many oak trees that stood along the banks of the Cell, and to stop the poor beasts from roaming too far, their masters were in the habit of placing iron shackles around their feet. Should one of these creatures have been heard or seen dragging their aching trotters homewards at night, it is hardly surprising that a superstition such as *Yr Hwch a'r Tshaen* was born.

The image of the boar in Welsh folklore is not unprecedented: *Y Twrch Trwyth* appears in the tale of *Culhwch ac Olwen*, one of the oldest Arthurian romances in existence. The significance of the pig in Welsh folkloric imagery is otherwise discussed in Chapter Ten: 'Death Omens'.

A notable folkloric pig which rears its head every *Nos Galan Gaeaf* (Hallowe'en) is the monstrous *Hwch Ddu Gwta* (Tailless Black Sow). A north Walian tradition in particular, she was said to be a devil in the form of a black pig. Bonfires represent one of the oldest and most consistent traditions from this time of year, associated with communal celebration and divination rituals. Once the flames subsided, a cry would be raised to warn of the *Hwch*'s coming, sparking a mad dash homewards for fear of being last, with frightened runners shouting:

> *Nos G'lan gaua'*
> *Ar ben pob camfa*
> *Hwch ddu gwta*
> *Gipio yr ola'*

Hallowe'en, atop every stile, the tailless black sow, takes the hindmost.

> *Adre', adre', am y cynta':*
> *Hwch ddu gwtta gipia'r ola'.*

Home, home, let us race: the tailless black sow will snatch the last.

There are, as with most folk customs, regional variations to this ritual: in Caergybi (Holyhead), for example, the *Hwch* was said to exhibit a tongue of flames. Clearly a device used by parents to encourage their terrified children home, with further incentive provided as she was said to sit atop every stile on the way (a motif that was discussed in Chapter Three: 'Ghosts in the Landscape').

A beast that cannot be so neatly explained was said to roam the woods near the village of Boduan, Gwynedd, known as 'Bwystfil Boduan' ('The Beast of Boduan'), a creature which is perhaps more in keeping with a cryptozoological entity than a ghost. The tale is recorded by Myrddin Fardd in *Llên Gwerin Sir Gaernarfon*: 'In form it was not dissimilar to a fox, but was larger in size, and had large spots here and there along it' ('*O ran ffurf nid anhebyg ydoedd i lwynog, ond ei fod yn fwy ei faint, ac ymsotiau mawrion draw ac yma ar hyd-ddo*').

Myrddin Fardd continues by stating that '[i]ts chilling cries at night, according to folklore, were enough to drive terror through the recesses of the bravest heart' ('*[y]r oedd ei oernadau yn y nos, medd llên werin, yn ddigon i yru arswyd drwy gilfachau y galon ddewraf*'). The sound that this animal made, by all accounts, did not fit its appearance as this creature's cry was akin to the braying of a donkey. If an observer imitated the cry, then the animal was always heard to reply, but would stop short of being close enough to be easily seen. Its brays seem to have been restricted to winter nights, especially when the weather was frosty, and it was entirely absent both in the summer months and during the daytime. It was known to attack cats, and it was said that if it got hold of one then the cat would never be seen again.

After a time, the apparition seemed to change location and was reported in the woods surrounding Plas Hen, in Llanystumdwy – a hall which also boasts a considerable number of other hauntings (see Chapter Six: 'Poltergeists'). It was thought to have remained there for a few years before disappearing completely. Some believed it may have been an exotic animal that had escaped from a ship moored at the nearby anchorage of St Tudwal or the like. Myrddin Fardd suggests some comparison can be made with the legendary creature from Welsh mythology, *Cath Palug*, who fought and was killed by Cai (Sir Kay) of King Arthur's Court.

It seems likely that this creature was flesh and blood rather than anything phantasmal. The account reads like an early big cat sighting, possibly that of a lynx, which (braying aside) has spots and could arguably be mistaken for a very large fox. Lynx can live between two and seventeen years in the wild and would roam from one territory to another to seek food, catching a variety of small animals which could easily have included domestic cats. They are not unknown in the wild even in modern times, with a Eurasian Lynx shot in Norwich in the summer of 1991. Most modern big cat sightings tend to be a result of creatures being released into the wild from private collections; the idea of such a beast having escaped from a foreign ship is certainly not outside the realms of possibility.

CHAPTER FIVE

Holy Ghosts

*

Ni ddaw bendith i dy ran,
Heb it newid sail y llan.
Nei chei syflyd o'r fan hyn,
Llanfihangel Pen-y-bryn.
Trad.

No blessings will come your way, without moving the foundations of the church. It shall not be moved from this spot, Llanfihangel Pen-y-bryn.

Historically, the relationship between ghosts and the Church is complicated. In centuries past, the two were inextricably linked. With the arrival of the Protestant Reformation and the subsequent rejection of the concept of purgatory and, by association, Catholicism, the relationship between the living and the dead fundamentally changed. However, with opposing post-Reformation Lutheran and Calvinistic beliefs in the appearance of spirits, there was a movement among Dissenting ministers, and both Protestant and Catholic clergymen across Britain, to use accounts of apparitions (of all denominations!) to prove the survival of the soul after death as a rebuke against atheism:

Are not all these numerous instances, together, sufficient to convince all the Sadducees and atheistical men of the age (or any age in the time to come) of the being of spirits, and of their appearance in the world?

It is the works of ministers and clergymen such as these that have given rise to some of Wales's most valuable ghost-lore, the main example being the accounts of the Reverend Edmund Jones, 'Yr Hen

Broffwyd' ('The Old Prophet') of Transh in Pont-y-pŵl (Pontypool), Monmouthshire, whom we have just quoted.

Here, we shall examine some of the Welsh ghost stories which intersect with church and chapel culture in Wales, and the folklore that lies behind stories and traditions relating to religion where spirit activity plays a part. An entire generation of terrified youngsters who grew up reading the Usborne classic *The World of The Unknown: Ghosts* (first published in 1977) might be under the misapprehension that holy ghosts are few and far between, as the book states that only 'one ghost is thought to exist in a graveyard. It is the "graveyard guardian", the spirit of the first person to have been buried there.' Welsh ghosts are here to disprove that theory.

We cannot discuss the bridging of the supernatural and Christianity within Wales without first considering the influence of the religious movements across the cultural landscape over the centuries; so much of the country's ghost-lore is directly intertwined with religious imagery and dogma. This concept is discussed more fully in the introductory chapter; however, this would seem like a prudent moment to introduce one such example within Welsh folklore: the phenomenon of *canu yn yr awyr* (singing in the sky), that is, hearing phantom, or angelic, voices from the heavens.

This supernatural – or rather, spiritual – experience is reported in connection with the religious revivals that are dotted through eighteenth- to early twentieth-century Wales. Ieuan Buallt (Evan Jones) of Ty'n-y-pant farm in Llanwrtyd, Powys, was a prolific chronicler and collector of local history, lore and custom, whose manuscripts are kept as part of the Amgueddfa Cymru (Museum Wales) archives in Nantgarw. His booklet of handwritten notes regarding *canu yn yr awyr* provide a valuable insight into the folk narrative associated with the Welsh revivals:

Fel yr oedd y bonheddwr David Jones, Llwyn-derw, Abergwesyn, a'i wraig un diwrnod yn dychwelyd o'r cwrdd yn Llanwrtyd, a phan yn rhywle yn Nghwm Irfon, clywsant ganu a moliannu uwch eu pennau yn yr awyr, yr hyn a ddilynwyd gan ddiwygiad mawr ar grefydd yn lled fuan. Gan mai yn y flwyddyn 1796 y daeth y teulu parchus yma o'r Fanog i Lwyn-derw, ac i Mr. D. Jones farw ym 1810, rhaid mai o flaen yr adfywiadau a gafwyd ym 1804, neu 1808 oedd hyn.

Dywedai'r hen bobl, hefyd, i 'ganu yn yr awyr', fel y galwent ef, gymeryd lle o flaen diwygiad mawr a rhyfedd hwnnw a fu yn y flwyddyn 1840. Clywyd hwn yn blaen iawn yn ardal Llechweddol, Llanwrtyd. Yr oedd y lleisiau i'w clywed mor eglur, fel y gellid clywed un llais mawr yn gryfach na'r lleill; ac yn adeg yr adfywiad yn yr ardal a nodwyd, yr oedd un dyn o'r enw Dafid Davies, Llawrdref fach, neu 'Dafydd Jac y Clochydd', yn hynod gynnes ei ysbryd gyda'r diwygiad, ac iddo lais mawr, cryf, ac amlwg, fel y clywid ef yn moliannu yn blaen yn nghanol torf fawr. Sylwai yr Hen Williams, gweinidog Llanwrtyd a Throedrhiwdalar, ei fod i'w glywed yn moliannu fel dafad Saesnig yn brefu yn nghanol defaid mynyddig.

Clywodd amryw 'ganu yn yr awyr' hefyd, o flaen y diwygiad a fu ym 1859–60. Yr oedd i'w glywed o flaen rhai oedfaon, fel y dywedir. Un noswaith fel yr oedd hen wr o'r enw Isaac Powell, Tir Ithel, ger Llanwrtyd yn myned tuag adref, a phan ar y llwybr ger y ty, clywai ganu a moliannu amlwg yn dod i waered ar hyd y ffordd o Gwm Irfon, safodd i wrando, a chlywodd ef yn dod lawr heibio'r Ffynon a Dôl-y-coed, tua'r pentref. Yn fuan wedi'ynu, torrodd y diwygiad allan gyntaf mewn cwrdd gweddi wythnosol yn yr Alltwineu, a daeth mintai o bobl i lawr o'r cyfarfod dan ganu a moliannu yr holl ffordd tua'r pentref.

As David Jones, a gentleman of Llwyn-derw, Abergwesyn, and his wife were returning one day from the service in Llanwrtyd, while somewhere in Cwm Irfon [the Irfon Valley], they heard singing and worship in the sky above them, which was followed by a great religious revival fairly soon afterwards. As it was in the year of 1796 that this respectable family came from the Fanog to Llwyn-derw, and that Mr D. Jones died in 1810, this must have been before the revivals seen in 1804, or 1808.

The elderly people also claimed that 'singing in the sky', as they called it, took place before that great and peculiar revival that took place in the year 1840. This was heard very plainly in the region of Llechweddol, Llanwrtyd. The voices were heard so clearly, that one loud voice was heard more clearly than the rest; and at the time of the revival in this same area, one man named Dafid Davies of Llawrdref Fach, or 'Dafydd Jac the Sexton', was extremely warm-spirited towards the revival, with a great, strong voice, and distinctive, so that he could plainly be heard worshipping in the middle of a large crowd. Old Williams, the minister of Llanwrtyd and Troedrhiwdalar, noted that he could be heard giving praise like an English sheep braying in the middle of mountain sheep.

Many also heard 'singing in the sky', ahead of the 1859–60 revival. It was heard, as is claimed, before some religious meetings. One night as an old man named Isaac Powell of Tir Ithel near Llanwrtyd was returning home, and when on the path near the house, he heard clear singing and worshipping coming towards him along the road from Cwm Irfon, he stood to listen, and heard it come down past Ffynnon and Dôl-y-coed, towards the village. Soon afterwards, the revival began at a weekly prayer meeting in Alltwineu, and a band of people came down from the meeting while singing and worshipping all the way to the village.

A further example of this phenomenon, widespread but rarely mentioned in folklore texts, is recorded by William Davies in his 1898 essay, 'Casgliad o Lên-Gwerin Meirion' ('A Collection of Meirion Folklore'):

Am yr hen gred swynol hon, diau ei bod yn dra chyffredinol yn Nghymru hyd o fewn oes neu ddwy yn ol. Yn hanes 'Yr Hynod William Elis, Maentwrog,' dywedir:— 'Byddai yn myfyrio llawer ar y byd ysbrydol a'i breswylwyr. Soniai am yr angylion da a drwg fel pe buasant ei gymydogion agosaf. Rhoddai rhai yn ei erbyn ei fod yn ofergoelus, gan y byddai yn rhoddi coel ar freuddwydion, ymddangosiad ysbrydion, a gweinidogaeth angylion. Dywedai wrth bregethwr unwaith, pan yn ymddyddan ar hyn, "Y mae yr angylion yn ymladd llawer drosom i gadw y cythreuliaid rhag ein niweidio. Y mae yn swydd ddigyn sal iddynt hefyd, a ninnau yn rhai mor ddrwg." Gofynai y pregethwr, "A ydych yn meddwl eu bod yn dyfod i'n byd ni o gwbl?" "O, ydynt," ebe yntau, "ac y mae guard ohonynt yn dyfod i nol pob dyn duwiol. Daethant i nol Richard Jones o'r Wern dipyn bach yn rhy fuan; yr oedd o heb fod yn hollol barod. Darfu iddynt hwythau ganu penill uwch ben y tŷ, i aros iddo fod yn barod, ond 'doedd neb yn deall y geiriau na'r dôn ychwaith : iaith a

*thôn y nefoedd oeddynt.'" Yr oedd rhai o'r cymydogion yn dweyd fod
swn canu nefolaidd uwch ben Rhosigor – y ty lle bu Richard Jones
farw ynddo ychydig amser cyn iddo ehedeg ymaith; a dyna ydoedd
esboniad William Ellis arno.*

Regarding this charming old belief, it was certainly quite common in Wales within the past one or two generations. In the
history of '*Yr Hynod William Elis, Maentwrog,*' ['The Remarkable
William Elis of Maentwrog,'] it is said that:— 'He would often
meditate on the spiritual world and its inhabitants. He spoke of
the good and evil angels as if they were his closest neighbours.
Some accused him of being superstitious, as he believed in the
legitimacy of dreams, the appearance of ghosts, and in the min-
istry of angels. He told a preacher once, as they were conversing
on the subject, "The angels often battle on our behalf in order
to stop the demons from harming us. It's a poor enough job for
them too, with us being so wicked." The preacher asked, "Do
you think that they visit our world at all?" "Oh, yes," he replied,
"and a guard of them comes to fetch every godly man. They
came a little too early for Richard Jones of Wern; he wasn't quite
ready. It came to pass that they sang a verse above the house,
while waiting for him to prepare himself, but no one understood
the words nor recognised the melody: they were the language
and music of heaven."' Some of the neighbours claimed that
heavenly sounds of singing were heard above Rhosigor – the
house where Richard Jones died shortly before he left us entirely;
and that was the explanation given by William Ellis.

An experience similar to *canu yn yr awyr* is recorded in *Hanes Methodistiaeth Arfon* (The History of Methodism in Arfon) (1910) by William
Hobley, who describes the appearance of angelic spirits associated with
the unusual death of J. C. Vincent, the vicar of Eglwys Sant Baglan
(St Baglan's Church), otherwise known as Hen Eglwys Llanfaglan in
Gwynedd. The word *llan* in Welsh means church or parish, and the
suffix of a place-name beginning with Llan- usually denotes the saint
in whose name the church is consecrated. In this instance therefore,
Llanfaglan denotes the church/parish of St Baglan.

The thirteenth-century church stands overlooking Afon Menai (the Menai Straits), and is arguably one of the most picturesque churches in the country. Now under the care of the Friends of Friendless Churches charity, the churchyard configuration is suggestive of possible pre-Christian origins. Its age is exemplified further by the repurposing of a fifth- or sixth-century inscribed stone slab which may be found above the door, featuring Latinised forms of Brythonic, forerunner of Welsh.

Appointed as Llanfaglan's vicar in 1862, J. C. Vincent was well liked within the parish because of the dedication he had previously shown to those members of the community who were affected by a cholera epidemic which had hit the area in 1866. He unfortunately died at a relatively young age: 'and it was said at the time that he was dying, in full possession of his senses, asking those around him, didn't they see the angels in the room?' ('*ac fe ddywedid ar y pryd ei fod ar ei farw-ysgafn, mewn llawn feddiant ar ei synwyrau, yn gofyn i'r rhai o'i amgylch, onid oeddynt hwy yn gweled yr angylion yn yr ystafell?*')

The line between *ysbrydion* (ghosts) and *ysbrydoedd* (spirits) in Welsh ghost-lore is tenuous, with angels, demons, fairies and 'ghosts' proper often being lumped together, especially in earlier seventeenth- and eighteenth-century accounts. This has already been exemplified in the discussion pertaining to the haunting of Camfa Angharad, Abererch, in Chapter Three: 'Ghosts in the Landscape'.

This is not the only account of an angelic spirit being witnessed by the sick and dying in Wales. A much earlier example is recorded in the anti-witchcraft treatise, *Cas Gan Gythraul* (The Devil's Hatred), first published in 1711 by T.P., who describes a ghost appearing to a young and sickly man, with imagery arguably closer to that of an angelic figure than a ghoul:

> *Y mae Hanes arall yn breintiedig o berthyd Dŷn iefangc o oedran 29 oedd yn glaf, i ba un yr ymddangossod yspryd mewn gwisg wen ddisclair, hyd onid oedd yn goleuo'r 'Stafell, ymmha un yr oedd y dŷn claf, ac y gyffyrddodd ac ef ac ai iachaoedd ef, ac a archodd, i'r dŷn arferyd ffurf o Weddi, pa un oedd a geiriau da ynthi, eithr fod yn rhaid iddo fyned i ddywedyd neu adrodd y cyfryw weddi wrth ddrws y garghell, &c. Ac ar yr amserau oedd 'n erchi iddo ac yr oedd yn erchu iddo annog dynion i edifarhau, ac i ymadel ai*

beiau eithr fel y mae ychydig o wenwyn, yn fawr ei herigl, er rhoddi
llawer o Sugar iw felyssu; Felly er bod y dŷn hwn wedi cael ei
annog gan y cyfryw Yspryd i gyflawni rhai pethau da, ar ddibenion
drwg twyllodrus, felly efe oedd ynghyd a'r rhain wedi erchu iddo
newid y Sabboth, a rhai pethau cyfeiliornus eraill, ac er dim a'r
oedd y Gweinidog oedd yn y lle hwnnw a gwyr da eraill yn allu
i wneuthur, nid oedd yn gallu attal dynion rhag canlyn y cyfryw
un, trwy gymmerd i fyny fath o grefydd newydd, a thybied mae
Prophwyd didwyll ydoedd, nes yn y diwedd iddynt glywaid fod eu
Prophwyd oedd yn ei hannog hwy i fod yn Sanctaidd ac yn ddiwair
i hunan, yn euog o odineb.

Another History is printed in relation to a young Man of 29
years who was ill, to whom appeared a spirit in shining white
robes, so that it lit up the Room, in which was the patient, who
touched him and healed him, and who ordered, that the man
should practice a form of Prayer, which was nobly worded, and
that he had to say or recite this particular prayer at the chancel
door, &c. And it was requested and demanded that he encourage men to repent, and to atone for their sins but just as as a
little poison is greatly dangerous, even having been sweetened
with a lot of Sugar; So though this man was encouraged by this
particular Spirit to accomplish some good things, they were for
deceitful and evil purposes, so that he along with these had commanded him to change the Sabbath, and other devious things,
and despite all that the local Minister and other good men could
do, he could not stop men from following this particular one, in
taking up a kind of new religion, and consider him a Prophet in
good faith, so that in the end they heard that their Prophet who
encouraged them to be Sacred and chaste, was guilty of adultery.

Religious mania of the revivals aside, while congregational encounters
with angelic figures might be considered acceptable, and even believable,
their infernal counterparts were also frequently used as 'proof' of the divine – a tool most often deployed by the Dissenting clergymen of Wales.

A classical example is provided below in a letter from 1771, sent by
a native of Ynys Môn (Anglesey) who recounts the tale of a travelling

preacher, 'the Rev. Mr. Hughes', and his encounter with a demonic spirit. The letter is included in the Reverend Edmund Jones's *A Relation of Apparitions of Spirits, in the Principality of Wales* (1780):

> At one time going by night to preach, and his way being by an artificial circle upon the ground between Amlwch Village and St Elian Church, said to be haunted by an evil Spirit. When he came near or entred [*sic*] into the Circle, the similitude of a Greyhound came against him, and he was presently pulled off his horse and beaten. Next night, having occasion to go that way, he went with an intention to speak to the Spirit; he went, but was beaten again. It did not avail that he was a big, strong, courageous man, and such he was; for who could fight with a Spirit? He did indeed speak to him, but had no answer.

While passing the same artificial circle another time on foot, the reverend saw that the demonic entity was chained. The crafty preacher, seeing how far the chain could reach, stood just out of harm's way to attempt to question it once more. This time, he was able to elicit an answer:

> That going with a company when he was alive to offer a Silver-groat which is expected and received at Elian Church; for some Parish use he had hid it under a stone, said he had lost it to be excused from payment, told Mr. Hughes where it was, who found and paid it: and the trouble ceased.

This account, which appears rather fantastical at first glance, and even garners some scepticism from the usually credulous Jones, in fact contains many motifs which we have discussed in previous chapters: a ghost appearing in the form of a greyhound; a person only able to converse with a spirit on the third attempt; and the overarching theme of a restless ghost with unfinished business. That this spirit appears within an 'artificial circle' – undoubtedly referencing the age-old universally recognised technique of casting a 'magic circle' in an attempt to contain the demonic entity (a technique not unknown to the cunning folk and conjurers of Wales) – again represents another example of a supernatural boundary which has previously been seen in Chapter Three: 'Ghosts in the Landscape'.

While Edmund Jones remained sceptical, there are elements of truth in this tale. Eglwys Sant Eilian, Llaneilian, is an example of a *clas* church, comprising a hodge-podge of medieval and modern buildings, dating from the twelfth to the twentieth centuries. One of its most notable features is the surviving fifteenth-century rood screen which bears traces of a morbid painting depicting a skeleton with a scythe, and the words '*Colyn angau yw pechod*' ('Death's sting is sin'). Interestingly, the church also harbours a 1667 iron-banded wooden chest, used for collecting donations – probably the very same that saw neither hide nor hair of this unfortunate soul's silver groat.

An account of this same story is recorded by Peter Roberts in *Hynafion Cymreig* (Welsh Antiquities) (1823), the Welsh-language version of his earlier English text, *The Cambrian Popular Antiquities* (1815) – a version that is altogether poorer for its relative lack of writing on the supernatural and witchcraft in Wales. This account is provided below for the benefit of Welsh-language readers, as Roberts's translation is far superior for its nineteenth-century richness than we could hope to achieve:

Ar un amser pan oedd y Parch Mr. Hughes, offeiriad cyfrifol yn yr Eglwys Sefydledig, yn myned gwedi nos i bregethu yn Mon, efe a ddaeth i fan lle y gwelai efe gylch gwneuthuredig ar y llawr, rhwng Amlwch ac Eglwys St. Elian, yr hwn a ddywedid ei fod yn cael ei aflonyddu gan ysbryd aflan. Pan aeth efe i mewn i'r cylch, rhywbeth tebyg i filgi a ddaeth yn ei erbyn, ac yn union-gyrchol cymmerwyd ef ymaith oddiar ei geffyl, a churwyd ef yn enbyd. Y noson nesaf, gan ei fod yn myned yr un ffordd, yr oedd yn meddwl llefaru wrth yr ysbryd, ond pan ddaeth i'r lle curwyd ef eilwaith yr un modd; efe a ofynodd amryw bethau iddo, ond ni chafodd un atteb. Yn mhen ychydig amser efe a ddygwyddodd fyned heibio yr un lle heb geffyl, ac yna efe a welodd fod yr ysbryd wedi ei gadwyno; efe a ganfu mor bell y cyrhaeddai y gadwyn, a chan sefyll ymaith o'i chyrhaedd, efe a holodd yr ysbryd paham yr oedd efe yn aflonyddu y rhai a elent heibio y ffordd hòno. Yr ysbryd a ddywedodd wrtho, ei fod ef y myned, gydâ chymdeithion ereill, pan oedd yn y bywyd hwn, i offrymu dernyn o arian (yr hyn ddysgwylir ac a dderbynir yn Eglwys St. Elian) at wasanaeth yr eglwys, ond iddo ei guddio dan gàreg, a dweyd iddo ei golli, fel yr esgusodid ef rhag talu. Dywedodd hefyd wrth Mr. Hughes pa le yr oedd y dernyn, ac efe a'i cafodd ef yn y lle hwnw, ac a'i talodd, a gorphwysodd yr aflonyddwch.

There is a particularly infamous demonic spirit haunting Eglwys Sant Digain (St Digain or Dygain's Church) in Llangernyw, Conwy. The church building here was heavily re-modelled as part of the widely undertaken programme of nineteenth-century restorations, removing much of the original architectural detail; the oldest sections, such as the nave, are thought to date back to the thirteenth century. Two standing stones remain in the churchyard, one dating from the seventh to the ninth centuries, and the other, inscribed with a cross, dating from the ninth to the eleventh centuries.

These are not the oldest relics found in this churchyard, however, for Llangernyw is famous for being home to a giant yew tree that dwarfs the gravestones here, its split trunk giving the appearance of four separate trees – a defect from when the old church oil tank was harboured within its cavity and much of the dead wood in the hollow of the tree cleared away. With various sources citing its age at between 1,500 to 5,000 years old, it is arguably one of the oldest trees in Europe and stands as a remarkable survivor of the ages.

Another surviving relic from Eglwys Sant Digain is the folk tale of the Angelystor, a demonic calendrical spirit which, to the best of our knowledge, was first recorded by Elias Owen in *Welsh Folk-lore: A Collection of the Folk-Tales and Legends of North Wales* (1896), and widely retold since, with good reason. The term *angelystor* is the aphetic, or shortened, form of *efangelystor*, a term used to describe any of the four evangelists, i.e. Matthew, Mark, Luke or John. It may be a tongue-in-cheek reference to the fact that this particular spirit, rather than proclaiming good news, was instead said to announce from the altar of Eglwys Sant Digain every *Nos Galan Gaeaf* (Hallowe'en) the names of each parishioner who could expect death in the coming year:

Those who were anxious to know whether they or their neighbours had a longer time to live stood underneath the east window on that eve, and anxiously listened for the dreaded revelation.

Contemporary retellings often place the Angelystor in the yew tree itself when reciting its ominous list, rather than in the church – a development which is easy to appreciate given the age and striking appearance of the Llangernyw yew.

This divinatory practice is not an isolated tradition in Wales, as there was once a pervading and enduring folk belief that at a particular time of year, the spirits at a church would foretell who in a community was going to die in the following twelve-month period. The tradition is described in an earlier account by Peter Roberts in *The Cambrian Popular Antiquities*:

> The same has also been said to have followed the listening at the great door of the church in order to hear the names of those who were to die the following year, when a person has heard his own name called amongst the first of those mentioned.

In the Welsh version of this book, *Hynafion Cymreig*, this same excerpt is presented by the author as follows:

> *Y mae yn arferiad mawr hefyd i fyned i'r eglwys, ar y nos hon, i wrando ar ysbrydion holl drigolion y plwyf, y rhai ydynt yno wedi ymgasglu, yn galw rhes enwau y rhai ydynt i farw y flwyddyn gan-lynawl. Nid rhyfedd fod y gwrandaw-wyr, bob amser, yn clywed eu henwau eu hunain yn cael eu galw; yr hyn a wneir gan ryw un yn gwybod eu bod yno, i'r dyben o'u dychrynu.*

Numerous other ecclesiastical divinatory rituals were performed during *Nos Galan Gaeaf*. Myrddin Fardd in *Llên Gwerin Sir Gaernarfon* (The Folklore of Caernarfonshire) (1908) describes one of the less sinister examples performed in churches in north-west Wales (an account which appears to have been lifted near verbatim from Peter Roberts's text):

> *Arferid hefyd, fyned o amgylch yr Eglwys dan hau hadau cywrach, ychydig cyn deuddeg o'r gloch. Rhaid i'r personau fyddai yn hau, pa un bynag ai mab ai merch, fyned o amgylch yr Eglwys, a dywedyd ei fod yn hau, ac yn disgwyl i'w gariad ddyfod ar ei ol i fedi. Pan darawai cloch yr Eglwys yr ergyd diweddaf o ddeuddeg, yr hauwr a edrychai ar ei ol, ac nis methai un amser weled naill ai arch neu*

ysbryd ei gywely priodasol. Yr oedd yr ysbryd yma fynychaf yn anad-
nabyddus, ond pan welid y cariad gyntaf yn gorfforol, adnabyddid
ef yn union.

It was also the custom, to walk around the Church, sowing
hemp seeds, a little before twelve o'clock. Those who sowed,
whether they be men or women, travelled around the Church,
and stated that they were sowing, and expected their sweethearts
to harvest after them. When the Church bell struck the last of
twelve chimes, the sower would look behind them, and would
never fail to notice either a coffin or the spirit of their marital
companion. This spirit would usually be anonymous, but when
the sweetheart would first be seen physically, it would instantly
be recognised.

As well as *Nos Galan Gaeaf*, these various traditions were also often prac-
tised on *Dygwyl y Meirw* (literally translated as 'The Festival of the Dead',
or All Souls' Day) on 2 November, and on *Nos Galan* (New Year's Eve)
depending on the region, as exemplified by Cadrawd in his *History of
Llangynwyd Parish* (1887), describing the custom in Pen-y-Bont ar Ogwr
(Bridgend):

On New Year's night, tradition says, it was custom with the wise
and courageous old men of the Parish to sit up all night in the
Church porch. On that night, it was said, a voice, emanating
from beneath the altar table, pronounced the names of those
who should die within the coming year.

Variations on these rituals would also take place across England, but
more often associated with 24 April, St Mark's Eve. In some cases a
single ghost would appear; in others, the dead might rise from their
graves, or a phantom procession would emerge from the church. Sometimes the vigil needed to be kept for three years in a row, and sometimes
fasting was necessary, or one might need to walk around the building
three times before entering the church porch.

What makes the Angelystor an enduring folkloric figure, despite the
relative lack of earlier Welsh sources to confirm its ghastly presence, is

the combination of the Gothic romantic imagery of the church and its ancient yew, and the specific tale that accompanies Elias Owen's account:

> It is related of a tailor, who was reckoned a wit, and affected disbelief in the Spirit story, that he announced his intention to prove the thing a myth, and so, one Nos G'lan Geua', Shon Robert, as he was called, proceeded to the church just before midnight, and, to his horror, he heard his own name— 'Shon ap Robert,' uttered by the Spirit. 'Hold, hold!' said the tailor, 'I am not quite ready!' But, ready or not ready, it made no difference to the messenger of death, for that year the tailor died.

Eglwys Sant Deiniol (St Deiniol's Church) in the village of Llanfor, Gwynedd, previously known as Eglwys Sant Mor, is also associated with a haunting. This church was decommissioned in 1992 and is now in private ownership, but remains largely unchanged. The haunting would have occurred in the earlier building on the same site. The current structure was erected in 1875, using reclaimed bricks and tiles from the Llanfor Roman military camp.

The details of the apparition may be found again in Elias Owen's *Welsh Folk-lore*, in a story told to the author by Mr R. Roberts, a native of nearby Bala, as recalled by his grandmother who was born in 1744:

> He was said to have worn a three-cocked hat, and appeared as a gentleman, and whilst divine service was performed he stood up in the church. But at night the church was lit up by his presence, and the staves between the railings of the gallery were set in motion, by him, like so many spindles, although they were fast in their sockets. He is not reported to have harmed any one, neither did he commit any damage in the church.

The ghost was sometimes seen walking to the summit of Moel y Llan, and although it did not hurt anyone, its presence clearly terrified the community to the point that they decided to conduct a vestry in the local public house instead. Nobody would put themselves forward to collect the parish books from the church and, in the end, the landlady of the pub had to go. Every time she entered the church, the 'Evil Spirit' blew out the light that she was carrying and so she ended up making her way to the coffer to retrieve the books in the dark.

Eventually, and as is often the case in Welsh ghost tales from this period, two men 'skilled in divination' – cunning men – were brought in to deal with the haunting, and determined to banish the ghost to the nearby lake, Llyn y Geulan Goch, a pool in Afon Dyfrdwy (the river Dee) which snakes around the village. According to one slightly curious version of the story, the men first visited the church and conversed with the spirit, informing it they would return at a particular hour that night to remove it. While this all sounds very civil, amusingly, the men were late for their meeting, and as a consequence were met with a rather less compliant ghoul!

Eventually, they succeeded in removing the spirit from the church in the form of a cockerel, which they then transported on horseback to the lake in a bid to lay it as promised. While one last phantasmic scuffle ensued at the river bank, once bested, the ghost agreed to enter the water if its captors lay face down on the ground. Once in this position, a splash was heard as the ghost jumped in without further complaint.

The story tells that it was compelled to count all of the grains of sand on the lake floor before it would be able to leave again. At one point, there was some local concern that it had indeed succeeded in its task, with the storyteller's uncle himself having witnessed two phantom pigs disappear next to Llyn y Geulan Goch one night. Any rumours of escaped spirits were quashed, however, when another 'wise man' cast an inscribed stone into the pool and watched the waters boil and foam around it, 'proving' the spirit remained confined to its watery prison.

Interestingly, Elias Owen proceeds to record two other separate accounts of this same tale. The second was recalled to him by an old woman of the parish called Ann Hughes, who insisted that it was the parson himself, with assistance from an acquaintance, who laid this ghost. This particular spirit was not usually seen, but:

> was in the habit of coming down the pathway leading from Rhi-
> wlas to the church, making a great noise, as if dragging after him
> chains, or wheeling a wheelbarrow, and he went straight into the
> church, and there he stayed all night lighting up the church and
> making a great noise, as though engaged in manual labour.

The implication here is that manual labour is antithetical to the serenity of the church, and that the site of the ghost's haunting was therefore considered especially inappropriate. Her variant contains another interesting trope regarding the length of time for which the spirit banished:

> Ann Hughes could not tell me what plan was adopted to get rid of the Evil Spirit, but she knew this much, that he was laid in Llyn-y-Geulan-Goch, and that he was to remain there until a lighted candle, which was hidden somewhere in the church, when the Spirit was overcome, should go out. Often and again had she searched for this taper, but failed to discover it, but she supposes that it is still burning somewhere, for the Evil One has not yet escaped from the pool.

The motif of the burning candle measuring a period of time is found in many stories within folklore. The usual structure is that the spirit is bound until a candle has been entirely consumed. Once the contract is made, the candle is blown out and hidden away before the bargain can be realised.

The third version comes from *Y Gordofigion*, the transactions of the Liverpool and Birkenhead Eisteddfod (year unknown), and is translated by Owen. In this version, the troublesome ghost was exorcised by a man entering the church on horseback, no less. The spirit was removed in the form of a pig, the appearance of which caused an elderly woman to cry out, 'Good God! A pig in the Church!' ('*Duw annwyl! Mochyn yn yr Eglwys!*'). Enraged at her words, the spirit threw the man and his mare over the church, leaving behind the horse's hoofprints on a gravestone where it landed. But, as in all other examples of this tale, to Llyn y Geulan Goch the bogey eventually went, with such effort on the poor mare's part that she lost all her hair! This is also the version of the story provided by William Davies in 'Casgliad o Lên-Gwerin Meirion'.

Owen has clearly recorded the story of the ghost of Eglwys Sant Deiniol in some detail, providing an excellent example of the propensity for folk tales to evolve within a community over a relatively brief period of time, even one as close-knit as Llanfor. Owen was one of many clergymen of the period who served multiple roles as antiquarians, authors and scholars, and were responsible for collecting and recording many of the traditions, customs and stories that now make up a large volume of folklore for this period.

As already discussed in the introductory chapter, we need to be conscious of the inherent biases of these clergymen, specifically in relation to their position within the class structure. Supernatural encounters and belief systems, by this point, were often regarded as a quirk of the uneducated lower classes and a remnant of unenlightened times. Whilst this does not devalue the material, it is sensible to approach the accounts with this in mind.

In an effort to prevent religious places of worship from being built in the first instance, the Devil or a like-minded evil spirit were sometimes thought to interfere in their construction. In *Hanes Plwyfi Llangeler a Phenboyr* (The History of Llangeler and Penboyr Parishes) (1899) Daniel E. Jones recorded:

> *Ychydig i'r gogledd o Eglwys Llangeler mae maes a elwir Parc-y-Bwci. Mae y traddodiad fel ag yr oedd yn llawn ac yn ddethe wedi darfod gyda'r oes o'r blaen, ac nid oes sicrwydd am ddilysrwydd yr hyn a gyhoeddwyd yn ddiweddar am dano. Dywedir mai ar Barc-y-Bwci y dechreuwyd adeiladu yr Eglwys ar y cyntaf, ond fod cymaint a adeiledid yn y dydd yn cael ei symud yn y nos i'r lle y saif yr Eglwys yn awr. Mae'n werth sylwi fod y chwedl hon am lawer o Eglwysi heblaw Llangeler. Myn rhai fod yr un traddodiad am Eglwys Penboyr.*

Just north of Llangeler Church is a field called Parc-y-Bwci [Bogey Park]. The tradition which was once complete and detailed has died out with the previous age, and there is no certainty about the authenticity of what has recently been published about it. It is said that the construction of the Church was first started on Parc-y-Bwci, but that what was built during the day was moved at night to where the Church now stands. It is worth noting that this legend pertains to many Churches other than Llangeler. Some assert the same tradition exists for Penboyr Church.

Again, as is so often the case with these ghostly landmarks (discussed in more detail in Chapter Three: 'Ghosts in the Landscape'), it is unknown whether the park was so named after this particular ghoul, or whether the above tale was concocted retrospectively to explain the name.

Eglwys Llangeler was built in 1858 on the footprint of a medieval building, the more likely origin for the tale. The church is dedicated to Sant Gelert, also known as Celer, who is also the namesake for the village of Beddgelert (despite the best efforts of innumerable guidebooks over the years to convince tourists of the existence of a certain mythical dog). Sant Gelert was a cave-dwelling seventh-century hermit with a holy well to his name, who reputedly healed pilgrims visiting its waters. After bathing, the afflicted would lie on an old stone known as Yr Hen Lech (The Old Slate), in the hope of cure. The stone is mentioned by Sir John Lloyd in *A History of Carmarthenshire* (1935–9), and may be the one located in the old circular churchyard.

As a side note, the tale of Wales's most legendary dog, Gelert, was in fact the brilliant brainchild of David Pritchard, entrepreneurial landlord of the Royal Goat Hotel in Beddgelert from 1793, as a means of attracting more tourists to the village. While the story of a martyred animal guardian is a popular folkloric trope world-wide, Pritchard's version – further publicised by his grandson's great friend, the folklorist Glasynys (Owen Wynne Jones) – recounted the selfless acts of the loyal wolfhound of the Welsh prince, Llywelyn Fawr (Llywelyn the Great), in protecting his infant son against a wolf's attack, before being cruelly slain by his master in a classic case of mistaken identity. Pritchard, a native of south Wales, probably derived his tale from the 'martyred dog' story, a well-known tale told in south Wales during his childhood and found in one of Iolo Morganwg's manuscripts. The story was recounted to William Robert Spencer while staying in Dolgellau, who immortalised it in a poem, sealing the wolfhound's fate in Welsh mythology. Incidentally, David Pritchard was also said to haunt the Royal Goat Hotel for a time following his death, on account of having buried a hundred guineas under a hearthstone in the bar-room.

As the ghost of Eglwys Llangeler was said to hinder the building of the church, so too did the ghost of Eglwys Sant Mihangel (St Michael's Church), in Llandre, Ceredigion, otherwise known as Llanfihangel Genau'r Glyn. This record is provided by the Reverend Evan Isaac, in *Coelion Cymru* (Welsh Beliefs) (1938):

Bwriedid oesoedd yn ôl adeiladu'r eglwys gyntaf ar y lle y saif ama-
ethdy Glan Fred Fawr heddiw. Casglwyd y defnyddiau ac aed ati i
adeiladu. Gweithiai'r seiri maen yn ddygn drwy'r dydd, eithr yn y
nos dinistriai'r ysbrydion y gwaith a dwyn y meini i fan arall filltir
i ffwrdd. Aed ymlaen fel hyn am gryn amser; y seiri yn adeiladu a'r
ysbrydion yn chwalu. Ond un canol nos llefarodd yr ysbryd a chodi
ei lais fel y clywai'r holl ardalwyr ef:
    'Llanfihangel yng Ngenau'r Glyn;
    Glan Fred Fawr a fydd fan hyn.'
    Dechreuwyd adeiladu ar y man yng ngenau'r glyn lle y gosodwyd
y meini gan yr ysbrydion, ac ni fu ymyrryd mwy.

The intention many years ago was to build the first church on
the place where the farmhouse of Glan Fred Fawr stands today.
The materials were collected and the building work was begun.
The stonemasons worked tirelessly all day, but at night ghosts
destroyed their work and stole away the stones to another place
a mile away. It went on like this for some time; the masons
building and the ghosts destroying. But once at midnight the
ghost spoke and raised its voice so it could be heard by all of the
local residents:

'Llanfihangel at the Mouth of the Valley; Glan Fred Fawr will
stand here.'

Building work began at the spot in the mouth of the valley where
the ghosts laid the stones, and there was no more interference.

A further example is provided by Evan Isaac of the haunting of
twelfth-century Eglwys Penbryn (St Michael's Church) on the Ceredigion coastline, the story of which was collected from an address made
by the Reverend W. D. Jones for *Cymdeithas Hynafiaethol Sir Aberteifi*
(the Cardiganshire Antiquarian Society) in 1926:

Penderfynasai'r plwyfolion adeiladu ar fan a elwid Hen Glos, ar fferm
Pwll Glas, eithr nid cynt y casglwyd defnyddiau a dechrau adeiladu
nag yr aflonyddwyd arnynt gan fodau anweledig. Cariai'r bodau hyn
ymaith bob nos y meini a osodasid gan y gweithwyr yn ystod y dydd,
a'u gosod ar safle'r eglwys bresennol, a llafarganu wrth eu gwaith:

'Ni ddaw bendith i dy ran,
Heb it newid sail y llan.'
Wedi gorffen yr eglwys yn ôl dymuniad yr ysbrydion, clywyd lleis-
iau angylion yn cyhoeddi:
    'Nei chei syflyd o'r fan hyn,
    Llanfihangel Pen-y-bryn.'
    Ni wn am un esboniad ar y coelion hyn, ond gwn y byddai'n
fendith i lawer ardal petasai rhyw ysbryd a welsai'n gliriach ac ym-
hellach na dynion wedi penderfynu safleoedd rhai o gapelau Cymru.

The parishioners had decided to build on a spot named Hen Glos [Old Close], on Pwll Glas farm, but no sooner were the materials gathered and the work begun than they were interrupt- ed by invisible beings. Every night, these entities would carry away the stones laid down by the workers during the day, and lay them on the site of the present church, chanting while they did so:

    'No blessings will come your way, without moving the foun- dations of the church.'

After building the church according to the wishes of the ghosts, angelic voices were heard proclaiming:

    'It shall not be moved from this spot, Llanfihangel Pen-y-bryn.'

I do not know of any explanation for these beliefs, but I know that many areas would be blessed had some spirit who could see clearer and farther than mankind decided on the location of some of the chapels of Wales.

Again, we see a phenomenon not unlike *canu yr yn awyr* here, discussed at the beginning of this chapter.

Another example of spirits thwarting the building of churches is seen in association with Eglwys Ilan (St Ilan's Church) in modern-day Rhondda Cynon Taf, referred to in *Llen Gwerin Blaenau Rhymni: O Gasgliad Bechgyn Ysgol Lewis, Pengam* (The Folklore of Blaenau Rhymni: Collected by The Boys of Ysgol Lewis, Pengam) (1912) as 'Eilian Church' (and not to be confused with Eglwys Eilian in Abertawe (Swansea) or Amlwch). The account states that the original location for the church stood half a mile to the south of its present-day footprint, said to be easily recognisable because of its close proximity to a quarry. However, there are a number of disused quarries in the locality within the boundaries of the surrounding farmland, as is commonly found in the Welsh landscape.

Construction of the church on the original site was thwarted because every morning, those turning up for work would find their labours from the previous day destroyed, and the material and tools moved to the present-day location of Eglwys Ilan. After this had happened for some days, the workers surmised that the problems were due to spiritual intervention. The account concludes:

> *Brawychwyd hwynt, a chredasant mai man anffodus yr oeddent wedi ei ddewis i adeiladu yr eglwys arno, fod y llecyn yn cael ei fynychu gan ysprydion. Yr oeddynt yn ofergoelus iawn a meddyliasent fod y man, lle y cludwyd yr holl offerynau, yn llecyn ffodus, a bod yr ysprydion yn dangos y llecyn iddynt, trwy gludo y cerrig i'r fan honno. Felly oherwydd hyn, adeiladwyd yr eglwys lle saif yn awr.*

They were frightened, and they believed that it was an unfortunate place they had chosen to build the church on, and that the spot was frequented by spirits. They were very superstitious and thought that the place, where all the tools were transported, was a lucky spot, and that the spirits showed it to them, by transporting the stones to it. So because of this, the church was built where it stands now.

The ghostly troubles persisted in this area even after the church was built on the suggested location. The tale is recorded by the same budding folklorists of Ysgol Lewis (Lewis School) as follows:

> *Ar ol adeiladu Eglwys Eilian, am flynyddau wedi hynny – pe byddai rhywun yn cerdded ar hyd Heol Eglwysilan, rhwng dau lecyn, sef y llecyn gwreiddiol penderfynwyd adeiladu yr eglwys arno, a'r eglwys, clywai swn rhywbeth tua llath neu ddwy tu cefn iddo, ac yn naturiol iawn, oherwydd ni welai ddim, oblegid ar nosweithiau tywyll iawn yn unig y clywyd y swn, meddyliai mai ysbryd ydoedd. Os byddai y person yn aros, arhosai y swn ar yr un pryd. Rhwng y ddau lecyn hyn yn unig clywyd y swn a oedd yn debyg i rhywbêth yn cerdded.*

After the building of Eilian Church, for many years afterwards – if someone were to walk along Heol Eglwysilan, between two spots, the original spot on which it was decided to build the church, and the church itself, they would hear the sound of something about a yard or two behind it, and very naturally, because nothing was to be seen, as the noise was only heard on very dark nights, it was thought to be a ghost. If the person stayed still, the sound would also cease to move. The sound was heard between these two spots alone and was similar to the sound of something walking.

It would appear, however, that these ghostly footsteps may have been caused by something altogether more corporeal. A parishioner walking home towards Abertridwr along the same road one evening became aware of a second set of footsteps in the darkness. Well aware of the ghastly reputation of Heol Eglwysilan, he decided to continue to the point where the ghost was known to disappear, but was sorely disappointed when his companion continued onwards with him. Coming to a crossroad, he determined that he would find out exactly who or what was on his tail and so reached out into the night, only to grab Tango, the local innkeeper's faithful hound, who was wont to accompany his master home late at night. Perhaps this dog's charity extended to all parishioners traversing Heol Eglwysilan in the dark?

There is another ghost story in connection to Eglwys Ilan, which describes a strange light that was seen within the church during the seventeenth century:

> *Pe disgwylai rhywun i fewn trwy'r ffenestr, gwelai rhyw bethau tu fewn yn debyg iawn i ysprydion, wedi eu gwisgo i gyd mewn gynnau gwynion, a'u gwynebau yn wynion iawn. Dychrynwyd y gymdogaeth i gyd gan y newydd, ac yr oedd ofn ar bawb i fyned heibio yr eglwys unrhyw amser yn y nos.*

Should one peer through the window, they would see some things inside that looked very similar to ghosts, dressed in white robes, and with very pale faces. The entire community was frightened by the news, and every one was too scared to pass the church at any time of night.

This phenomenon was noted to occur on the third or fourth day following a burial within the church vaults, and it was not too long before a wily parishioner revealed this haunting to be due to the night-time escapades of the unscrupulous priest and his daughters, ransacking the coffins of the latest arrivals.

Another example of where an alleged ghost was seen to illuminate the interior of a church at night was recorded at Eglwys Sant Pedr and Sant Illtud (St Peter and St Illtyd's Church) in the village of Llanhamlach, Powys, and reported in the *The Tenby Observer* on 30 March 1882.

The lights were seen every evening at the same time, around 7 o'clock, and continued for some hours. After a few days, the newspaper article notes that 'a party of young gentlemen, having become interested in the tale, went to Llanhamlach for the purpose of "seeing these supernatural lights"'.

On further inspection, it transpired that between the church and nearby Peterstone House a number of yew trees were planted. Light from the house was being cast onto one of these trees and then through the church windows, throwing unusual shadows on the church wall. This simple phenomenon was the cause of all of the excitement surrounding the perceived ghost and, having laid the spirit once and for all, 'the party of scientific explorers returned to Brecon highly elated at their successful campaign'.

Such mundane explanations for ghosts are far from unusual in British folklore. At Beddington Church in the London Borough of Southwark, for example, a similar optical illusion persisted because people were too frightened to investigate further. The *Evening Express* carried a brief reference to the case on 17 September 1908:

> An alleged ghost in Beddington Churchyard has been laid by the discovery of a vertical tombstone faintly illuminated by the reflection of the light of a road lamp 250 yards distant off a horizontal memorial stone. The 'apparition' was about 100 yards from the boundary and the scared villagers looked and passed on rather than trespass among the tombs and investigate.

While a corporeal and light-fingered man of the cloth was behind the 'ghostly' events at Eglwys Ilan, not all priestly hauntings were such obvious fabrications. The Reverend William Jenkin Davies mentions such an example in *Hanes Plwyf Llandyssul* (The History of Llandysul Parish) (1896), which involves the spirit of the priest appearing near the village of Faerdrefawr (a location which also features in Chapter Three: 'Ghosts in the Landscape'):

> *Ar brydie, bydde ysbryd yn blino pobl y plwydd yn ombeidus. Ma cwm yn joino Blancwm a Ferdre Fowr wrth i gily; a ma 'no ffynon yn cal i galw'n 'ffynon ffeiriad,' am, medde nhw, fod hen ffeirad wedi bod yn byw 'no ryw oese nol. Ma nhw wedi gweld 'rhen ffeirad yn cerdded lawer gwaith o beitu'r lle, a'i wisc wen am dano; a rodd ofan ombeidus ar y dynion i weld e.*

> At times, a spirit would disturb the people of the parish terribly. The valley joins Blancwm and Ferdre Fowr together; and there's a well called 'ffynon ffeiriad,' [priest's well] because, they say, an old priest lived there some age ago. They've seen a priest walking many times around the place, with his white robe about him; and terribly frightened the men who saw him.

The well does not appear to be referred to in other accounts, and so it is possible that its location has been forgotten. Thankfully, however, its story remains very much alive.

CHAPTER SIX

Poltergeists

*

'Roedd ganddo arfer ffyrnig,
I guro gwyr â cherig,
Aeth pawb yn brudd o herwydd hwn,
A'i adwyth ddychrynedig.
Trad., 'Cân Ysbryd y Pentre' ('The Song of the Ghost of Pentre')

It had a fearful fashion, of striking, kicking, lashing, and throwing stones at timid folks, without grace or compassion.

During the twelfth century, the cleric and historian Gerallt Gymro (Giraldus Cambrensis) recorded two accounts of 'unclean spirits' on his tour of Wales, who were noted for manifesting by throwing dirt. The first was recorded in the house of Stephen Wiriet, and the second in the house of William Not, both of whom resided in Maenorbŷr, Pembrokeshire. In the Not household, they also cut holes in the family garments, while in the Wiriet home, they were said to converse with visitors, taunting them 'openly with everything they had done from their birth, and which they were not willing should be known or heard by others'. It is likely that these accounts, as detailed in *The Itinerary Through Wales and the Description of Wales* (1191), represent the first recorded Welsh poltergeists.

Over 800 years later, the phenomenon remains very much at the forefront of many people's minds thanks to the popularity of the 2022 BBC Radio series *The Witch Farm*, written and presented by broadcaster Danny Robins. Based on a book examining the case – *Testimony* (1996) by Mark Chadbourn – the series looks at the alleged haunting of a farmhouse called Heol Fanog in the Aberhonddu (Brecon) area during the 1990s. The case is controversial in many ways, but especially because of the involvement of a priest whose work with the occupants led to the property becoming the site of more exorcisms than any other building

in Britain. Whatever the truth behind the hauntings, it has certainly left its mark on the area and renewed interest in the subject.

The term poltergeist is generally applied to alleged hauntings that involve noises linked with, or escalating to, observable physical phenomena. The compound term comes from the German verb *poltern* (to crash or rumble) followed by the noun *geist* (spirit). While the word 'ghost' is found in Old English and comes from the same root as the Germanic *geist*, 'poltergeist' is very much a nineteenth-century addition to the language.

Because of the violent nature of many poltergeist cases, exorcism is frequently associated with such hauntings, as in the example of Heol Fanog. These spirits are often seen as malicious and, from here, it is an easy leap to ascribe their nature to dark supernatural forces such as demons, necessitating religious intervention. The role of the clergy in providing exorcisms is long-standing, but traditionally, ghosts could also be banished or laid by a local cunning person or conjurer.

Such was the case at Plas Hen, now known as Plas Talhenbont (Talhenbont Hall), in the village of Llanystumdwy, Gwynedd, where the ghost of a wealthy gentleman returned to haunt the family. This spirit was known for its extraordinary abilities, creating powerful gusts of wind, cracking the windows and violently rattling water pitchers outside the back door, until the whole mansion was described as shaking to its foundations.

A glass plate negative, dated circa 1885 and held in the National Library of Wales, shows that at the time of this haunting, Plas Hen stood bordered by trees on three sides with the front of the building left exposed. It would not be surprising for winds coming from the right direction to be funnelled towards the house, possibly explaining some of the reported phenomena.

The problem, perceived as supernatural at the time, became so severe that the household decided to call upon the services of what Myrddin Fardd, in *Llên Gwerin Sir Gaernarfon* (The Folklore of Caernarfonshire) (1908), refers to as a *dewin*. Although commonly translated as 'wizard', in this particular example the terms 'conjurer' or 'cunning man' are better suited, as the person concerned contrived to banish the restless spirit to a nearby wooded hollow between Plas Hen and Gwynfryn. Myrddin Fardd describes how the cunning man bound the ghost by assigning it a task which it could never complete, much like we have already seen in the previous chapter:

yr oedd yn rhaid i ysbrydion gwasanaethgar o'r fath gael gwaith
parhaus, onide deuent yn ol i aflonyddu drachefn; a'r gwaith a
gafodd yr ysbryd hwn oedd, cario ymaith ddwfr yr afon gerllaw â
rhidyll, nes cael o hono ei gwely yn sych; a chan fod mwy o dyllau yn
ngwaelod y rhidyll nag o ddim arall, cafodd yn ddiau orchwyl digon
anhawdd ei gyflawni; ac fel yr ymddengys, gwaith lled anghysurus
ydoedd i ysbryd hen foneddwr ag oedd wedi arfer byw mewn llawn-
der, seguryd, a phob moethau o'r fath!

such servile spirits had to have continuous work, should one
wish to prevent them returning to haunt again; and the work this
spirit was given was to carry away the water of the nearby river
with a sieve, until its bed was dry; and as there were more holes
in the bottom of the sieve than anything else, it was undoubtedly
a difficult enough task to accomplish; and as it seems, it was
rather uncomfortable work for the spirit of an old gentleman
who was used to living in fullness, idleness, and all such luxuries!

Emptying a body of water using a receptacle with a hole or holes in it
is one of a short list of very common tasks assigned to bound spirits.
Sometimes a sieve is employed. Sometimes it is a shell with a hole
in the bottom. These endless tasks serve to protect the living from
future disturbances from a troublesome entity. Usually they are fairly
foolproof, but over the Bristol Channel in Devon, there is an example
of a spirit given the same task as the Plas Hen ghost who found a way
around the problem.

Upon his death, the spirit of Benjamin Gayer, the unscrupulous
mayor of the town of Okehampton during the early 1700s, was bound
to Cranmere Pool on nearby Dartmoor where he was assigned the same
task as the ghoul at Plas Hen. Having tried unsuccessfully for some
time, Gayer found a solution to the problem when he came across the
carcass of a dead sheep, the flesh of which he used to line his sieve. Such
was the exuberance with which he then emptied the pool that the water
flowed down the valley, flooding the town.

Of course, the spirit in such a story cannot be seen to triumph and
so was again banished by the local clergy, this time with the task of
spinning ropes out of the sandy bed of the pool – another common task

given to the ghosts of the restless, and one which is replicated in several ghost-laying tales across Wales.

Another notable example is relayed by Myrddin Fardd, where the many troublesome poltergeists of Castellmarch mansion in Llanbedrog, Gwynedd, were banished to the nearby beach to construct a rope of sand:

> *eithr tebygol eu bod yn glynu wrth y gwaith yn ddiwyd, gan nad oes y fath eiriau a 'rhoddi heibio waith heb ei orphen' yn ngeirlyfr ysbrydion, hyd y gwyddon; er nad oes i lygad o gnawd unrhyw argoel o wneuthuriad rhaff yn y lle …*

it's likely they have been diligently glued to the task, as there are no such words as 'giving up on unfinished work' in the ghost's handbook, as far as we know; though to eyes of flesh there is no sign of a rope being made here …

Not all spirits were so compliant with their tasks. Down the road in Gelliwig, Botwnnog, Myrddin Fardd recounts the tale of a mischievous ghost who crossed swords with the minister of nearby Llanengan, Mr Williams:

> *daeth yr hen Ficer allan o'r ystafell, lle buasai ef a'r ysbryd yn ym-godymu, a'i ddillad yn garpiau, a'r fath arogl ddrewedig arno, fel y gorfuwyd golchi pob cerpyn oedd yn ei gylch, a'i rwbio yntau à sebon meddal o'i goryn i'w sawdl. Mynai y gwr eglwysig fod i'r ysbryd aros dros ysbaid hanner can' mlynedd mewn twll ebill, wedi ei dori yn un o ddylaethau y tŷ, yn gauedig à thopyn digon tỳn, fel ag i'w ddiogelu rhag aflonyddu o hono neb yn nghorff yr amser appwyntiedig; eithr yr ysbryd a wrthwynebai y fath benyd a hyny, drwy ymladd a dadlu yn egniol fod deng mlynedd yn llawn ddigon o gosp arno, yn ngwyneb cyfartaledd ei droeddau; a'r diwedd fu, iddynt gyttuno ar i'r ysbryd lochesu yn y twll pennodol dros yr ysbaid o ugain mlynedd; a dyna derfyn ei hanes fel yr ymddengys hyd yn hyn.*

the old Vicar came out of the room, where he and the spirit had been wrestling, with his clothes in rags, and such a stinking smell on him, that he had to wash every piece of clothing which he wore, and to scour himself with soft soap from top to toe. The cleric wanted the spirit to remain over a period of fifty years in an auger hole, cut in one of the house's beams, closed with a sufficiently tight top, to make it safe so that it could not disturb anyone in the appointed time; but the spirit opposed such a penance as that, by fighting and arguing energetically that ten years was quite sufficient punishment for him, considering the sum of his crimes; and the result was, they agreed that the spirit should take refuge in the specified hole for the period of twenty years; and that is the end of his story as it seems so far.

Restless spirits in folklore are usually banished to stretches of water (often the Red Sea) or shrunk into a receptacle which is then hidden away to stop them from returning. The concealment in a beam of the house, as in this case, is unusual, and we have to wonder at its significance. Often, the beams of older houses were inscribed with apotropaic markings, or otherwise deliberately burnt with the naked flame from a candle or taper as a form of supernatural protection. To the best of our knowledge, to trap a spirit within a beam is unprecedented.

In *The Bard's Museum; Or Rational Recreation* (1809), author Robert Fitzpatrick includes a poem called 'The Hostess, The Friar and Ghost'. The poem tells the story of a woman who is being haunted and a friar who passes by and stops to help:

> Thro' the whole mansion he each crevice tried,
> For ghosts, they say, in auger-holes can hide.
> He met no spectre, goblin, shade or spright,
> All lull'd to rest, wrapt in the arms of night

If ghosts can hide in auger-holes, then perhaps they can be stoppered into one as well.

The detail of Mr Williams, Llanengan's minister, having to remove a foul smell from himself after battling the spirit is one which seemingly has few parallels outside Welsh accounts. It is usually described as a sulphurous smell, more commonly associated with the manifestation of the Devil or his demons, as described by William Davies in *Hanes Plwyf Llanegryn* (The History of Llanegryn Parish), first published in 1948:

Brwydr fawr a fu rhyngddynt; ymladdodd yr ysbryd â holl ystrywiau'r fall ei hun, a dywedai chwaer yr hen Ficer Williams fod ei gnawd ef yn arogli'n enbyd gan sawr satanaidd am ddyddiau lawer wedi'r ornest. Edrydd y chwedl fod y Ficer wedi llwyddo i botelu'r ysbryd, a'i fod wedi ei roddi i orwedd yn dawel yng ngwely'r afon wrth bont Dysynni.

There was a great struggle between them; the spirit fought with all its base chicanery, and the old vicar's sister later reported that his flesh gave off a Satanic stench for many days after the struggle. The tale is told of how the vicar managed to bottle the spirit and that he laid it to rest quietly on the bed of the river near the Dysynni bridge.

The haunting described by Davies took place at Gwyddfryniau, a house not far from the village of Bryncrug, Gwynedd. The ruins of the building can still be seen to this day. The spirit at the heart of the poltergeist activity here was named Cadi'r Forwyn, or Cadi the Maid, who worked as a servant at Gwyddfryniau. The story describes the activity as being so disruptive that on a number of occasions, the living inhabitants were forced to flee during the night to a neighbouring property. Unusually, it was said that the ghost pursued them there and continued to cause disruption.

One of the witnesses was Lewis William, a schoolmaster described as being 'employed by the Reverend Thomas Charles of Bala' (1755–1814), a highly influential Calvinistic Methodist clergyman. Lewis William made his observations while 'on watch-duty' in the house one night, which suggests that there had been sufficient concern to arrange an organised investigation. While there, he 'heard and felt things too horrible to express in human language' ('*iddo glywed a theimlo pethau rhy ofnadwy i'w mynegi mewn iaith ddynol*'). William had elected to spend the night in what was said to be the most haunted room, taking with him a candle and his Bible, thinking that he would spend the night alternately praying and reading. Long before midnight, however, the schoolmaster was driven from the room by the spirit after having been overpowered by its vile stench.

Cadi'r Forwyn was said to have been as active during broad daylight as she was at night, on one occasion throwing and scattering sheaves of wheat around a field while the farmhands were busy reaping: 'In the end there was nothing for it but to send for old Vicar Williams, known as a clergyman who knew how to subdue the devil' ('*Yn y diwedd nid oedd dim i'w wneuthur ond anfon am yr hen Ficer Williams, a adwaenid fel yr offeiriad a fedrai ostegu'r cythraul*').

The old vicar was successful in his attempts to imprison the spirit, before throwing the bottle into the Dysynni River, as described in the earlier quotation.

In *Bywyd Cymdeithasol Cymru yn y Ddeunawfed Ganrif* (The Social Life of Wales in the Eighteenth Century) (1931), Erfyl Fychan describes how tales such as the ghost of Cadi'r Forwyn would be recounted at the traditional *Noson Lawen* (Merry Evening), which was discussed in the introductory chapter:

> *Byddai raid cael dawnsio, ac yn sŵn y delyn byddai'r ieuanc wrthi a'u holl egni, a'r gwragedd yn brysur yn gweu hosanau. Rhaid oedd trafod holl newyddion y fro, ac yna wedi iddi hwyrhau, neu yn hytrach yn gynnar yn y bore byddai rhywun yn adrodd am ryw ysbryd.*

> There would have to be dancing, and to the sound of the harp the young would be at it with all their energy, and the women would be busy knitting stockings. All the local news had to be discussed, and then after it got late, or rather early in the morning someone would report about some ghost.

Erfyl Fychan provides an example of a poltergeist case which was recorded by lexicographer, poet and founder of the Honourable Society of Cymmrodorion, Lewis Morris, in a letter to his brothers. The original letter can be found in the two-volume *The Letters of Lewis, Richard, William and John Morris of Anglesey (Morrisiaid Mon) 1728–1765*, published between 1907 and 1909, and edited by J. H. Davies.

The events are centred around the estate of Hafod Uchtryd, Ceredigion, which housed an impressive Gothic mansion, rising to prominence in the second half of the eighteenth century when its owner, Thomas Johnes, used it as an example of the aesthetic landscape ideal of the 'Picturesque'. It is worth noting that this building is not the later mansion of which many photographs exist; this was demolished in the 1950s and had replaced the house in which the poltergeist was recorded in 1751.

The Hafod poltergeist was known to steal candles in front of people and to kiss unsuspecting women before screaming with laughter. One witness observed, in broad daylight, a number of potatoes, which had been peeled ready for boiling, jump out of their basket – 'as you have seen maggots jump out of cheese in hot weather' – and disappear, only to reappear in the basket later on.

One night, a curious party were gathered in one of the rooms to see if they could witness any unexplained phenomena. After the doors had been shut to prevent any intrusion, a number of stones appeared in the hearth. One of the party removed the largest of them, which was about the size of an adult hand, and put it on the floor in front of him, placing his foot on top of it. The stones were suddenly removed to the other end of the room, including the one under the man's foot. At the time this occurred, according to the letter, there came a tinkling sound from a brass pan in the room, which no one was near.

Other phenomena included a large hall table, heavy enough that it would need four men to manoeuvre, being lifted and turned over so that its legs knocked against the ceiling, and a piece of window glass flying through the air and landing on a table without breaking. On one occasion, when making bread, the mistress of the house instructed her maid to bring a large bowl of oatmeal, at which point the ghost 'heaped up the tub with oatmeal, and threw it on the table without spilling a grain'.

Two attempts to banish the spirit failed for very different reasons. A parson who tried to control it received a violent blow to the head for his trouble, while a cunning man brought in from Breconshire to lay the ghost deliberately left it unbanished because the household refused to pay him for his work.

The ability to cause physical injury to witnesses is one of the aspects which mark poltergeist cases apart from other hauntings. This is also described by Myrddin Fardd:

Ysbryd hynod iawn oedd yr un a aflonyddai breswylwyr Cae-llwyn-grydd, Llanllechid, yr oedd yn curo pawb o'i amgylch! Efe a darawai ddyn yn ei wegil â chareg, pan y byddai yn sefyll a'i gefn ar bared, hyd nes y dysgynai ar ei wyneb! Pa mor uchel bynag ydoedd y gwalch hwn yn ei fedrusrwydd i luchio ceryg, yr oedd yn ei fryntwch yn gyfartal ddigon, fel yr ymddengys oddiwrth ei ymddygiadau isel a chreulawn.

A very extraordinary spirit was the one that disturbed the residents of Cae-llwyn-grydd, Llanllechid, who was beating everyone around it! It hit a man in the neck with a stone, when he was standing with his back against a wall, until he fell on his face! This rascal's skill in throwing stones was only matched by his viciousness, as was proven by his base and cruel behaviour.

The Reverend Edmund Jones also describes a poltergeist case from 1758 in Llanllechid. As Myrddin Fardd recounts how an old ballad was printed in 1784 to commemorate the events at Cae-llwyn-grydd, Edmund Jones's account most probably represents the same haunting.

Jones describes how a witness who was struck by one of the stones told a member of the clergy that it weighed around five pounds, and that rocks as heavy as twenty-seven pounds had been thrown, said to have come from the river which ran past Cae-llwyn-grydd farmhouse. Priests from nearby Bangor came to try and lay the spirit, but it was said to have been too strong for them and they were forced to leave after also suffering physical attacks.

Stone throwing is a common feature of poltergeist cases from all over the world, succinctly epitomised by the Reverend D. G. Williams of Ferndale in his 1895 essay, 'Casgliad o Len-Gwerin Sir Gaerfyrddin' ('A Collection of Carmarthenshire Folklore'): 'ghosts sometimes like to throw stones' (*'mae yr ysbrydion weithiau yn hoff o daflu cerryg'*). He provides a further example from the morning of 21 May 1719 – the Thursday following Whitsunday – in Llangeler, Carmarthenshire, whereby a poltergeist began throwing stones at farmhands working on the threshing floor. This activity intensified over the course of the following week with injuries to workers and household members, and damage to the farmhouse, culminating in the barn and all the grain being burnt to the ground.

Further international examples include the 1931 case investigated by the former governor of Jamaica, Lord Olivier, revolving around a 14-year-old girl called Muriel McDonald, whose invisible assailant's stone-throwing seemed to follow Muriel around the house. In the 1980s, a house in Tucson, Arizona, was frequently battered by stones thrown by unseen hands, witnessed by the primary investigator in the case. For four months in 1998, stones were thrown in a poltergeist case at Humpty Doo in Australia. Here, the spirit also allegedly used the stones to spell out the word 'car' on the floor. Three priests failed to exorcise the property. As recently as 2019, a family home in Bhutan, south Asia, was hit by stones from an unknown source. The cases are numerous and exemplify the often violent nature of the poltergeist.

The remains of the Cistercian abbey in Hendy-gwyn ar Daf (Whitland), Carmarthenshire, founded in 1151, is now registered as a Historic Monument of National Importance, but was thought lost for many years. Following its closure in 1539, the site was plundered and the stones reused for the construction of other properties, the foundation only being rediscovered in 1837. One such property was the iron forge, known locally as Y Fforge, which was built on the abbey's estate. The earliest surviving records of the forge come from 1636, stopping around the start of the nineteenth century as it most likely fell out of use while more efficient modern methods of iron-working came into effect. Nothing survives of the building now, although the trace of a leat (aqueduct) can still be seen.

According to the Reverend William Thomas in his book *Hynafiaethau yr Hendygwyn-Ar-Daf* (Antiquities of Whitland) (1868), Y Fforge used to be well known for its poltergeist activity:

Ymddangosent i rai ym mhob ffurf. Trystient yn yr ystafelloedd y nos. Symudent y llestri o un man i'r llall, fel y tybid. Rhedent i fyny ac i lawr y grisiau. Yr oedd un hen frawd er ys ychydig yn ol yn tystio iddo weled y diafol yn chwythu y tân a'r meginau nes oedd y cwbwl yn wenfflam, pan nad oedd y rhodau yn symud dim.

They appeared to some in all forms. They clattered in the rooms at night. They moved vessels from one place to another, as was supposed. They ran up and down the stairs. An old fellow a little while ago testified that he saw the devil blowing the fire and the bellows until the whole thing was ablaze, when the wheels did not move at all.

Ironworks have traditionally been closely associated with the supernatural, and with the Devil in particular, as he is said to be the source of the blacksmith's abilities. The folk tale of the 'Blacksmith and the

Devil', in which the smith strikes a bargain with the Devil for his soul in exchange for the knowledge of working metal only to trick the Devil out of the arrangement, is claimed by some to originate in the Bronze Age. That the disturbances at Y Fforge were down to the Devil's work would seem to be supported by the Reverend Thomas, stating that '[t]he hammer was heard working one Sabbath when no worker was near'. The implication here is that only the Devil or one of his imps would dare work on a Sunday.

Stories of ghostly happenings at Y Fforge were not restricted to poltergeists and devils, and in Chapter Ten: 'Death Omens', we shall also see how the owners, the Morgan family, were connected with another very prominent Welsh ghost motif: the *toili*, or phantom funeral.

While it was often claimed that blacksmiths acquired their skills through supernatural means, other highly skilled workers could also sometimes fall foul of similar superstitions. An example is noted near the village of Cwm Clydach, in what is now Rhondda Cynon Taf. The ghost in this case was that of a fuller who worked in the area. Historically, the role of a fuller was to treat wool by kneading a clay-based material (known as fuller's earth) into it, absorbing lanolin and other oil impurities, before the finished product was used by weavers. The process is very old and equally unpleasant, and can be traced back as far as Cuneiform texts.

A fulling mill was located in this area, and its flannel laid out in a field called Twyn-y-Ddeintir to be dried after treatment. Referring to the case in *Plwyf Llanwyno* (Llanwynno Parish) (1913), Glanffrwd states that the spirit of the fuller was known there 'until living memory of those who are alive now' ('*o fewn cof rhai sydd yn fyw yn awr*'). As is usual with poltergeists, the ghost is not seen but heard, particularly in this case as an omen of bad weather. Glanffrwd writes:

> *Yr oedd yn pannu yn anferthol cyn dyfodiad ystorm a thywydd garwach na chyffredin. Yr oedd yn eistedd ar Dwyn-y-Ddeintir i weithio, ac i gadw stwr erchyll am hyd o'r nos yn fynych, a gwyddai yr hen drigolion yn dda os byddai y Pannwr wrthi fod tywydd creulon wrth y drws. Byddai weithiau yn dod oddiar y Ddeintir i fyny at y Cwm, a'r Ty-canol, a'r Ty-draw, ac yn curo y ddaear, neu yn lachio y coedydd, neu yn gwneud swn annaearol iawn, nes*

*byddai y trigolion yn chwysu gan ddychryn. Aeth llawer cenhedlaeth
o drigolion y plwyf i'w beddau ac arnynt gymaint o ofn yr Hen
Bannwr ag angeu ei hun.*

It fullered greatly before the arrival of a storm and rougher
weather than usual. It sat on Twyn-y-Ddeintir to work, and
often to keep a horrible din all night long, and the old residents
knew well that if the Fuller was at it there would be cruel weather
at the door. It would sometimes come from the Deintir up to
the Cwm, and Ty-canol, and Ty-draw, and beat the ground, or
shake the woods, or make a very unearthly noise, until the inhabitants were sweating with fright. Many generations of parish
inhabitants went to their graves as full of fear of the Old Fuller
as of death itself.

This ghost was only once reported to have physically harmed anyone.
The victim in question was a weaver named Dafydd Cadwgan:

*Ymddygodd yr Hen Bannwr yn lled ddirmygus ac annheg tuag ato
ef, oblegyd dywedai Dafydd iddo ddyfod ato ar ben Coed-y-Cwm,
a neidio ar ei gefn, a chwipio Dafydd druan bob cam o'r ffordd o
Goed-y-Cwm hyd Glwyd Cae'r Defaid.*

The Old Fuller behaved rather contemptuously and unfairly
towards him, because Dafydd said that it came to him at the top
of Coed-y-Cwm, and jumped on his back, and whipped poor
Dafydd every step of the way from Coed-y-Cwm to Clwyd
Cae'r Defaid.

That someone with so unpleasant an occupation as the fuller should, in
death, mercilessly torment someone who enjoyed a significantly higher
standing in life is perhaps unsurprising, and is consistent with other accounts we have presented which offer some degree of social commentary.

One element which seems to be missing from many of these historic
Welsh poltergeist cases is the involvement of a young child, unusually
so for hauntings of this type as children are often cited by those who
study poltergeist phenomena as being the focus of events.

An exception to this is a case in Dyffryn, Maesteg, where the pol tergeist seems to have been held responsible for the misbehaviour of a young boy, turning cattle from their sheds and setting fire to hay ricks in the fields. It was said that the spirit appeared to the boy and informed him that he had been watching him even more closely than his own mother, and if he did not do as the ghost commanded, the boy would be severely punished. On one occasion, it was alleged that the spirit threw the lad over the house, but that he was saved from harm because he landed in the branches of an old oak tree.

The poltergeist broke many of the windows of the boy's home by throwing stones, consistent with the stone-throwing tradition in many other cases described earlier in this chapter. Despite this, and the rough treatment of the boy, nobody is described as having suffered any injuries as a result of the phenomena.

In his account of this case in the 1885 essay, 'The Folklore of Glamorgan', Cadrawd states that the 'ghost was at last made to depart by application of the Black Art'. We might now imagine that this was perhaps some kind of official-looking ritual designed to scare an unruly child into behaving more respectably!

As you would expect, Wales has its share of haunted inns, many of which boast of poltergeist activity. One case which was particularly well covered in the press took place at the Old Emlyn Arms (previously the Paxton) in Llanarthne, Carmarthenshire, at the start of the twentieth century. The landlord at this time, John Morgan Meredith, lived there with his wife and a servant girl whom they had recently adopted. The story broke in the *Evening Express* on 1 January 1910 under the headlines:

REAL GHOST AT LAST
PROSAIC POLICE TALK OF BURGLARS
ARE ASSAILED BY HOT ASHES
FUSILLADE OF STONES, CANDLESTICKS, AND DOG CHAINS
BEER CELLAR FITTINGS WALK UPSTAIRS

Again, in this case, the spirit is never seen but makes itself known through physical phenomena:

On Wednesday night Mrs. Meredith and the girl were alone in the house, the husband having gone to visit his relative at his native place of Machynlleth. During the evening Mrs. Meredith went out to fetch the cows, and when she was crossing the yard stones were thrown at her. She did not take much notice, but when she was returning to the house the key of the cellar door was hurled towards her from the passage. A little later the servant informed Mrs. Meredith that someone was knocking at the door outside, whereupon the old lady told her not to open it, as it was after 'stop-tap' and a policeman might come. The knocking, however, continued, and Mrs. Meredith ultimately opened the door when she was startled to see no one there, but a candlestick flew past her, having been thrown from outside.

To those unfamiliar with the phrase, 'stop-tap' is a commonly used slang term in Wales for calling last orders at the bar before closing time.

Having initially been concerned about police involvement, Mrs Meredith ended up calling for a policeman after an 'unearthly noise' was heard. She and her adopted daughter went to stay in a neighbouring house out of concern for their safety.

Upon arrival, the local constable, Gwilym Jenkins, arranged for the house to be surrounded while he went inside to investigate, as he thought there might be a burglar in the property. He did not find anyone there but, while searching underneath a bed upstairs, a heavy ornament from the mantelpiece was thrown at him, along with other objects, including empty bottles and glasses, saucepan and teapot covers, corks, and even hot coals, while he made his way around the house.

The events were witnessed by many different people, and continued until the following afternoon. A dog chain coated in lime was thrown into the building; the Meredith family did not recognise it and nobody saw where it originated from. A toasting-fork fell from a fireplace and a mat fell from the upstairs landing onto someone's head. Many of the stones being thrown were also covered in lime and seemed to be similar to the ones found outside the building.

While the servant girl was initially accused, this was later dismissed on account of her young age and her being present in the kitchen when some of the objects were being thrown from outside. Constable Jenkins was of the opinion that the incident was a practical joke, although he could not work out how such a thing was possible. The Merediths, who were in their sixties at the time, had lived in the Emlyn Arms for over twenty years and nothing unusual had been previously reported.

Two days later, the *Evening Express* printed an article which confirmed the police constable's story. A neighbour, who had entered the property at the height of the disturbance, described his version of events in his own words:

'I entered the room behind the bar at the Emlyn Arms soon after ten o'clock on Wednesday night. There was a crowd gathered outside, it being thought there was a burglar on the premises. The door and the windows of this room were closed, and all of a sudden I felt a large stone whizzing past me. It did not come through the window, because all the glass is intact, nor could it have come through the door, because that was closed. Immediately afterwards some hot coals fell, scattering on the table and about the room. I picked one up, and there could be no question about it being hot. If you ask me where they came from I cannot tell you. All I can say is that the room was absolutely closed from the outside world, and I was standing near the fireplace, and am certain there was no one there. I was naturally frightened, and went outside and called in a neighbour. As soon as we came back into the room a bottle dropped at our feet, and was smashed into a thousand pieces, while stones from various directions whizzed past both of us. I can't explain these things, but as to their having taken place I can vouch for them, because I speak that which I do know.'

The story was also reported in various other Welsh newspapers such as the *Weekly Mail*, *The Carmarthen Weekly Reporter* and *The Welshman*, as copy was often recycled from one publication to the other. None of the newspaper reports at the time were able to offer a satisfactory resolution to the events at the Emlyn Arms, but we might be able to offer one with hindsight. A few months later, on 18 June 1910, *The Cardiff Times* ran a short article headlined 'Ghost Story Recalled':

John Morgan Meredith (62) was a land surveyor under the Ordnance Survey Department when he married, in June 1887, the licensee of the Emlyn Arms, Llanarthney, a business which he had carried on since that year. He failed through insufficient trade and the ill health of his wife. His gross liabilities came to £343 5s 6d, his deficiency being £333 11s 10d. The Official Receiver observed that debtor's [*sic*] was the inn at which a 'ghost' had been discovered. It may be remembered that it caused quite a sensation. The examination was closed.

It is not too much of a stretch to imagine that Meredith, with or without the cooperation of his family, fabricated these events in order to garner public interest in his ailing business. It would not be the first haunting that had arisen through a need for advertising, and it certainly will not be the last.

CHAPTER SEVEN

Ladi Wen

*

Mae sôn am wrach-y-rhibyn,
Y Tylwyth Teg a'r goblin,
A son am ysbryd Ladi Wen
Yn dychryn plwyf Penderyn.
Trad.

There is talk of gwrach-y-rhibyn, the fairies and the goblin, and talk about a White Lady, frightening the parish of Penderyn.

There are certain motifs in ghost-lore which are so common as to become stereotypical in some respects. The *Ladi Wen* (White Lady) is one such example, found in folklore records across all of Britain and Ireland as well as further afield. Whether Wales can boast more sightings than anywhere else is debatable, but the figure of the *Ladi Wen* has long formed an integral part of its culture.

Even within those few Welsh communities where accounts of ghost stories are relatively lacking, a *Ladi Wen* can often be found lurking. Such an example can be seen in Llannon, a small village in Carmarthenshire:

Ni fu'r stori ysbryd mewn bri mawr yn y plwyf. Ceir sôn am ychydig o dai a oedd yn gartref i ysbrydion, ac am ymddangosiad y Ladi Wen wrth Farchoglwyn, ac wrth hen goeden gerllaw lle mae'r ysbyty yn awr.

The ghost story was not very popular in the parish. There is talk of a few houses that were home to ghosts, and of the appearance of the *Ladi Wen* at Marchoglwyn, and at an old tree near where the hospital is now.

In a 1970 article for the journal *Folklore*, 'The White Lady of Great Britain and Ireland', the American folklorist and historian Jane C. Beck posited that in Wales, distinction is made between two variants of this particular ghost: *Dynes Mewn Gwyn* (Lady in White), a term used to describe the more traditional figure of a revenant in white garb, and *Ladi Wen*, depicting an ethereal spectre claimed to specifically haunt locations where a violent death has occurred.

However, when examining the primary sources, there is little tangible evidence to suggest that these two distinct categories exist in any significant form within the Welsh folkloric tradition. The use of *Dynes Mewn Gwyn* as a label is rarely found, while the term *Ladi Wen* is pervasive, and used to denote most apparitions which present in this particular way. We therefore discount Beck's suggestion, and use the term *Ladi Wen* as the original sources present it.

Similarly, the image of the White Lady is considered by some to be very old, said to result from pre-Christian beliefs being subsumed into modern religious doctrines. Links have been suggested between the *Ladi Wen* and the fairies, and even early goddess or deity worship. In Wales, however, these links are tenuous at best, and at worst exemplify misinterpretation and over-romanticisation of the texts. As ever, we need to exercise caution when looking for lineage in folkloric concepts, especially as in this instance, many of those assumptions made by previous authors overlook the evidence presented within the original Welsh-language sources.

Although the *Ladi Wen* can appear at any time of the year, it is more generally prevalent in Wales around *Nos Galan Gaeaf* (Hallowe'en) (as discussed in Chapter Three: 'Ghosts in the Landscape'):

> *Nos Glangaea', twco 'fala',*
> *Pwy sy'n dod ma's i chwara'?*
> *Ladi wen ar ben y pren*
> *Yn naddu coes ymbrelo.*

Hallowe'en, bobbing for apples, who's coming out to play? A *Ladi wen* atop the tree, whittling an umbrella handle.

There are frequent traces in the landscape relating to the appearance of White Ladies, in place-names such as Traeth y Ladi Wen (White Lady Beach) at Porth Padrig, Ynys Môn, or the mass of rock in Bwlch y Rhiwgur, near Abermaw (Barmouth), Gwynedd, known simply as Y Ladi

Wen following the murder of a young lady at this location. According to William Davies, who records the tale in his 1898 essay, 'Casgliad o Lên Gwerin Meirion' ('A Collection of Meirion Folklore'), the old folk believed 'that it was her ghost that turned the rock in question into the form and image of a girl. They also believed that the nearby waterfall murmured throughout the ages, – "Revenge! revenge!"' (*'mai ysbryd hono a drodd y graig dan sylw ar ffurf a llun merch. Credent hefyd fod y pistyll dw'r sydd gerllaw yn sisial yn oesoesoedd, – "Dial! dial!"'*).

Another ghostly lady in white associated with a body of water is recorded in the manuscripts held at the Nantgarw archives of Amgueddfa Cymru (Museum Wales), in a story entitled 'Parlwr y Glyn'. A contemporary record in 1977 by John Morris Jones recounts how a maid called Susan Scott from Garthmeilio country house in Llangwm, Conwy, once drowned herself in one of the deep pools that can be found near the present site of the A5 between Cerrigydrudion and Corwen. This particular pool lay in close proximity to a cave called Parlwr y Glyn (Parlour of the Valley), from which came:

> *[y]sbryd ar ffurf benyw wen, yn ymsymud rhwng y parlwr ar llyn dwfn lle y boddodd Susan Scott. Yr oedd llawer wedi ei weld tua chan mlynedd yn ol, ond bu tawelwch am flynyddoedd lawer, a thybiau y to iau, mae dychymig oedd y cwbwl.*

> a ghost in the form of a white lady, moving between the parlwr [Parlwr y Glyn] and the deep lake where Susan Scott was drowned. Many had seen it around a hundred years ago, but there had been silence for many years, and the younger generation suspected that it was all imagined.

One evening before the Christmas of 1915, four girls on their way from Llangwm to Dinmael to sing carols were met by the ghost, who they claimed sported a pair of wings, and who told them tenderly that 'Susan Scott is still alive', and that death would surround them over the next few days. The terrified girls found they were unable to move while in the presence of the winged spirit, which on leaving, made a terrible sound 'akin to five or six owls screeching over each other' (*'fel pump neu chwech o dylluanod yn gwaeddi ar draws eu gilydd'*).

The *Ladi Wen*'s predictions were soon realised, as one of the girls subsequently lost her father, the other a sister, and the remaining two, who were sisters, lost their mother.

While the suggestion of a winged spirit might usually offer some reassurance to the witness, it is clear that the subversion of angelic imagery in this instance made for a suitably terrifying spectre. Indeed, the image of the *Ladi Wen* was often used as a useful bogey by parents who wanted to encourage their young children to behave. In general, however, she is presented as a peaceful and serene spirit unless provoked or annoyed. Cadrawd offers the following description in his 1885 essay 'The Folklore of Glamorgan':

> The Ladi Wen or White Lady, was a gentle, silent, melancholy sort of spectre, generally haunting some lonely spot, a field, a style, a cross road; and in no way to be dreaded, poor creature! Her appearance was always sudden – a bright vision, clothed in white, with glossy coal-black locks hanging over her shoulders, with a pale and care-worn face, and having an expression of intense pain.

In Carmarthenshire, the Reverend D. G. Williams lauded her as 'one of the most honourable bogeys of the county' ('*un o fwciod mwyaf anrhydeddus y sir*'). He further suggests that if one wished to see the apparition in all her glory, the reader could do no better than to find a particular location between Abergwili and Felin Esgob where they might see a piece of old pavement in the middle of the road where she is known to dwell:

> *Y mae ganddi drigfan o dan y palmant, ac yno y treuliai ei hamser y dydd. Na feddylied neb fod y cyfleusderau yn brin yn y sir i'w gweled, ond nodwn un llecyn arbennig er mantais i ddiethriaid. Nid yw bell oddiwrth ffordd haiarn. Aed yr ymwelydd dros y ffordd blwyf yn y lle a nodais, a gofynned am Glwyd Llainyfelin. Treulied y nos yno, ac oni cha gwmni yr urddasol Ladi Wen na ddyweded neb mwyach fod ein breintiau yn lluosogi a'n cyfleusderau'n cynyddu.*

She has a dwelling under the pavement, and there she spends her time in the day. No one should think that the opportunity to see her in the county is lacking, but one special location is noted for the benefit of travellers. It is not far from a railway. The visitor is encouraged to venture across the parish road in the place mentioned, and ask for Clwyd Llainyfelin. Spend the night there, and if you would not have the graceful company of the *Ladi Wen*, let no one claim again that our privileges multiply nor our opportunities increase.

While this Carmarthenshire spook seems to while away her hours lurking under the road, other apparitions of the *Ladi Wen* have a particular purpose behind them. In some cases, they have an association with some form of buried treasure, the location of which they can reveal to those who ask. The motif of ghosts disclosing their hidden possessions was discussed in more detail in Chapter Two: 'Unfinished Business'. Such is the case with the apparition of a *Ladi Wen* associated with Castell Ogwr (Ogmore Castle) in the Vale of Glamorgan.

Castell Ogwr originally existed as an earthwork and wood defence in the twelfth century before being fortified in stone around the thirteenth century. It is one of three such castles which were built to defend the old county of Glamorgan against attack from the west.

There are two variants of the story of the *Ladi Wen* at Castell Ogwr. In the first, the apparition appeared at a local man's bedside, whereas in the second, the man approached the ghost himself at the castle. In both cases, the *Ladi Wen* led him to a stone in the castle tower, under which was buried a cauldron of gold. He was granted half of its contents, and while this sum of gold made him a very wealthy man, his greed prevailed. One night he elected to return to the castle in order to claim the other half of the treasure. Caught in the act, the *Ladi Wen* appeared to him again, this time tearing at him with clawed fingers. While the man was able to escape home, he fell ill and could not be cured. He eventually confessed his deeds and, once he had done so, passed away.

Folklore has frequently been used as a teaching aid, particularly by the Victorians, who used such tales to instruct the 'less educated' on the correct way to live life and set a moral compass, as has been noted several times within the scope of this book. We cannot say for certain when it originated, but the tale of Castell Ogwr is clearly offering a commentary on the sin of greed.

The motif of the castle, White Lady, and buried treasure is certainly not unique to Ogwr, nor indeed to Wales. Blenkinsopp Castle in Northumberland, for example, boasts a similar spirit who remains trapped there until a buried chest of gold is removed. In *English Fairy and Other Folk Tales* (1890), Edwin S. Hartland describes how she appeared to a young boy whose family occupied the castle at the turn of the nineteenth century. He described her to his parents who had rushed to his room having been roused by his shouts:

> She looked so angry at me because I would not go with her. She was a fine lady and she sat down on my bedside and wrung her hands and cried sore. Then she kissed me and asked me to go with her, and she would make me a rich man as she had buried a large box of gold many years since down in the vault; and she would give it to me as she could not rest as long as it was there. When I told her I durst not go, she said she would carry me, and she was lifting me up when I cried out and frightened her away.

Cadrawd provides us with another *Ladi Wen* in the south of the country, this time at Sain Tathan (St Athan), in the Vale of Glamorgan. This story is a complex and yet fascinating tangled web of differing information which may prove impossible to unpick. Cadrawd's version recounts the local tale of how a man had been buried alive: 'in a standing position, in a field at Baslay's Farm; and ever since no animal was ever known to eat the grass which grew over the spot'.

The *Ladi Wen* in question was often sighted walking at night past the stile which led into the field. Again, we find another reference to spirits appearing in association with stiles, with the physical barrier once more representing a significant supernatural boundary, as discussed in Chapter Three: 'Ghosts in the Landscape'. Stiles, in particular, feature as the preferred haunting perch for the *Ladi Wen*, especially around *Nos Galan Gaeaf* (Hallowe'en).

In an earlier source, *The History of the Princes, the Lords Marcher, and the Ancient Nobility of Powys Fadog* (1881) by Jacob Youde William Lloyd, the internment in the field is ascribed not to the body of a man, but to a woman named Matilda, said to be the daughter of Sir Thomas Despenser, lord of Glamorgan, who in 1411 was buried alive as punishment for the purported poisoning of her husband.

The husband in question was Sir Lawrence de Berkerolles, whose ancestors claimed descent from one of the alleged 'twelve knights' of the Marcher, Robert FitzHamon, credited with having conquered Glamorgan in the eleventh century. Sir Lawrence's medieval manor house, most commonly referred to as East Orchard Castle, had supposedly been handed to the FitzHamons following the conquest. A local legend tells of how Sir Lawrence was said to have lost his voice after inadvertently harbouring the disguised Owain Glyndŵr, the prince of Wales and leader of the Welsh revolt, believing him to be a travelling Frenchman. Having boasted of his plans to capture the prince for a number of days, the knight was struck dumb on the departure of his new companion as Glyndŵr finally revealed his true identity. Sir Lawrence was said to have never spoken again.

But there remains even more of a problem with this earlier account, because according to genealogical records, Matilda was the name of one of Sir Lawrence's daughters, rather than his wife. That is, until we realise that this tale of Sir Lawrence originates from the manuscripts of none other than Wales's master forger, antiquarian and poet, Iolo Morganwg. Iolo, in turn, notes that the genealogies presented in *Llyma Wehelyth Rial y Coetty* (The Royal Lineage of Coetty) were transcribed by himself from the manuscripts of Thomas Hopkin of Coychurch. Given Iolo's penchant for romanticising Welsh history, it should come as no surprise that such an account of Glyndŵr's cunning against the dimwitted English invaders would be his invention.

Further confusion is introduced by yet another story which suggests that the woman buried alive in the field was Phelice de Vere, the wife of Lawrence's ancestor, Sir William de Berkerolles, who incorrectly believed that she was having an affair. He had her buried up to her neck and left for dead. It is said that her sister used to walk past in a long dress so that she might suck moisture from its hem in an effort to save her, but Phelice died after ten days. Sir William later learned that she was innocent, and took to drinking heavily before losing his wits and perishing.

Another version penned by Marie Trevelyan in *Folk-Lore and Folk-Stories of Wales* (1909) names the *Ladi Wen* as Lady de Clare, ascribing the infidelity claim to her husband, Sir Jasper Berkerolles. Apart from being completely different people, the story follows that of Sir William and Phelice. Trevelyan notes this account as having been taken from the *Iolo MSS*, but as we have seen above, this is evidently not the case.

It is possible that Baslay's Farm, as mentioned by Cadrawd, is what is now named as Batsley Farm, lying some two and a half miles away from East Orchard Castle. Iolo Morganwg also penned the location of the haunting as 'near the by-road leading to Bat's Lays (possible Beast's Lays), an ancient residence a little to the west of St Athan village'.

Furthermore, Marie Trevelyan records an account from 1863 of milkmaids sighting a beautiful woman dressed in white in a field in this same location. They described her as circling a particular spot, but could not fathom why. Unfortunately, this tale is unreferenced. A report in *Fortean Times* magazine in 2001 stated that people were still sighting the *Ladi Wen* at Sain Tathan that year.

Whether the body was ultimately male or female, the mention of it being in a standing position is only explicitly referred to in Cadrawd's account. In folkloric terms, standing burials are often associated with deviant internment; in particular where there is concern that the corpse may dig its way out of the grave after death. One exception to this is found at Box Hill, Surrey, where Major Peter Labilliere was buried head-down at his own request. This, however, was a result of eccentricity – he is indeed described as such on his own tombstone.

Important Irish figures such as chieftains or royalty would sometimes be buried in a standing position facing their enemies, perhaps as a way of protecting their people even after death. There are other examples of standing burials without any particular protective nature attached to them, such as Ben Jonson who is famously buried in Westminster Abbey in a standing position, allegedly as his poverty would not allow him to pay for a six foot plot, although this is likely to be apocryphal.

A similarly curious account of the *Ladi Wen* is recorded by Evan Davies in *Hanes Plwyf Llangynllo* (The History of Llangynllo Parish) (1905), and concerns 'The White Lady of Gernos'. Located near Maesllyn, Ceredigion, Mount Gernos was a mansion constructed in the seventeenth century, and is described in some detail in Samuel Meyrick's *The History and Antiquities of the Country of Cardigan* (1808), an excerpt of which is also provided within Evan Davies's book.

In the nineteenth century, Mount Gernos was owned and inhabited by the Tyler family and was part of an estate covering many square miles; however, by the twenty-first century, the only remaining evidence of the grand property were two crumbling two-storey-high window sections, posing a stark juxtaposition to the relatively flat green fields surrounding them.

Among several other possible etymologies, Davies suggests that the original form of the word Gernos was *Caerynos* – 'night camp' – taking its name from the settlement at this location during the Roman occupation. It was here that the events were said to unfold which led to the legend of the *Ladi Wen*.

One night a young Irish lady, who had lost both her lover and her father to Roman capture, visited the camp to try and secure their release. One of the Roman officers, having grown weary with the Irish people, decapitated the poor woman. She was said to have been instantly transformed into a cat, which then proceeded to haunt the area for many hundreds of years. In the seventeenth century, reports of the ghost changed to that of a *Ladi Wen*, said to appear on the road to the north-west of the Mount Gernos entrance, from where she would walk with her hands clasped behind her head in despair. By the early twentieth century, the ghost was no longer being seen, but its memory still lingered sufficiently to cause some people to be wary of passing the place at night.

The *Ladi Wen*, according to Davies, appeared 'when the present mansion was built'. It may well be that the presence of a spectral lady haunting the entrance to the mansion proved a more successful deterrent against potential intruders than the legend of a ghostly cat. Further examples of 'protective' ghost-lore are provided in other chapters.

The mid-fifteenth-century medieval gentry hall house, Penarth Fawr, near Chwilog, in the community of Llanystumdwy, Gwynedd, now a scheduled monument and Grade 1 listed wedding venue (and incidentally, where Delyth was married), was said to be haunted by a *Ladi Wen*, the story of which may also have served a protective purpose. The tale is recorded in *Llên Gwerin Sir Gaernarfon* (The Folklore of Caernarfonshire) (1908) by Myrddin Fardd:

Y Ladi Wen oedd cynllun ysbrydol y bwgan hwn, yn arddull o ferch ieuangc hynod brydferth o bryd a gwedd a ymgartrefai yn y lle, yr

hon ag yr oedd balchder ac uchder yn elfen ryfygus yn ei chyfan
soddiad, a charu yn ei bus hoff ganddi, ond byddai raid iddi gael
boneddwr o waed uchel i'w rheoli, onide gwrthodedigaeth fyddai y
canlyniad, ac felly yr oedd ei sylfaen garwriaethol yn ei phrydferth-
wch, a disgwyliai i foneddwr trwyadl ei hoffi o'r herwydd. Ond un
tro yn lled hwyr, wele yr eneth yn dyfod adref ar gefn ceffyl, wedi
ymwisgo mewn dillad claer-wynion yn ol ei dull arferol. Ond pwy
ddaeth o hyd iddi cyn cyrhaedd y tŷ ond gŵr bonheddig o ran golwg,
ar farch fel hithau, rhoes ei serch arni, aeth yn garwriaeth; ond
diwedd yr ymdrafodaeth oedd i'r carwr ysbrydol fyned yn olwyn o
dân drwy'r simdde; ymaflodd braw yn ei chyfansoddiad o'r herwydd,
a bu farw mewn ychydig ddyddiau.

This ghost took the spiritual appearance of the *Ladi Wen*, in
the style of a very beautiful young woman who called the place
home, to whom pride and grace were formidable elements in her
constitution, and love was a favourite cause to her, but she would
need a gentleman of high blood to control her, otherwise rejection would be the result, and so the foundation of her romance
was in her beauty, and she expected a thorough gentleman to like
her because of that. But at a late hour on one occasion, behold,
the girl was coming home on horseback, dressed in pale-white
clothes according to her usual style. But who found her before
she reached the house but an apparent gentleman, on a horse
like herself, he gave her his love, it became a romance; but the
end of the incident was for the spiritual lover to transform into
a wheel of fire and travel through the chimney; terror took hold
of her constitution because of this, and she died in a few days.

Again, the theme of the victimised woman plays a strong role within
this account; however, it is interesting to note another common motif in
Welsh folklore – the appearance or disappearance of a ghost as a 'wheel
of fire'. The significance of this phenomenon was discussed in the introductory chapter of this book and exemplified within subsequent chapters.
    A further amalgamation of the *Ladi Wen* and the ghostly 'ball of fire'
can be seen in an account from Brogynin house in Penrhyn-coch, Ceredigion, the alleged birthplace of renowned fourteenth-century poet

Dafydd ap Gwilym. Some of Iolo Morganwg's first forgeries are thought to have been included in the earliest printed collection of Dafydd ap Gwilym's work, *Barddoniaeth Dafydd ap Gwilym* (The Poetry of Dafydd ap Gwilym) (1789), which Iolo claimed to have found anew.

The story of the *Ladi Wen* of Brogynin is found in *Folk-lore of West and Mid-Wales* by Jonathan Ceredig Davies (1911), later translated by Reverend Evan Isaac for *Coelion Cymru* (Welsh Beliefs) (1938):

> *Gwelid ef ganol nos ar brydiau gan weision y ffermydd cylchynol, yn croesi'r buarth ar ffurf 'Ladi Wen' dal a hardd mewn gwisg laes, eithr pan aent tuag ati diflannai mewn pelen o dân.*

> It was seen in the middle of the night at times by servants from the surrounding farms, crossing the courtyard in the form of a tall and beautiful '*Ladi Wen*' in a long gown, but when they approached her she disappeared in a ball of fire.

This particular *Ladi Wen* account also incorporates an element of 'unfinished business' with reference to hidden treasure, as the ghost is only laid to rest one late Sunday evening in winter, when a young lad is brave enough to follow the spirit to a low roofspace within Brogynin out of which, with shaking hands, he recovers an old woollen sock full of gold. Like all good ghosts, she immediately vanishes when business is considered concluded, and the house is left in peace.

A peculiar motif found exclusively within Welsh folklore can be seen in the story of 'Ysbryd Ladi Wen y Goppa' ('The White Lady Spirit of y Goppa'), recorded in *Hanes Bro Trawsfynydd* (The History of the Trawsfynydd District) (1973) by local members of Merched y Wawr (mentioned earlier as an organisation roughly analogous to the Women's Institute). The lady in question was said to have been in love with a man named Hwfa:

> *a gwnaethant â'i gilydd i gyfarfod un noson wrth rhyw lyn oedd ymhen draw Nyrs y Goppa. Ond erbyn i Ladi Wen fynd yno at yr amser penodedig, nid oedd ond dillad Hwfa ar y lan, ac yntau yn y llyn wedi boddi.*

and they made up to meet one night at a lake which was situated at the end of Nyre y Goppa [Goppa Nursery]. But by the time *Ladi Wen* went there at the appointed time, there were only Hwfa's clothes on the shore, and he had drowned in the lake.

Local tradition states that the spirit of the woman, as a *Ladi Wen*, can still be heard crying and wailing in the dead of night, 'The night is long to wait for Hwfa' ('*Hir yw'r nos i aros Hwfa*') – a ghostly cry that appears in several Welsh accounts as we have already discussed in Chapter Two: 'Unfinished Business'.

While the story provides no detail regarding the circumstances that caused Hwfa to drown in the first instance, one needs only to know a little of the history of Trawsfynydd to be able to draw some conclusions as to the origins of this particular tale.

Y Goppa farm remains one of the oldest buildings in the area, dating back to at least 1608, and stands on the banks of Llyn Trawsfynydd (Trawsfynydd Lake), where it is probable that Hwfa met his unfortunate end. Created in the 1920s to supply water to the nearby hydro-electric power station at Maentwrog, Llyn Trawsfynydd, with a total surface area of 1180 acres, represents the largest man-made reservoir in Wales. The drowning of such a vast area of land, including twenty-five farms, a number of houses, and Cae Adda chapel, unsurprisingly resulted in some local opposition. The lake was further expanded in the 1960s to serve the reactors for Atomfa Trawsfynydd, the nuclear power station (now decommissioned).

With this history in mind, it is entirely plausible that this particular *Ladi Wen* tale, featuring the horrific consequences of a local man drowning in the man-made reservoir, as the inhabitants of Trawsfynydd had watched many of their homes being submerged, may in fact serve as a response to the creation of the lake and the irreversible changes this brought about within the landscape. If there is any truth behind our interpretation of this story, then perhaps there was more for the local communities to fear from the living than from the spectre of the *Ladi Wen*.

CHAPTER EIGHT

Water Spirits

*

Yr avanc er ei ovyn
Wyv yn llech ar vin y llyn;
O dòn Llyn Syvaddon vo
Ni thynwyd ban aeth yno:
Ni'm tỳn mèn nag ychain gwaith,
Oddiyma heddyw ymaith.
Lewys Glyn Cothi, 'I Llywelyn ap Gwilym ap
Thomas Vychan, Bryn Havod'
('To Llywelyn ap Gwilym ap Thomas Vychan, Bryn Havod')

I am the suppliant *afanc* sheltering beside the lake; once he was there he was not drawn from the wave on Llyn Syfaddan: neither a cart nor working oxen will today draw me away from here.

Folkloric boundaries are never truly anchored; the same can be said for spirits connected with bodies of water. Tales of strange maidens emerging from lakes and wells in Wales are numerous. Over the centuries, several communities across the country have laid claim to farmers making their fortune from the prolific aquatic dairy cows of the *Tylwyth Teg* (fairies), not to mention various sightings of lake monsters of all shapes and sizes. In this chapter, we shall focus predominantly on the 'ghost' proper, and its place within the watery depths of Welsh lore.

We begin with Myrddin Fardd in *Llen Gwerin Sir Gaernarfon* (The Folklore of Caernarfonshire) (1908). He records a story that takes place along a short stretch of the river Colwyn, near Beddgelert in Eryri, known colloquially as Llyn Nad-y-Forwyn (Lake of the Maiden's Cry):

Yn nghymdogaeth Llyn-Nad-y-Forwyn yr oedd deuddyn ieuangc
wedi eu dyweddio i briodi; ond yr oedd y mab wedi rhoddi ei serch

*ar ferch arall; a'r noson cyn y briodas rhoddodd hwth i'w ddyweddi
i'r llyn uchod, er mwyn bod yn rhydd oddwrhi i gael priodi y llall.
Byth ar ol hyny yr oedd y gymmydogaeth yn cael eu haflonyddu gan
ysbryd. Ambell dro ceid ei weled yn dyfod i lawr ar hyd yr afon
Golwyn fel olwyn o dân; bryd arall gwelid boneddiges yn rhodio
oddeutu yr afon, mewn gwisg o sidan; dro arall byddai cwynfanau
dolefus yn dyrchafu o'r llyn; ac ambell dro gwelid merch ieuangc yn
dyfod i fyny o'r llyn yn hanner noeth, a'i gwallt gwlyb yn hongian i
lawr dros ei hysgwyddau; ac yn cwynfan yn chwerw a thorcalonus
uwchben y llyn, yr hwn, ar ol hyny, a elwid 'Llyn-Nad-y-Forwyn.'*

In the neighbourhood of Llyn-Nad-y-Forwyn a young couple
were engaged to be married; but the young lad had given his
love to another girl; and the night before the wedding he threw
his fiancée into the lake above, to be free from her in order to
marry the other. Ever since the community was disturbed by
a ghost. Sometimes it was seen coming down along the river
Colwyn like a wheel of fire; another time a lady was seen walking
around the river, in a dress of silk; at another time there would
be loud moans rising from the lake; and sometimes a young
woman was seen coming up from the lake half naked, with her
wet hair hanging down over her shoulders; and moaning bitterly
and heartbroken above the lake, which, after that, was called
'Lake of the Maiden's Cry.'

This account can also be found in an earlier record by Elias Owen in
Welsh Folk-lore: A Collection of the Folk-Tales and Legends of North Wales
(1896), again with reference to the heartbroken spirit appearing as a
'ball of fire, rolling along the river Colwyn' – a sight which we are now
very familiar with. The image of the lake-bound ghost of a 'victimised
woman' dressed in silk is also reminiscent of the *Ladi Wen* motif discussed in the previous chapter.

Another water-bound ghost with a tragic backstory is found in Carmarthenshire, in an altogether more tourist-friendly setting. The National
Botanical Garden of Wales, open to the public since 2000, now stands
on the site of what was Middleton Hall. The hall was built around 1600
by the high sheriff, Sir Henry Middleton, from wealth accrued from the

estate's heavy involvement in the East India Company. Through personal debts and mortgages, the hall changed hands several times during the eighteenth century, eventually being bought in 1776 by William Paxton, the Master of the Mint of Bengal for the East India Company. Paxton, on his return to Britain in 1785, commissioned an impressive new hall as well as extensive landscaped grounds, which were particularly notable for a string of seven lakes surrounding the building. The most impressive lake was Pond Du (Black Pond), overlooked by the front of the hall.

The events that are said to be connected with this haunting happened during Edward Hamlyn Adams's ownership, and are recorded in *Llanarthne Ddoe a Heddiw* (Llanarthney Past and Present) (2002). Adams, a wealthy merchant born in Kingston, Jamaica, in 1777, moved to Wales with the purchase of Middleton Hall in 1824 following William Paxton's death. Once settled, he went on to become the Member of Parliament for Carmarthenshire.

It was believed that Pond Du was haunted by the ghost of one of Adams's grandchildren, known as 'the black baby'. Adams had a number of grandchildren, one of whom is said to have died in India as an infant. The body was sent home to Middleton Hall at the request of the family, but the mummification process was apparently not well executed and by the time the corpse arrived in Carmarthenshire, it had turned black. When he saw it, Adams refused to believe that the baby was his kin, and so he instructed that the coffin and the remains should be thrown into the pond.

The historical veracity of this story should probably be questioned. Edward Adams, known as an unpleasant character, had made his fortune trading in slaves from Jamaica and Barbados. Owing to the family's reputation for 'eccentric behaviour' (more so due to the conduct of his eldest son, Edward Abadam), several other legends also flourished, and told of secret tunnels through the estate, with a locally held belief that Adams had been buried in the park on his estate following his death in 1842 and a coffin full of stones had instead been buried in Llanarthne churchyard. The grim tale of the black baby sounds very much like a possible tall tale concocted by the local community on the back of his reputation, rather than one which describes actual events.

A second ghost is also reported at the site of Middleton Hall in the form of a figure dressed in 'old military uniform', walking towards the hall from the road that led to Waunlas Farm. This was an unusual calendrical spirit: it was only seen twice a year, at the end of June and at the end of November.

Another doleful watery ghost is said to have been sighted in Trawsfynydd, Gwynedd. *Hanes Bro Trawsfynydd* (The History of the Trawsfynydd District), edited in 1973 by the local members of Merched y Wawr, recounts a tragic tale from Wern-fach farm in Cwm Cefn Clawdd:

> *Dywedid bod gŵr Wern Bach [Wern-fach] yn hynod angharedig wrth ei wraig. Aeth allan un noson a gwaeddodd un o'r plant fod ei fam allan yn chwilio amdano. Meddai yntau: 'Be' sydd ar y d...l eisiau rwan?' Pan aeth yn ôl i'r tŷ roedd yn waed i gyd. Pasiodd gŵr y Fotty ar gefn ei ferlen, a phan edrychodd at yr afon gwelai ysbryd gwraig yno fel petai'n golchi. Dychrynodd y ferlen a rhedodd adref bob cam.*

It was said that the master of Wern Bach [Wern-fach] was extremely unkind to his wife. He went out one night and one of the children shouted that his mother was out looking for him. He said: 'What does the d...l want now?' When he went back to the house he was covered in blood. The master of Fotty passed on the back of his pony, and when he looked at the river he saw the ghost of a woman there as if she was washing. The pony got scared and ran straight home.

The river in question is likely the Crawcwellt, which runs alongside the prehistoric settlement at Cefn Clawdd and what are now the ruins of Wern-fach farm.

Another local ghost story is found in association with this same farm. It was said that someone crossing the mountain at night in the vicinity of Wern-fach noticed a light moving towards the cowshed. They speculated that perhaps one of the cows was calving, and went to the shed to see if they could offer any help to the farmer. When they reached the shed, the witness was surprised to see that it was deserted and so, naturally, 'there must be a ghost around' (*'mae'n rhaid fod ysbryd o gwmpas'*).

The most common attribution to 'supernatural' lights in British folklore is the phenomenon known as 'will-o'-the-wisp'. Refered to as *tân ellyll, mall-dân* or *hudlewyn* in Wales, the glow is caused by natural bio-luminescence as organic materials in the ground decay and oxidise. In folk tales, these lights were said to lure those travelling in darkness away from the path; because they tended to occur in marshy or boggy areas, straying therefore posed a very real danger. In some areas, conversely, there are stories of these lights leading people away from harm too.

While most stories of supernatural lights relate to the *cannwyll gorff* (corpse candle), the motifs of the will-o'-the-wisp and *Jac y Lantarn* (jack-o'-lantern) are also common in Wales. Whereas both of these latter entities are often described separately within Welsh folklore texts, in practice, their names were frequently used interchangeably. They are discussed further in Chapter Ten: 'Death Omens'.

An example is recorded by the Reverend William Hobley in *Hanes Methodistiaeth Arfon* (The History of Methodism in Arfon) (1913), where lights would sometimes attempt to lead people to drown in stretches of water. Hobley quotes a senior Methodist minister, Gruffydd Prisiart:

> *Yr oedd rhyw ellyll a elwid yn Jac y Lanter yn gwibio yn y nentydd. Dywedid y byddai'n ceisio denu rhai dros y clogwyni i dorri eu gyddfau, ac eraill i'r dwfr i foddi.*

> There was a demon known as Jac y Lanter which darted in the streams. It was said that it would try to coax some over the cliffs to break their necks, and others to drown in the waters.

The Welsh origin story for *Jac y Lantarn* is best summarised in one of the most notable nineteenth-century collections of Welsh fables and folklore, *Cymru Fu* (The Wales That Was) (1862) by Llyfrbryf (Isaac Foulkes). This was an early publication by Llyfrbryf who originally published it in three parts between 1862 and 1864. The volumes were a collection of Welsh fables, folklore and traditions, mainly recorded by the author himself. He writes how an old rogue from Arfon called Sion Dafydd, who was known to consort frequently with 'the children of the bottomless pit' (*'plant y pwll diwaelod'*), once tricked the Devil. He is said to have sold his soul to his cloven-footed acquaintance for a large sum of money, on the understanding that if he could keep his hold on anything, the Devil would not be able to drag him away – a trick Sion used to thwart his foe at every opportunity. As he could not be carted to Hell, and was considered too immoral for Heaven, he became *Jac y Lantarn* on earth, mirroring the similar Irish folk legend of Stingy Jack, or Jack the Smith.

Another example of a malevolent spirit was recorded in Dolgellau, Gwynedd, in association with Ffynnon Cnidw (Cnidw Well), or Ffynnon Gwenhudw as it is more commonly known, recorded by William Davies in his 1898 essay, 'Casgliad o Lên-Gwerin Meirion' ('A Collection of Meirion Folklore'). This well stands near Tŷ Blaenau, home of the eighteenth-century antiquarian and poet Rhys Jones, between Dolgellau and Garnedd Wen, its water famous for curing rheumatism. According to William Davies, the well was troubled by a ghost that would leap onto Rhys's grandfather's horse as they journeyed home from church, clinging to the beast's back until the grandfather had dismounted a mile or so away.

Interestingly, the word *gwenhidwy* is Welsh for sprite, goblin or apparition, and the name has strong connections with the sea; it can also mean mermaid. *Maes Gwenhidwy* (the field of Gwenhidwy) serves as a poetic name for the ocean, while *meirch Gwenhidwy* (the horses of Gwenhidwy) is a similar term used to describe waves, referenced by many Welsh poets from the sixteenth century onwards. *Cnidw* is the colloquial form.

Haunted watery locations were also used within Welsh folklore to serve as warnings, a theme we have already encountered in several chapters of this book. Such an account can be found in the essay 'Chwedlau a Thraddodiadau Plwyf Llanfachraith' ('The Legends and Traditions of Llanfachraith Parish') in the journal *Taliesin* (1859), by 'Cofiadur'. An ungodly man lived in Y Friog, Gwynedd, who refused to pay his tithe as regularly as he refused to say his prayers or listen to sermons. Due to his 'reluctance and corrupted behaviours' ('*[c]yndynrwydd a'i lygredig ymddygiadau*'), he was excommunicated by the Grey and Black Friars who jointly ran the monastery.

Nid ymwnaeth â chyffes na chymmun hyd ei awr olaf, a'r canlyniad fu iddynt ei orfodi i dderbyn y Viaticum, ar bwys pennyd o gael ei boeni ym mhistyll y Cain fel arwydd glanhad am ei losgach, a

*dywedir y byddai ysgrechfeydd ofnadwy yn dod o'r ogof ar amserau:
yn enwedig felly pan fyddai llifogydd yn yr afon, neu ynte pan fyddai
rhewogydd wedi clöi y dwr.*

> He did not partake in confession or communion even at his last
> hour, the result of which was that they obliged him to accept
> the Viaticum [last rites], on pain of being tormented in Cain
> waterfall as a sign of being cleansed of his unnatural lust, and it
> is said that terrible screams came from the cave at times: espe-
> cially so when the river was flooded, or when frost had solidified
> the waters.

The location of this haunting is the impressive Pistyll Cain, a waterfall
that can be found along the picturesque walking route through Coed
y Brenin, a popular destination for tourists visiting Eryri, blissfully
unaware of its gruesome place in Welsh folklore.

As we have already discussed the significance of various folkloric
boundaries (and arguably, a waterfall like the one above could be considered one of them), it would be remiss of us not to mention haunted
bridges. Several examples can be found within local lore, such as Pont
Glyn-diffwys (Glyn-diffwys Bridge), located next to the A5 in Llangwm,
Conwy. You may have noticed that this tale is located in the same area
as the screeching winged lady in the previous chapter. This account,
however, comes from William Davies in 1898, and describes how this
area at the time was something of a hot-spot for murders – so much so
that it harboured a reputation for being a 'nesting place' ('*nythle*') for
ghosts, and no one would dare pass this bridge at night. Again, we see
ghost-lore being used to serve as a warning within the community to
steer clear of a particular ill-reputed location, and to protect travellers
from the treacherous terrain encountered at Glyn-diffwys, which literally translates as 'precipice-valley'.

A spring-dwelling ghost is recorded in the parish of Llandysul, this
time a former minister rather than a damned soul or evil spirit. The
scholar and preacher, Reverend David Dafis, was known through his
writing as Dafis Castellhywel. He was born in 1745 at Goitre-isaf farm
in the village of Betws Bledrws, Ceredigion, and ordained as a minister
at eighteen years of age in 1763. It was in 1782 that he acquired his

bardic name when he moved to the fourteenth-century Castell Hywel, where he kept a school at which he taught for the next thirty years to widespread acclaim.

After his death in 1827, while he was buried in the churchyard at Eglwys Santes Gwenog (St Gwenog's Church), his restless ghost haunted a particular spring for some considerable time and for reasons otherwise unknown. The circumstances were recorded by the Reverend William Jenkin Davies in *Hanes Plwyf Llandyssul* (The History of Llandysul Parish) (1896):

> *Buodd yspryd 'rhen Ddafis Castellhŵel yn pistyll gwyn clos pori, am lawer o flynydde wedi 'ddo farw. Eithe'r merched ddim am lawer i 'ol dŵr o'r pistyll wedi 'ddi ddachre twyllu, o achos fod i ysbryd e'n cerdded o boti'r lle.*

Old Dafis Castellhywel's ghost haunted the pasture of pistyll gwyn (white spring) for many years after he died. The women wouldn't for any price fetch water from the spring once darkness fell, because his ghost walked about the place.

In the seminal text, *Observations on the Snowdon Mountains* (1802), David Dafis's peer, the antiquarian William Williams of Llandygái, describes the folklore associated with Llyn Marchlyn Mawr, today a reservoir used as a water source for the nearby Dinorwig hydroelectric power station. Despite Williams's deep-rooted love of Eryri, his description of this particular lake is less than flattering:

> The stupendous cliffs of Lidir [Elidir] Fawr hang over it, and give it an awful and dismal appearance, which I suppose has been the occasion of fabling it the abode of evil spirits, doomed to be confined there for a certain term of years by those skilled in magical charms, or exorcism, as a punishment for haunting houses and frightening people.

Its onerous reputation clearly persisted, and by the turn of the twentieth century, Marchlyn Mawr had acquired an altogether different type of bogey – the *Ceffyl Dŵr* (Water Horse). A spectre that rears its head in a number of locations across Wales, described with some minor regional differences in size and temperament, the *Ceffyl Dŵr* generally shares many characteristics with the Scottish *kelpie*. James Motley, author of *Tales of the Cymry* (1848) draws further, albeit perhaps more tenuous, comparison with the mischievous nature of the 'Phoocah of the Irish', the shapeshifting abilities of the 'English Puck', and, by association therefore, the will-o'-the-wisp, who also lure their victims to their demise.

The Reverend William Hobley records in the fifth volume of *Hanes Methodistiaeth Arfon* (The History of Methodism in Arfon) (1923):

> *Unwaith ar gefn Ceffyl y Dwr yn iach weithian am yr hoedl, oblegid cyn meiddio dyn gwac dyna farch a'i farchog yngwaelod llyn! Ac am yr ellyll hwn, cig a chnawd yw ei arbennig amheuthun; ac yn arafdeg y traflynca efe'r ysglyf, gan gymaint blasyn a gaiff arnynt.*

> Once on the back of *Ceffyl y Dwr* then goodbye to his life, for before the man has ventured a cry, the horse and its rider would be at the bottom of the lake! And as for this demon, meat and flesh are its special delicacy; slowly it swallows the prey, because it is so partial to them.

The reader could be forgiven for thinking that the name 'Marchlyn Mawr' derives from this local legend; this is indeed Williams's own interpretation, stating that '*Marchlyn* means ~~The Horse Lake, or Mere~~'. ~~This is unlikely~~ to be the case, and the more probable translation of *march* in this context would be 'large'. The *Ceffyl Dŵr* story may well have been concocted later to fit the alternative interpretation of the name, especially given the lake's existing uncanny reputation.

Hobley also describes another demonic Welsh water spirit that was believed to haunt the waters of Eryri – the *afanc*, which, as we will see, has variously been described as a mythological water monster and a ghost, as well as everything in between:

> *Diau fod Nant y Ffrancon i'w ddeall am yr afancwn neu'r ellyllon a lechai yng ngwaelodion y llynoedd, afanc ym mhob i lyn, er, yn eithaf tebyg, y bu'r beaver bychan yma hefyd, a elwir wrth yr un enw. Yr oedd Sarn yr Afanc yn y Ceunant yng nghwrr isaf y nant,*

*ac y mae Llyn yr Afanc yn agos i Gapel Garmon. Creaduriaid gwir-
ioneddol unwaith, yr un adeg neu gynt na'r adeg y troediai'r anifail
cors y ddaear, ond a aethant wedi hynny yn ellyllon dychmygol.*

It is doubtless that Nant y Ffrancon is known for the *afancwn*
or the demons that lurked in the depths of the lakes, an *afanc* in
every lake, although, it is probable, the small beaver also dwelt
here, called by the same name. Sarn yr Afanc [Afanc Causeway]
was in the Ceunant [Gorge] in the lower reaches of the stream,
and Llyn yr Afanc [Afanc Lake] is close to Capel Garmon. Once
real creatures, at the same time or earlier than when the swamp
animal trod the earth, but which then became imaginary demons.

The *afanc* which, as explained by Hobley above, is also the Welsh word
for 'beaver', was a monster known from Welsh mythology as early as
the fourteenth century, and is referred to by several poets of the time,
including Lewys Glyn Cothi in the fifteenth century, an excerpt of
whose poem, 'I Llywelyn ap Gwilym ap Thomas Vychan, Bryn Havod',
is quoted at the opening of this chapter. Lady Charlotte Guest's 1838
translation of the *Mabinogion* names the beast slain in the romance of
Peredur fab Efrawg as the *Addanc*.

What is less clear is whether *afanc* served as the translation of 'beaver'
during the late medieval period, when the word first appears, or exclusively referred to the supernatural creature. The first reference to '*afangc*'
being synonymous with the 'castor' or 'bever' only appears in 1632 in
John Davies's *Antiquae Linguae Britannicae et Linguae Latinae, Dictiona-
rium Duplex*.

William Williams in *Observations on the Snowdon Mountains* includes
a footnote with a wonderfully florid description of the beaver, quoting
from David Powell's *Historie of Cambria, Now Called Wales* (1584):

It is a beast not much unlike an otter, but that it is bigger, all
hearie saving the taile, which is like a fishe taile, as broad as
a man's hand. This beaste useth as well the water as the land,
and hath a verie sharp teeth, and biteth cruellie, till he perceive
the bones cracke: his stones be of great efficacie in physicke.
He that will learn what strong nests they make, which Giraldus

called Castells, which they build upon the face of the water with great bowes, which they cut with their teeth, and some lie upon their backs holding the wood with the fore feet, which the other draweth with a crosse stick, the which he holdeth in his mouth, to the water-side, and other particularities of their natures, let him read Giraldus, in his Topographie of Wales.

We therefore turn to Giraldus Cambrensis and *The Itinerary Through Wales and the Description of Wales* (1191), where he wrote about the beaver surviving in the river Teifi alone of all the rivers of Wales. He notes that the creature's skin was much 'sought after in the west' (the price being specifically mentioned in the medieval Welsh laws of Hywel Dda) as were its medicinal castor sacs, erroneously echoing the long-held belief that the mammal used to self-castrate in order to avoid capture. What is clear is that all evidence points to the beaver having become extinct in Wales (and the rest of southern Britain for that matter) by 1300.

With its unusual appearance and behaviour compared to other aquatic creatures, as well as its rarity in Welsh rivers, it is easy to see why the beaver might have been viewed as something more demonic. However, the evidence suggests the term *afanc* was used to denote the water spirit long before its association with the toothy mammal.

Arguably the most well-known account of the *afanc* is the tale of Llyn yr Afanc in Betws-y-coed, Conwy, recorded by the antiquarian, naturalist, and linguist, Edward Lhuyd in 1693. Hobley recounts a later version, interestingly with very little having changed from the original:

Uwchlaw Betws y Coed y mae Llyn yr Afanc. Merch a hudodd yr afanc hwn o'r drigfan, a rhwymid ef â thidau heiyrn tra'r ydoedd yn cysgu â'i ben ar ei glyn hi, fel Samson ar liniau Dalila. Pan ddefrodd yr afanc, ffwrdd ag ef i'w loches a bron y ferch yn ei grafanc. Eithr yr oedd y dîd â digon o hyd ynddi, a rhwymwyd ychen bannog o efeilliaid wrthi a thynnwyd yntau'r afanc allan o'i loches. Hwn oedd yr afanc a gludwyd i Lyn Cwm Ffynnon Las [Llyn Glaslyn] uwchben Llyn Peris.

Above Betws y Coed lies Llyn yr Afanc. A girl lured this *afanc* out of its dwelling, and it was bound with iron chains while it slept with its head on her thigh, like Samson on Delilah's knees. When the *afanc* awoke, it took off to its den and held the girl in its claws. But the rod had enough length in it, and a twinned pair of horned oxen were tied to it and dragged the *afanc* from its shelter. This was the afanc that was taken to Llyn Cwm Ffynnon Las [Llyn Glaslyn] above Llyn Peris.

The motif of oxen being tasked to pull a demonic entity out of its lair is replicated across Wales. In *The Myvyrian Archaiology of Wales: Collected Out of Ancient Manuscripts* (1801–7), Iolo Morganwg fabricated a story of how at Llyn Llion (most likely Llyn Tegid in Bala, Gwynedd), 'the Horned Oxen of Hu Gadarn [Hu the Mighty], dragged the *Afanc* of the river to land and the lake was disturbed no more' ('*Ychain Bannog Hu Gadarn, a lusgasant Afanc y llynn i dir ac ni thorres y llyn mwyach*').

A similar tale is recounted by William Davies, this time in Corwen, Denbighshire, in connection with Nant y Fieren (Bramble Stream). The Devil and his minions were said to dwell here, taking great delight in terrifying the community. Eventually, enough was enough, and it was decided that the Devil would be dragged away 'with two horned oxen' ('*efo dau ychain banog*'). Once two beasts of suitable strength and a willing priest were found, the Devil was caught, and off they went along the stream to a lake called 'Cefn y Cloion'.

It was said that the imprints left by the oxen's hooves could be seen in the rock above the stream; similarly the marks left by their horns digging into the land while pulling gave rise to the name Moel Gyrn (Horn Hill), which is situated between Corwen and the village of Gwyddelwern. Slightly less palatable is 'Maes y Perfedd' (Field of Entrails') further on, where one of the poor oxen was said to have been disembowelled in its struggle with its stubborn cargo!

While sightings such as this would be expected to have dried up during the twentieth century, the *afanc* surprisingly continues to play an active role within Welsh folkloric belief and even modern-day hauntings. The Old Rectory at Bae Rhosili, Penrhyn Gŵyr (Gower Peninsula), boasts a number of unpleasant and unusual ghosts, the details of which may be found in any good coffee table book relating to Welsh hauntings, but are perhaps best recorded in *Portrait of Gower* by Wynford Vaughan-Thomas in 1976:

One person who stayed at the house, after the Church authorities had wisely built a new Rectory near to Rhossili church, told me that on a certain winter's night 'something very unpleasant indeed comes out of the sea and comes into the house.' Another story suggests that you can suddenly walk into a cold pool of air in the corridor and hear a low voice in your ear saying, 'Why don't you turn around and look at me?' No one has ever dared.

While this case is very well known across the country, the more contemporary account, and its unexpected links to the *afanc*, is not. At least, not unless you happen to have grown up in Welsh-speaking Wales during the 1990s with a fondness for late-night S4C paranormal television programmes. There is an entire generation of children left traumatised by *O'r Ochr Draw* (From the Other Side), which followed the dramatised re-enactions of Anglican priest and modern-day exorcist, J. Aelwyn Roberts, the vicar of Llandygái. The series was based on his 1990 book, *Holy Ghostbuster*, which he followed up with the 1991 Welsh-language version, *Yr Anhygoel* (The Unbelievable). It is in the Welsh text that we find his interesting 'professional take' on this case:

> *Clywais sôn am afanc arall yn dod o'r môr i hen reithordy yn ymyl Caerdydd, ac yn sefyll tu ôl i aelodau'r teulu a dweud 'Os beiddiwch, trowch ac edrychwch arnaf.' Ond mae'r teulu a'r ymwelwyr wedi eu disgyblu i beidio â throi ac edrych os digwydd hyn iddyn nhw.*

I heard of the *afanc* coming out of the sea to an old rectory near Cardiff, and how it would stand behind members of the family and say 'If you dare, turn around and look at me.' But the family and the visitors are instructed not to turn around and look if this happens to them.

This version seems to fuse both accounts of the rectory haunting, with Roberts appearing to suggest that the ghosts are one and the same.

He continues by providing another contemporary account of the *afanc* which appeared to a colleague, known only as 'W.R.', when he first slept at his new home in the parish of Yr Hen Briordy, Ynys Môn:

'Yna,' meddai, 'mi clywais i o. Rhyw sŵn fel sŵn anifail yn brwydro am ei wynt ac roedd y stafell i gyd yn ogleuo. Roedd fy nghorff wedi cyffio cymaint gan yr oerni rhyfedd fel ei bod yn ymdrech i droi i gyfeiriad y sŵn meginol yma. Ar ôl troi fe'i gwelais; roedd o'n eistedd yn y lle tân ac roedd cymaint duach na'r grât fel y gallwn ei weld yn blaen. Rhyw ddüwch seimlyd, mawr, di-siâp a dau lygad creulon yn treiddio drwof.

'Roedd y ddau lygad yn gallu siarad, a'r funud honno roedden nhw'n dweud wrtha i fy mod yn mynd i farw. Roedd y peth yn hollol sicr ei fod yn mynd i fy lladd ac na fuaswn yno erbyn y bore. Roedd o'n chwerthin am fy mhen ac yn graddol wasgu'r nerth allan o'm corff. Ceisiais beidio ag edrych arno er mwyn torri ei bŵer ond fedrwn i ddim, roedd yn rhaid i mi edrych ar y ddau lygad uffernol oedd yn crechwenu wrth fy lladd.'

'Then,' he said, 'I heard it. A noise like that of an animal fighting for its breath and the whole room stank. My body had stiffened so much from the strange coldness that it was an effort to turn towards the direction of that bellows-like noise. After I had turned I saw it; it was sat in the fireplace and was so much blacker than the grate that I could see it plainly. Some slimy blackness, large, shapeless and two cruel eyes boring through me.

'Those two eyes spoke, and that second they were telling me that I was going to die. That thing was completely sure that it was going to kill me and that I wouldn't be here by the morning. It was laughing at me and slowly squeezing the life from my body. I tried not to look at it in order to break its power but I couldn't, I had to look at those two hellish eyes that were smirking at me while it killed me.'

W. R. eventually breaks the demonic spell by reciting prayers until dawn. In Chapter Two: 'Unfinished Business', we have previously discussed the hallucinatory and physical symptoms of sleep paralysis and its role in folklore; this particular account reads similarly to such stories.

Regardless of origin, there is something more to be said of the tenacity of the *afanc* – not only that such a fantastical spirit as this might not only survive within the national folkloric narrative with very little variation between early and more contemporary retellings of the legend, but that it has also evidently evolved into an entity which can be held responsible for modern-day Welsh hauntings.

Having read of the sea-dwelling *afanc*, it would be remiss of us not to conclude this chapter with another kind of sea-borne spirit. While the portentous screeches of the *cyhyraeth* and the *wawch* (discussed later in Chapter Ten: 'Death Omens') were sometimes said to be heard along the coastline of south Glamorgan and Meirion, respectively, as a warning of impending disasters at sea, it is to the ghost ships of Wales that we now steer.

Gwennan Gorn was reportedly sighted several times from the shores of Abergele, Conwy. The phantom ship is believed to have been built there by the prince and voyager, Madog ab Owain Gwynedd, who in 1170, as legend has it, sailed to America aboard it. Having arrived at a strange new land, his party returned to Wales in search of willing volunteers with whom to form a colony. While the tale is most probably fictitious, it did not prevent several Welshmen from the seventeenth through to the nineteenth centuries from travelling to America to 'find' Madog's lost descendants, with tall tales of Welsh-speaking tribes touted by none other than Thomas Jefferson himself.

In sixteenth-century Dinbych-y-pysgod (Tenby), Pembrokeshire, during a bout of stormy weather, it was said that a strange ship was sighted, in difficulty, sailing quickly through Bae Caerfyrddin (Carmarthen Bay). Its sails and masts were wrecked, and all that could be seen aboard from the shore were strange lights and ghostly shapes moving along the deck. At night, terrible wailing noises were heard rising above the storm from its direction. By morning, a semi-conscious man was found washed ashore, wearing foreign clothing and unable to speak a word. He eventually moved to live on Ynys Santes Catrin (St Catherine's Island), a small tidal island which links to the beach at low tide.

One stormy night, the stranger relayed his tale to a local shepherd from the mainland who had befriended him. He confessed to having been a pirate who had murdered his wife in a fit of jealousy. His entire crew had perished on their journey and so the ship had been sailed towards Tenby by spirits. Since arriving on the island, he could hear mermaids calling to him, telling him his wife was content. Suddenly jumping to his feet and waving furiously at the waves, he shouted 'I'm coming! I'm coming!' and leapt into the water, never to be seen again.

While this story could be interpreted as a cautionary tale in relation to the untrustworthiness of strangers from outside the community, the following late eighteenth-century account from Glamorgan, recorded by the Reverend Edmund Jones, is a little more pointed:

> Many years ago there came an Englishman into Swansea, who was a Deist, who corrupted several people and disgusted others (who were aggrieved at his blasphemies against the Scripture and scriptural men). But the judgement of God reached him, and set him into the hands of the destroyer – for he shot himself to death. The people were not willing to put him into the earth and therefore cast his cursed body into the sea, to carry it away. But, as if the sea would not have him, it cast him back upon the sand. The people threw him into the sea again; the sea again rejected him, and then they buried him in the sand. Indeed, his unclean body defiled both the water and the earth about it, as being full of sin and rendered the curse of God. And as his burial was ignominious, so his resurrection will be to damnation – according to the Scripture (John 5:29).

It is rather telling that despite the litany of malicious water spirits and bloodthirsty aquatic monsters mentioned within this chapter, perhaps the most callous act here was committed by the good people of Swansea!

CHAPTER NINE

Fantastical Ghouls

*

Mi glywais i ers dyddiau
Fod bwgan yn y Pentre'
Weithiau'm mrig y coed yn dân
Yn chware'r mân ganghenau.
Attributed to Dafydd Ddu Eryri

I've heard for many a day, of a ghost in Pentre', sometimes aflame in the treetops, playing the little twigs.

In the introductory chapter, we saw how the appearance of ghosts in Wales was heavily influenced by concurrent historical events, in turn leading to an array of abstract phantoms and outlandish spectres – in other words, fantastical ghouls. While such examples have been noted elsewhere throughout this book in the form of wheels of fire, monstrous lake spirits, and talkative poltergeists, this chapter serves as a home for some of Wales's weirdest spectres.

We start this chapter with a type of phantom that is highly unusual within Welsh ghost-lore:

Nid yn gyffredin y mae bwcïod neu ysprydion plant i'w gweled neu i'w clywed, ac nid yn fynych y cofnodir eu bod yn arfer ymrithio ar lun plentyn; ond y mae hyny yn dygwydd ambell waith; a hyny, mae yn debyg, pan y byddo plentyn diniwed wedi cael cam gan rywrai, neu, efallai, wedi cael ei lofruddio gan ryw anghenfil neu anghenfiles yn dwyn delw dyn. Eithr y mae yspryd plant weithiau yn ymlwybran ar hyd y ddaiar, ac yn aflonyddu tawelwch marwolion.

It is not common for children's bogeys or ghosts to be seen or heard, and it is not often recorded that they appear in the form of a child; but that has happened a few times; and that, apparently, when an innocent child has been wronged by someone, or perhaps, murdered by some monster or she-monster bearing the image of man. But the spirits of children sometimes roam the earth, and disturb the silence of the dead.

One such example was said to haunt Cwm Coednerth farmhouse in the village of Troed-yr-aur, Ceredigion – 'Bwci Melyn Bach y Cwm' ('The Little Yellow Bogey of the Valley'), so named because of its yellow attire. The account appears (along with the quotation above) in *Ysten Sioned* (Sioned's Pitcher) by Daniel Silvan Evans and Ivon (first published in 1882), and whereas 'his voice was the sweet voice of an innocent child' ('*llef alaethus plentyn diamgeledd ydoedd ei lef*'), he was also noted to bare his teeth and snarl at unwary passers by.

While the apparition of a child might therefore be considered fantastical on its own merit, the *Bwci Melyn Bach* has another trick up its little yellow sleeve that sets it apart from other Welsh accounts:

> *Ar ryw dro arall gwelodd dyn diethr ef yn rhywle o gwmpas y tŷ, a phlygodd i'w godi a'i amgeleddu; ond aeth y plentyn melyn wylofus yn llynwyn o waed rhwng ei ddwylaw!*

> On another occasion a stranger saw him somewhere around the house, and stooped to pick him up and embrace him; but the weeping blonde child became a pool of blood between his hands!

While there are plenty of shapeshifting ghosts within Welsh folklore, with many examples noted in this book, we are not aware of any other examples where a ghost becomes a pool of blood in this way. Silvan Evans suggests that:

> *nid oes dim sicrwydd beth oedd achos y bwci bychanig hwn; ond barnai y dysgedigion, a sisialai y werin, fod plentyn diniwed wedi cael ei lofruddio ryw bryd gan rai o hen breswylwyr y Cwm.*

there is no certainty as to what was the cause of this very small bogey; but scholars believed, and peasants whispered, that an innocent child had been murdered at some point by some of the old inhabitants of the Valley.

Surprisingly, this is not the only account of a little yellow boy in Welsh ghost-lore, nor even from the same county! A similar story is found in the manuscripts kept at the Nantgarw archives, Amgueddfa Cymru (Museum Wales), in a handwritten book of ghost stories collected and edited by Adran Penmorfa, Cylch Aberteifi (Penmorfa Ward, Cardigan Group), for the 1932 Urdd Eisteddfod. This particular tale is entitled 'Y Penfelyn Bach' ('The Fair-Haired Child'):

Un nos serlog olau, ond oer anghyffredin, yr oedd gwr o'r ardal yn dyfod adref yn bur hwyr – o ran hynny yr oedd yn ddyfnder nos arno. Nid oedd ganddo ond tua gwaith chwarter awr o gerdded, ond fod y ffordd oedd ganddo i fyned ar hyd-ddi yn enwog am ysbrydion. Ond yr oedd ef yn hollol ddiarswyd, oherwydd oedd ef yn gyfarwydd a'r ffordd a'r ysbrydion. Fel yr oedd yn nesu at gartref, yn hollol ddisymwth ac anisgwyliadwy, safodd o'i flaen, yn hollol noeth, blentyn bychan penfelyn, braf yr olwg ar ganol y ffordd. Pa fodd, ac o ba le y daeth nis gallasai ddirnad, gan fod y ffordd yn berffaith glir y funud cynt. Credodd mai plentyn gwirioneddol ydoedd, a dywedodd, – 'Wel y bwlyn penfelyn bach, beth wyt ti'n wneud allan ar noson mor oer a heno.' Gyda hyn, diflannodd y plentyn, ac ni welodd olion ohono mwy.

One bright but unusually cold starry night, a man was coming home very late – in actual fact it was in the middle of the night. He only had around a quarter of an hour's walk left to do, but the road he had to travel along was famous for its ghosts. But he was completely unafraid, because he was familiar with the road and with the ghosts. As he was nearing home, very suddenly and unexpectedly, there stood before him, completely naked, a small fair-haired child, of a friendly disposition in the middle of the road. How, and from where it came he could not perceive, as the road had been perfectly clear the minute before. He believed him to be a real child, and said, – 'Well you little fair-haired rascal, what are you doing out on a night as cold as tonight.' With that, the child disappeared, and he saw no further sign of it.

The gentleman in question returned home, much shaken by his experience. Familiar as he was with the local ghouls of Penmorfa, 'he considered this particular encounter more mysterious than any other' ('*ystyriai fod mwy o ddirgelwch yn gysylltiol a hwn nac a'r un arall*'). In any case, this ghost seemed more welcoming than the Bwci Melyn Bach located less than half an hour's drive down the road!

Another fantastical account is recorded in *Ysten Sioned*, this time in the parish of Llanilar in Cardiganshire. Here, there was a piece of land which was known as Bryn Rhosog. Local belief was that the ground was cursed because, despite there being a number of surrounding farms, all attempts to cultivate this area had failed. Along with being a 'paradise' for frogs, plovers and herons, it also served as a habitat for the local shapeshifting bogey.

Although sometimes said to appear in the form of a man, and at other times as 'some beast of mixed species' ('*rhyw fwystfil cymmys-gryw*'), the usual form adopted by the Bryn Rhosog bogey was that of a large ball of fire which rolled speedily around on the ground – again, a common motif in Welsh ghost-lore discussed and exemplified elsewhere in this book.

The people of the area were too nervous of the ghost to approach and speak with it which, as we discussed in Chapter Two: 'Unfinished Business', was required in order for a spirit to be able to deliver any message it might have. One man in the village, named Siacci Lletty Sinsir, believed himself to be the only person who could undertake this task.

Siacci fancied himself a poet, and so composed a rhyming couplet to address the ghost:

Rhyw noson dywell aeth wrtho ei hun (nid yw ysprydion byth yn dewis cwrdd â dau) tua'r Rhos; arosodd yno hyd hanner nos i'w ddisgwyl; a thoc dyma y bwci yn dyfod ar lun 'rhywbeth tebyg iawn i ddyn,' ac yn sefyll ar gyfer Siacci, yr hwn a'i cyfarchodd fel hyn:
   '*Bwci Bryn Rhosog,*
   Ar bwy'r wyt ti'n gosod?'

*Ond druan o Siacci! yr oedd y bwci yn gystal bardd ac yntau, a
gwell hefyd, o herwydd fe'i hatebodd mewn mynyd â'r ddwy linell
a ganlyn:*
'Arnat ti, Siacci,
Os dali di ati.'
*A chyda hyn gwelai dân yn saethu allan o eneu y bwci, a hefyd o'i
ddau lygad, y rhai oeddynt (fel y dywedai ein harwr) gymmaint o
faint a'r ddwy lamp a welsai yn yr eglwys fore'r plygain.*

Some dark night he went by himself (spirits never choose to appear
before two people) towards the Rhos; he stayed there till midnight
to wait for it; and eventually here was the bogey appearing in the
guise of 'something very like a man,' and standing near Siacci,
who greeted him this way:
'Bryn Rhosog bogey, whom do you prey on?'
But poor Siacci! the bogey was as good a poet as he was, and
better too, because he soon answered with the following two lines:
'On you, Siacci, if you keep at it.'
And with this he saw fire shooting out of the bogey's mouth, and
also from his two eyes, which were (as our hero claimed) as
big as the two lamps he had seen in the church on the morning
of plygain.

Plygain is a traditional Welsh carol service, held at any time over the old
Christmas period between early December and late January, wherein
members of the congregation would sing traditional (and often very
old) Welsh-language carols without accompaniment, either as soloists
or within larger groups. Very few words would be spoken throughout,
and while there was often no particular order to the service, no same
song would be sung twice. It is one of several old Welsh traditions which
communities today have thankfully revived.

The ghost's threat that it would prey on Siacci if he kept troubling it
had the desired effect. He was found the next morning some six miles
away, scared out of his wits, and was laid up with a fever for five weeks.
He eventually recovered but, as is often the case when confronted with a
particularly horrifying phantom, he was described as never being quite
the same again.

'Rhyming battles' are not unprecedented within Welsh folklore. The previous reference to the *plygain* especially brings to mind another unusual Christmas tradition in which a battle of wits, through the medium of verse, features at its heart. The infamous cavorting mare, Mari Lwyd, is predominantly associated with the south of the country, but was first recorded in 1798 by John Evans in *A Tour Through Parts of North Wales*. Here, Mari and her troupe of wassailers attempt to gain entry into each house on their tour through the parish, with a doorstep performance called *pwnco* – not unlike Siacci's efforts with the *bwci*.

Poetry figures in another unusual haunting from Y Faenol estate, comprising some 1,000 acres of land near Bangor, Gwynedd, its history steeped in the slate quarrying industry. Here, there exist several versions of the same tale, each revolving around a rhyming ghoul.

The ghost is first reported in the January 1893 issue of the periodical *Bye-Gones*, and is said to have been copied from an otherwise unspecified manuscript by the poet Bleddyn:

> It used to be very troublesome, often appearing to wayfarers in the night in the shape of a large bird screeching amongst the branches of the trees, and uttering in a shrill voice
>
> *Gwae! gwae! imi erioed*
> *Ro'i bwyall mewn troed*
> *I dori coed y Faenol!*
>
> Woe! woe's me that I ever put
> A handle to my axe,
> To fell the trees of Faenol!

The bird, it is said, is the lingering spirit of a rogue who was executed for felling trees on the Faenol estate; a story most likely concocted to deter potential thieves.

In later sources, the cry of the *bwgan* has evolved into something altogether more sinister, as recounted in the tale of 'Ysbryd Coed y Faenol' ('The Spirit of Faenol Woods') by Myrddin Fardd in *Llên Gwerin Sir Gaernarfon* (The Folklore of Caernarfonshire) (1908):

Gwae i mi erioed,
Ro'i esgid am fy nhroed
I ladd yn nghoed
Y Faenol.

Woe that I ever, put a shoe on my foot to kill in the woods of Y Faenol.

Myrddin Fardd states that local folk believed the ghost was that of a man who had been guilty of various robberies and murders, and was subsequently hanged at one of the crossroads for his crimes. Others said that he had been killed in Y Faenol woods themselves, and that the words cried out were instead:

Gwae fi erioed
Ro'i bwyell mewn troed,
I ladd yn nghoed y Faenol.

Woe that I ever, put an axe in a foot, to kill in the woods of Y Faenol.

With a span of less than twenty years between these two accounts, the subtle variances may be explained by regional differences, and the effects of poetic licence on an evolving folk tale which was undoubtedly popular within the area during the turn of the nineteenth century, becoming more fantastical and gruesome with every retelling.

A similarly fantastical woodland bogey is associated with Glodd-aeth woods in Llandudno, Conwy – land which was owned by the Mostyn Baronetcy from the fifteenth century, the oldest landowning family in Wales after the Crown, and the family responsible for the nineteenth-century development of Llandudno as a holiday resort. The story was recorded by the Reverend Elias Owen in *Welsh Folk-lore: A Collection of the Folk-Tales and Legends of North Wales* (1896), and tells of Thomas Davies from Tŷ Coch in Rhyl, a trapper employed to hunt foxes on the estate, who one evening found a foxhole containing cubs – a haul that would undoubtedly bring in money if he could catch them all. Re-turning in the evening when he knew the vixen would be out foraging, he made himself comfortable on the bough of a large oak tree opposite.

Just as he had settled down, Davies heard a 'horrible scream in the direction of the sea', sounding like the distant cry of a man in distress. As it seemed far away, he opted to continue with his vigil, but every so often the cry would be heard again, and seemed to move closer in his direction. As darkness fell, Davies beheld a frightful figure coming towards him through the trees:

> There, he saw before him, a nude being with eyes burning like fire, and these glittering balls were directed towards him. The awful being was only a dozen yards or so off. And now it crouched, and now it stood erect, but it never for a single instant withdrew its terrible eyes from the miserable man in the tree, who would have fallen to the ground were it not for the protecting boughs. Many times Davies thought that his last moment had come, for it seemed that the owner of those fiery eyes was about to spring upon him.

Closing his eyes, the trapper clung to the oak for his life until he heard the cockerel crowing at around 4 o'clock the following morning, at which point the spectre had vanished.

This story is understandably well represented within Welsh folklore texts, most probably due to the particularly ungodly aesthetic of the phantom, which again shares its burning eyes of fire with the *bwci* of Bryn Rhosog, and is a common motif with regards to ghostly Black Dog sightings, as described in Chapter Four: 'Spectral Beasts'. As in the case of 'Ysbryd Coed y Faenol', the Gloddaeth ghoul might also have served as a warning to potential poachers who would represent competition to the trapper, Thomas Davies, for his 'half-a-crown per head'. Perhaps the apparition also offered a convenient excuse for him falling asleep on the job. In either case, it is entirely possible that the Gloddaeth ghost was his own invention.

We have previously considered talkative ghosts in Chapter Two: 'Unfinished Business', when discussing those wailing spirits who bemoan how long the day and night are while waiting for a particular individual – be that Noe, Noah, Owen, Hwfa, Aron or Arawn. There is another particular type of wailing Welsh ghost which seems even more fantastical, haunting the lakes surrounding Dolgellau in Gwynedd.

The most contemporary accounts recorded in coffee table books on Welsh ghosts, such as *Ghosts & Legends of Wales* by John Attwood Brooks (1987), relate the story of a:

man-shaped monster which drags itself from the water crying 'The hour is come but not the man', and if anyone happens to be near he will be dragged below the surface of the lake and never seen again.

The story is repeatedly found mentioned in relation to the folklore of Llyn Cynwch, the reservoir that provides drinking water to the town of Dolgellau and forms part of the Nannau Estate.

However, this lies in contrast to some of the older sources that record this tale. One early example can be found in the journal *Folk-lore* from 1928, in an article entitled 'Welsh Folklore Items III', as collected by L. Winstanley and H. J. Rose. They note that while staying in Dolgellau, they found 'a pool in the neighbourhood which is said to be haunted; a man comes out of the water and drags people in'.

T. Gwynn Jones in the seminal text, *Welsh Folklore and Folk-Custom* (1930) suggests that the 'pool' was Llyn Cynwch. However, a more bizarre figure may be seen and heard from the nearby Llyn Gwernan. The tale is first recorded (to the best of our knowledge) by the poet and Welsh folk song collector Ceiriog (John Ceiriog Hughes) in his 1863 text, *Y Bardd a'r Cerddor: Gyda Hen Ystraeon am Danynt, Llyfr IV* (The Bard and Musician: With Old Stories About Them, Book IV):

Y mae un chwedl modd bynnag yn gysylltiedig â'r llyn hwn, fel pe bai rhai o rïeni plant y gymydogaeth wedi ei dyfeisio i gadw eu teuluoedd mân rhag perygl boddi.

Dywedir fod nifer o bobl a ddychwelent o ffair Dolgellau wedi gweled dyn mawr, yn rhodio o amgylch y llyn gan floeddio mewn llais cwynfanus

'MAE'R AWR HEB DDYFOD A'R DYN HEB BASIO.'

Dychrynasant a rhedasant adref. Erbyn cyraedd cartref, clywent gan eraill oedd wedi dod yn gynt o'r ffair, fod y dyn rhyfedd hwnw wedi bod yn amgylchu Llyn Gwernen er's amryw oriau. Clywyd ef gyntaf tua deg o'r gloch y nos, a pharhaodd i floeddio:

'Mae'r awr heb ddyfod a'r dyn heb basio,'
tan dri yn y boreu. Dyma'r amser olaf y clywyd ei lais, gan ddynion
ifeinc a ddychwelent i Ddolgellau ar ol bod yn hebrwng eu cariadau
adref.
   Bore tranoeth gwelid ffon ar wyneb y llyn – yna caed cap – ac yna
ddyn dieithr wedi boddi.

There is one legend however associated with this lake, as if in-
vented by some of the parents of local children to keep their little
families from the dangers of drowning.

   It was said by many people returning from Dolgellau fair that
they had seen a large man, striding around the lake while shouting in a plaintive voice

'THE HOUR HAS NOT COME AND THE MAN HAS
NOT PASSED.'

They got scared and ran home. By the time they arrived home,
they heard from others who had returned sooner from the fair,
that the strange man had been circling Llyn Gwernen for several
hours. He was first heard at ten o'clock at night, and continued
shouting:

   '*The hour has not come and the man has not passed,*'

   until three in the morning. That was the last time his voice
was heard, by the young men coming home to Dolgellau having
accompanied their sweethearts home.

   The following morning, a stick was seen on the lake's surface
– and then a cap was found – and then the stranger was found
drowned.

This account is recorded verbatim by William Davies in his 1898 essay,
'Casgliad o Lên-Gwerin Meirion' ('A Collection of Meirion Folklore');
he does not mention this type of apparition in connection with Llyn
Cynwch at all. In fact, it is a tale of the *Tylwyth Teg* (fairies) that Davies
associates with this lake instead.

   It is interesting to note that by the time the tale is recorded by T. Gwynn
Jones, the cry said to be emitted by the lake-dwelling phantom is: 'The
hour is come but not the man', which is replicated in all later retellings of
this tale, and certainly lends a more sinister and threatening tone to the

spirit's message. It is also curious that any mention of Llyn Gwernan is erased from contemporary folklore accounts, despite the original sources suggesting this as the earliest location for the ghoul. Whether the origin of the legend as recorded by Ceiriog is a genuine haunting – or just the tragic demise of a distressed stranger after a day spent at Dolgellau fair – is up to the reader's discretion.

Another fantastical watery apparition can be found in association with Cors Fochno in Ceredigion, one of the largest active raised peat bogs in Britain, which lies along the Dyfi estuary near the village of Borth, and forms part of the Dyfi National Nature Reserve. In *Coelion Cymru* (Welsh Beliefs) (1938), the Reverend Evan Isaac, who lived in nearby Tre Taliesin, paints an image of the bog at the turn of the twentieth century:

> *Ar ei chanol y mae math o ynys led fawr, ac arni rai ffermydd da, a cheir hefyd ambell dŷ annedd, a hen waith mwyn plwm sy'n segur ers ugeiniau o flynyddoedd. Ond y mae'r gweddill o'r gors, a'r rhan fwyaf ohoni, yn siglen ddiwaelod a pheryglus. Tyf arni frwyn cryf a hesg sidanaidd, ac yma a thraw glystyrau o helyg.*

> In the middle of it is a fairly large island, and on it some good farms, and a few dwellings, and the old lead ore works that have been idle for many years. But the rest of the bog, and the greater part of it, is a bottomless and dangerous quagmire. On it grow strong rushes and sedge like satin, and scattered around are clusters of willow.

On the oceanic borders of this bog, the legendary Welsh bard Taliesin Ben Beirdd is said to have been born; his alleged grave – the cairn at Bedd Taliesin – is also not too far away. Here too lurked *Hen Wrach Cors Fochno* (The Old Hag of Cors Fochno), a malevolent spirit who plagued the bog and the people of Llangynfelyn parish, and was much feared in the area during the nineteenth and twentieth centuries.

In *Bro Ddyfi a Machynlleth: Rhamant ei Hanes a'i Llên Gwerin* (Bro Ddyfi and Machynlleth: The Romance of its History and Folklore) (1936), author Oswald Rowlands provides a succinct account of the unusual attributes of this creature:

Y mae llawer o chwedlau am Hen Wrach Cors Fochno. Doi allan o'r gors ar nosau niwlog a mynd i'r tai trwy bob rhwystr a ddyfeisid i'w hatal. Anadlai yn wynebau pobl a pheri afiechydon. Aflonyddwyd arni unwaith a hithau'n swperu ar fwyd llyffant a ffa'r gors. Sïodd fel sarff a diflannu. Yr oedd, meddid, yn saith droedfedd o daldra, yn denau ac yn esgyrnog. Yr oedd ganddi groen melyn a gwallt du fel muchudd yn ymdorchi o'i phen aruthrol hyd ei thraed.

There are many legends about *Hen Wrach Cors Fochno*. She rose out of the swamp on foggy nights and entered houses through every obstacle that was devised to stop her. She breathed in people's faces and caused diseases. She was disturbed once while she was supping on fungus and marsh beans. She hissed like a serpent and disappeared. She was, they say, seven feet tall, and was thin and bony. She had yellow skin and pitch-black hair that curled from her enormous head to her feet.

Isaac notes that he is only aware of one witness to the phantom – a woman called Betsen of Llain Fanadl, a dilapidated cottage on the edge of the bog. One night while returning home from collecting gorse roots for the fire, she spotted the *Hen Wrach* sat on a pile of rushes, describing her as having an enormous head, with pitch-black hair falling thickly down her back and lying in tangles across the floor:

Swpera yr oedd ar ffa'r gors a bwyd llyffaint. Ar ei gwaith yn myned heibio, cyfarchodd Betsen hi â 'Nos da.' Neidiodd y Wrach ar ei thraed – yr oedd yn llawn saith droedfedd o daldra, ac yn denau ac esgyrnog a melyngroen – a throi at Fetsen ac ysgyrnygu arni ddannedd cyn ddued ag afagddu, chwythu i'w hwyneb fel y chwyth sarff, a diflannu yn y gors. Dywedir na fu Betsen byth yr un ar ôl y noson honno.

She was feasting on bogbeans and toadstools. While passing on her rounds, Betsen greeted her with a 'Good night.' The *Gwrach* jumped to her feet – she was a full seven feet tall, and thin and bony and yellow-skinned – and turned to Betsen and snarled at her with teeth as black as hell, blew into her face like a snake, and disappeared into the bog. It was said that Betsen was never the same after that night.

Isaac claims the *Hen Wrach* is unique in Welsh folklore, and that this type of haunting is not found in the rest of the country:

> *Y mae llawer o draddodiadau a choelion Cymru yn gyffredin i'r holl siroedd, ond ni chlywais am draddodiad yr Hen Wrach yn unman ond ym mhlwyf Llancynfelyn.*

There are many traditions and beliefs in Wales that are common to all counties, but I never heard of the tradition of the *Hen Wrach* anywhere else but Llancynfelyn parish.

In fact, many valid parallels can be drawn between the appearance and character of the *Hen Wrach* and that of the infamous Welsh death portent, *gwrach-y-rhibyn*, discussed further in Chapter Ten: 'Death Omens'. This is nowhere more apparent than in the description provided by Myrddin Fardd of the hag-like death omen:

> *Tybir mai yn y niwl tew y preswyliai, ac mai anfynych, os byth, yr oedd yn cael ei gweled, eithr yn cael ei chlywed yn ysgrechian yn uchel, ac yr oedd ei hysgrech bob amser yn cael ei hystyried fel argoel o ryw ddrwg ar ddisgyn i ran y sawl a'i chlywai ... Yr oedd hon yn ofnadwy yr olwg arni – ei breichiau gieulyd, ei hewinedd hirion, ei gwallt attwf, ei danedd duon, a gwelwder marwol ei holl wedd yn ei gwneuthur yn amcan-ddesgrifiad o'i llef hir-llaes, yr hon oedd yn ddigon arswydus i rewi gwythenau pawb a'i clywent.*

It is thought that she dwelt in the thick fog, and that she was rarely, if ever, seen, but was heard screaming loudly, and her scream was always considered an omen of some evil that would befall the person who heard it ... She was monstrous to look upon – her sinewy arms, her long nails, her unkempt hair, her black teeth, and the deathly pallor of her whole countenance was objectively befitting of her lingering wail, which was terrifying enough to freeze the veins of all who heard it.

Similarly, the *Hen Wrach* was also said to conjure a thick, damp fog that would spread through the bog and to the village on dark nights, which she would use to access parishioners' homes to spread her curse. As *gwrach-y-rhibyn* is an omen reported in many regions across Wales, it is entirely possible that she may pre-date the legend of the *Hen Wrach* in Llangynfelyn, with the latter representing the evolution of folklore within the parish to accommodate the changing landscape.

In many ways, the *Hen Wrach* was a stereotypical description of the hag as we know her in folklore – ugly, frightening and malicious – but the element of this story where she causes disease by breathing in people's faces is interesting. It is certainly not a motif limited to Wales, and has also been described as an attribute of evil spirits from Eastern European folklore; the Albanian *Shtriga*, for example, presents as a hag and is said to survive by sucking the life force from its victims, usually children. This causes them to develop immune dysfunction and become ill, contracting conditions such as pneumonia which ultimately lead to death.

While unusual, the clue to the origins of this folkloric entity lies in her name. *Yr Hen Wrach* was the name given to a specific illness in Wales – the ague, a medieval term given to an acute, intermittent fever. The term is now almost exclusively used in association with malaria, which presents similarly. The disease was associated with swampy areas akin to the bog at Cors Fochno, such as in East Anglia where marsh fever was known as Fen Ague. Evan Isaac describes the sickness that plagued his community:

> *Dechreuai mewn teimlad llesg a chlafaidd, tebyg i saldra'r môr, ac yna ceid crynu mawr drwy'r holl gorff a barhâi am awr gron. Unwaith bob pedair awr ar hugain y deuai'r crynu, ac awr yn ddiweddarach bob dydd. Parhâi felly am wyth neu ddeng niwrnod, a phan ballai grym y clefyd, a'r claf wedi troi ar wella, ceid diwrnod rhydd rhwng dau grynu, ac yna ddau ddiwrnod rhydd, ac wedyn dri, a'r dyddiau rhydd yn parhau i gynyddu hyd oni ddiflannai'r cryndod yn llwyr.*

It started with a faint and sickly feeling, akin to seasickness, and then came violent shaking through the entire body that lasted for a whole hour. The shaking came once every twenty-four hours, and would start an hour later each day. It continued like this for eight to ten days, and when the worst of the disease was over, and the patient showed signs of recovery, there would be a day of rest between two of shaking, and then two restful days, and then three, and the period of restful days would lengthen until the shaking disappeared completely.

It is clear that the *Hen Wrach* not only literally means ague, but the imagery also represents a personification of the inhabitants' fears of disease spreading from the bog. A similar example may be found in Victorian London, where a panic over giant pigs living in the sewer systems around Hampstead emerged immediately following an epidemic of typhoid and cholera, spread by dirty water.

Isaac states that the only way to rid the bog of the *Hen Wrach* was through fire:

> *Nid oes a'i dinistria ond tân, a chan y trig mewn cors sy'n siglen ddyfrllyd, nid oes obaith am ei thranc hyd oni ddêl y dilyw tân, a rhaid i hwnnw losgi'n hir i'w llosgi hi.*

> Nothing destroys her but fire, and as she dwells in a bog that is a watery quagmire, there is no hope for her destruction other than the deluge of fire, and that would need to burn for a long time to burn her.

While it is worth noting here that the reverend's 'deluge of fire' may well be interpreted as the biblical end of days, in fact, the burning of Cors Fochno's vegetation was a common agricultural practice that occurred annually to accompany the grazing of cattle – a practice which continued until 1986.

Oswald Rowlands suggested that the *Hen Wrach* disappeared when people switched from peat to coal as fuel, though peat cutting continued on the bog until the 1950s. Isaac confirms this suggestion, stating that the *Hen Wrach* was largely believed to have disappeared at the turn of the twentieth century, but issues a foreboding warning to his readers:

*Deugain mlynadd yn ôl peidiodd y cryd, ac ni flinwyd ganddo neb
o'r pentrefwyr byth wedyn, a chredwyd yn sicr farw o'r Hen Wrach
yng ngaeaf y flwyddyn y diflannodd yr afiechyd. Yn gyfamserol â'i
marw hi bu llawer o gyfnewidiadau ym mwyd yr ardal, ac yn eu
plith roddi heibio losgi mawn, a defnyddio glo yn eu lle. Eithr y mae'r
Hen Wrach yn fyw o hyd. Cysgu y mae yn y gors, a phan dderfydd
glo Morgannwg a Mynwy deffry hithau, a bwrw melltith fel cynt, a
gwelir y pentref yn crynu gan y cryd eto. Cysgu y mae'r Hen Wrach.*

Forty years ago the ague came to an end, and none of the vil-
lagers were troubled by it ever again, and it was believed with
certainty that the *Hen Wrach* had died in the winter of the year in
which the disease disappeared. There were many changes in the
area concurrent with her death, and among them the practice of
burning peat was put aside, and coal used in its stead. However
the *Hen Wrach* yet lives. She sleeps in the bog, and when the coal
of Morgannwg and Monmouthshire is spent, she will awaken,
and cast curses as before, and the village will be shaken by the
ague once more. The *Hen Wrach* sleeps.

Away from the maliciousness of the *Hen Wrach*, at Bryn Bachau farm
in Llanarmon, Gwynedd, we meet a ghost of an altogether different
fantastical nature – one who was punished for being too nice. While
household spirits are often banished because they are considered malevolent, in this case, the family who lived in this particular farmhouse
were troubled by an unusually philanthropic phantom. Myrddin Fardd
recounts how the ghost:

*bob amser a ymddygai yn hynaws, tosturiol a charedig wrth y tlawd.
Pan y delai gardotyn at y drws, pa hwyl bynag fyddai ar deulu y tŷ,
gofalai ef, nid oes achos i ddywedyd ar draul pwy, am daflu iddo
dorth o fara, heb nag edliw na grwgnach dim yn ngwyneb amledd
ymweliadau y cardotwyr, &c.*

always appeared reverent, compassionate and kind to the poor.
When a beggar came to the door, whatever mood the family
of the house were in, he ensured, there is no cause to say at

whose expense, that they were given a loaf of bread, without reproach or grumbling nor complaint regarding the frequency of the beggar's visits, &c.

The living residents of Bryn Bachau gradually became annoyed that the ghost 'took advantage of their labours and property' ('*yr hyfdra a gymmerai efe ar eu llafur a'u heiddo hwy*'), and so slipped away from the house to find someone with the right arcane knowledge to rid them of the spirit. That person was an infamous cunning man known as Sion y Llyfrwr, or 'Sion of the Books' – so called because of his illustrious collection of texts. He subsequently visited the farm and was apparently successful in banishing the ghost 'over the point of Penychain to the sea' ('*dros drwyn Penychain i'r môr*'), where the Hafan y Môr holiday park (formerly Butlins, Pwllheli) now stands.

Another example of an unusual household haunting is one described by Cadrawd and found in both his essay of 1885, 'The Folklore of Glamorgan', and his book, *History of Llangynwyd Parish* (1887). It occurred at the Grade II listed seventeenth-century Gelli-siriol farmhouse, which sits above the river Llynfi in Llangynwyd, Bridgend. At the time of the haunting, it had recently been vacated by the previous owner, Richard Hugh. Cadrawd describes the common room in the farmhouse as having an upper storey and corresponding windows with sills that were too high to be comfortably reached, on which an old straw basket had been left by a former tenant.

One day, a man by the name of Sion Bifan Fawr visited the farm. His name alludes to the fact that Sion was particularly tall and so it was decided to make use of this fact and ask him to retrieve the basket from its ledge. Upon inspection, it was found that the basket contained a quantity of hazelnuts:

> of an excellent quality. No one could tell how long they had been there; and as a superstition prevailed that it was possible to bewitch or charm such products, the family declined to touch them.

There had been a widespread belief around the Llangynwyd area that Gelli-siriol farmhouse was home to a ghost. It was thought that anyone approaching the property at night would be accompanied by a shadowy figure in the form of a man but, after the basket containing the untouched hazelnuts was removed from the property, the ghost was never seen again.

Nuts were used in various ritualistic practices across Wales at one time, with the hazel tree being particularly associated with divination, and so their association with the supernatural is not unprecedented. What is more interesting here are the uncanny properties attributed to such a mundane object by the family, and the tenuous link made by the community between the removal of the basket and the disappearance of the ghost.

Many of the most fantastical accounts of ghosts in Wales arise from the exploits of its various cunning folk and conjurers, no doubt as a marketing ploy – the more extraordinary the vanquished bogey, the more talented the ghost layer. Several such exploits are recorded in Wales in relation to folk magician and alchemist, Huw Llwyd. Born around 1568, Llwyd was also a scholar, soldier, musician and bard who lived in Cynfal Fawr in the parish of Maentwrog, a home which he is thought to have re-built on the site of a previous dwelling, and still stands to this day. The bard Huw Machno wrote the following *cywydd* (a measure of Welsh poetry) circa 1630, describing Llwyd's colourful personal chamber at Cynfal Fawr, which provides an excellent insight into the lifestyle and habits of the conjurer and healer in Wales:

> *Os dyfod i'w ysdafell,*
> *(hon sy waith hardd yn saith well)*
> *i lyfrau ar silffau sydd*
> *deg olwg, gida'i gilydd,*
> *i flychau'n elïau lân*
> *ai gêr feddyg o arian*
> *ai fwcled glân ar wanas,*
> *ai gledd pur o'r gloyw-ddur glas,*
> *ai fwa yw, ni fu i well,*
> *ai gu saethau, ai gawell,*
> *ai wnn hwylus yn hylaw,*
> *ai fflasg, hawdd i caiff i'w law,*
> *ai ffon enwair ffein iown-wych,*
> *ai ffein gorn, ai helffyn gwych,*
> *ai rwydau, pan f'ai'r adeg,*
> *sy gae tynn i bysgod teg,*

ai ddrych oedd wych o ddichell,
a wyl beth oi law o bell,
ar sies ai gwyr, ddifyr ddysg,
a rhwydd loyw dabler hyddysg.
Beth yw'r holl bethau hyn
Mae dialedd am delyn.
Pa blesser rhag trymder trwch?
I ddyn, pa fwy diddanwch.

If entering his room, (it is well-built, seven times better) his books arranged a fair sight, together on shelves, his boxes of pure ointments and his medical instruments made of silver, his clean buckler hanging on a nail, and his pure sword of shining blue steel, and his yew bow, than which there is none better, and his beloved arrows, and his quiver, and his gun conveniently placed, and his flask, close at hand, and his fine and excellent fishing-rod, and his fine horn, and his excellent hunting-staff, and his nets, when the time comes, a tight trap for fine fish, and his telescope splendid its cunning, for seeing distant objects right from his hand, and his chess-set and pieces, a pleasant education, and an expert in backgammon. What are all these things, there is immensity in the harp. What pleasure from its heavy depth? For a man, what other entertainment.

Unsurprisingly, several very well-known legends have circulated in relation to this character – each one as fantastical as the next. This particular tale relates to Huw's encounter with a ghost, and is taken from *Cymru Fu* (The Wales That Was) (1862). This story takes place at a natural outcrop of rock that became known as Pwlpud Huw Llwyd (Huw Llwyd's Pulpit) – a landmark which survives to this day. It is situated amongst the Cynfal waterfalls, and it was here that Llwyd used to come at night to reflect.

This was much to the annoyance of Huw's wife, who fretted over his absence while she lay in bed for hours waiting for his return, invariably 'as cold as a frog' ('*cyn oered a llyffant*'). One night, she hatched a plan to stop his nocturnal excursions, instructing her brother to disguise himself as a ghost in a white sheet, to visit Huw at his stone pulpit and scare him home. The altercation does not seem to have gone as planned:

'Holo! pwy wyt ti?' ebai Huw Llwyd wrth ei ganfod yn nesu ato, 'Ai ysbryd wyt ti? Pa un ai ysbryd da ai ysbryd drwg wyt ti?' Ond ni feddai y ffug-ysbryd air i'w ateb. 'Os ysbryd da wyt ti, ni wnei ddim niwad i mi er mwyn Morgan fy mab; ac os ysbryd drwg wyt ti, ni wneid dithau ddim niwaid i mi, 'does bosibl, a minau yn briod â dy chwaer di.' Yr oedd y dyn yn y gynfas yn dechreu crynu erbyn hyn: 'yr'wan am dani hi, 'r gwyn,' ebai H. Llwyd, 'gwylia di'r Du yna sy'n sefyll wrth dy sodlau di!'

'Hullo! who are you?' asked Huw Llwyd when he noticed the ghost approaching, 'Are you a ghost? Are you a good ghost or a bad ghost?' But the counterfeit ghost had no words with which to answer him. 'If you are a good ghost, you will do me no harm for the sake of my son Morgan; and if you are a bad ghost, you will do me no harm either, surely, what with me being married to your sister.' The man in the white sheet was starting to tremble by now: 'and now for it, white,' exclaimed H. Llwyd, 'watch out for Black who is stood at your heels!'

Huw Llwyd was evidently no fool. His brother-in-law ended up fleeing in fright back to the house, firmly believing that he was being chased by a spirit, while Huw shouted after him, 'There goes Black! There goes White' ('*Hwi, 'r Du! Hwi, 'r Gwyn*'), from his perch.

The white-sheeted ghost, as we have already discussed in the introductory chapter, is not a significant figure in Welsh ghost-lore. However, it was often used as a means of 'playing the ghost', examples of which are not difficult to find in Welsh folklore texts. While there were certainly no written accounts of ghosts in white sheets in Wales during Huw Llwyd's lifetime, the imagery itself was still universally understood, with examples of tricksters in shrouds recorded as far back as the first century CE, in accounts such as *Philopseudes sive Incredulus* by Lucian of Samosata, describing young fellows playing pranks 'in black palls and skull-masks'. We must also remember that this tale was penned 200 years following Llwyd's death, having probably evolved and altered with every retelling, as folk tales are wont to do; while white sheets might not necessarily have featured in the original account, they now form an integral part of this particular legend.

It should also be noted that the use of the racially charged terms 'white' and 'black' to describe good and evil respectively have now rightly fallen out of favour in folklore studies.

William Davies in his essay of 1898 also describes a haunting relating to Huw Llwyd, this time associated with his burial place, which he calls 'Ysbryd Ceunant Cynfal' ('The Ghost of Ceunant Cynfal'). An earlier reference to the same story can be found in Griffith John Williams's book *Hanes Plwyf Ffestiniog o'r Cyfnod Boreuaf* (History of Ffestiniog Parish from the Earliest Period) (1882):

Yr oedd ar lawer o'r hen bobl ofn myned heibio Ceunant Cynfal ym mhell ar ol claddu Huw Llwyd, gan y credent fod yr ysbrydion yn parhau i fynychu y lle, a bu y wlad hyn yn ddiweddar iawn heb ei chwbl glirio oddiwrth yr ofergoelion hyn. Ryw dro oddeutu diwedd y ganrif ddiweddaf, yr oedd Gaynor Morris, merch y Parch. David Morris, M.A., offeiriad Ffestiniog, yr hwn a breswyliai yn Cynfal, wedi myned allan yn y nos. Gan na ddychwelai aed i chwilio am dani. Methwyd a'i chanfod hyd y boreu, pan y cafwyd hi wrth ddrws beudy Tŷ'r Ynys, wedi colli ei synwyrau, a chredai yr hen bobl yn ddiysgog mai yr ysbryd drwg oedd wedi ei llusgo yno.

There were many of the old folk who were scared of passing Ceunant Cynfal long after Huw Llwyd was buried, as they believed that ghosts continued to frequent the place, and the country was not until very recently rid of these superstitions. One time around the end of the last century, Gaynor Morris, the daughter of Rev. David Morris, M.A., the priest of Ffestiniog, who dwelt in Cynfal, had gone out at night. As she had not returned a search was conducted for her. She could not be found until the morning, where she was discovered by the barn door of Tŷ'r Ynys, having lost her senses, and the old folk steadfastly believed that the evil spirit had dragged her there.

The fantastical element in this particular account lies only in the community's willingness to attribute this poor young woman's fate so easily to the acts of an 'evil spirit'.

A further example of the conjurer's ghost-laying skills is found recorded in the manuscripts held at the Nantgarw archives, Amgueddfa Cymru (Museum Wales), entitled *Ysbrydion, Chwedlau a Dipyn o Hiwmor* (Ghosts, Legends and a Little Humour) and collected by Gwilym Vaughan Jones of Pencoed, Bangor. This tale is called 'Yr Ysbryd Drwg' ('The Evil Spirit'), told to the author by Robert Henry Edwards of Llwyngwril, Gwynedd. He tells how over a century ago, an old woman lived in Llanegryn, where a particularly creative spirit was noted to trouble the parish. After a while, its activity became increasingly unbearable, and so the old woman and the son of Rhyd-y-rhiw farm went on horseback to Bala to seek the aid of a cunning man:

> *Daeth y gŵr hysbys gyda hwy yn ôl i Lanegryn. Darganfu fod yr ysbryd drwg yma yn gallu myned i mewn i wahanol greaduriaid, weithiau â i mewn i gi, a thro arall i'r gath. Cafodd hyd i'r ysbryd mewn tŷ. Gorchmynnodd y gŵr hysbys i bawb ddod allan o'r tŷ iddo gael dechrau ar ei waith. Llesteiriwyd ef am fymryn, oherwydd 'roedd y forwyn wedi cuddio yn y llofft. Bu ymladdfa fawr rhwng y gŵr hysbys a'r ysbryd drwg. Yn y diwedd daliwyd yr ysbryd ganddo, a trodd ef yn 'bry glas. Rhoddodd y pry yn ddiogel mewn potel.*

The cunning man came back with them to Llanegryn. He found the evil spirit could enter different animals, sometimes entering a dog, and other times the cat. He found the spirit in a house. The cunning man ordered everyone to leave the house so he could begin his work. He was frustrated for a while, as the maid had hid in the loft. There was a great battle between the cunning man and the evil spirit. In the end the spirit was caught by him, and he turned it into a blue fly. He put the fly safely in a bottle.

The bottle was promptly carried to Pont Dysynni (Dysynni Bridge) and thrown into the river, as was the custom, and an act we have already seen performed in several accounts of ghost-laying throughout this book – even from this very bridge (see Chapter Six: 'Poltergeists').

While ghostly beasts are so numerous in Wales that we have been able to dedicate an entire chapter to them (Chapter Four: 'Spectral Beasts' – including another example from Llanegryn), this is the first time we have encountered a spirit possessing corporeal animals. This is a rare phenomenon which carries biblical connotations, such as in Mark 5:11–13:

> A large herd of pigs was feeding on the nearby hillside. The demons begged Jesus, 'Send us among the pigs; allow us to go into them.' He gave them permission, and the impure spirits came out and went into the pigs. The herd, about two thousand in number, rushed down the steep bank into the lake and were drowned.

While the Church, and in particular, the Protestant churches, often protested that cunning folk worked in league with the Devil, conjurers and folk healers in Wales would have completed their tasks with heavy use of Christian iconography and written words derived from the Bible, as is evidenced through surviving handwritten books of incantations and charms. Whereas the account of an evil spirit possessing animals is therefore fantastical in its own right, it is not otherwise surprising given the particular details of this case.

Incidentally, it is recorded that the butchers of Dinas Mawddwy, Gwynedd, believed that the small puncture marks that could be identified on the inner aspect of a pig's hind legs after removing the hair by scalding indicated where the Devil had entered the swine in the above passage.

The reputation of cunning folk within the community is also exemplified in a story recorded by John Rhosydd Williams in *Hanes Rhosllannerchrugog* (The History of Rhosllannerchrugog) (1945). He tells of a local man who claimed to have been so skilled in the art of summoning and banishing spirits, that he raised too many!

> *Ymddengys fod cymydog wedi ei dramgwyddo, ac ar noson leuad aeth ati o ddifri i dalu'r pwyth yn ôl, drwy godi ysbrydion i daflu cerrig ar dir y cymydog. Ond pan ddaeth y bore, nid oedd arwydd fod dim allan o'r cyffredin wedi digwydd. Fodd bynnag am hynny, mynnai ef iddo godi cymaint ohonynt fel nad oedd digon o waith ar eu cyfer, ac y bu rhaid iddo eu rhannu yn ddwy fintai – rhai i daflu'r cerrig ar y cae, a'r lleill i'w taflu'n ôl i'r afon!*

It seems that a neighbour had offended him, and on a moonlit night he set out in earnest to do him mischief, by summoning spirits to throw stones on to the neighbour's land. But when morning came, there was no sign that anything out of the ordinary had happened. Regardless of this, he maintained that he had summoned so many of them that there was not enough work for them, and he had to divide them into two groups – some to throw the stones onto the field, and the others to throw them back into the river!

The suggestion in this case is that the conjurer was going to render his neighbour's land unfit for cultivating by covering it in stones. There seems to have been little evidence for the veracity of the man's abilities, despite his bold claim that he had been overly effective.

We have seen many other examples of ghosts throwing stones in Chapter Six: 'Poltergeists'; however, the following example is particularly unusual in that the spirit responsible is that of a witch.

Local tradition within the hamlet of Llandecwyn, Gwynedd, tells of how Dorti'r Wrach (Dorti the Witch) was thrown to her death in a cask from the clifftops above the northern shores of Llyn Tecwyn (Tecwyn Lake), and buried on its shore, where she fell. William Davies describes the legend which was ascribed to Dorti's grave:

> *Parha i fod yn ddychryn i blant yr ardal er's cenedlaethau lawer. Ar y bedd y mae nifer o gerig gwynion bychain; a pha blentyn bynag a gymer un o'r ceryg hyn ymaith, cyfyd ysbryd Dorti ato, a theifl ef i'r llyn, ac aiff hithau a'r gareg wen yn ol ar y bedd.*

It has continued to frighten the children of the area for many generations. On the grave there are a number of small white stones; and whichever child takes one of these stones away, the ghost of Dorti will rise to find them, and throw the child into the lake, before taking the white stone back to the grave.

A nonsense rhyme would also have to be recited to keep the *gwrach* at bay:

Dorti, Dorti,
Bara gwyn yn llosgi,
Dŵr ar y tân
I olchi'r llestri.

Dorti, Dorti, white bread burning, water on the fire to wash the dishes.

We have previously discussed how folklore has been used as a way of keeping people away from particular places. In stories such as this one, we can also see an illustration of the lasting belief that communities had in the powers of cunning folk or witches.

We shall conclude this chapter on Wales's fantastical ghouls with an exceptionally unusual excerpt from the biography of the Reverend William Williams of Wern, Llanfrothen, entitled *Cofiant Darluniadol y Parchedig William Williams, o'r Wern: Yn Cynwys Pregethau a Sylwadau o'i Eiddo* (The Pictorial Biography of the Reverend William Williams, of Wern: Including his Comments and Sermons) written by the Reverend David Samuel Jones of Chwilog in 1894. Williams was an Independent minister born in 1781 at Cwm-hyswn-ganol in Llanfachreth, Gwynedd. This account was given to him at Pen-y-stryd chapel in Trawsfynydd:

Traethid wrtho am y lluaws ysbrydion oeddent yn weledig mewn lleoedd neillduol yn yr ardal, i lawr o'r lluaws ysbrydion hyny, y traethai yr henafgwr hygoelus hwnw am danynt, yr hwn a sicrhai ddarfod iddo weled myrdd o ysbrydion duon yn cerdded ymylon cantel llydan ei het, ond heb ei bensyfrdanu ganddynt, hyd at y bwgan sicr a hynod hwnw, a welid yn ymddangos wrth bont y Cilrhyd, ar ffurf dyn heb ben iddo. Nid yw yn gwbl hysbys pa ddyddordeb a gymerodd ein gwrthddrych yn y campau annuwiol y crybwyllwyr am danynt yn flaenorol; ac ni wyddis i ba raddau y credai efe yn modolaeth ac ymddangosiad dychmygol, yr ysbrydion y sonid cymaint wrtho am danynt.

He was told of the numerous ghosts that could be seen in specific places around the area, from those numerous spirits, spoken of by the credulous old fellow, he who swore that he saw a myriad of black ghosts walking along the wide brim of his hat, but was not amazed by them, to that irrefutable and remarkable bogey, whom he saw appearing near Cilrhyd bridge, in the form of a headless man. It is not entirely known how interested our subject already was in the ungodly claims about them made by the storyteller; and it is not known to what degree he believed in the existence and illusory appearance, of the spirits which he was told so much about.

Why the witness would find the sighting of the headless phantom near a bridge 'remarkable' and yet remain unperturbed by his myriad of hat-dancing bogeys is quite the mystery! And yet, therein lies the joy of recounting some of Wales's most fantastical ghouls.

CHAPTER TEN

Death Omens

*

Ac o'r nant acw clywid anamserol sŵn,
Yr heliwr marw fyddai'n galw ar ei gŵn.
Cwn annwn udent yn nyfnderau'r nos
Wrth weld rhyw ffurfiau rhithiol ar y rhos.
Eos Bradwen

And from that brook was heard an untimely roar, the lifeless
huntsman would be calling his pack. The hounds of hell would
howl in the dead of night, seeing some phantom shapes on the
moor.

Venturing back into the more superstitious past, we don't have to look
very hard to find that portents of death are common in cultures across
the world. Ghostly materialisations, strange lights, and the unusual
behaviour of wildlife may all have signified that your time, or that
of someone close to you, was almost up. In an age of rudimentary
medical knowledge where unexpected death was commonplace, it is
easy to see how any sign, however innocuous, might be perceived as
premonitory.

Omens in Wales, as with much of Britain and Ireland, exist in
abundance. From the mundane to the fantastical, numerous folkloric
texts of the seventeenth to the twentieth centuries describe how innumerable natural phenomena could prognosticate everything from
births and marriages, to the weather and the harvest. In particular,
Wales has a certain unique propensity for portents of death. Hearing
a rooster crow at an unusual time, the screech of an owl, the howl of
a dog, or the sounds of a small bell ringing in the ear (a noise now
easily recognisable as tinnitus) would be enough to chill the stoutest
of hearts. To witness the unseasonable blossoming of a fruit tree, a
robin hop over the threshold, or to see a white fox, weasel or crow,

or a murder of crows congregating on a moonlit night were similarly ominous signs. Cynddelw (Robert Ellis) provides such an example in *Manion Hynafiaethol* (Antiquarian Details) (1873):

> *Clywed Ceiliog yn canu gamamser a roddai fraw ym mhob calon ofnus, rhag ofn fod prophwyd y boreu yn rhagfynegu tranc anesgorawl un o'r teulu.*

Hearing a Rooster crow at an unusual time would strike terror into every fearful heart, for fear that the prophet of the morning was predicting the inevitable demise of one of the family.

One could sometimes expect to be told directly by phantom voices of their impending demise, or that of someone in the parish. An early example is provided in the *Iolo MSS* (1848), which describes how a greedy lord heard that a cockerel had crowed three times, and was followed by a phantom voice proclaiming, 'To-night,– this very next night, shall the greatest and richest man in this parish die' ('*Heno nesaf, y nos heno nesaf y bydd marw y gwr mwyaf a chyfoethoccaf yn y Plwyf*'), only to find by morning that the poorest peasant on his land had succumbed to cold and hunger. The lord, as the story goes, in a state of sorrow for his past misdeeds, became a religious and charitable man.

A similar, albeit more sinister, account is also seen in *A Relation of Apparitions of Spirits, in the Principality of Wales* (1780) by the Reverend Edmund Jones, who describes how a supernatural 'cloud' approached John the son of Watkin Elias Jones while ploughing in a field in Mynyddislwyn parish in Monmouthshire, and asked him: 'of which of three diseases, the Feaver, the Dropsy or the Consumption he would chuse to die, for one of them he must chuse in order to his end'.

John chose consumption (tuberculosis), and having fallen asleep in the field, awoke in a state of ill health and died a year later. While there are elements to this tale suggestive of angelic visitation, the reverend believed it to be the spirit of a departed ancestor, proclaiming such a message to be beneath the work of angels.

Death omens were particularly prevalent among those communities whose life expectancy was demonstrably shorter than average. The mining towns and villages of the south Wales valleys serve as one of the most notable examples, with various omens said to have presented before many a disaster. On 17 July 1902, *The Aberystwyth Observer* reported that Glyncorrwg colliery, Cwmafan, was reputedly haunted, with some 300 men refusing to enter the mine on the Monday morning:

> Some of them said they considered the workings in danger of being flooded by water from an abandoned mine adjoining, whilst others say they have seen the figure of a woman waving a lighted lamp in the mine, and have heard screams as from a woman. The men assert that they have heard cries for help and sounds of falls, and seen flashes of light, all of which they say are evil omens.

A dove was also reported to have been sighted hovering above the colliery – an irrefutable omen of disaster. While it is apparent this sighting did not bear fruition in Cwmafan, similar sightings of loitering doves, as well as a litany of other portentous signs, were also reported prior to the Llanbradach and Senghenydd colliery explosions in 1901, and the Morfa colliery disaster in 1890.

A report from 11 December 1895 may be found concerning a later panic among the miners of the Morfa colliery in the *Evening Express* by none other than Morien, a prominent and eccentric journalist for the *Western Mail*, and author of several texts concerning local history and the nineteenth-century neo-Druidic movement in Pontypridd, the contents of which were often prone to a generous degree of artistic licence:

> The story of the fright is briefly as follows:— A short time before the explosion six years ago several workmen declared they had heard strange noises in the workings. It is stated that several men were so frightened by what they had heard that they left of their own accord and went to work in the Rhondda Valley. Among other things then said was that an apparition, dressed in a black oil-cloth suit, had ascended from the shaft by the side of a tram of coal on the cage, and that it had been seen walking across the yard to the place used as a deadhouse after the explosion. One of the officials of the colliery, dressed exactly in the same manner, did as the apparition had done immediately after the disaster had happened. On the present occasion, in addition to finding the

dove as stated on Sunday night, two men declared they heard a few day ago groans issuing from a part of the workings unoccupied. In addition to this, it is stated a heavy door on one of the roadways was seen to open and shut of its own accord, and a canvas door was seen fluttering in a most mysterious fashion. The entire locality is much moved in reference to the affair, and among other things, as indicating the possibility of things supernatural appearing, refer to the witch of Endor raising by the request of King Saul the ghost, of the prophet Samuel. It must be admitted that it seemed that a small minority laughed merrily over the tales told.

Cadrawd in particular collected several ominous accounts from miners within the Llangynwyd area, which he recorded in his 1885 essay, 'The Folklore of Glamorgan', and in *History of Llangynwyd Parish* (1887):

Upwards of twenty years ago a man was employed doing repairs at the bottom of a 'shaft.' Everything was perfectly still, excepting such noise as emanated from his own work. Suddenly he heard the sound of something falling down the shaft, and he stepped aside out of its way. He distinctly heard it strike the bottom with a dull thud, and it sounded to him like the fall of a sack of sawdust, but he could see nothing. He felt greatly surprised, and even frightened, and had not the courage to continue his work. He went up the pit, and meeting some of his fellow-workmen on the landing, told them of the strange circumstances he had heard. They stood wondering around him, and all concluded that he must have heard some ominous sound before a death. They had not long to wait for a verification of their fears, for the very next night, about the same hour, two men were down in the pit doing repairs near to the spot the first man had been at work. They had availed themselves of the swing door, to protect themselves from anything falling down the shaft. All at once they heard a sound as of something coming down, and the next instant it fell upon the door. They at first took it to be a bag of chaff for the horses, but on lifting up their lights they discovered, to their horror, a man's hand forced through the doorway. It

proved to be one of the fellow-workmen, who, having to cross
the shaft in the upper workings, had not observed in the dark
that the bridge over which he would have to pass had been with-
drawn; so the poor fellow perished.

Akin to seeing wraiths of the living, discussed in the introductory
chapter, hearing a death act out before the event was also considered
a portent of doom. These phantom noises were commonly reported
phenomena across Wales, and are often referred to within several folklore and parish history texts as the *tolaeth* – a term which is discussed
later in the chapter. A further example is provided by Daniel Silvan
Evans and Ivon in *Ysten Sioned* (Sioned's Pitcher) (first published in
1882), far from the perils of the mines, in the slightly less treacherous
surroundings of Aberystwyth High Street:

> *Amryw flynyddoedd yn ol daethai un o Weinidogion enwog o Sir
> Gaernarfon, a chydag ef flaenor parchus ac adnabyddus iawn i
> lawer drwy Gymru yr amser hwnw, i Gymdeithasfa y Methodistiaid
> Calfinaidd, a gynnelid yn Aberystwyth; a rhoddent i fyny gyda'r
> diweddar Robert Davies, Masnachydd, yn yr Heol Fawr, tŷ yr hwn
> oedd yn llawn o ddiethriaid, fel llawer o dai ereill yn y dref, yn
> amser y Gymmanfa; a chan fod mwy o helaethrwydd yng nghalon
> y gwr da hwnw nag oedd yn ei dŷ, talai am welyau i amryw mewn
> tai oedd yn derbyn diethriaid.*
>
> *Y tro hwn cymmerodd wely i'r ddau wr y sonir am danynt uchod
> gyda Mrs. Lewis, yn y Coburg House, ar y Terrace; mae tŷ hwnw
> yn bresennol yn rhan o'r Belle Vue Hotel. Ar ol swpera yn nhŷ Mr.
> Davies, hebryngwyd hwynt i lawr i'w lletty; aethant i'r gwely; ond
> cyn hir clywent lawer o symmudiadau yn yr ystafell nesaf, a dawnsio,
> yng nghyd ag offerynau cerdd yn lleisio, fel nad oedd yn ddichonadwy
> iddyn gysgu; ac yn ddisymmwth clywent ryw beth trwm yn cwympo
> ar y llawr; a dyna y dawnsio a'r beroriaeth ar ben; a rhai yn rhedeg
> i fyny ac i lawr y grisiau, a phob peth yn profi fod rhyw beth pwysig
> wedi cymmeryd lle; a chyn hir wele ddrws eu hystafell hwythau
> yn agor, fel pe buasai llawer o ddynion yn dyfod i mewn yn dwyn
> rhywbeth a'i ddodi ar y bwrdd. Ac yn y man aeth y cwbwl yn hollol
> ddistaw. Yr oedd y ddau wr dieithr wedi dychrynu yn anarferol, ac*

ni chysgasant drwy y nos. Drannoeth adroddasant yr holl helynt wrth
Mr. Davies; nis gallent ddyfalu beth oedd yn bod.

Yr wythnos ganlynol, ar ol iddynt ddychwelyd adref, derbyniasant
lythyr oddi wrth Mr. Davies yn eu hyspysu am y peth a ddygwyddasai
'neithwyr' yn y Coburg House; sef bod teulu o Saeson wedi cymmeryd
yr ystafelloedd hyny gan Mrs. Lewis, a'u bod wedi cadw dawnsfa
neu gorelwest yno y nos o'r blaen, ac ar ganol y dawnsio, syrthiodd
boneddiges ieuanc i lawr yn farw ar ganol yr ystafell. Defnyddiwyd
pob moddion er ei hadferyd, ond yr oedd y 'wreichionen fywiol' wedi
dianc; a rhoddwyd hi 'heibio' ar fwrdd yn yr ystafell lle y gorphwysai
y ddau wr o Sir Gaernarfon yr wythnos o'r blaen!

Several years ago one of the famous Ministers from Caernarfon
County, and with him a respected elder well known to many
throughout Wales at that time, came to the Assembly of the
Calvinistic Methodists, which was held in Aberystwyth; and they
stayed with the late Robert Davies, Merchant, in the High Street,
a house which was full of strangers, like many other houses in the
town, at the time of the Assembly; and since there was more abundance in the heart of that good man than there was in his house,
he paid for beds for several in houses that received strangers.

This time he took a bed for the two men mentioned above with
Mrs. Lewis, at the Coburg House, on the Terrace; that house is
now part of the Belle Vue Hotel. After dinner at the home of Mr.
Davies, they were escorted down to their accommodation; they
went to bed; but before long they heard many movements in
the next room, and dancing, together with musical instruments
sounding, so that it was not possible to sleep; and suddenly they
heard something heavy falling on the floor; which brought an
end to the dancing and music; and some began running up and
down the stairs, everything proving that something important
has taken place; and before long the door of their room also
opened, as if many men were coming in bringing something and
putting it on the table. And then everything went completely
silent. The two strangers were terribly frightened, and they did
not sleep all night. The next day they reported everything to Mr.
Davies; they could not imagine what was going on.

The following week, after they returned home, they received a letter from Mr. Davies informing them about the thing that had happened 'last night' at the Coburg House; namely that an English family had taken those rooms from Mrs. Lewis, and that they had held a dance or a ball there the night before, and in the middle of the dancing, a young lady fell down dead in the middle of the room. All means were used for her recovery, but the 'living spark' had escaped; and she was 'laid out' on a table in the room where the two men from Caernarfon County rested the week before!

Ghostly bangs and shuffles are perhaps the least strange of Wales's numerous phantasmal portents. Below, we have included examples of the country's most unique and distinctive omens of death.

Cannwyll Gorff

Of all the phantasmal death omens, the *cannwyll gorff* (corpse candle) is arguably the most universally recognised and well established across Wales. While this motif is also recorded throughout the British Isles, the earliest written record of the apparition arises in Wales in 1656. In a letter dated 14 February, and later published in Richard Baxter's *The Certainty of the World of Spirits* (1691), John Lewis, Justice of the Peace from Glascrug in Llanbadarn Fawr, Ceredigion, proclaims that 'all the parts I know of *Wales*, as our Neighbouring Counties (as I hear) have Experience of them'.

The *cannwyll gorff* was a supernatural light or flame which foretold the death of an individual, whose identity might be surmised by the flame's appearance. These lights were more frequently mobile, and under these conditions were usually related to corpse roads – the tracks traditionally used to transport a coffin to a church or other burial place for internment. The manuscripts of Ieuan Buallt, held at the Nantgarw archives, Amgueddfa Cymru (Museum Wales), describe how in Llanwrtyd, Powys: 'It is an old saying that every man carries his own corpse candle towards the cemetery' ('*Y mae yn hen ddywediad fod pob dyn yn cario ei gannwyll gorff ei hun tua'r fynwent*').

The earliest account from John Lewis recalls how:

two Candles were seen, one little, and a great one passing the Church way, under my House, my Wife was then great with

Child, and near her time, and she feared of it, and it begot some fear in us about her; but just about a week after, her self first came to me (as something joyed that the fear might be over) and said (as true it was) an old Man, and a Child of the Neighbour-hood passed that same way to be Buried.

In a later letter, dated 20 October 1656, Lewis also refers to the *cannwyll gorff* as 'Dead Mens Candles':

This is ordinary in most of our Counties, that I never scarce heard of any sort, Young or Old, but this is seen before Death, and often observed to part from the very Bodies of the persons all along the way to the place of Burial, and infallibly Death will ensue.

Similarly, William Williams of Llandygái in *Observations on the Snowdon Mountains* (1802), refers to the apparition in north Wales as 'corpse-tapers gliding along as harbingers of death'. The image of a spectral taper would perhaps be more recognisable among the lower classes, who would have been reliant on inexpensive rushlight tapers to light their homes.

Richard Baxter also includes a letter dated 19 March 1656 by John Davies from Genau'r Glyn, Ceredigion, who further confirms the probable Welsh origins of the *cannwyll gorff*, stating there was no record of 'those fiery Apparitions' outside Wales at that time – an account which was later reprinted by the antiquarian, John Aubrey, in his seminal book, *Miscellanies*, in 1696.

Myrddin Fardd, in *Llên Gwerin Sir Gaernarfon* (The Folklore of Caer-narfonshire) (1908), noted that while there was some disagreement over the period of time between sighting a *cannwyll gorff* and the subsequent death, it was generally accepted that the end would come within the year. However, the meanings attributed to the size of the candle and the colour of its flame were more generally agreed upon:

nid oedd un gwahaniaeth yn nghylch fod lliw a maintioli y Ganwyll bob amser yn dynodi oedran a rhyw y sawl yr argoelid ei ddiwedd. Lliw coch fyddai i fflam y ganwyll a ragflaenai angladd mab, a lliw llwyd-oleu i'r un a ragflaenai angladd merch; a chanwyll fawr o flaen person mewn cyflawn faint, ac un fechan o flaen plentyn, ac

*yn gwahaniaethu yn gymmesur i wahaniaeth oed a maint plentyn
bychan a pherson llawn twf Byddai y dyn a dorid i lawr yn llawn
nerth ei yni, yn cael ei ragflanu gan fflam anferth a disglaer; a hen
wr neu hen wraig, wedi hir ddihoeni gan afiechyd a henaint, yn cael
argoel o'u diwedd gan oleuni salw a gwelw, ond o faintioli cyffredin.*

there was no variation in that the colour and size of the Candle
always indicated the age and gender of the person whose end
was predicted. Red would be the colour of the candle flame that
preceded a boy's funeral, and a light grey colour for the one that
preceded a girl's funeral; and a large candle in front of a person of
full size, and a small one in front of a child, and differing propor-
tionately to the difference in age and size of a small child and a
fully-grown person. The man who was cut down in the prime of
his life, would be preceded by a huge and bright flame; and an old
man or an old woman, long ravaged by disease and old age, were
portended their end by a sickly and pale light, but of ordinary size.

Over a century after the *cannwyll gorff* made its debut in Richard Baxter's
volume, the Reverend Edmund Jones wrote of the omen's supposed
origins:

The prevailing opinion is, that it is an effect of St David's Prayer;
some will say of some other Bishop; but the more intelligent
think it of St David, and none indeed so likely as St David ...
Being a very Spiritual man, and living much under a sense of
eternity, after this short life, as all very Spiritual men do, and
observing that the people in general were careless of the life to
come, and could not be brought to mind it, and make a prepa-
ration for it, tho' he laboured much to bring them to it, prayed
God to give a sign of the immortallity [*sic*] of the foul, and of a
life to come, a presage of death and a motive to prepare for it;
and that God in answer to his prayer sent the Corpse-Candles,
and likely the *Kyhirraeth* to answer the same pious end.

We shall learn of the *kyhirraeth* – or *cyhyraeth* – later in this chapter.

Given that this origin story is notably absent from the letters sent to Baxter in 1656, and in view of the Reverend Jones's proclivity to ground supernatural events in Christian doctrine, it would seem reasonable to assume a degree of folkloric licence here. Regardless, it is this origin story that has prevailed within Welsh folklore to this day, retold with little variation from the original in 1780.

Tudur Clwyd, writing in *Ofergoelion yr Hen Gymry: Mewn Pymtheg Dosparth* (The Superstitions of the Old Welsh: In Fifteen Categories) some time at the turn of the twentieth century, also made a link between the *cannwyll gorff* and Christianity:

> *Ond os oedd rhywbeth heblaw achosion anianyddol iddi, credwn iddi ddyfod fel coel o ganol coelion ereill y Babaeth yn y canol oesoedd yn nghylch canwyllau, y rhai a oleuid ar yr allorau ddydd a nos, ac a oleuid hefyd yn ngwylnosau y meirw: yr ymgais egniol i oleuo rhyngddynt â'r byd anweledig.*

> But if there was something other than natural causes behind it, we believe that it came as a belief amongst all the other beliefs of the Papacy in the middle ages relating to candles, which were lit on the altars day and night, and were also lit in the vigils of the dead: the vigorous attempt to light the invisible world between them.

Similarly in *History of Pontypridd and Rhondda Valleys* (1903), Morien records the memories of an old lady named Shan Yniscrug when she was a maid in the Rhondda Valley. She told how funerals would stop to rest at 'Aber'orchwy Bridge' (Treorchy):

> There in the dark nights, I have seen Corpse Candles congregated. Near the bridge was a stable, and I have known the servant man, on visiting the stable, requiring no other light to enable him to see objects inside, than the light from those Corpse Candles.

In this case, and despite his Druidic leanings, Morien stands in agreement with Edmund Jones, clear in his personal view that the *cannwyll gorff* is a Christian superstition:

Down to the Protestant Reformation in Britain (1535) the Roman Catholic clergy were fond of object lessons in Divine Service. On a funeral reaching the Lychgate, bordering on the churchyard, the clergy would pass out of the church to meet the coffin under the roof of the Lychgate. In their midst was carried a lighted candle, to represent the soul of the corpse in the coffin. Then in the return journey into the church, the candle was carried in front of the coffin into the building. It appears the ceremony was based on the following verse: 'He was a burning and shining light' – (candle in the Welsh version) – St. John, v, 35. 'Efe oedd ganwyll yn llosgi ac yn goleuo.'

As is often the case with ghosts, the *cannwyll gorff* was said to be visible only to a select few. In Talacharn (Laugharne), Carmarthenshire, for instance: 'The belief in "Funeral Lights" was very strong up to a few years ago, but it was acknowledged that this gift or power – of seeing lights – was held by few.'

In Brynaman village, which sits on Y Mynydd Du (the Black Mountain) range on the Carmarthenshire border, Dafydd Williams of Cwmgarw, fondly referred to as 'Newyrth' ('Uncle') Dafydd, was noted to be such a man by Enoch Rees in *Hanes Brynamman a'r Cylchoedd* (The History of Brynamman and the District) (1896):

> *Yr oedd wedi gweled canwyllau cyrff yn ddi-rif, a drychiolaethau, ac ysbrydion, ac yr oedd yn gyfarwydd a'r tylwyth teg, a bendith y mamau, ac yr oedd yn gallu rhoi darluniau o'r pethau dyeithr hyn gyda'r fath arddeliad, nes peri i ni 'ofni a chrynu' wrth ei wrando, ac yr oedd eu darluniau mor fyw nes y gwelem y canwyllau, ac y clywem y cyhirathod wrth fyned gartref o Gwmgarw, a byddem yn cadw look out dros ein hysgwydd rhag i'r ysbrydion ein cipio i'r lleoedd y clywsom mor rhagorol am danynt.*

He had seen countless corpse candles, and apparitions, and spir-its, and he was familiar with the fairies, and the *bendith y mamau* [blessing of the mothers], and he was able to create images of these strange things with such conviction, that he made us 'fear and tremble' when we listened to him, and his imagery was so vivid that we saw the candles, and we heard the *cyhirathod* when going home from Cwmgarw, and we would keep a look out over our shoulder lest the spirits took us to the places we heard so excellently about.

Cadrawd remarks upon another attribute of the *cannwyll gorff*, which seems to go unmentioned in other texts: 'In some instances, where two persons were together, one only saw the corpse candle passing: if that one would but place his hand on the other's shoulder, he also was made to see it.'

On some occasions a *cannwyll gorff* did not appear as an isolated light, but rather was seen being carried by the apparition of a recently buried person, or by a spectral skull, the latter having been recorded by the Reverend Edmund Jones. Llyfrbryf claimed in *Cymru Fu* (The Wales That Was) (1862) that the candles were never seen in stormy weather, but were witnessed 'as often as flies in July evenings' ('*mor aml a gwybed min nos yn Ngorphenaf*'). Sometimes the light was seen about a person's body before death, as in Carmarthenshire, where a small light was witnessed coming 'out of the servant's nostrils, which soon became a Corpse-Candle', again recorded by Edmund Jones in 1780. Cadrawd similarly observed that the flame of a *cannwyll gorff* might be seen emanating from the mouth of a person who was close to death, and Wirt Sikes in *British Goblins* (1880) recorded that staff in a London hospital reported seeing a blue flame in the mouth of a person who was about to pass away. Sikes postulated this was the result of spontaneous ignition of hydrogen from the decomposing body.

A more unusual manifestation is recorded by Tudur Clwyd:

Pan yr odd hon yn myned i lawr i afon yn ganwyll, ac yn dyfod i fyny yn hwch a pherchyll yr ochr arall, yr oedd yn bryd synn! Gwibiai hon yn y nos o fan i fan: weithiau cludid hi, bryd arall, meddir, gwibiai o honi ei hun ... Oni chiliai dynion o'i ffordd, y mae engreiphtiau am rai a darawyd i lawr gan ei grym; a haerir mewn rhai engreiphtiau iddi daflu gwŷr oddiar eu ceffylau.

When this one went down to the river as a candle, and came up as a sow and piglets on the other side, it was a surprising sight!

It would dart from place to place at night: sometimes it was carried, other times, it is said, it would roam by itself … There are examples of some men who did not get out of its way, and were struck down by its power; and it is claimed in some examples that it threw men from their horses.

He notes instances where the light would materially, and sometimes violently, affect those who stood in its way (both on land and in the water) including the overturning of a stagecoach and a coracle.

The mention of the candle transforming into a sow and piglets is certainly curious. While we have already discussed the appearance of ghostly pigs elsewhere in this book (Chapter Four: 'Spectral Beasts'), phantom animals are not usually linked with the *cannwyll gorff*. It is worth noting that pigs were frequently associated with the supernatural in Wales, even within the earliest prose texts, appearing repeatedly throughout the *Mabinogion*. There can be few Welsh people who would not recall the story of *Culhwch ac Olwen* and its antagonist, *Y Twrch Trwyth*, the enchanted boar from whose bristles the young squire Culhwch has to retrieve a magical comb and razor. By doing so, he will impress the giant Ysbaddaden Bencawr, father of Olwen, the girl with whom he is in love.

Belief in the appearance of the *cannwyll gorff* was sufficiently strong that when mysterious lights were sighted, it was often all too easy to jump to the wrong conclusion. An example is recorded by Thomas Morgan in *Hanes Tonyrefail: Adgofion Am y Lle a'r Hen Bobl* (The History of Tonyrefail: Memories of the Place and the Old People) (1899):

> *Yr wyf yn cofio yn dda fy mod yn sefyll ar Dwyn y Ton ar noswaith dywyll, ac amryw o'r gwehyddion gyda mi. Dyna Dic yn tynu ein sylw at ganwyll gorff yn dod oddiwrth Groesol Tynybryn tua'r Waunrhydd. Yr oedd Dic yn sicrhau mai arwydd fod angladd i ddyfod y ffordd hono yn sydyn ydoedd. Ond dygwyddodd i Hopkin Morgan chwerthin cyn i Dic ddybenu. Digiodd drwyddo, a dywedodd nad oeddyn hwy, y Sosiniaid, a thylwyth Rees Evans, ddim yn credu mewn Duw na diawl, ond eu hunain. Ac yn y cythrwfl, fe ddiffoddodd y ganwyll. A wyddoch chi pwy oedd y ganwyll? Dim ond Abram Lloyd o Gelli'rhaidd, yn dyfod at Bili Dafydd, y Bwtsiwr, a defaid mewn panierau, a chanwyll a 'lantern' i'w oleuo.*

I remember well that I was standing on Twyn y Ton on a dark evening, and several of the weavers were with me. Dic drew our attention to a corpse candle coming from Croesol Tynybryn towards Waunrhydd. Dic assured us that it was a sign that a funeral would be coming that way soon. But Hopkin Morgan happened to laugh before Dic finished. He was consumed with anger, and said that they, the Unitarians, and the family of Rees Evans, did not believe in God or devil, only themselves. And in the turmoil, the candle went out. Do you know who the candle was? None other than Abram Lloyd from Gelli'rhaidd, coming to visit Bili Dafydd, the Butcher, with sheep in panniers, and a candle and 'lantern' to light the way.

It is tempting to consider, in light of all of the descriptions that we have just examined, that the *cannwyll gorff* is a variation on the more widely recognised folklore pertaining to the 'will-o'-the-wisp', known as *tân ellyll*, *mall-dân* or *hudlewyn* in Welsh – ethereal lights seen floating over boggy ground or marshy areas. These lights were said to lead travellers to either doom or safety depending on the story, as discussed in Chapter Eight: 'Water Spirits'. It must be understood that these two are, in fact, quite distinct. Even by the end of the nineteenth century, the will-o'-the-wisp was generally accepted to be a natural phenomenon, caused by the spontaneous ignition of gases from underground, whereas the *cannwyll gorff* continued to be regarded as supernatural.

Y Toili

Proclaimed by Peter Roberts in *Hynafion Cymreig* (Welsh Antiquities) (1823) as being 'the most dangerous thing for a man to meet of all types of apparitions' ('*y peth mwyaf peryglus i ddyn gyfarfod âg ef o bob math o'r drychiolaethau*'), the *toili*, or phantom funeral, also represents a significant phantasmal omen within Welsh folkloric tradition. The phenomenon is less commonly referred to as a *tolaeth*, which we have already encountered, and occasionally, would also be termed a *drychiolaeth* in parts of Powys, and a *cyhyraeth* in parts of Caernarfonshire (usually considered a separate entity which we discuss later in the chapter).

To the best of our knowledge, the oldest surviving text to describe this apparition is *A Geographical, Historical, and Religious Account of the*

Parish of Aberystruth in the County of Monmouth (1779) by the Reverend
Edmund Jones (there are no known surviving copies of his first volume
of Welsh spirits from 1767). He describes it as an omen enacted by the
Tylwyth Teg (fairies), which the reverend believed to be 'Spirits of Evil'
who 'infallibly foreknew the time of Men's death'.

The term *toili* is considered a vernacular corruption of *teulu* (family) –
a word which, depending on the region, was sometimes used interchangeably with *toili* to describe these omens. This etymology may explain
its early association with the *Tylwyth Teg*, as *tylwyth* is also synonymous
with 'family'. It is an omen deeply rooted in Welsh folklore although,
much like the *cannwyll gorff*, numerous accounts are recorded across the
British Isles, most notably in Ireland and Scotland.

The Welsh clergyman and scholar Daniel Silvan Evans, writing in
Ysten Sioned, lamented the dwindling sightings of the *toili*, and provided a very useful introduction to the apparition as it was regarded a
century after Edmund Jones's initial description:

> *Y mae y toeli bob amser, pan y dygwyddo, yn myned o flaen mar-*
> *wolaeth mewn rhyw deulu neu gilydd. Cychwyn y ddrychiolaeth allan*
> *o'r tŷ yr â'r corff marw o hono, ar hyd y ffordd angladd tua'r eglwys, aiff*
> *i mewn i'r adail gyssegredig honno, ac wedi aros amser cymmesur yno,*
> *daw allan drachefn at y bedd; ac wedi darfod y claddu, ymwasgara y*
> *dyrfa ledrithiol, a derfydd am y toeli hwnw. Mewn gair, y mae'r toeli*
> *yn gyffelyb ym mhob dim i'r angladd gwirioneddol, ond yn unig nad*
> *oes gan y gwyddfodolion toeïlawl gnawd ac esgyrn, nac, hyd y gwyddys,*
> *un sylwedd arall. Nid oes, fel yr ymddengys, un amser pennodol i doeli*
> *gychwyn o'r tŷ y bydd marwolaeth i ddygwydd ynddo, ac wrth bob*
> *tebygolrwydd y mae cryn ryddid wedi ei roddi iddo o ran yr amser.*
> *Gall y farwolaeth a ragarwyddir ganddo ddygwydd yn ebrwydd iawn;*
> *ond nid oes rhaid iddi ddamweinio am rai wythnosau; eto bernir nad*
> *oes un toeli uniongred i'w ganfod am fwy na rhyw fis o amser cyn y*
> *gwelir angladd yn teithio ar hyd yr un ffordd.*

The *toeli* always, when it happens, precedes death in one family or
another. The apparition starts out of the house which is home to the
dead body, along the funeral road towards the church, it goes into
that sacred building, and after staying a proportionate time there,

it comes out again to the grave; and when the burial is over, the illusory crowd disperse, and that *toeli* comes to a close. In a word, the *toeli* is similar in all respects to the actual funeral, but only that the presences of the *toeli* do not have flesh and bones, or, as far as is known, any other substance. There is, as it seems, no specific time on which a *toeli* proceeds from the house in which death will occur, and in all probability it has been given considerable freedom in terms of the time. The death it foretells can happen immediately; but the incident need not occur for a few weeks; yet it is believed that a *toeli* is not usually seen for more than a month's time before a funeral is seen travelling along the same road.

By the nineteenth century, the role of the *Tylwyth Teg* had clearly diminished, and the funeral was largely regarded as a ghostly procession, as described in the manuscripts of Ieuan Buallt of Llanwrtyd.

> *Dywedir fod rhai personau yn cael gweledigaeth mor eglur ar y drych-iolaeth rhyfedd hyn, fel y gwelent yr holl ddynion, yr arch ar yr elor, y pedwar dyn oddi tani, y bobl ar geffylau, a'r cerbydau, oll yn cydsymud yn union fel y gynhebrwng wironeddol!*

It was said that some people would experience such a clear vision of this strange apparition, that they saw all the men, the coffin on the bier, the four men underneath it, the people on horseback, and the carriages, all moving together exactly like the real funeral procession!

Even so, some later accounts continued to contain subtle elements which one might associate with the *Tylwyth Teg*. Daniel Silvan Evans recorded such an example from Moeddyn, Ceredigion, where a husband and wife, while out binding corn in their field one evening, witnessed a large crowd heading towards the nearby village:

> *Clywai y ddau rwymydd y siarad a'r sibrwd, y trwst a'r berw, fel pe buasai yno gynnifer o bobl yn myned heibio mewn gwirionedd, ond ni deallent gymmaint a gair a leferid gan neb. Clywent drwst a hustyng y dyrfa yn myned heibio, ond ni ddeallent yr un sill, ac nid adwaenent un wyneb.*

The two binders of corn heard the talking and the whispering, the noise and hubbub, as if there were actually a number of people passing by, but they did not understand so much as a word that was spoken by anyone. They heard the noise and clamour of the passing crowd, but they didn't understand a single syllable, and they didn't recognise a single face.

Accounts of the strange language of the *Tylwyth Teg* are far from unprecedented within Welsh folklore, having been documented as early as the twelfth century by Giraldus Cambrensis.

A similar account suggestive of fairy involvement is found in a handwritten book of ghost stories collected and edited by Adran Penmorfa, Cylch Aberteifi (Penmorfa Ward, Cardigan Group) for the 1932 Urdd Eisteddfod, entitled 'Bwci a Thoili'. The account relays the experience of the author's father one unfortunate night while on his way home:

> *Yn awr, yr hyn oedd waethaf ganddo oedd myned heibio'r fynwent a oedd ynghanol y pentref. Ffrwynwyd y golau ymhob ty, a theimlai fel yr unig berson byw yn y lle. Pan oedd gyferbyn a chlwyd y fynwent yn sydyn odiaeth daliwyd ef yn dyn, a chlywai swn yn dod o'r fynwent fel myrdd aneirif yn pesychi'n ddibaid. Ymdrechai a'i holl egni i ryddhau ei hun, ond methai. Yna ni wyddai ddim pellach nes oedd wedi gadael y pentref ymhell ar ol. Nid oedd ganddo un cyfrif sut y daeth y rhan arall o'r ffordd, hyd nes oedd gerllaw ei gartref.*

Now, what he disliked most was to go past the cemetery which was in the middle of the village. The lights were snuffed out in every house, and he felt like the only living person there. When he was opposite the cemetery gate he was very suddenly held tightly, and could hear a sound coming from the cemetery like an innumerable horde coughing endlessly. He tried with all his might to free himself, but failed. Then he knew no more until he had left the village far behind him. He had no recollection of how he came the rest of the way, until he was near his home.

This account reads similarly to many tales of poor unfortunates who lose their bearings, or lose track of time, in the presence of fairies.

Unusually, the *toili* could appear at any time and not just under the cover of darkness. The Reverend William Thomas, in *Hynafiaethau yr Hendygwyn-Ar-Daf* (Antiquities of Whitland) (1868) recounts how the *toili* was seen in association with David Morgan, owner of Y Fforge ironworks, whose family we have already met in Chapter Six: 'Poltergeists': 'There is one very remarkable thing about his funeral. The crowd was seen in broad daylight by a person from the neighbourhood before the incident took place' ('*Y mae un peth yn hynod iawn yng nglyn a'i angladd. Gwelwyd y dorf liw dydd goleu gan berson o'r gymydogaeth cyn i'r amgylchiad gymeryd lle*').

In this case, the observer relayed the tale to Morgan, describing all of the local people whom he had seen in the cortege. When Morgan asked if his own apparition had been seen in attendance, the witness replied that he had not been present. Morgan immediately understood that his own funeral had been witnessed and, true enough, it was not long until events played out exactly as foreseen.

Accompanying auditory phenomena were frequently reported, as exemplified by an account recorded by Cadrawd, whose witness stated:

> When I arrived near to Pontrhydycyff, on a cross-road that led to the main highway, my horses suddenly halted, and, looking before me through the darkness to discover the cause, I thought I could see a great crowd of people coming out of the cross-road into the main, on which I was proceeding. It was too dark to see anything very distinctly, or to recognise features; but I could plainly distinguish the footsteps and bustle of a moving crowd. After a time, something resembling a coffin borne on men's shoulders passed by, followed by a number of horses and horsemen, amongst them being prominently a white horse. After they had passed on, I followed them slowly, and could distinguish the sounds of movements in front of me.

The witness continues to report that a few weeks after his encounter, an old neighbour died, and his funeral procession, complete with a mourner on a white horse, was noted to have taken the same route.

Sometimes, the auditory echoes of a funeral procession were experienced in isolation, without accompanying visual phenomena. In *Hanes a Hynafiaethau Llansamlet* (History and Antiquities of Llansamlet) (1908), the Reverend William Samlet Williams recounts how some members of the community reported hearing:

> *penill neillduol yn cael ei ganu cyn cyfarfod gweddi wylnos yn cael ei roddi allan gan hwn a hwn, sydd heddyw yn fyw, a llais y canwr yn eglur. Hysbyswyd hyn gan y claf cyn ei farw, ac felly y bu, canys daliwyd sylw ar hyn yn yr wylnos. Clywyd llais pregethwr cyn i angladd gymeryd lle, yn rhoddi penill allan, ger y tŷ, ac ar y ffordd. Daliwyd sylw, ac felly y bu.*

a particular verse being sung before a *gwylnos* [vigil] prayer meeting being conducted by such and such, who is alive today, with the singer's voice being clear. This was declared by the patient before he died, and so it was, because attention was paid to this in the *gwylnos*. A preacher's voice was heard before a funeral took place, reciting a verse, near the house, and on the road. This was noted, and so it was.

While the *toili* might serve as a useful harbinger for those who might wish to consider getting their papers in order, so too could these phantom sounds act as an early warning for some of the local craftsmen, as per the following example from Llanegryn, Gwynedd:

> *Gwyddai Thomas Thomas, y saer, noson ymlaen llaw bob amser ei fod i wneuthur ysgrîn (arch) i ryw druan neu'i gilydd drannoeth. Clywai sŵn llifio, plaenio, a morthwylio yn ei weithdy yn ystod y nos bob amser yn rheolaidd cyn gwneuthur ysgrîn.*

Thomas Thomas, the carpenter, always knew the night before that he was to make a coffin for some poor fellow the following day. He would hear the sound of sawing, planing, and hammering in his workshop, always during the night before he was due to make a coffin.

As we've seen already, this particular type of auditory omen is generally known as a *tolaeth*, a term which, while sometimes used interchangeably with *toili*, usually describes 'death rapping or knocking', and can sometimes relate to the sounds of a phantom corpse, furniture or coffin being moved, mirroring the sounds of the preparations to come. The Reverend Elias Owen notes the phenomenon in his 1887 collection of north Walian lore: 'The death rappings are said to be heard in carpenter's workshops, and that they resembled the noise made by a carpenter when engaged in coffin-making.'

Sometimes, only the pushing and shoving of a ghostly procession was reported, without any auditory or visual components. Cadrawd writes of how two miners returning home late one evening down a steep and narrow path:

> found themselves struggling with what seemed to be a crowd of people, and they found it impossible to keep their footing on the steep path, and were pushed on either hand against the furze and underwood. They did not recover a proper footing until they got to the bottom of the steep. They could distinctly realize the bustle of the crowd that they seemed to be amongst. They could see nothing, and yet they were crushed, and even trampled upon. Alarmed beyond measure, they were glad to get away from the spot where they had been subjected to such remarkable experiences. The next day a man was killed at the level, and all the workmen came out to assist in carrying the body to its home over the identical path down to the road. The two friends found in this circumstance ample explanation of the difficulties they had suffered from on the previous night.

In this vein, Cadrawd also reports how elderly folk, while walking the roads after dark, were in the habit of keeping to the very edge of the path to avoid coming into contact with 'a bier conveying a phantom corpse'.

In *Hanes Plwyfi Llangeler a Phenboyr* (The History of Llangeler and Penboyr Parishes) (1899), Daniel E. Jones records various *toili* encounters as told by the 'responsible old people' ('*hen bobl gyfrifol*') of the parish. One tale from near Carmarthen tells of similar invisible forces:

Rodd hen wraig o Manllegweun yn dod adre o Gaerfyrddin ryw nosweth, a rochor isha Bwlchclaw dynai 'n teimlo'n hunan hwldwp

yn erbyn rhwbeth; treiodd droi naill ochr, ond rodd rhwbeth wedi
crnoi o bytiddi o bob cyfeiriad. Diallodd whap iawn ma engla odd
no, a doith gydag e hyd ben lon Penboyr.

An old woman from Manllegweun was coming home from
Carmarthen one night, and just below Bwlchclaw she felt herself
pushed up against something; she tried to turn either side, but
something had surrounded her from every direction. She understood very quickly that it was a funeral, and she came with it as
far as the end of Penboyr road.

The witness ended up being swept along by the ghostly procession until
she reached the church gate, at which point she felt the invisible crowd
part and was able to continue her journey home untroubled. Daniel E.
Jones also refers to a similar case of an unsuspecting man being swept
up on the road to Llangeler Church – an experience that left him so
terrified that he died shortly after the encounter.

Unlike the *cannwyll gorff*, which was usually only observed by an individual, it was not at all uncommon for multiple people to witness the
toili. The Reverend William Hobley records such an example in *Hanes
Methodistiaeth Arfon* (The History of Methodism in Arfon) (1910):

Gwelodd dau o lanciau ym mhentref Clynnog gynhebrwng yn dod
drwy'r ffordd ganol, a dyn adnabyddus iddynt yn eistedd ar gaead
yr arch. Yr oedd y dyn hwnnw yn cael ei gladdu ymhen ychydig
wythnosau yn ol hynny.

Two youths in the village of Clynnog saw a funeral procession
coming down the main road, and a man well known to them sitting on the lid of the coffin. That man was buried a few weeks later.

While many a *toili* was said to consist of strangers, such as in the account
discussed earlier from Moeddyn, Ceredigion, just as many of these phantom funerals consisted of recognisable members of the congregation, as
with the case of David Morgan's *toili* from Hendy-gwyn ar Daf. Should
one wish to identify the phantom attendees however, Cadrawd suggests
an unusual method for doing so in the old county of Glamorgan:

It was said that one could recognize everyone in a phantom funeral, who might be sufficiently nerved for such an unearthly sight, if he would run in front when he happened to see one approaching, and look into a pool of water, if such a thing was to be found on the side of the road over which the cortege was passing. He would also see the name of the deceased on the coffin-plate. Some were said to have been foolish enough to do this, and to have seen their own names, and the date at which they would die.

The latter part of this excerpt could be interpreted as a warning for the curious – a theme which we have encountered multiple times during the course of this book. While the details of Cadrawd's suggestion do not seem to replicated elsewhere, the people of Llanwrtyd parish had their own method:

Y mae yn hen ddywediad, pan gyferfydd person â thoili, os na fydd ef yn ei gweled mor blaen ag y dymunai, ond iddo orwedd ar ei gefn wrth ochr y ffordd, ac edrych ar y toili rhyngddo a'r goleufer, y bydd iddo adnabod pawb felly.

There is an old saying, when someone meets a *toili*, if they do not see it as clearly as wished, they only need lie on their back by the side of the road, and look at the *toili* between themselves and the light, and they will recognise everyone in that manner.

We learnt at the beginning of our discussion on the *toili* that Daniel Silvan Evans feared its gradual exodus from the collective consciousness. Indeed, the Reverend Gomer Morgan Roberts, regarded as a leading modern historian of Welsh Calvinistic Methodism as well as a diligent recorder of folklore, wrote in *Hanes Plwyf Llandybïe* (The History of Llandybïe Parish) (1938) that one William Miles of Caer-bryn was the last to observe the phantom funeral in the parish, having been 'pressed tightly to the edge of the bank by the force of the invisible crowd' ('*cael ei wasgu'n dynn i ymyl y clawdd gan rym y dyrfa anweledig*').

However, Silvan Evans need not have worried, as sightings of the phantom funeral were still being recorded as recently as the 1960s, such as the following example from Ceredigion, penned by Evan Jones in *Ar Ymylon Cors Caron* (On the Outskirts of Cors Caron) (1967):

> *Gŵr arall a alwai ar dro oedd Mr. Jones yr arwerthwr ac adroddai yntau storïau cynhyrfus hefyd. Un hwyrnos pan oedd ef a'i gyfaill yn mynd i'w gartref, sef fferm Esgerhendy, sylwasant wrth basio capel Blaenpennal fod yno olau. Aethant ymlaen at y ffenestr yn ddistaw bach a gwelsant fod yno wasanaeth angladdol. Clywsant y canu a gweled y gynulleidfa yn mynd i'r fynwent gerllaw. Methasant aros yn hwy gan ofn ac ni ddywedodd yr un o'r ddau air arall am weddill y ffordd adref. Ymhen pythefnos, meddai ef, 'roedd eu gwas hwy yn orweiddiog ar ystyllen a bu gwasanaeth angladdol yn hollol fel y gwelsant ac y clywsant hwy ef. Gwnâi'r straeon hyn i ni feddwl fod yna doili neu ysbryd yn llechu ymhob llwyn yn yr ardal.*

Another man who occasionally called was Mr. Jones the auctioneer and he also told exciting stories. One evening when he and his friend were going to his home, which is Esgerhendy farm, they noticed while passing Blaenpennal chapel that there was a light in the window. They went on to the window in silence and saw that there was a funeral service. They heard the singing and saw the congregation going to the nearby cemetery. They couldn't wait any longer out of fear and neither of the two said another word for the rest of the way home. After two weeks, he said, their servant was lying on a board and there was a funeral service exactly as they saw and heard. These stories made us think that there was a *toili* or a ghost lurking in every hedge in the area.

While contemporary sightings may be infrequent, it is clear from the innumerable accounts recorded over the centuries that the *toili*, much like the *cannwyll gorff*, has succeeded in establishing itself firmly within Welsh folkloric tradition.

Gwrach-y-rhibyn

Gwrach-y-rhibyn is the name given to a particularly unpleasant hag-like spectre whose appearance presages death. While some folklore texts record her as being an omen bound to the old county of Glamorgan, she is in fact recorded in numerous locations across the length and breadth of the country. We have already seen the traces of her legacy within the landscape of Llangeler, Carmarthenshire, in Chapter Three: 'Ghosts in the Landscape', and discussed her in association with *Hen Wrach Cors Fochno* in the previous chapter, 'Fantastical Ghouls'.

In her book *Atgofion Ceinewydd* (Memories of New Quay) (1961), the author Myra Evans recalls:

> *Yn nhŷ fy modryb tynnai dau ddarlun fy sylw bob amser. Darlun o 'wrach-y-rhibyn' oedd un ohonyn' hw', a llwyddai bob tro i yrru ar-swyd drwof. Meddai'r wrach ar wallt du fel y muchudd. 'R oedd ei chroen yn dywyll, ei chefn yn gam, a'i chorff yn denau fel ysgerbwd. Medrwn weld ei hadenydd, fel slumyn-bacwn, yn cyhwfan y tu ôl i'w mantell laes, ddu.*
>
> *Gyrrai ei llygaid tanbaid a'i thrwyn crwca ias o arswyd drwof bob amser. A pham lai? Onid hon oedd gwrach-y-rhibyn a godai ofn ar bawb? Yn ôl yr hanes, byddai ambell waith yn hedfan o amgylch y pentre' wedi nos, gan daro yn erbyn cwareli ffenestri golau gyda'i bysedd ewinog. Pan wnai hynny, deuai anffawd neu angau i'r bwthyn hwnnw.*

In my aunt's house two pictures always caught my attention. One of them was a picture of '*gwrach-y-rhibyn*', and it managed to drive terror through me every time. The gwrach had pitch-black hair. Her skin was dark, her back was crooked, and her body was as thin as a skeleton. We could see her wings, like lean bacon, spread out behind her long, black cloak.

Her burning eyes and her crooked nose always sent a chill of terror through me. And why not? Was this not *gwrach-y-rhibyn* that scared everyone? According to the story, she would some-times fly around the village at night, tapping against lighted window panes with her clawed fingers. When she did that, misfortune or death would come to that cottage.

She is described by David Erwyd Jenkins in *Beddgelert: Its Facts, Fairies, & Folk-Lore* (1899) as being:

a girl of immense size, and of an extremely hideous appearance. She had bright red hair, as coarse as a horse's tail, falling down in rough ringlets over her bony shoulders. Her two cheek-bones projected like two ridges, and her curved nose reached almost to her pointed chin. Her eyes flashed red fire from their deep sockets, and when she opened her mouth to give forth her awful howl or shout she showed two or three teeth like the spikes of a harrow, lying the one across the other.

As proclaimed by the Reverend D. G. Williams in his 1895 essay, 'Casgliad o Len-Gwerin Sir Gaerfyrddin' ('A Collection of Carmarthenshire Folklore'): 'her glory is her ugliness' ('*ei gogoniant hi yw ei hagrwch*')! Obvious similarities might be drawn with the figure of the Irish *banshee*. Indeed, much like the *banshee*, *gwrach-y-rhibyn* is often sighted close to areas of water although, like many witch figures in folklore, is said to be unable to cross it easily herself.

Gwrach-y-rhibyn would generally stay concealed, shrouded in mist or fog, until an unwary traveller came upon a crossroads or an estuary – two examples of significant folkloric and supernatural boundaries, a concept we have previously discussed in Chapter Three: 'Ghosts in the Landscape'. If at an area of water, she was said to beat upon its surface, screaming 'my husband, my husband!' ('*Fy ngŵr, fy ngŵr!*'), or lamenting for 'my wife' ('*fy ngwraig*') or 'my child' ('*fy mhlentyn*'). Depending on the identity of the traveller, the words spoken by the *gwrach* would foretell which of the unfortunate witnesses' loved ones was to die shortly. If her screams were devoid of words, then the witnesses themselves were believed to be doomed.

The following account of *gwrach-y-rhibyn* is recorded by the Reverend William Jenkin Davies in *Hanes Plwyf Llandyssul* (The History of Llandysul Parish) (1896):

> *Ie, Grach-y-rhibyn, fe'i gwelwd e'n y plwydd filodd o weithe. Grondwch: Un tro pan odd Sali Ffynonllewlin yn sâl iawn, gwelodd crwt y bugel hen wraig a'i gwallt brithwyn yn cuddio'i holl gorph yn myn'd ar yr hewl, a phan y cyrddodd Rhydwên sgrechodd nes hela ofan ar yr holl ardal, oblegid rodd pob Grach-y-rhibyn yn sgrechen yn ofnadw wrth wel'd a chroesi dwr. Ar ol iddi fynd lawr i Landyssul, âth yn union i fynwent Eglwys y Plwydd, a diflanodd yno.*

Yes, *Gwrach-y-rhibyn*, she was seen in the parish a thousand times. Listen: Once when Sali Ffynonllewlin was very ill, the shepherd's boy saw an old woman with her greying hair hiding her entire body travelling along the road, and when she reached Rhydwên she screamed so much as to frighten the whole area, because every *Gwrach-y-rhibyn* screams terribly when seeing and crossing water. After she went down to Llandysul, she went straight to the churchyard of the Parish Church, and disappeared there.

Myrddin Fardd in *Llên Gwerin Sir Gaernarfon* suggested that *gwrach-y-rhibyn* might be seen to represent Andras, or the Mother of Evil, referred to by the author as an old Welsh goddess figure to whom human sacrifices were offered. While the idea is replicated in other antiquarian sources of the time as being a variant of the goddess of fury, Andrasta, otherwise known as Malen, or Y Fall (for example, the 1753 *Antiquæ Linguæ Britannicæ Thesaurus: Being a British, or Welsh-English Dictionary*), in fact, the word is more likely a variant of *anras* (without grace, ungodly).

Y Cyhyraeth

The figure of *gwrach-y-rhibyn* is often conflated with that of the *cyhyraeth*, with folklorists such as John Rhŷs in *Celtic Folklore: Welsh and Manx* (1901) having described them as one and the same. It is also a term which may infrequently be used to describe a phantom funeral in parts of north Wales. The word *cyhyr* in Welsh denotes muscle, tendon or sinew, and therefore *cyhyraeth* can either refer to a skeletal, corporeal person of skin and bone, or the better-known wailing wraith of folklore. It is a figure that precedes that of *gwrach-y-rhibyn* within Welsh accounts, and unlike *gwrach-y-rhibyn*, is described within the earliest records as an auditory phenomenon, later described by Llyfrbryf in *Cymru Fu*: 'This warning was not a vision, but a *hearing*' ('*Nid drychiolaeth mo'r rhybudd hwn, eithr clywolaeth*').

The first probable accounts of the *cyhyraeth* as a portentous entity are recorded once more in 1780 by 'Yr Hen Broffwyd' ('The Old Prophet'), the Reverend Edmund Jones, in *A Relation of Apparitions of Spirits, in the Principality of Wales*, where it is predominantly said to haunt those areas running alongside the river Tywi on its course from Ceredigion through Carmarthenshire. It is also strongly associated with Pembrokeshire, in particular 'the middle part of the bishopric of St David's', which Jones declared harboured the greatest number of its manifestations. The reverend describes the *cyhyraeth*'s howls as follows:

> That it is a doleful disagreeable sound heard before the deaths of many, and most apt to be heard before foul weather: that the voice resembles the groaning of sick persons who are to die; heard at first at a distance then comes nearer, and the last near at hand; so that it is a three fold warning of death, the King of terrors. It begins strong, and louder than a sick man can make, the second cry is lower; but not less doleful, but rather more so; the third yet lower, and soft like the groaning of a sick man, almost spent and dying ... If it meets any hindrance in the way, it seems to groan louder.

Cadrawd describes this omen as 'a frightful form of lamentation that proceeded from the house of death to the parish church', while in *Plwyf Llanwyno* (Llanwynno Parish) (1913), Glanffrwd claimed that it was not unusual in times gone by to 'hear the screams of the *cyhyraeth* on the bridge above the house' ('*clywed ysgrech cyhyraeth ar y bont uwchben y tŷ*').

Charles Redwood, in *The Vale of Glamorgan* (1839), claims the shrieks of the *cyhyraeth* may be heard along the southern coast, warning fishermen of coming stormy weather and impending shipwrecks. Here, it is heard moaning:

> at first at a distance, gradually approaching towards them along the edge of the waves, and then dying away, as it were upon the gale. And when they fancied it had entirely gone, it would suddenly shriek with a fearful loudness near them, and petrify them with horror, the sound was so terrific and unearthly.

Wirt Sikes also includes this unreferenced passage in *British Goblins*.

A similar auditory phenomenon, known as the *wawch*, was sometimes reported screeching along the shores of the old county of Meirionnydd. The entity is described by William Davies in his 1898 essay, 'Casgliad o Lên-Gwerin Meirion' ('A Collection of Meirion Folklore'):

*Ni ddywedid i neb erioed weled y Wawch ond y byddai yn ehedeg
yn yr entrych, ac oddeutu glanau y môr, gan floeddio yn hirllais,
'Gwae, gwae,' yn rhag-rybudd o ystormydd a damweiniau ar y môr,
yr hyn a barai i'r pysgotwyr ymogel amryw ddyddiau rhag anturio
allan â'u rhwyfau i'r môr.*

It was not said that anyone ever saw the *Wawch* but that it flew
up high, and away from the sea shore, bawling in a drawn-out
cry, 'Woe, woe,' in advanced warning of storms and accidents
at sea, such that the fishermen avoided venturing out to the sea
with their oars for a number of days.

While the onomatopoeic word *gwawch* means to shriek or yell, it is also
the Welsh name for the grebe, an aquatic bird which can sometimes be
seen at sea, and whose doleful cry rising over the crashing waves could
easily be mistaken for its ominous namesake.

Aderyn Corff

Shrieking sea birds aside, it was the terrible cry of the *aderyn corff*
(corpse bird), 'the infallible herald of death' (*'blaengenad anffaeledig
angau'*) that, according to Cynddelw in *Manion Hynafiaethol*, proved
'effective enough to sober the hardest of the children of superstition and
ignorance, and make them wish for a good end' (*'yn ddigon effeithiol
i ddifrifoli y caletaf o blant ofergoeledd ac anwybodaeth, a pheri iddynt
ddymuno diwedd da'*).

Traditionally, a bird said to cry within earshot of a sickbed, or more
commonly beat its wings day and night against the window panes behind
which the sick person lay, was regarded as an *aderyn corff*. In this regard,
the owl was often the main culprit. However, as Jonathan Ceredig Davies
in *Folk-lore of West and Mid-Wales* (1911) states: 'every bird is not a corpse
bird', and there is a clear distinction between the *aderyn corff* and the
portentous behaviour of birds discussed at the beginning of this chapter.

These phantasmal creatures were reported in a variety of guises depending on the region. It is often described without wings or feathers,
sometimes crying 'Come, come!' (*'Dewch, dewch!'*). The Reverend
Evan Isaac claims in *Coelion Cymru* (Welsh Beliefs) (1938) 'that it is
black in colour and the size of a thrush, with its large eyes capable of

shooting out piercing beams as cold as ice' ('*ei fod yn ddu ei liw ac o faintioli ûronfraith, a'i lygaid mawr yn saethu allan belydrau treiddiol â'u ias fel ia*').

A little grey bird would appear to an old woman, Miss Griffiths of Henllan, near Eglwyswrw, Pembrokeshire, to forewarn of a death in the family, as told to Jonathan Ceredig Davies. In the Caerffili and Rhymni areas, Marie Trevelyan claimed the bird was dark in colour with a grey breast, and had a 'smooth fur-like coat and small fin-like flappers'. In Breconshire, it was said to resemble a grey, bedraggled robin with eyes like 'balls of fire'.

In the tape recordings held at the archives at St Fagan's National Museum of History, Cardiff, transcribed by John Owen Hughes in *Straeon Gwerin Ardal Eryri* (Folk Tales of Eryri) (2008), one storyteller, William Roberts, described a recent encounter with the strange creature in the village of Dolbenmaen, Gwynedd: 'Well, something like an owl or something like that. Wid! Wid! Wid! Wid! Wid! Wid! Wid! That's how it does it. We didn't hear it then after that happened' ('*Ol rh'wbath tebig i ddylluan ne' r'wbath felly 'de. Wid! Wid! Wid! Wid! Wid! Wid! Wid! Fel'a mae o'n g'neud. Chlywsoni mo'no fo wedyn wedi hy ddigw'dd*').

Ieuan Buallt writes how in Llanwrtyd, Powys:

> *Clywyd ef weithiau â llais oer diethr yn dywedyd yn blaen, 'dere-whip, dere-whip,' a hynny amryw weithiau; ac yna ymadael gan adael pawb o'r teulu wedi eu llenwi a difrifoldeb a sobrwydd mawr.*

It was sometimes heard speaking plainly with a strange cold voice, '*dere-whip, dere-whip*,' and did so often; and then departed having filled everyone in the family with a great seriousness and sobriety.

The *aderyn corff* has even been recorded as having visited Welsh people living abroad, with accounts reported in Perth, Australia, and in Patagonia, Argentina.

Cŵn Annwn

Supernatural hounds whose howling was believed to foretell death, *Cŵn Annwn* (the Hounds of Annwn), represent perhaps one of the oldest omens within Welsh tradition. They are first recorded in the

First Branch of the *Mabinogi* as the hunting dogs of Arawn, king of the Welsh otherworld, Annwfn (also known as Annwn), a figure already familiar to us from Chapter Two: 'Unfinished Business'. They are most commonly described within Welsh folklore as they first appear to Pwyll, prince of Dyfed, while hunting a stag in Arberth (Narberth):

> And of all the hounds he had seen in the world, he had never seen dogs of this colour – they were a gleaming shining white, and their ears were red. And as the whiteness of the dogs shone so did the redness of their ears.

The colours red and white are indicative of their supernatural origins. Early nineteenth-century antiquarians such as Edward Davies in *The Mythology and Rites of the British Druids* (1809) fancied the colours represented 'a mystical transformation of the *Druids*, with their *white robes* and *red tiaras*'. In reality, *Cŵn Annwn* are described in all manner of sizes and coat colours in Welsh folklore accounts – from the 'dark, dun' and 'blood-red hounds' of James Motley, 'always dripping in gore', to the 'great Mastiff Dog' of the Reverend Edmund Jones, and the fire-breathing beasts of old Meirionnydd recorded by William Davies.

Generally speaking, spectral dogs such as these are particularly connected with the Germanic mythology of the Wild Hunt – ghostly sky riders accompanied by their demonic hounds, in pursuit of evil souls to convey to the afterlife. Odin is often recognised as the leader of the Hunt, but is replaceable with regional historical or folkloric figures; we find versions of the Hunt being led by King Arthur, the Devil, and Sir Francis Drake, to name a few. In Wales, the leader tends to appear as King Arawn, or his psychopompic counterpart, Gwyn ap Nudd, king of the *Tylwyth Teg*; alternatively, the hounds are said to be led by an unnamed black, horned figure.

In *Ofergoelion yr Hen Gymry: Mewn Pymtheg Dosparth*, Tudur Clwyd provides a description of the spectral pack:

> *Cwn Annwn a Chwn Uffern, am y credid wrth eu sŵn ar noson dymhestlog mai o ardaloedd y trueni y deuent. Teithient trwy yr awyrgylch, ac yn yr ystyr yma yr oedd eu llwybrau megys llwybrau*

yr adar; am byny y gelwid hwynt 'Cwn Awyr.' Pan glywid sŵn yn mrig y coed yn ystod y gauaf, dywedid fod Cwn Annwn yn dyfod. Os y gofynid pa fath rai oeddynt, atebid mai helgwn bychain oeddynt, wedi dyfod i'r wlad i 'hela eneidiau y meirw.' Denwyd llawer o blant a phobl mewn oed i'w cylch erioed, ac anifeiliaid, a chipiwyd hwynt ynmaith fel nas gwelwyd hwynt byth mwy!

Hounds of Annwn and Hell Hounds, because it was believed by their noise on a stormy night that they came from the regions of woe. They travelled through the atmosphere, and in this sense their paths were like the paths of birds; this is why they were called 'Sky Dogs.' When a noise was heard in the tree-tops during winter, it was said that the Hounds of Annwn were coming. If it was asked what kind they were, it was answered that they were small hounds, having come to the country to 'hunt the souls of the dead.' From the beginning, many children and adults were attracted to their circle, and animals, and were snatched away so they were never seen again!

As we can see from this excerpt, terminology is generally quite inter-changeable in regard to ominous hounds, with names largely dependent on the area in which they were sighted or heard. Alternative terms include *Cŵn Wybr*, or *Cŵn Awyr* (Sky Dogs), *Gwyllgwn* (Wild Dogs), and even sometimes *Cŵn Du* (Black Dogs), the latter discussed in Chapter Four: 'Spectral Beasts'. The Reverend Edmund Jones provides an early description from Llanhilleth, Blaenau Gwent, which proves these terms were interchangeable as far back as 1780. The account details how the dogs were heard hunting by Thomas Andrew, 'an honest religious man', when coming home one evening:

He feared they were hunting the sheep, and hastened on to meet and hinder them; he heard them coming towards him, tho' he saw them not. When they came near him, their voices were but small, but increasing as they went from him; and down they went the steep way towards the river *Ebwy*, dividing between this parish and Monithisloin, whereby he knew that they were, what are called *Cwn wybir*, i.e. Sky Dogs; but in the inward parts of Wales, *Cwn-annwn*, i.e. Dogs of Hell. I have heard say that these spiritual hunting dogs have been heard to pass by the eves of some houses before the death of some in the family.

Here, Edmund Jones also exemplifies an unusual attribute of *Cŵn Annwn*, which is not generally associated with the broader characteristics of spectral hunting dogs – that their howls are louder at a distance and fade on approach. This peculiarity seems to have originated here, and has been repeated so many times by later antiquarians and folklorists that it has now embedded itself as 'canon'.

The dogs were also commonly termed *Cŵn Bendith y Mamau* (The Hounds of the Blessing of the Mothers), or hounds of the fairies, as seen in the following account by the Reverend William Jenkin Davies in *Hanes Plwyf Llandyssul*:

> *Tro arall, pan odd Ifan Blancwm yn mynd adre ar y gaseg fal o Lambed, dyna gwn bendith y mame yn rowndo am dano; fe gishodd Ifan i whippo nhw, ond rhynty nhw i'r llawr rodd y whip yn mynd. Bu Ifan bron colli i fowyd, oblegyd rodd y cwn yn crechen fel bytheued, ac yn hela ofan ar y gaseg yn ombeidus; ond erbyn hyn ma'r cwn wedi diflanu.*

Another time, when Ifan Blancwm was going home on the mare from Llambed, the *bendith y mame* dogs surrounded him; Ifan tried to whip them, but the whip fell through them to the floor. Ifan almost lost his life, because the dogs screamed like hounds, and scared the mare terribly; but by now the dogs have disappeared.

Bendith y Mamau, or 'Blessing of the Mothers' are the fairies of south Wales lore, and are often connected with the stories of *Cŵn Annwn*. However, the terminology is also found in north Wales, and is mentioned by William Davies in 'Casgliad o Lên-Gwerin Meirion'. By virtue of their association with the *Tylwyth Teg*, they are sometimes noted to accompany the *toili*, and are said to tread the corpse roads from the home of the ill-fated individual to the cemetery.

In *Hanes Plwyfi Llangeler a Phenboyr*, Daniel E. Jones notes the shapeshifting nature of *Cŵn Bendith y Mamau*: 'These were often seen in the parishes until about the middle of this century. They took many forms – dogs, mice, and sometimes sows and piglets.' ('*Gwelid y rhai hyn yn fynych yn y plwyfi hyd tua haner y ganrif hon. Cymerent lawer o ffurfiau – cwn, llygod, ac weithiau hwch a pherchyll.*')

Again, we see reference to the image of the sow and piglets, as previously discussed in the section on the *cannwyll gorff*. It is also worth observing that shapeshifting dogs are not unique to Wales; for example, there are a number of stories relating to the Black Shuck, another omen of death or ill-fortune from the northern counties of England, where the dog may appear in other forms.

Daniel E. Jones continues with his tales of shapeshifting hell hounds, before neatly summarising why these omens have survived and flourished within the collective consciousness:

> *Ryw ddeng-mlynedd-ar-hugain yn ol gwelsom ddyn, un noswaith, wedi ei ddychrynu ganddynt. Ymddangosant iddo fel llygod ar Ben Moelgyni, a dilynasant ef a gryn dipyn, hyd nes y gallodd gyrhaedd ty a diogelwch.*
>
> *Mor bell ag y gwyddom, nid oes son yma am Gwn Annwn a Chwn Wybr ardaloedd eraill, ond dichon taw yr un ydynt a Chwn Bendith-y-mamau. Pan gofir fod y plwyfi hyn yn ffinio a Chenarth a Chilrhedyn, yn y rhai y gorwedd Glyn Cuch, i'r lle y daeth Pwyll Pendefig a'i gŵn i hela, ac y cwrddodd ag Arawn brenin Anwn a'i gŵn yno, a'u bod, fel y tybiwn, yn ffurfio rhan o diriogaeth brenhinoedd Anwn, nid rhyfedd fod cŵn yn cael lle pwysig yn ofergoelion y plwyfolion.*

Some thirty years ago we saw a man, one night, having been frightened by them. They appeared to him like mice on Pen Moelgyni, and they followed him a long way, until he was able to reach a house and safety.

As far as we know, there is no mention here of the Hounds of Annwn and Sky Dogs from other areas, but they may be the same as *Cŵn Bendith-y-mamau*. When it is remembered that these parishes border on Cenarth and Cilrhedyn, in which Glyn

Cuch lies, where Pwyll Pendefig and his dogs came to hunt, and met Arawn the king of Anwn and his dogs there, and that, as we suppose, they form part of the territory of the kings of Anwn, it is not surprising that dogs have an important place in the superstitions of the parishioners.

Epilogue

*

According to the cuneiform scholar Irving Finkel, assistant keeper of ancient Mesopotamian script, languages and cultures at the British Museum, an ancient Babylonian tablet dating to around 1500 BCE, and acquired by the museum in the nineteenth century, may well contain the earliest known depiction of a ghost. The small clay artefact contains detailed instructions on how to exorcise this troublesome spirit.

The exorcist was instructed to create two figurines, one of a man and one of a woman, and to prepare two vessels of beer. At sunrise, the sun god Shamash would be invoked through incantation and the ghost would be transferred to one of the figurines, where it would be trapped. While around 3,500 years have elapsed since the creation of this tablet, some of these ritualistic elements may be familiar by now. The supernatural or folkloric boundary of sunrise, the laying of spirits through incantation, and the trapping of a spirit in a vessel are all themes we have encountered in Welsh ghost-lore throughout this book.

Although the thematic elements of ghost-lore remain remarkably consistent throughout the world, and throughout the ages, we hope that we have shown how Wales possesses its own extremely specific imagery, rituals and belief systems which are not precisely replicated anywhere else. The wheels of fire that thunder across the Welsh countryside at night, the wailing phantoms still searching for Arawn, and those hat-dancing bogeys from Trawsfynydd – to name but a few examples – all combine to form folk traditions which are truly unique.

The popularity of Welsh ghost-lore is steadily increasing with the rise of the popular radio show or podcast series, the flamboyant ghost tour, and even through the modern concept of legend tripping – visiting and interacting with a site of folkloric significance. Yet, many of Wales's modern hauntings mirror the same motifs as times gone by. We have seen how the distorted, abstract ghouls collected by the Reverend Edmund Jones in 1780 were echoed during the 1904–5 religious revival, and how the first written account of the *cannwyll gorff* (corpse candle) in the seventeenth century reads much like late twentieth-century sightings. The medium through which these stories are told may change, but the roots of these tales have remained firm.

That many of these unique aspects of Welsh ghost-lore develop and evolve independently of the pervasive influence of neighbouring countries is made all the more extraordinary by the fact that they have not only survived, but flourished. While it is likely that many of the tales we have presented here will rarely, if ever, have travelled outside the borders of Wales, none of them can be described as 'lost' or 'forgotten'. Instead, perhaps, they can be better understood and circulated when we contextualise them within broader Welsh history and culture.

There are undoubtedly many Welsh ghosts which remain unearthed. We would invite readers to share their own experiences with us so that we can archive them for the future and ensure they are included within the canon of Welsh ghost-lore still to come.

Glossary

Translations based on entries from *Geiriadur Prifysgol Cymru*
(The University of Wales Dictionary)

Afanc: aquatic monster, beaver, crocodile, alligator

Bendith y Mamau: Blessing of the Mothers, fairies, spirits

Bolól: bogey, hobgoblin; the Devil

Bwbach: bugbear, bogey, ghost, spectre, phantom, scarecrow

Bwci: bogey, goblin, ghost, spectre

Bwgan: ghost, hobgoblin, bugbear

Cannwyll gorff: corpse candle, fetch-light

Cŵn Annwn: hounds of Annwn, hounds of Hell

Cŵn Bendith y Mamau: dogs of the fairies

Cŵn Du: Black Dogs

Cythraul: devil, demon, fallen angel, unclean spirit; the Devil, Satan

Cyhyraeth: skeleton, apparition, ghost, spectre, death portent, wraith

Diafol: devil, demon

Drychiolaeth: apparition, ghost, spectre, phantom funeral, illusion, vision, revelation

Ellyll: goblin, elf, fairy, apparition, phantom, ghost, bogey, evil spirit, devil, demon

Gwiddon: giantess, female monster, hag, witch, sorceress, satyr, nymph

Gwrach-y-rhibyn: portentous apparition in the guise of a hag

Gwyllgwn: Wild Dogs, a spectral mastiff of huge size

Hen Wrach Cors Fochno: The Old Hag of Cors Fochno

Hudlewyn: will-o'-the-wisp, jack-o'-lantern, ignis fatuus

Hwch Ddu Gwta / Gwtta: tailless black sow said to chase people on Hallowe'en

Jac y Lanter / Lantarn: jack-o'-lantern, will-o'-the-wisp, ignis fatuus

Ladi Wen: ghost, usually that of a woman dressed in white (literally, white lady)

Lledrith: apparition, spectre, phantom, magic, spell, charm, enchantment; illusion

Mall-dân: will-o'-the-wisp, jack-o'-lantern, ignis fatuus

Nos Galan Gaeaf: Winter's Eve, Hallowe'en

Nos Galan Mai: May-day Eve

Noswyl Ifan: St John's Eve

Rhith: shape, form, figure, appearance, guise, disguise, illusion, ghost, apparition

Tân Ellyll: will-o'-the-wisp, jack-o'-lantern, ignis fatuus

Toili: phantom funeral

Tolaeth: phantom funeral, auditory omen of death

Tylwyth Teg: fairies, spirits

Y Tair Ysbrydnos: The Three Spirit Nights

Ysbryd: spirit, soul, ghost, spectre

Bibliography

*

Newspaper articles

'A Breconshire Ghost', *The Tenby Observer* (30 March 1882), 3.

'A Ghost!', *Pontypool Free Press and Herald of the Hills* (28 November 1868), 4.

'A Tondu Apparition', *The Cardiff Times* (10 September 1904), 4.

'An Apparition at Tondu', *Evening Express and Evening Mail* (5 September 1904), 2.

'Fighting Ghost', *The Peak Hill Express* (25 November 1904), 4.

'Ghost Story Recalled', *The Cardiff Times* (18 June 1910), 8.

'Llanarthney Ghost', *Evening Express* (3 January 1910), 2.

'Mine Believed Haunted', *The Aberystwyth Observer* (17 July 1902), 4.

Morgan, Owen (Morien y Gwyddon), 'Omens of the Mine', *Evening Express* (11 December 1895), 2.

'Real Ghost at Last', *Evening Express* (1 January 1910), 2.

'Spooks in a Welsh Village', *Dundee Evening Telegraph* (22 May 1902), 4.

'Tombstone as Ghost', *Evening Express* (17 September 1908), 2.

'The Tondu Ghost', *The Cardiff Times* (17 September 1904), 3.

Evans, Thomas Christopher (Cadrawd), 'Welsh Tit-Bits', *The Cardiff Times* (20 June 1903), 1.

Books, pamphlets and journal articles

Aaron, Jane, *Cambria Gothica: Gothic Tales from Nineteenth-Century Wales* (Aberystwyth: Llyfrau Cantre'r Gwaelod, 2012).

Adran Penmorfa, Cylch Aberteifi, 'Bwci a Thoili', in *Casgliad o Straeon am Ysbrydion a Bwciod yn Unrhyw Ardal yng Nghymru* (From the collections of Amgueddfa Cymru 1925/2, 1932).

Adran Penmorfa, Cylch Aberteifi, 'Crochon Aur Dyffrynbern', in *Casgliad o Straeon am Ysbrydion a Bwciod yn Unrhyw Ardal yng Nghymru* (From the collections of Amgueddfa Cymru 1925/2, 1932).

Adran Penmorfa, Cylch Aberteifi, 'Y Penfelyn Bach', in *Casgliad o Straeon am Ysbrydion a Bwciod yn Unrhyw Ardal yng Nghymru* (From the collections of Amgueddfa Cymru 1925/2, 1932).

Anon., *Y Breuddwydiadur; Neu Ddehonglydd i Freuddwydion, Wedi ei Gasglu o Ysgrifeniadau yr Hen Gymry* (Lerpwl: Argraffwyd dros y Llyfr-Werthwyr, n.d., circa 1900).

Aubrey, John, *Miscellanies Upon Various Subjects* (London: Reeves & Turner, 1890).

Baxter, Richard, *The Certainty of the World of Spirits. Fully Evidenced by the Unquestionable Histories of Apparitions, Operations, Witchcrafts, Voices, &c. Proving the Immortality of Souls, the Malice and Misery of the Devils, and the Damned, and the Blessedness of the Justified* (London: T. Parkhurst at the Bible and Three Crowns in Cheapside; and J. Salusbury at the Rising Sun near the Royal Exchange in Cornhill, 1691).

Beck, Jane C., 'The White Lady of Great Britain and Ireland', *Folklore*, 81/4 (1970), 292–306.

Beynon, Tom, *Cwmsêl a Chefn Sidan* (Caernarfon: Llyfrfa'r Methodistiaid Calfinaidd, 1946).

Birch, Walter de Gray, *A History of Margam Abbey* (London, 1897).

Bleddyn, 'The Faenol Ghost', *Bye-gones*, 3 (1893), 3.

Brooks, John Attwood, *Ghosts & Legends of Wales* (Norwich: Jarrold Publishing, 1987).

Cangen Merched y Wawr, Trawsfynydd (ed.), *Hanes Bro Trawsfynydd* (Trawsfynydd: Merched y Wawr, 1973).

Brown, Theodora (papers of) (University of Exeter Library Heritage Collections, EUL MS 105, 1965).

Caldas, Thomas Corum, *The Hangman, The Hound and Other Hauntings: A Gazetteer of Welsh Ghosts* (Llanrwst: Gwasg Carreg Gwalch, 2010).

Cambrensis, Giraldus, *The Itinerary Through Wales and the Description of Wales* (London: J. M. Dent & Sons, 1908).

Cofiadur, 'Chwedlau a Thraddodiadau Plwyf Llanfachraith', *Taliesin*, 1/2 (1859), 132–7.

Cothi, Lewis Glyn, *Gwaith Lewis Glyn Cothi* (Oxford: The Cymmrodorion, or Royal Cambrian Institution, 1837).

Cowdell, Paul, 'A Giant Bedsheet with the Holes Cut Out: Expectations and Discussions of the Appearance of Ghosts', in O. Jenzen and S. Munt (eds), *The Ashgate Research Companion to Paranormal Cultures* (Surrey: Ashgate Publishing Ltd, 2013), 159–69.

Daniel, John, *Archæologica Lleynensis, Sef Hynafiaethau Penaf Lleyn* (Bangor: Nixon a Jarvis, 1892).

Davies, David (Dewi Cynon), *Hanes Plwyf Penderyn* (Aberdâr: Pugh a Rowlands, 1924).

Davies, Edward, *The Mythology and Rites of the British Druids, Ascertained by National Documents: And Compared with the General Traditions and Customs of Heathenism, as Illustrated by the Most Eminent Antiquaries of our Age. With an Appendix, Containing Ancient Poems and Extracts, with Some Remarks on Ancient British Coins* (London: J. Booth, 1809).

Davies, Evan, *Hanes Plwyf Llangynllo: Traethawd Buddugol yn Eisteddfod Coedybryn, Tachwedd 8, 1901* (Llandysul: Gwasg Gomer, 1905).

Davies, Jonathan Ceredig, *Folk-lore of West and Mid-Wales* (Aberystwyth: Welsh Gazette Offices, 1911).

Davies, Owen, *The Haunted: A Social History of Ghosts* (Hampshire: Palgrave Macmillan, 2007).

Davies, Sioned (ed.), *The Mabinogion* (Oxford: Oxford University Press, 2018).

Davies, William, 'Casgliad o Len-Gwerin Meirion', in *Eisteddfod Genedlaethol y Cymry: Cofnodion a Chyfansoddiadau Buddugol Eisteddfod Blaenau Ffestiniog, 1898* (Liverpool: Cymdeithas yr Eisteddfod Genedlaethol, 1900).

Davies, William, *Hanes Plwyf Llanegryn/A History of the Parish of Llanegryn* (Talybont: Y Lolfa, 2002).

Davies, William Jenkin, *Hanes Plwyf Llandyssul* (Llandysul: J. D. Lewis, 1896).

Deio Bach, *Can yr Ysbrydion* (Cwmafon: Griffiths & Sons, n.d.).

Drane, Robert, *Castell Coch: A Gossiping Companion to the Ruin and its Neighbourhood* (Cardiff: Robert Drane, 1857).

Ellis, Robert (Cynddelw), *Manion Hynafiaethol: Neu Loffyn o Hen Gofion Cymruaidd, Wedi eu Casglu a'u Dethol o Gronfa Cynddelw* (Treherbert: Isaac Jones, 1873).

Evans, Daniel Silvan and Jones, John (Ivon), *Ysten Sioned: Neu y Gronfa Gymmysg* (Gwrecsam: Hughes a'i Fab, 1894).

Evans, Isaac, *Coelion Cymru* (Aberystwyth: Cambrian News Cyf, 1938).

Evans, John, *A Tour Through Parts of North Wales, in the Year 1798, and at Other Times; Principally Undertaken with a View to Botanical Researches in that Alpine Country: Interspersed with Observations on its Scenery, Agriculture, Manufactures, Customs, History, and Antiquities* (London: J. White, 1800).

Evans, John Gilbert, *Llyfr Hwiangerddi y Dref Wen* (Caerdydd: Gwasg y Dref Wen, 1981).

Evans, Myra, *Atgofion Ceinewydd* (Aberystwyth: Cymdeithas Lyfrau Ceredigion Gyf., 1961).

Evans, Thomas Christopher (Cadrawd), 'The Folklore of Glamorgan', in *Eisteddfod Genedlaethol y Cymry: Cofnodion a Chyfansoddiadau Buddugol Eisteddfod Aberdar, 1885* (Caerdydd: Cymdeithas yr Eisteddfod Genedlaethol, 1887).

Evans, Thomas Christopher (Cadrawd), *History of Llangynwyd Parish* (Llanelli: Llanelly and Country Guardian, 1887).

Fitzpatrick, Robert, *The Bard's Museum; or Rational Recreation: Containing the Serious, the Moral, and the Comic; Also, Several Songs, &c. Throughout the Work* (Dublin: H. Fitzpatrick, 1809).

Foulkes, Isaac (Llyfrbryf), *Cymru Fu; yn Cynnwys Hanesion, Traddodiadau, yn Nghyda Chwedlau a Dammegion Cymreig* (Wrexham: Hughes & Son, 1862).

Frimston, Thomas (Tudur Clwyd), *Ofergoelion yr Hen Gymry: Mewn Pymtheg Dosparth: Yn y Rhai yr Olrheinir eu Tarddiad o'r Cyfnod Boreuaf* (Llangollen: W. Williams, Swyddfa y 'Greal' a'r 'Athraw', n.d., circa 1906–10).

Fynes-Clinton, Osbert Henry, *The Welsh Vocabulary of the Bangor District* (Oxford: Oxford University Press, 1913).

Gibbard, Noel, *Hanes Plwyf Llan-non: Hen Sir Gaerfyrddin* (Llandysul: J. D. Lewis a'i Feibion Cyf, 1984).

Griffiths, Kate Bosse, *Byd y Dyn Hysbys: Swyngyfaredd yng Nghymru* (Talybont: Y Lolfa, 1977).

Gruffydd, Eirlys, *Ffynhonnau Cymru, Cyf. I – Ffynhonnau Brycheiniog, Ceredigion, Maldwyn, Maesyfed a Meirion* (Llanrwst: Gwasg Carreg Gwalch, 1997).

Gruffydd, Eirlys, *Gwrachod Cymru* (Caernarfon: Gwasg Gwynedd, 1980).

Hartland, Edwin Sidney, *English Fairy and Other Folk Tales* (London: Walter Scott, 1890).

Harvey, John (ed.), *The Appearance of Evil* (Cardiff: University of Wales Press, 2003).

Hobley, William, *Hanes Methodistiaeth Arfon: Dosbarth Bethesda (O'r Dechre Hyd Ddiwedd y Flwyddyn 1900)* (Caernarfon: W. Gwenlyn Evans, 1923).

Hobley, William, *Hanes Methodistiaeth Arfon: Dosbarth Caernarvon, Ardaloedd Waunfawr a Beddgelert (O'r Dechre Hyd Ddiwedd y Flwyddyn 1900)* (Caernarfon: W. Gwenlyn Evans, 1913).

Hobley, William, *Hanes Methodistiaeth Arfon: Dosbarth Caernarvon, Eglwysi'r Dref a'r Cylch (O'r Dechre Hyd Ddiwedd y Flwyddyn 1900)* (Caernarfon: W. Gwenlyn Evans, 1915).

Hobley, William, *Hanes Methodistiaeth Arfon: Dosbarth Clynnog (O'r Dechre Hyd Ddiwedd y Flwyddyn 1900)* (Caernarfon: W. Gwenlyn Evans, 1910).

Hobley, William, *Hanes Methodistiaeth Arfon: Dosbarth Dinorwig (O'r Dechre Hyd Ddiwedd y Flwyddyn 1900)* (Caernarfon: W. Gwenlyn Evans, 1921).

Holland, Richard, *Haunted Wales: a Guide to Welsh Ghostlore* (Gloucestershire: The History Press, 2011).

Howells, William, *Cambrian Superstitons, Comprising Ghosts, Omens, Witchcraft, Traditions, &c. to which are Added a Concise View of the Manners and Customs of the Principality, and Some Fugitive Pieces* (Tipton: Thomas Danks, 1831).

Hughes, Herbert (ed.), *Cymru Evan Jones* (Llandysul: Gwasg Gomer, 2009).

Hughes, Hugh Derfel, *Hynafiaethau Llandegai a Llanllechid* (Caernarfon: Cyhoeddiadau Mei, 1979).

Hughes, John Ceiriog (Ceiriog), *Y Bardd a'r Cerddor: Gyda Hen Ystraeon am Danynt, Llyfr IV* (Gwrecsam: R. Hughes a'i Fab, 1863).

Huws, Howard, *Llên Gwerin Bangor a'r Cyffiniau* (Bangor: Gwasg Gwŷr Rhyddion, 2022).

Huws, John Owen, *Straeon Gwerin Ardal Eryri, Cyf. I* (Llanrwst: Gwasg Carreg Gwalch, 2008).

Huws, John Owen, *Y Tylwyth Teg* (Llanrwst: Gwasg Carreg Gwalch, 1987).

Huws, Sara, 'Welsh Keywords: *Gwiddon*', *Planet*, 241 (2021).

Ifan, Dafydd Guto, *Llên Gwerin y Môr: Arferion, Chwedlau, Coelion, Dywediadau, Mytholeg, Traddodiadau* (Llanrwst: Gwasg Carreg Gwalch, 2012).

Ifans, Rhiannon, *Stars & Ribbons: Winter Wassailing in Wales* (Cardiff: University of Wales Press, 2022).

James I and VI, *Dæmonologie* (London: John Lane, 1924).

James, Annie, 'Correspondence: The White Dog', *Folklore*, 56/1 (1945), 228.

Jenkins, David Erwyd, *Beddgelert: Its Facts, Fairies, & Folk-Lore* (Porthmadog: Llewelyn Jenkins, 1899).

John Williams (Ab Ithel), 'Elis Wynn o Lasynys', *Taliesin*, 2/8 (1861), 275–82.

Jones, D. S., *Cofiant Darluniadol y Parchedig William Williams, o'r Wern: Yn Cynwys Pregethau a Sylwadau o'i Eiddo* (Dolgellau: W. Hughes, 1894).

Jones, Dafydd Glyn (ed.), *Cerddi'r Bardd Cwsg* (Bangor: Dalen Newydd, 2014).

Jones, Dafydd Glyn (ed.), *Rhywbeth yn Trwblo: Straeon Ysbryd gan ein Prif Awduron* (Bangor: Dalen Newydd, 2012).

Jones, Dafydd Glyn, *Un o Wŷr y Medra: Bywyd a Gwaith William Williams, Llandygái (1738–1817)* (Dinbych: Gwasg Gee, 1999).

Jones, Daniel E., *Hanes Plwyfi Llangeler a Phenboyr: Traethawd Buddugol yn Eisteddfod Drefach-a-Felindre, Awst 18, 1897, Gyda Chwanegiadau* (Llandysul: Gwasg Gomer, 1899).

Jones, David Watkin (Dafydd Morganwg), *Hanes Morganwg* (Aberdâr: Jenkin Howell, 1874).

Jones, Delyth and Jones, Tom, *Llanarthne Ddoe a Heddiw (Llanarthney Past and Present)* (Caerfyrddin: Carmarthenshire County Council, 2002).

Jones, Edmund, *A Geographical, Historical, and Religious Account of the Parish of Aberystruth in the County of Monmouth. To Which are Added, Memoirs of Several Persons of Note, Who Lived in the Said Parish* (Trevecka, 1779).

Jones, Edmund, *A Relation of Apparitions of Spirits, in the Principality of Wales; To Which is Added the Remarkable Account of the Apparition in Sunderland, With Other Notable Relations from England; Together with Observations About Them, And Instructions from Them: Designed to Confute and to Prevent the Infidelity of Denying the Being and Apparition of Spirits; Which Tends to Irreligion and Atheism* (Trevecca, 1780).

Jones, Edmund, *A Relation Of Apparitions Of Spirits, In The County Of Monmouth, And The Principality Of Wales: With Other Notable Relations from England, Together with Observations About Them, And Instructions from Them: Designed to Confute and to Prevent the Infidelity of Denying the Being and Apparition of Spirits, Which Tends To Irreligion and Atheism* (Newport, Monmouthshire: E. Lewis, etc., 1813).

Jones, Evan (Ieuan Buallt), 'Canwyllau Cyrph' (From the collections of Amgueddfa Cymru 1793/501, n.d.).

Jones, Evan (Ieuan Buallt), 'Swn Canu yn yr Awyr' (From the collections of Amgueddfa Cymru 1793/503, n.d.).

Jones, Evan (Ieuan Buallt), 'Y Toili' (From the collections of Amgueddfa Cymru 1793/501, n.d.).

Jones, Evan, *Ar Ymylon Cors Caron* (Aberystwyth: Cymdeithas Lyfrau Ceredigion Cyf., 1967).

Jones, Geraint Vaughan (ed.), *Dating Old Welsh Houses: Cynfal Fawr* (Discovering Old Welsh Houses Group, 2012).

Jones, Gwilym Vaughan, 'Yr Ysbryd Drwg', in *Ysbrydion, Chwedlau a Dipyn o Hiwmor* (From the collections of Amgueddfa Cymru 3920/13, 1998).

Jones, Gwilym Vaughan, 'Ysbryd ar Foto-beic', in *Ysbrydion, Chwedlau a Dipyn o Hiwmor* (From the collections of Amgueddfa Cymru 3920/13, 1998).

Jones, John (Myrddin Fardd), *Llên Gwerin Sir Gaernarfon* (Caernarfon: Cwmni y Cyhoeddwyr Cymreig, 1908).

Jones, John Morris, 'Parlwr y Glyn', in *Cyfarfod Cystadleuol y Groes Nos Wener Ionawr 28ain, 1977* (From the collections of Amgueddfa Cymru 2440/2, 1977).

Jones, Owen (Myvyr), Edward Williams (Iolo Morganwg) and William Owen Pughe (Idrison), *The Myvyrian Archaiology of Wales: Collected Out of Ancient Manuscripts* (Denbigh: Thomas Gee, 1870).

Jones, Robert William (Erfyl Fychan), *Bywyd Cymdeithasol Cymru yn y Ddeunawfed Ganrif* (Llundain: Gwasg Gymraeg Foyle, 1931).

Jones, Tegwyn, *Tribannau Morgannwg* (Llandysul: Gwasg Gomer, 1976).

Jones, Thomas Gwynn, *Welsh Folklore and Folk-Custom* (London: Methuen & Co. Ltd, 1930).

Lewis, Thomas, *Ymddangosiad Ysprydion Drwg: Sef Sylwedd Araeth a Draddodwyd Mewn Dadl Gyhoeddus yn Nghyfarfod Blynyddol Cymdeithas Cymreigyddol Bangor, Nos Wyl Dewi Sant, Mawrth 1af, 1844* (Llanrwst: John Jones, 1844).

Lloyd, Jacob Youde William, *The History of the Princes, the Lords Marcher, and the Ancient Nobility of Powys Fadog, and the Ancient Lords of Arwystli, Cedewen, and Meirionydd* (London: T. Richards, 1881).

Lloyd, John Edward, *A History of Carmarthenshire in Two Volumes* (Cardiff: London Carmarthenshire Society, 1935–9).

Maynard, Christopher, *The World of the Unknown: Ghosts* (London: Usborne Publishing Ltd, 2019).

Merrick, Rice, *A Booke of Glamorganshires Antiquities* (London: Dryden Press, 1887).

Morgan, Owen (Morien y Gwyddon), *History of Pontypridd and Rhondda Valleys* (Pontypridd: Glamorgan County Times, 1903).

Morgan, Thomas, *Handbook of the Origin of Place-Names in Wales and Monmouthshire* (Merthyr Tydfil: H. W. Southey, 1887).

Morgan, Thomas, *Hanes Tonyrefail. Adgofion am y Lle a'r Hen Bobl* (Caerdydd: Western Mail, 1899).

Morris, Robert Prys, *Cantref Meirionydd: Ei Chwedlau, ei Hynafiaethau, a'i Hanes* (Dolgellau: E. W. Evans, 1890).

Motley, James, *Tales of the Cymry; with Notes Illustrative and Explanatory* (London: Longmans, 1848).

Owen, Elias, *Welsh Folk-Lore: A Collection of the Folk-Tales and Legends of North Wales, Being the Prize Essay of the National Eisteddfod, 1887* (Oswestry and Wrexham: Woodall, Minshall, & Co., 1896).

Owen, Trefor Meredith, *Welsh Folk Customs* (Llandysul: Gwasg Gomer, 1987).

Powell, T., 'A Stair Passage in a Church Wall. The Black Dog', *Archaeologia Cambrensis*, 19/6 (1919), 537–8.

Redwood, Charles, *The Vale of Glamorgan: Scenes and Tales Among the Welsh* (London: Blatch & Lampert, 1839).

Rees, Alwyn and Brinley Rees, *Celtic Heritage: Ancient Tradition in Ireland and Wales* (London: Thames & Hudson, 1961).

Rees, Enoch, *Hanes Brynamman a'r Cylchoedd: O'r Flwyddyn 1819*

Hyd y Flwyddyn 1896, Yng Nghyd ag Attodiad Yn Cynwys Manylion Dyddorol a Gwerthfawr yn Nglyn a Dosbarth y Glo Garreg (Ystalyfera: E. Rees a'i Feibion, 1896).

Rhŷs, John, *Celtic Folklore: Welsh and Manx, Vol. I* (Oxford: Clarendon Press, 1901).

Rhŷs, John, *Celtic Folklore: Welsh and Manx, Vol. II* (Oxford: Clarendon Press, 1901).

Richards, Melville, 'The Supernatural in Welsh Place-names', in G. Jenkins (ed.), *Studies in Folk Life: Essays in Honour of Iorwerth C. Peate* (London & Beccles: Routledge & Kegan Paul Ltd, 1969), pp. 304–13.

Richards, Thomas (ed.), *Antiquæ Linguæ Britannicæ Thesaurus: Being a British, or Welsh-English Dictionary* (Bristol: Felix Farley, 1753).

Roberts, Gomer Morgan, *Hanes Plwyf Llandybïe* (Caerdydd: Bwrdd Gwasg Prifysgol Cymru dros Gyngor yr Eisteddfod Genedlaethol, 1939).

Roberts, Joe Aelwyn, *Holy Ghostbuster: a Parson's Encounters with the Paranormal* (London: Robert Hale, 1991).

Roberts, Joe Aelwyn, *Yr Anhygoel* (Caernarfon: Gwasg Gwynedd. 1991).

Roberts, Peter, *Hynafion Cymreig: Neu, Hanes am Draddodiadau, Defodau, ac Ofergoelion, yr Hen Gymry; yn Nghyd a Sylwadau ar eu Dechreuad, &c. &c.* (Caerfyrddin: J. Evans, 1823).

Roberts, Peter, *The Cambrian Popular Antiquities: or, an Account of Some Traditions, Customs, and Superstitions, of Wales; with Observations as to their Origin, &c.* (London: E. Williams, 1815).

Roberts, William (Nefydd), *Crefydd yr Oesoedd Tywyll: Neu, Henafiaethau Defodol, Chwareuyddol, a Choelgrefyddol: yn Cynwys y Traethawd Gwobrwyol yn Eisteddfod y Fenni ar Mari Lwyd, y Traethawd Gwobrwyol yn Eisteddfod y Blaenau ar Ddylanwad yr Ysgol Sabothol er Cadwraeth y Gymraeg; Ynghyd â Sylwadau ar Lawer o Hen Arferion Tebyg i Mari Lwyd* (Caerfyrddin: A. Williams, 1852).

Rowlands, Oswald, *Bro Ddyfi a Machynlleth: Rhamant ei Hanes a'i Llên Gwerin* (Aberystwyth: Cambrian News, 1936).

Sikes, Wirt, *British Goblins: Welsh Folk-Lore, Fairy Mythology, Legends and Traditions* (London: Sampson Low, Marston, Searle, & Rivington, 1880).

Stevens, Catrin, *Cligieth, C'nebrwn ac Angladd* (Llanrwst: Gwasg
Carreg Gwalch, 1987).

T.P., *Cas Gan Gythraul Neu Annogaeth i Bawb Ochelyd Myned i
Ymghynghori a Dewiniaid, Brudwyr, a Chonsyrwyr, Gydac Eglurhad
Ynghylch y Perigl Mawr a Fyned i Ymgynghori â Hwynt a
Chrybwylliad Ynghylch Llawer o Arferion a Thraddodiadau Drygionus
Sydd yn Cael eu Harferyd yn Nghymru* (Amwythig, 1759).

Thomas, J. Ann, 'Ysbryd y Gist Dderw' (From the collections of
Amgueddfa Cymru 2428, 1976).

Thomas, R. J. et al. (ed.), *Geiriadur Prifysgol Cymru: A Dictionary of
the Welsh Language* (GPC Ar lein, Canolfan Uwchefrydiau Cymreig
a Cheltaidd Prifysgol Cymru), *www.geiriadur.ac.uk*.

Thomas, Thomas Henry, 'Some Folk-Lore of South Wales', in *Reports
and Transactions (Cardiff Naturalists' Society) 1900–1981*, XXXVI
(1903), pp. 52–64.

Thomas, William (Glanffrwd), *Plwyf Llanwyno: Yr Hen Amser, Yr Hen
Bobl, Yr Hen Droion* (Aberdâr: Pugh a Rowlands, 1913).

Thomas, William, *Hynafiaethau yr Hendygwyn-Ar-Daf* (Llanelli: B. R.
Rees, 1868).

Trevelyan, Marie, *Folk-Lore and Folk-Stories of Wales* (London: E.
Stock, 1909).

Tyler, Robert Henry, *Laugharne: Local History and Folk Lore* (Llandysul: Gwasg Gomer, n.d.).

Vaughan-Thomas, Wynford, *Portrait of Gower* (London: Robert Hale,
1976).

Williams, D. G. (Lloffwr), 'Casgliad o Len-Gwerin Sir Gaerfyrddin',
in *Eisteddfod Genedlaethol y Cymry: Cofnodion a Chyfansoddiadau
Buddugol Eisteddfod Llanelli, 1895* (Cymdeithas yr Eisteddfod
Genedlaethol, 1898).

Williams, John Ellis Caerwyn (ed.), *Llên a Llafar Môn* (Llandysul:
Gwasg Gomer, 1963).

Williams, Griffith John Williams, *Hanes Plwyf Ffestiniog o'r Cyfnod
Boreuaf* (Wrexham: Hughes & Son, 1882).

Williams, John Rhosydd, *Hanes Rhosllannerchrugog*
(Rhosllannerchrugog: Pwyllgor Lleol Eisteddfod Genedlaethol
Rhosllannerchrugog, 1945).

Williams, Robert Thomas (Trebor Môn), *Derwyddiaeth: Tomenau,*

Crugiau, Carneddau, Cromlechau, Cistfeini, Meini Sigl, Meini Hirion, Llwyni, a Chylchau Derwyddol, yn Ynys Môn, yn ol Traddodiad a Dysg (Merthyr Tydfil: Farrant & Frost, 1890).

Williams, Taliesin (Taliesin ab Iolo) (ed.), *Iolo Manuscripts. A Selection of Ancient Welsh Manuscripts, in Prose and Verse, from the Collection Made by the Late Edward Williams, Iolo Morganwg, for the Purpose of Forming a Continuation of the Myfyrian Archaiology; and Subsequently Proposed as Materials for a New History of Wales* (Liverpool: I. Foulkes, 1888).

Williams, William, *Observations on the Snowdon Mountains; with Some Account of the Customs and Manners of the Inhabitants* (Oxford: S. Collingwood, 1802).

Williams, William Samlet, *Hanes a Hynafiaethau Llansamlet* (Dolgellau: E. W. Evans, 1908).

Winstanley, L. and H. J. Rose, 'Welsh Folklore Items, III', *Folklore*, 39/2 (1928), pp. 171–8.

Wood, Juliette, 'A Welsh Triad: Charlotte Guest, Marie Trevelyan, Mary Williams', in C. Blacker and H. E. Davidson (eds), *Women & Tradition: A Neglected Group of Folklorists* (Durham: Carolina Academic Press, 2000), 259–76.

Wynne, Ellis, *Gweledigaethau y Bardd Cwsg* (Caerfyrddin: J. Ross, 1767).

Ysgol Lewis, *Llen Gwerin Blaenau Rhymni: O Gasgliad Bechgyn Ysgol Lewis, Pengam* (Rhymni: Mr G. J. Jacobs, 1912).

Diolchiadau/ Acknowledgements

*

While this book seems to have materialised out of the ether based on a chance encounter with Mark while discussing the folklore surrounding sleep paralysis in north Wales, in hindsight, it has been years in the making. The folklore and, in particular, the ghost stories of Wales have featured prominently throughout my life, not least due to the efforts of my family, to whom I extend my gratitude first and foremost.

To Nick and Rhian Badder, Luned and Chris, for reading, editing and encouraging beyond measure throughout this strange and uncanny journey. Their remarkable and unflappable faith in my abilities often far exceeds my own. And to my husband, Dr Elidir Jones, a master of retelling creaky old Welsh ghost stories in his own right. Following countless hours of reading draft after draft, commenting, correcting, translating and editing, all while keeping our own two *Gwyllgwn* in check (as well as ensuring ongoing encouragement with a continuous supply of strong coffee), his contribution to this book cannot be understated. *Byddai'r llyfr yma cymaint tlotach heb dy gyfraniad, dy gefnogaeth, a dy gariad diysgog.*

So too the contribution of Dafydd Glyn Jones, my father-in-law, whose expertise in both Welsh folklore and the beautiful intricacies of the language ensured that both content and translations provided within these pages are as accurate as possible – *diolch yn dalpe i chi.*

To all the staff at Calon and the wider team, in particular Amy, Abbie, Maria, Georgia, Elin, Adam, Rebecca, Caroline, Agnes, Lucy and Ruth, for their keen observations and support throughout this process, and for putting such faith in a first-time writer. To Katie, for being able to bring to life the darker side of Welsh ghost-lore so marvellously in her illustrations – the text is all the richer for your involvement in this process. And to Mark, for his unwavering confidence and trust, and his impeccable humour when the two of us were drowning in *bwganod.*

I owe a significant debt of gratitude to Dr Juliette Wood for her mentorship and for always setting me on the right path. *Diolchiadau mawrion* also go to Dr Dylan Foster Evans for introducing me to the wonderful Leckwith Ghost, and to the remainder of the staff at Cardiff University's School of Welsh for their ongoing support. Warm thanks also to Dr Lisa Tallis at Cardiff University's Special Collections and Archives, and Amgueddfa Cymru staff at both Sain Ffagan and Nantgarw archives (in particular, Lowri Jenkins and Meinwen Ruddock-Jones) for their invaluable knowledge, guidance and patience. My heartfelt thanks also go to Dr Lee Raye, for their impressively niche expertise in medieval Welsh beavers. I would also like to thank Sara Huws for her encouragement and friendship, and for being a continuing source of inspiration and strength.

Lastly, I would like to offer my overwhelming gratitude to my beloved late mentor and dearest friend, Wil Jones, whose infallible ability to relate the most gruesome of ghost stories far outshone any of the attempts made within these pages. Without the profound influence of his own bright and brilliant spirit, it is fair to say that I would never have considered it possible to attempt this book, let alone build a career in studying the folklore of my *milltir sgwâr*. This book was written in celebration of his memory and his own undeniably significant contribution to Welsh culture. As noted in my dedication, I live in the hope that his spirit is never too far away.

Delyth Badder
April 2023